UNDENIABLE PASSION

"I didn't want to hurt you," he whispered. "I don't want anyone to hurt you."

He kissed her again. And in that moment when their defenses were down, when all he thought was to console, to comfort, and when all she sought was peace, passion sneaked in.

He kissed her now with a fierceness that was at once earthy and innately spiritual. And she responded in kind. They became one, inseparable.

Even when he lifted his face, it was as if they were still one. His gaze delved into hers with pure, undiluted passion, passion too long denied.

Gradually sensibility returned, and with it a wild kind of joy. The world and its problems whirled away and left her here in his arms, like she had craved. Like she had dreamed. And oh, how wonderful it was.

BOOK YOUR PLACE ON OUR WEBSITE
AND MAKE THE
READING CONNECTION!

We've created a customized website just for our very special readers, where you can get the inside scoop on everything that's going on with Zebra, Pinnacle and Kensington books.

When you come online, you'll have the exciting opportunity to:

- View covers of upcoming books
- Read sample chapters
- Learn about our future publishing schedule (listed by publication month *and author*)
- Find out when your favorite authors will be visiting a city near you
- Search for and order backlist books from our online catalog
- Check out author bios and background information
- Send e-mail to your favorite authors
- Meet the Kensington staff online
- Join us in weekly chats with authors, readers and other guests
- Get writing guidelines
- AND MUCH MORE!

Visit our website at
http://www.zebrabooks.com

CHANCE OF A LIFETIME

Vivian Vaughan

Zebra Books
Kensington Publishing Corp.
http://www.zebrabooks.com

TO MY FAMILY

With Special Thanks for the fabulous bows to
Elaine Raco Chase

ZEBRA BOOKS are published by

Kensington Publishing Corp.
850 Third Avenue
New York, NY 10022

Zebra, the Z logo and Splendor Reg. U.S. Pat. & TM Off.

First Printing: March, 1999
10 9 8 7 6 5 4 3 2 1

Printed in the United States of America

After the Great Spirit created the earth and the heavens, He hung the moon and flung a handful of stars into the ebony sky. In that single moment before the People were fashioned from the rock of the sacred mountain, an errant star slipped from the hand of the Great Spirit. Falling to ground, it formed a crater that reached to the heart of Our Mother Earth. From the depths of this crater sprang a pool so rich with the blood of life that only a man of great powers dared drink from it. And the Word came down that he who drank of the water and lived would be chief of all he surveyed. Should this chief become lonely he had only to bathe in these sacred waters to find love everlasting. But for those who would bring harm to the People the water would become fire, and they would be consumed by it.

—*The Legend of Apache Wells*

Chapter One

Fort Davis, Department of Texas, 1868

Fiery red hair loose and flying, Sabrina Bolton dashed into the road that ran beside the house she shared with her parents on Officers' Row. Scarcely breathing, she squinted against the dazzling afternoon sun for a glimpse of the long-overdue troops, admonishing herself all the while.

What kind of fool rushed into the road half-dressed to view her own fate? Sabrina knew what kind of fool. She was like that; nineteen years of her mother's chastisement hadn't changed her. If she were to hang at the gallows, she would want to look her executioner in the eye. If Captain Lon Jasper should propose to her, as everyone at Fort Davis expected, she wanted to feel the fluttering butterflies Carrie Young claimed every woman in love felt—*now*. The instant Lon rode into view Sabrina wanted his pale blue eyes to pierce her heart, a phrase gleaned from romances she read in *Godey's Lady's Book*. And she wanted to feel butterflies, hundreds and thousands of them.

In truth, Sabrina had never felt a single fluttering butter-fly in her life. She was, in the words of her father, Quarter-master Edward Bolton, "a sensible young woman with her head attached squarely to her shoulders." To which her mother, Martha, invariably huffed, "All daughters are sensible in their fathers' eyes."

It was Martha who decided the time had come for Sabrina to wed. And Lon Jasper was Martha's lucky choice—or victim, Sabrina sometimes thought.

Transferred to Davis from Fort Bliss, Lon had barely settled into bachelor quarters before Martha set her cap—rather, Sabrina's cap—for the handsome, eligible officer. "Trust me, Sabrina, Captain Jasper is your chance of a lifetime."

For reasons beyond Sabrina's comprehension, she did not share her mother's enthusiasm. Not that there was anything wrong with Lon. He was an officer and a gentle-man in everyone's book—obviously the perfect marriage candidate her mother claimed. In truth, however, Sabrina wasn't ready for marriage, not even with the perfect mate. At nineteen, that made her not sensible at all, but some kind of misfit. While her mother pined for grandchildren, Sabrina wanted something else first—something intangi-ble, elusive, but, she sensed, intrinsically important—before she became a virtual servant to husband and chil-dren.

Perhaps she had seen too much of life. Or, perhaps, as her mother insisted, she read too many romances. Never-theless, if fluttering butterflies meant love, she wanted butterflies. She wanted singing birds and shooting stars and a racing pulse. . . .

A sudden thundering of hooves erupted from out of nowhere. One minute Sabrina was immersed in fantasy. The next, a horse plunged out of Sleeping Lion Mountain behind her.

Startled, she turned, only to gape, disbelieving her eyes. No riders came that way. There was not even a trail, which did nothing to discourage the huge black stallion. He took the rocky hillside as if it were a grassy racecourse, eyes flashing and nostrils flaring. *A runaway.*

Sabrina glanced from horse to rider—a mistake, for the first thing she spied was the trailing end of a red headband, the kind favored by Apache warriors.

Apache! The word spawned terror in stouthearted men. *She was about to be run down by a savage.* Staring fate in the eye suddenly lost its appeal. Yet, like in a bad dream from which she struggled to awaken, she stood unable to move. She felt trapped by her own body.

The horse came closer. The man began to shout. "Get out of the way!"

Move. Yes, she must. This was no time to stand her ground even if she wanted to, which at the moment was the furthest thing from her mind.

Turning, she ran. One step. Two. Then she was falling. The red earth rushed to meet her. A sob of terror lodged in her throat. She fought for balance, caught it, glanced back to gauge the approaching danger. Another mistake.

The horse had reared on its hind legs. It was enormous, like a charger out of a medieval fairy tale. Unshod hooves pawed the air.

Heart thrashing, Sabrina attempted again to run. This time when her toe caught in the gold swag her mother had not quite finished attaching to the hem of the fancy green gown, she fell to her knees.

With an earth-shattering blow the animal's hooves crashed to the roadbed beside her. Terrified, Sabrina tried to scramble to her feet, only to trip on her hem again.

Think, she admonished through the thundering in her head. *Stop acting like a numbskull and think.*

"Are you hurt?" The man had dismounted and stood

over her, fists thrust to hips, enraged. Ends of that frightful headband and strands of long dark hair dangled dangerously close to her face.

A savage. Other telltale signs confirmed her terrible assessment—a calico shirt belted low over leather britches, Apache-style. Moccasins that ended in cuffs just below the knees, Apache—

"Are you hurt?" he repeated.

He had the harshest voice she had ever heard, and up close his eyes were ferocious, like those of a wild animal. She had never been this near an Apache before, never looked into the eyes of one of these savages the army had come west to tame, never expected to. His green eyes filled her with . . . *green* . . . ?

Did Apaches have green eyes? Regardless, looming over her, he looked every inch the savage. Just when she thought she might faint, his words registered. "You speak English," she said.

"And you obviously understand it, so answer me. Are you hurt?"

"No." She felt marginally better for having used her voice, if not her legs. But when she gathered her skirts to rise, she noticed the disheveled state of her gown. Lord in heaven! Mama would . . .

Prompted by thoughts of her mother, Sabrina glanced toward the house. No sight of Martha, who was probably still searching for the right pair of gloves to wear for the arrival of Senator Carmichael.

The senator . . . The soiree . . .

In a sudden, sickening flash of memory Sabrina recalled that her dress was unfastened down the back. She reached to grip the loose edges together. When the bugle sounded her mother had been fitting the hand-me-down gown but had not yet let out the bodice enough for it to fasten from the waist up.

Martha had been certain the bugle heralded the arrival of the senator. Sabrina recognized it as sounding the return of Company G. She had come out for a look, not truly expecting to see the troops yet, since sound traveled far in this clear mountain air. Certainly, she never imagined getting caught in the road with her dress undone.

"If you aren't hurt, get out of my way," the savage was saying. "You spooked my horse."

"Spooked your horse?" The conversation was nothing like she would have imagined, if in her wildest dreams she had ever imagined herself sitting in the road talking to a savage who had borne down on her like one of the three Furies—in this case, one was enough.

The brilliant midday sun glinted from his feral eyes and burnished his dark hair, which hung in waves from the red headband to past his shoulders. *Waves?* On an Apache?

A matter of little consequence. This man could have rosy cheeks, and his green eyes would still be straight out of her fiercest nightmare.

He swept her with searing contempt. "Get up, I said." He was still angry.

Well, Sabrina was angry, too. Angry that he dared confront her here on the sanctity of the post, her domain, beside her own house. Angry that by coming into her life he had taken away the intangible and up to now untested sense of freedom she had enjoyed. In doing so he made her fearful.

And fear magnified her anger, prompting her to act with uncharacteristic boldness. She, who always acquiesced, who strove to please, who yielded a point whether or not she had truly lost it, had had enough. That it took a savage bearing down unexpectedly to rouse her temper mattered not. Sabrina Bolton was angry, and she did not intend to let this man get the best of her.

"I do not spook horses." With a defiant jerk, she yanked

on her skirt and tried to stand. "You are the one in the way. This post is off limits to sav—" Her skirt held fast. She jerked again. Something ripped. She gaped at the length of gold swag that had torn away from the hem. Her initial reaction was incredulity. Mama would die! Then elation.

She wouldn't have to wear this atrocious gown to the commander's soiree. She would never have been able to stand up to her mother, but now the dress was ruined.

When she saw the cause of the mishap, however, thoughts of soirees and inelegant gowns fled. The savage stood with one moccasin-clad foot planted solidly on the glittering gold fabric.

In the second it took her to consider the consequences of engaging in a tug-of-war with a savage, he noticed it, too. Braced against the worst, whatever unimagined horror that might be, she watched him go down on one knee. It took every ounce of fortitude she could muster not to scream.

But his attention was not on her. He lifted the gold silk in a rough brown hand. She watched him study it, as though mesmerized. He draped the glittering swag over his palm, let it fall through long, thick fingers. Coarse fingers, she noticed. Work-hardened. In this moment of stillness curiosity stirred.

Who was this man? He didn't look Apache, but he certainly dressed the part. No man in his right mind would come onto a military post disguised as a savage.

In the midst of her thoughts he lifted his eyes and caught her staring at him. His gaze held hers for a heartbeat, until she realized he was handing her the swag. Disconcerted, she reached for the cloth. It began to slip through his fingers, then stopped. *He wasn't turning it loose.*

No sooner had she thought it than he released the golden silk. She watched it fall from his hand to her lap.

When she raised her face, she found his gaze on her, curious and probing.

Fascination danced dizzily inside her. She had bewildered this strong, wild man. Fascination, followed closely by panic. What was she doing sitting on the ground gaping at a savage?

Senses restored, she scrambled to her feet. The swag, however, had torn away from the gown in more than one place. She tripped again, flailed wildly with her arms, struggled to keep her balance, determined against all odds not to fall in this man's presence one more time.

She didn't, but only because he caught her. The same hands that had held the silk grabbed her by the shoulders. His touch sent waves of terror shimmying down her spine. She found his gaze, willed him to hear the plea she could not voice, and read his own startled expression.

Quick as lightning, his hands released her bare shoulders and landed on her back. Before she could think how to stop him, one large hand slipped inside her dress. She wore only a chemise.

In that instant Sabrina knew why ladies wore corsets. She would never have to be told again. Not in this lifetime. They wore them for armor. For protection against large, hot hands that spanned backs and sent terror tingling down the spines of proper ladies. Mortified, she realized her behavior was anything but proper.

As though he, too, were disconcerted, he jumped aside and stood glaring at her from beneath that ghastly headband. His fierce gaze unnerved her. She slumped limply to the ground.

"Can't you stand on your own two feet?" he demanded.

Weak-kneed, she searched for her footing again, this time with a firm grip on her bodice. Inexplicably, she felt the need to assure him that it wasn't her practice to run around half-dressed. "Mama was fitting . . ." She stopped at his deepened frown. He wouldn't know what fitting a gown meant. And she certainly didn't need to defend herself to a savage

Notes of the cavalry bugle came again, drifting on a clear spring breeze, closer now. Sabrina staggered to her feet. Company G had come into sight; its blue standard waved proudly against the backdrop of rose-colored hills. When she looked back to the Apache, he was staring down the road toward the soldiers.

"Company G of the Ninth," she explained, wondering why she bothered. He might speak English, but he certainly wouldn't know army jargon. He surprised her yet again.

"Led by Captain Lon Jasper, the son of a bitch I've come to see." Without a backward glance, he mounted and galloped toward the advancing company. He rode down the center of the road, so ambush wasn't his intent. But what was? What could he, a savage, want with Lon?

Savage. The term didn't seem right, yet his voice had seethed with savagery.

"Sabrina!" Martha Bolton arrived in a panting rush. "Is it the senator?" Her expression fell at the sight of the torn gown. "Oh, my . . ."

Brief though her encounter with the Apache had been, to Sabrina it seemed a lifetime. She struggled to focus on her fidgeting mother, a task comparable to returning from another world. Her first contact with a savage, and it had left her benumbed.

"My dear, my dear," Martha fluttered, "what have you done to this gown?" She reached for the length of gold China silk. Sabrina watched it slip through her fingers.

Dazed, she glanced back to the Apache. He was farther away now, a miniature rider on a toy horse. But this man had not come for child's play. Swept by a nameless premonition, she wondered again what he wanted with Lon. Whatever, Lon had a company of men to back him up, while the savage was but one. Yet she had the strangest feeling he needed no one.

At the house she changed into the first gown that came to hand, a gray percale weeding dress, twice-turned but clean, and struggled to shake the stupor that had befallen her. Buttoning her cuffs, she gathered up a bag of flour-sack bandages, collected from officers' wives, and left her room.

Martha waited beside the lace-draped mantle in the typically cluttered Victorian parlor of their small home. She clutched the ruined silk gown to her ample bosom. A sturdy woman of medium height, with a strong back, broad Germanic features, and salt-and-pepper hair that straggled perpetually from the bun at her nape, Martha Bolton was forever somber-faced. Her brown eyes never twinkled. Sabrina could not recall ever hearing her mother laugh. Today, she discovered, would not be the exception. Martha faced her, stolid and grim.

Sabrina often thought there must be an X marking the spot on the worn floral-patterned carpet where her mother now stood, for Martha never failed to use that particular place from which to strike her deadliest blow for sympathy. Like a preacher had a pulpit and a politician a soapbox, Martha Bolton had the portrait of what it might have been to stand beneath and silently dare her one remaining daughter to make life any worse.

And Sabrina never failed to succumb. She knew she was a disappointment to her mother. Regardless how hard she tried, she could never please. Today, however, along with her usual sense of futility, she experienced an uncustomary flash of resentment. Why must she always be the one to give comfort? She needed comforting, too. Today, she could use a mother with whom to discuss her unnerving encounter with a man who dressed like a savage and held gold silk as if it had fallen from heaven and whose hot hand on her back felt both frightening and reassuring. What did that mean? Whom could she ask?

Her mother would be scandalized. First she would want to know who saw the savage touch her. Then she would berate Sabrina for going out in a dress that didn't button, in a gown she had worked her fingers to the bone to redesign for the upcoming soiree.

"You know I disapprove of you going to that hospital," Martha was saying. "Proper young ladies do not . . ."

Proper young ladies? The spot on Sabrina's spine where the savage touched her burned at the term. She shook off the memory. "I won't do anything unladylike." A familiar promise, offered today in an attempt to forestall Martha's most recent and ardent fear, that Sabrina would ruin her chance for a good marriage by volunteering at the hospital.

The work was important to Sabrina, meaningful. She couldn't imagine giving it up for trivialities. Besides, she thought defiantly, what else was she supposed to do? Reba Applebee flashed to mind. Reba, who had lost a child, now whiled away her hours gluing together wedding china, broken on the overland journey from New York.

"I must go for a little while, Mama," Sabrina insisted when Martha's silent censure continued unabated. "With the troops returning, Doc Henry will need me."

"And you need your reputation, child. What if that doctor is inebriated?"

Another familiar topic. To be fair, it wasn't only Martha who believed the post surgeon indulged in spirits. His "condition" was one of several favorite topics of gossip when officers' ladies gathered for bridge.

"Doc Henry doesn't imbibe, Mama." A remark she had repeated at least a hundred times during the past two years. Eager to be away before the situation deteriorated, she headed for the door. Already her chest was tight, and her head swam with self-recriminations.

Be patient with Mama, her conscience warned. *She has suffered enough.* Martha Bolton was an expert at bringing to light Sabrina's innermost failings as a daughter.

"Your mama could wring guilt out of a turnip," Papa suggested once, upon finding Sabrina hidden behind the well house sobbing after one of Martha's tirades. "Don't let it get you down, sugar. She means well."

"I'll be home in time to help with supper," she called now.

Stalwart to a fault, however, Martha followed. "Captain Jasper doesn't want you tending those men, Sabrina. He told me so himself."

Sabrina stopped in her tracks. She never argued with her mother. She had learned early and well that the results were too devastating. But this was a different matter. Whether or not her mother and Lon had discussed her work at the hospital, the idea inflamed her.

"What else does he expect me to do, Mama? I don't have any broken wedding china to glue back together." The retort slipped out. Sabrina was immediately sorry. She might as well have slapped her mother on the face.

"For shame, child. With that attitude you will never have a *wedding.* Captain Jasper has his eye on you. Trust me, Sabrina. Marriage to a man of his ilk is the chance of a lifetime."

Now look what you've done. Chastised by the voice in her heart, Sabrina retraced her steps and pecked a kiss on her mother's cheek.

"I'm sorry about the gown, Mama. It can't be ruined. Put it on the dress form and see if you can mend it."

"You think I should?"

Encourage her, the voice prompted. *She's your mother. She deserves your support.* "Of course, Mama."

"But you don't like it."

"Of course I like it." She swallowed the lie, because it was white and necessary, and hugged Martha's stiff shoulders. "You will remember to let out the bodice?"

Martha shrugged, not placated.

Struggling to escape the familiar maze of guilt, Sabrina hugged her mother again. "I'll have the loveliest gown at the soiree, Mama, as always, because I have the loveliest mother."

Today for the first time in memory the acquiescence left her with the bitter aftertaste of resentment. Why was she always the one to console? Today she needed consoling, too, or at the least, guidance. *And inner courage,* she thought sadly.

The savage had been right to question her ability to stand on her own two feet. She couldn't, neither physically nor any other way. In despair, she doubted she would ever learn.

Soft new grass sprouted in the clearing between Officers' Row and the post hospital to the rear. Around them on three sides jumbled red cliffs of the Davis Mountains reached to a cloudless blue sky, sheltering the sprawling hospital and nearby steward's house as at the back of an open palm. Hospital Canyon, it was commonly called. In the short time since the bugle sounded, it had come alive with activity.

Officers, wives, enlisted men, even the regimental band hurried to welcome the long-awaited troops. Sabrina set off across the clearing, eager to escape before her mother returned to her original topic of discontent—Sabrina's work at the hospital. The revelry in the air was contagious; it soothed the ragged edges of her guilt. Soon she was skipping to a sprightly rendition of "When Johnny Comes Marching Home."

Strange as it seemed when she thought about it, the post

hospital—with its surgeon, gentle Doc Henry—served as an island of escape in her turbulent world. There, among the wounded she felt accepted. There, unlike at home, she was confident and at ease. There, she could bring comfort and a reasonable amount of pleasure to people who asked nothing of her but a cheerful countenance. There, her guilty conscience was somewhat assuaged.

By now several wagons of wounded had drawn up to the hospital steps. Off to the side, white officers and the buffalo soldiers they commanded had begun to dismount. Sabrina spotted Lon Jasper without any trouble. She watched him step down from his saddle and pace the line of troops, clapping one man on the shoulder here, pausing for a word with another there. Tall and blond, he drew one's attention even from the distance and in a trail-grimed uniform.

Butterflies, she prayed. This must surely be the time for a swarm of them. Lon had been gone twenty-four days. Carrie was certain he would propose marriage the moment he returned. If so, weren't butterflies a tad overdue? She wasn't clear about what caused a woman to feel flutters in her stomach. . . .

A hand to the back?

The thought flashed through her like an errant heat wave, when, for the second time that day, the sleek black warhorse and its wild rider galloped into view. It reared to a halt in front of Lon. The savage slid to the ground amid a swirl of red dust.

Mesmerized, she watched him stride toward Lon, who, half a head shorter than the Apache, stood his ground. When the savage grabbed him by the shoulder, Lon shook him off. They exchanged what appeared to be heated words. Around her others stopped to stare at the lithe, fair-complexioned officer and the dark and rugged savage.

Doc Henry jogged past, struggling with his suspenders. "You bringing bandages, Sabrina?"

"Yes, sir." Snapping back to the task at hand, she lifted her skirts to continue through the ankle-deep grass only to be taken aback again, for her mind played tricks. Instead of faded gray percale she felt silk. Visions spun in her head, memories of gold silk slipping through the savage's rough hand, the look of bewilderment on his strong face.

The green and gold gown Mama worked her fingers to the bone for you to wear when Lon proposes, the voice in Sabrina's heart accused. She glanced back to Lon, feeling guilty, as if by some unfathomable deed she had betrayed him.

Seeing her, he lifted a hand in greeting.

Chapter Two

Sabrina hurried up the broad front steps of the multi-winged hospital, working her way through litters of wounded. Outside the enlisted men's ward, a familiar voice stopped her.

"Lordy, Miss Breena, ain't you a sight fer sore eyes?"

"Jedediah! What are you doing here?"

The orderly lay near the back of the austere ward, with its whitewashed native stone walls and gray-painted wooden floor. Twice her age and wiry, Jedediah was Sabrina's personal favorite among the hospital staff. They laughed and worked easily together, side by side, even though Sabrina knew if her mother ever found out she would have the devil to pay.

"What would the ladies say, child?" Mama would ask. "You mustn't be caught consorting with that . . . uh, class of people."

Martha's objections didn't stop with Jedediah's *class*, of course. But when Sabrina reached him now any qualms faded. One look at his leg took her breath. "Oh, Jedediah."

The orderly's eyes, dulled by pain, glowed at her attention. "Could be worse, Miss Breena. If they'd left me out there, them redskins would've used this ol' black hide for target practice."

"As stubborn as you are? Why, they'd know right off you would blunt their arrows."

Privates Hedgewick and Jones, the two other orderlies, had arrived carrying fresh water and were already at work relieving the thirst of the wounded troopers.

"Weren't no redskin broke this leg." Pain etched fine lines to either side of his eyes and left his lips virtually colorless. "My ol' horse took a fall and pitched me off."

"I warned you not to go out with that patrol." Seeking a way to ease his pain, Sabrina removed scissors from a chatelaine she kept in her rag sack. "I'll cut away your trouser leg so the doc won't waste time when he comes."

"Jones can do that, Miss Breena."

"Jones is busy. And Hedgewick, too, since you ran off and busted your leg and left them with all the work." Jesting, she sat on the edge of the cot and began to cut through the heavy, blood-encrusted blue wool. She concentrated on the fabric, cautioning herself not to show a reaction to the wound, but when the uniform fell away, she couldn't stifle a gasp.

"There goes my chanct at bein' steward."

"Not necessarily."

"Aw, Miss Breena, don't worry 'bout foolin' me. I's from a long line of folks had worse trouble than this. It was a long shot, anyhow, that steward job. I didn't get my hopes up none." He winked. "But weren't it the chanct of a lifetime for a black feller like me?"

Chance of a lifetime? The phrase seemed infinitely more

appropriate applied to Jedediah's situation than when her mother used it to describe Lon Jasper's marriage potential.

"Sabrina?" As if she had conjured him by her thoughts, Lon appeared at her side. "They told me I'd find you here, but I didn't believe . . ." His frown deepened at the sight of Jedediah's leg. Before he could comment on the severity of the wound, she jumped to her feet.

"My, my, don't you look fit?"

Indeed, he did. His fair complexion had turned swarthy from twenty-four days under the Texas sun. It made a stunning backdrop for his pale blue eyes, which she had always credited with softening his otherwise sharp features. Today a gentle warmth exuded from his starched military bearing.

Cap clamped to left ribcage by a rigid arm, he stood before her in a uniform that looked freshly brushed. Blond hair swept in a neat wave from his forehead. He must have stopped by quarters to freshen up before. . . .

Before coming to see her? Her heart skipped a beat. Disconcerted, she glanced away. Had he come to propose marriage? *Not yet,* she prayed, *not today.*

Every officer's wife on the post awaited the betrothal announcement with bated breath, if not held tongue. Her mother expected Lon to propose at the commander's soiree for Senator Carmichael—thus the extravagantly redesigned gown.

Carrie was certain he would not wait that long. "If lengthy separations have any advantage," the bubbly newlywed assured Sabrina, "it is to encourage a man to make a commitment."

When Lon reached for her arm, Sabrina wished she had taken Carrie more seriously. What would she say? How would she respond to a marriage . . . ?

"Come outside with me," he was urging.

"Outside? Oh, no. I'm—" But he had already dragged her a couple of feet away from Jedediah's cot.

"June Willart is coming for her husband. I want you to help them home."

"Captain Willart is wounded?" Why hadn't he said that in the first place?

"Shaken up," Lon amended. "His horse stepped in gopher hole a few miles back. He took a tumble."

A tumble? What did that mean? Sabrina glanced to Jedediah. Did Captain Willart stand to lose his leg, his position in the army, possibly his life?

"Run along, Miss Breena. I ain't goin' nowhere till the doc comes."

Sadly, that was true, but she would have liked to stay and offer emotional support. Reviling herself for possessing a weak spine in addition to weak knees, she returned the scissors to the chatelaine, gathered her rag sack, and, smiling fondly at Jedediah, allowed Lon to draw her through the ward and out onto the veranda. He didn't pause until he had rounded the south corner of the building.

"Sabrina, I—"

She glanced around nervously. They were in a partially secluded area, with only the vacant steward's house ten yards distant. "Where is Captain Willart?"

Lon's tone turned petulant. "I guess you didn't miss me very much."

Miss him? Coming straight from the wounded ward, missing Lon Jasper was the furthest thing from her mind. When she chanced another look at his face, her heart sank. Carrie was right. He intended to propose. Unless she forestalled him.

"Of course I missed you," she said quickly. *Just don't propose.* "I worried about you, too. Twenty-four days. What a nightmare . . ."

Lon stopped her babbling, not with the proposal she

dreaded, but with a pair of firm, strong lips that were straight out of every romance she had ever read, lips any girl in the world would swoon to kiss. *Any girl but a misfit like Sabrina Bolton.*

To give herself credit, she endured the intimacy without fidgeting or pulling away. Closing her eyes, she concentrated on conjuring butterflies. They were kept at bay, she decided, by an even more desperate prayer—that he not propose.

Not today. Relief came with the sound of footsteps.

"Lon, stop. Someone's coming." She freed herself by pushing against his chest and hurried around the corner, tucking loose strands of red hair behind her ears as she went. Lon caught up in time to watch an out-of-breath June Willart rush across the veranda and fall into the arms of her husband, who had stepped out of the officers' ward with a wide smile. On his own two feet. Without a bandage in sight.

"There, there, June darling. I'm fine. Walk me home."

"You're sure, dear?" Arm in arm the Willarts crossed the porch and descended the steps, eyes only for each other.

When Sabrina turned back to Lon, his expression was sheepish. "There goes your excuse to get me out of the ward."

"He did fall off his horse." Lon's petulance turned to bitterness. "I only wanted a little time alone with you, Sabrina. Don't I rate that?"

Dispirited, she avoided his eyes. What was wrong with her? Why did everyone in her life want pieces of her that did not exist? And why didn't those pieces exist? What kind of misfit was she? Her guilty conscience emerged full-blown.

"And for another equally good reason," he added.

Here it comes. Weakened by dread, she somehow managed

not to close her eyes against the inevitable. But she gazed out across the clearing, not at Lon, for this was one part of her fate she was not anxious to stare in the eye. The truth would surely be written all over her face.

"To invite you to the commander's soiree for Senator Carmichael," he explained.

"The senator has arrived?" She welcomed the change of topic like some girls would a new frock.

"I ran into his aide at Headquarters. Carmichael is due in tonight. The commander's wife set the soiree for day after tomorrow." When he reached to stroke a loose strand of hair off her face, she let him. "Will you come with me?"

"To the soiree? Of course." *Mama will be thrilled. So will I,* she vowed. Magnanimous now that the worst had not transpired, she relaxed. "That is, if you're up to Mama's latest design."

"You mean it beats that maypole costume?"

Sabrina smiled, remembering Lon's reaction to the gown her mother designed for the post's May Day celebration.

"Looks like she tarred and feathered you in flowers," he had joked good-naturedly. Lon Jasper was an uncommonly good sport.

It occurred to Sabrina then that with a mother like Martha Bolton, a girl needed a good sport infinitely more than she needed fluttering butterflies.

"She hasn't finished this one yet. It may surpass the May Day monstrosity by a country mile."

Lon popped his brows, as if an idea had been prompted by the conversation. "Why don't I walk you home? I could give my regards to your mother, maybe get a peek at this new creation."

"Oh, no. I can't leave yet. Doc Henry needs me. I—"

"Don't force me to be blunt, Sabrina." He turned steely blue eyes on her. "You had no business in that ward."

"I know, Lon, but . . ." Caught off guard, she stumbled for an excuse.

"You were holding that man's leg in your hands."

"That was Jedediah. Didn't you see how badly he's injured? His leg will probably—"

"Setting broken legs is the doctor's job."

"I cut his trousers away," she argued weakly. "That's all."

"That's all?"

Sabrina stared grimly across the clearing, while Lon's acerbic jab accentuated her inner turmoil. Certainly she had held Jedediah's leg. If she could have, she would have mended it, put it back together, molded it into a new and healthy limb. These thoughts distressed her. She wanted to talk about them but didn't know how, or with whom. Lon would never understand. She wasn't sure she understood herself. Mostly she wanted to continue her work at the hospital, but she couldn't expect Lon to understand that, either. It was improper, or considered so by everyone she knew.

"Fortunately I was the only one who saw you," he was saying.

The statement made no sense, at least not that Sabrina allowed herself to admit. The ward had been full of men, some of whom were well enough to have witnessed her cutting away Jedediah's trouser leg. If black troopers didn't count as witnesses, how could it matter that she touched one's leg?

Before she could gather her wits, their attention was diverted to a company of men who galloped up to the hospital. Major Harry Applebee led the troop and was the first to dismount.

"Sabrina, thank God you're here." The major carried a bundle wrapped in an army blanket. Something protruded from one end. A small foot.

A child.

Sabrina went cold. Images of another child struck her like a blast of frigid air. Long ago visions assailed her—so long ago she wouldn't remember were it not for the portrait hanging above their mantle.

Major Applebee took the steps two at a time. "Look what we found."

Terror gripped Sabrina. Terror, like on that long ago day, or as a result of it. With the passage of time, which came first was impossible to decipher.

Beside her Lon snapped to attention. "Major Henry is inside, sir. Sabrina was just leaving. The doc can—"

Without speaking, Sabrina extended trembling arms and Harry Applebee placed the child in them.

"I think she's alive," he said, "but she hasn't moved or opened her eyes in hours."

With bated breath Sabrina lifted a corner of the blanket, exposing the frailest child she had ever seen. Her head was wrapped in some trooper's bloody bandanna; her arms and legs were limp. Sabrina lowered a cold cheek to her face.

"She's breathing."

"Thank God," Major Applebee muttered—Major Applebee, who only a year earlier had lost his own small daughter.

"Come." Sabrina turned toward the dispensary. Her heart pounded so loudly that she hardly heard Lon's surrender.

"I'll be back for you, Sabrina."

"Fine." Then Lon Jasper was forgotten.

The dispensary was considered Sabrina's office. In the absence of a hospital steward she filled in by, among other duties, interviewing troopers who reported for morning Sick Call. Her job was to determine whether their complaints were legitimate or feigned, say the result of having imbibed too heavily of spirits. Hangovers were not grounds for missing daily activities. Here she carried the child, followed by the major.

"She was the only person left alive in that damned village," he explained.

"Her parents were killed?"

"Or ran away."

"They left her?" The possibility sickened Sabrina.

"For dead, I suppose. Mex raiders were hot on their trail. If they were among the survivors, which I doubt."

Crooning to the frightfully still child, Sabrina set her on the cluttered oaken desk. "Would you light a lamp, Major? Then find Private Hedgewick. I'll need hot water and bandages. I must have dropped my sack somewhere."

By the time the major returned, Sabrina had removed the blanket, gingerly unwrapped the bandanna, and determined that the child's wounds were superficial—lacerations on her forehead and one shoulder, but no broken bones. She looked to be about four-years-old, with straight hair, black as coal. Sabrina thought of the green-eyed savage and his wavy hair. This child made him look even less like an Apache.

"Will she make it?" the major asked, a whisper at her side.

"I don't see anything that won't heal." Sabrina dabbed the child's head wound with antiseptic and was relieved to see a wince. "Anything physical, that is."

"Well, I . . ."—Harry cleared his throat—"I thought maybe Reba and I . . ." Turning his back on Sabrina, he crossed to one of the tall windows that faced east toward Officers' Row. Hands clasped behind his back, the seasoned officer continued with uncharacteristic hesitation. "You know how sick Reba's been since we lost the babe, Sabrina. I thought . . . I mean, maybe we could . . . if no one else wants her—"

"That's a wonderful idea, Major."

"I don't want to get Reba's hopes up," he hedged. "What if the child dies? Or doesn't respond to us?"

"Fetch your wife," Sabrina advised. "Stop and see if Thelma McCandless has clothes to fit her."

"You really think it'll be all right?" He was beside her again, gazing at the child with a faraway look.

"It's a grand idea. Hurry, now. The sooner she has a family, the sooner she will come around."

After Harry Applebee left, Sabrina removed the torn calico dress and cleansed the frail body with a soft cloth and warm water. Finding no other injuries, she wrapped the child in one of the larger flour sacks. The little girl had yet to open her eyes, but her chest rose and fell in a steady rhythm.

She looked nothing like the portrait of the auburn-haired three-year-olds hanging in the Bolton's parlor. Yet the sight of this child brought back the old memories as nothing had in years.

Crooning softly, Sabrina carried her outside to the front veranda to await the return of the Applebees. By now it was late afternoon. The air was soft and cool. She paced the length of the porch, singing a song her father once sang to her, in the good old days before lullabies were banned from the Bolton household.

"Hush, little baby, don't say a word. Mama's gonna buy you a mockingbird. And if that mockingbird don't sing, Mama's gonna buy you a diamond ring."

Against her chest, the child's breathing warmed Sabrina. She wondered at the horrors the little thing had witnessed, and whether she would ever forget them.

She wondered if Reba Applebee would make a good mother. Now Reba would have something to do besides glue broken china back together. Sabrina shifted the child and paced to the opposite end of the porch. The sun was sinking fast behind the Davis Mountains. Already Hospital Canyon was in shadow. Turning, she watched the row of whitewashed officers' houses glow in the last dazzling rays of the sun. They looked as though a celestial artist had been at work with a pallet of fuchsias and reds and golds. What a glorious sight! What a glorious land!

The thought brought instant denial. Beautiful, yes, but barbaric and violent. Sabrina tightened her arms around the little orphaned child, while a curious sense of restlessness gnawed inside her. "And if that diamond ring turns brass . . ."—singing again, she turned toward Sleeping Lion Mountain—". . . Mama's gonna buy you a looking glass. And if that—"

As though someone had clamped a hand over her mouth, Sabrina's words stilled. Her breath caught. Instinctively she clutched the child to her bosom, focusing on the man who stepped away from the shadowed corner of the vacant steward's house not ten yards distant.

The Apache. Again she was struck by incongruities. He was too tall for an Apache. His hair wasn't right. Nor his eyes. Those intense green eyes were in shadow now, but she could feel them as surely as if it were high noon.

Across the distance their gazes held. The impact stunned Sabrina. The bottom fell out of her stomach. She couldn't catch her breath; for a moment she was certain she would never be able to breathe again.

Her brain was abuzz. She recalled the ridiculous way she had tripped in front of him, the fury with which he spoke of Lon, how he later confronted Lon in obvious anger. What did he want?

And why did he stand there, still as a statue? He looked like a dark-haired Apollo or Bacchus come to wreak retribution. He spoke not, nor did his gaze waver. Her skin seemed afire with the intensity.

Enthralled, she watched shadows play on his features,

creating angles and planes, rendering his face narrow where an Apache's was broad, blunt where an Apache's was full.

Her body hummed, aquiver with some nameless emotion—fear mixed with curiosity and an unfamiliar sort of expectancy. Who was this man? Her fascination of earlier increased insidiously. What could he want?

The truth struck her a jarring blow that practically knocked her off balance. The world stopped spinning. She knew what he wanted.

The child.

A second revolting thought dealt another blow, this one straight to her heart.

His child?

Sabrina clutched the little girl protectively in arms that felt leaden. Had he come for his child? No wonder he charged down the hill in a rage. No wonder he confronted Lon. If this were his daughter . . .

What should she do? Never had Sabrina been handed a decision of such magnitude. She glanced down at the little girl, then desperately back to the man. What should she do? Reba was coming. . . .

But if he were the father . . . She had no choice, no choice at all, if he were the father. Stiffly, she moved toward him, extending the child. "If she is yours . . ."—her voice broke, but she continued helplessly—"take her and be quick about it."

He made no move to come forward. She watched his gaze drop to the child, linger briefly, then find hers again. His pain thrust to the very heart of her; she felt it as surely as if he had struck her in the face.

Behind her came footsteps. That would be Reba. The anxious woman's heels clattered over the porch floorboards like a wagon over a rutted road. "Sabrina, is it true?"

Stricken to the core, Sabrina froze. "Take her," she cried to the man in a half-whisper.

"Sing to her," he called softly, a plea, intense and desperate. Then he was gone.

She cradled the child against her pounding heart.

"Harry said . . ."—Reba arrived at her elbow, lifted a tentative hand to the bundle—"is she . . . ?"

"She's fine, Reba." *But I'm not.* He was out there; she could feel him, not see him. Feel him—his eyes, his pain. Like a magnet, she felt drawn to his pain.

Sing to her. His words rang like a dirge through her distress. She felt weak. And sick. What should she do? Call to him? If she did, would he come? And if he came, would Harry put him in chains? She wished she had asked Lon what he wanted.

"I brought clothes," Reba was saying.

Quickly, before all courage fled, Sabrina turned her back to the shadows and handed the child to Reba, whose arms trembled as much as her own, albeit for far different reasons. To take a child from its father would be unforgivable; to take a child from Reba, after all she had lost, would be equally reprehensible.

Sing to her. They were the saddest words Sabrina had ever heard. She watched Reba lift the sack and plant a kiss on the child's forehead. Tears stung Sabrina's eyes. She hoped the man saw Reba's tenderness. Maybe it would make giving her up easier.

If give her up he must.

If this were, indeed, his child.

Her heart ached. She felt strangled by warring emotions. She fought tears. "Sing to her, Reba."

"What?" Reba asked.

Sabrina shook her head to settle her senses.

"I brought clothes," Reba said again.

It was almost the final straw for Sabrina, the thought of

Reba dressing the child for the man to see. She recalled her mother's enduring pain. She had seen the same pain in the man's eyes, heard it in his voice. Could he bear to watch Reba dress his daughter, prepare her for a new life? Could *she* bear it?

"Take her home, Reba. Dress her there."

"Yes. Yes, of course. Bless you, Sabrina. A girlchild! Oh, the glory of it. God has answered my prayers."

As nothing had before, Reba's claim stunned Sabrina. How could that be? Did God take from one to give to another? If so, how ever did He choose from whom to take, to whom to give? She turned aside, searched the shadows, anxiously seeking a sign from the man who had been there.

Harry Applebee gripped her shoulder. "Thank you, Sabrina. This is right, I know it now. Thank you for convincing me."

Unable to draw her eyes from the shadows, Sabrina spoke over her shoulder. "What if her parents return for her, Harry?"

For a moment the major said nothing. In the heavy silence, Sabrina heard Reba's footsteps retrace their earlier path across the porch. How anxious she would be to get home with her precious gift. When Harry spoke, it was with the military brusqueness that irritated Sabrina when it came from Lon Jasper.

"They perished," Harry told her. "I am as certain of it as I am that the sun will rise tomorrow. We will call her Emily. When the chaplain arrives, she will be baptized. Come. I promised Captain Jasper to see you home."

Unbearably shaken by all that had transpired and her part in it, Sabrina resisted. "I still have work to do here."

"Harry, darling, come quickly. We must get our little Emily out of the night air."

Sabrina's chest might as well have been ripped open

and her heart torn out. She watched the Applebees walk through the gathering shadows toward their home on Officers' Row, but in her mind's eye she saw only the strange man who dressed like an Apache and looked like he had stepped out of a book of ancient myths. His intense gaze burned into her memory, tingled along her spine, fluttered in her stomach, issuing some insidiously mysterious warning.

Had she given his daughter to another? What else could she have done? And if she had made such a terrible mistake, how would she right it?

Rather, where would she find the courage? For there was only one solution, of course, as terrifying as it was to consider. She must speak with him. Sabrina knew herself. Unless she learned the truth and tried to set things right, she would find no peace.

Anxiety crawled along her skin like a corps of angry ants. When the Applebees were safely out of sight, compelled against her will and better judgment, she swallowed her fear and headed for the man in the shadows.

Chapter Three

The ten yards that separated the hospital and steward's house were the longest ten yards Sabrina had ever walked. What made her think she was brave enough to stare fate in the eye? What made her think she even wanted to try? Her legs trembled. Dread swelled inside her. Maybe the Apache wasn't still there. She hoped he wasn't. She prayed he was.

She owed him an explanation, even though she knew from her mother's experience that nothing anyone could say would relieve the pain she had seen in his eyes.

When her foot struck a rock, she caught her balance deliberately. Call it pride, but she was not going to fall flat on her face in front of him again today. Not that it mattered. She had bigger problems. What was she thinking? What would she say to him? Maybe he had already gone. Maybe he—

When she came within two steps of the shadowed corner, he grabbed her. A hand darted from the shadows, a fist caught her arm. He snatched her around the side of the steward's house as if she were a sack of horse feed. The speed with which he struck erased all thought from her mind.

"Did Jasper force you to give up the child?"

For a moment all she could hear was her wildly thrashing heart. "Lon?"

"Did he?" To punctuate his angry demand, the savage slammed her against the wall and held her in place with a heavy forearm across her chest. He might as well have lopped off the top of a volcano, for that one act erased nineteen years of training in obedience, acquiescence, and ladylike deportment. Sabrina exploded.

"Turn me loose!" She jerked to free herself, kicked at his legs, felt her toes stub the rough leather moccasins. *Moccasins. A savage.* Still she could not hold her tongue.

"You have no right to attack me. I did nothing—" Her fury shocked her, but suddenly she had had enough. She had acquiesced and appeased and tried her best to please everyone who made demands on her, and many who had not. Her weakness made her sick. Suddenly she could tolerate it no longer.

Not another acquiescent breath was left in her, not another passive remark, not another ounce of the need to please. Suddenly she was through. Of all times to find courage lurking in the recesses of her soul!

He stopped her tirade by clamping a rough, hot hand over her mouth. "I asked why you gave up the child." He stood so close his hot breath blew against her face. His labored breathing echoed in her own chest. Her pulse drummed, leaving her dizzy.

"Answer me."

"Then turn me loose," she mumbled into his palm.

He didn't respond. Seconds passed while neither of them moved. Her heart pounded against his restraining arm. She was all too conscious of his presence. Every place

their skin touched, a heated trail reminded her of the way
he touched her in the road—his strong, hot hand to her
back with only a chemise to separate his skin from hers.
She wondered if he remembered.

"I mean you no harm." His tone held more weariness
now than anger. His voice was deep and solid, and sounded
as if it might have rumbled down from the mountains; it
drove straight to the core of her guilty conscience. "If I
release you, will you not call for help?"

She considered for a heartbeat, then agreed. When he
removed his hand, the night air chilled her lips. Inadvertently she licked them, tasted the saltiness left on her skin
by his and felt her pulse skitter erratically again. But her
fascination was grounded in reality, for his arm remained
like a bar across her chest. He was the wildest thing she
had ever been this close to, animal or human. She feared
him, even as her startling curiosity flourished.

He studied her, unspeaking, silent, waiting, she sensed,
for an answer to his question. "I couldn't keep the child,"
she said at length.

"Why not?"

"I . . . I'm not married."

"You're Jasper's woman. Did he forbid—"

"Jasper's woman?" Lord in heaven, did everyone on the
face of the earth believe that? And did their belief make
it true? Did she have no say in the matter? No control over
her own future? "I am not Lon Jasper's *woman!*" Fur-
iously, she spat the words. She had to let him know. Had
to set the record straight. "I'm not his anything. I am
nobody's woman. Do you hear—"

"Don't lie to me."

Like in a puzzle, jagged pieces of the day's events fell
into place. After confronting Lon, he must have waited
beside the steward's house. He would have seen Lon kiss
her. Dear God! Why did that leave her weak? Why did it

rouse her anger? If Lon were here right now, she would slap his face.

Which was absurd. Even if she found the courage to slap Lon, he didn't deserve her wrath. This savage was the one who—

"I offered you the child." Now she was the angry one. "Why didn't you take her?"

"I decided to give her to you."

"To me? You don't know me. If you wanted to give her away, why did you come here? Tell me that! Why did you come to this post?" She wondered again at her sanity. After nineteen years' dearth of it, why had her courage chosen this particular moment to surface—with a savage looming over her, for heaven's sake?

And he was definitely a savage, dark and powerful and frightening. When he moved, the ends of his headband blew against her cheek. Tied diagonally across his broad forehead, it served the dual purpose of holding his hair off his face and drawing one's attention to his eyes.

Although those eyes were indistinct here in the shadows, she remembered their striking green color and startling intensity. They were certainly not black Apache eyes.

Yet in other ways he was all savage. He reminded her of a wild animal, a predator. His nearness dried her skin and took her breath away.

For a long moment, he moved not a muscle, only returned her stare, still and silent. Then again he surprised her, this time by removing his arm. Instead of answering her question, he asked another quietly.

"How is she? They said she was injured." The simple query, spoken in that deep, rock-solid voice, was sickening in its implications. *Dear God. It was his child.*

Sabrina's mouth was so dry her tongue felt swollen. Although he touched her nowhere now, his presence lay heavily upon her chest. She had trouble drawing enough air to speak. "Only a few scratches," she managed.

Moments passed in silence while she studied him closely. Shadows across his face prevented her from reading his expression, but she knew he watched her, too. What did he see? Her hair must rival Medea's wild tresses, except instead of wriggling curls her own hair was plank-straight and a frightful red color. Why did it matter? Of all the foolish times to worry about her appearance. His next demand brought her back to the grave essence of the matter.

"Who was that you gave her to?" Beneath his fierce defiance was a wistfulness that reached out to her.

"Major Harry Applebee and his wife, Reba."

He stood so near, she felt him stiffen. Compassion rose inside her, prompting a mad desire to touch him, to comfort him. She gripped her hands into fists to keep from reaching for him. Who was this man?

Slashed by shadows, half his face was hidden, the other half an enigma. He neither looked nor sounded Apache, yet again she thought that no sane man would come onto a military post disguised as one.

In an attempt to ease his pain, she explained, "They lost a child a year ago. Reba grieved so long everyone was afraid she might die, too. When the major found this child, he . . . he thought she was orphaned . . . or abandoned."

"Apaches do not abandon their children!" His raw anger shattered Sabrina's hard-won composure. Compassion swelled, and again she resisted the compelling temptation to touch him. Sanity held her back, for it would surely be a mistake, comparable to trying to soothe a savage beast.

But of all the emotions that waged war within her at this moment, guilt was the strongest. Guilt for the part she played in this man's pain engulfed her. One question, however, remained to be asked, no matter how painful the answer for either of them. "Are you her father?"

He went instantly still—so still all she could hear was her own breathing, all she could feel was her own heart beating in her throat. After an indeterminable time, she felt his tension ebb into the heavy silence that had fallen between them. Fainter than any ghost, she heard his heart resume its beat.

"No." The word whispered across her face.

More seconds passed in silence while Sabrina listened with relief to the cadence of his heart.

When he spoke his tone was as reverent as a priest committing a soul to God. "Her father was called Chi Caliente." A long moment later he added, "He was my brother."

His brother? Tears sprang straight from Sabrina's heart and rolled in hot streams down her face. The child was his niece.

"You must take her." The words tumbled out, and they were right, regardless how difficult it would be to take the child from Reba.

"No."

"Take her home."

"I said no."

Night fell around them and became oppressive. Then, while his harsh voice still rang in her ears, she felt him touch her. At first she thought she imagined it. But no, his hands were on her face. Large, rough thumbpads wiped tears from her cheeks.

His touch was electrifying. It raced through her body like lightning skipping across the spine of the toothy red ridges above them. Yet it was gentle, the gentlest of touches, a caress that seemed to bind his pain to her. And she felt, irrationally, that she would always share it, his pain.

Without removing his warm hands from her face, he asked again, "Why didn't you keep her?"

"I told you. I have no home."

"No home?" His tone was lighter now and carried a trace of amusement. "You live someplace."

"With my parents."

"Keep her there."

"You don't understand. A child needs two parents—"

"A child needs love. I saw how much you would learn to love her. You sang to her."

"Singing isn't everything," Sabrina snapped. But wasn't it? Songs and laughter. Love and hope. Simple words for things most people took for granted. This man put them first, and the profound meaning of that stopped Sabrina's racing heart. His words spoke of trust in a stranger, of insight into another person that went far beyond the superficial. He saw her as a strong and compassionate woman. The assessment couldn't be more wrong. Yet wasn't it a portrait of the woman she wanted to become?

"Reba will sing to her." Strangely at ease with his silences now, she waited patiently for his reply. His next question addressed a valid concern.

"Will they raise her to be a servant?"

"No." This, Sabrina knew for certain. Harry and Reba would love and protect their little Emily. "She will be their daughter. She will have the best, everything."

Except her birth parents. Except her own people, her own way of life, her own . . .

Lost in thought, they both fell silent. His dark silhouette covered her like a warm and favored garment. He smelled sweetly of the desert. They stood so close she felt his breath caress her face, heard the cadence of his heart. Although he had released her, she felt his touch—his hand over her mouth, his arm across her chest, his rough fingers brushing away her tears.

"What is her name?" she asked at length.

This time his response came quickly. "You heard the major. They will call her Emily."

"Her real name. She would adapt more—"

"She has no other name." His voice shook with rage. "It died by the soldier's gun that murdered her parents."

Soldier? "No! It was raiders from across the Rio Grande."

"They are dead."

She trembled at the fury in his voice, yet not from fear. Instinctively, she knew his anger was not directed at her. His anger was for the system, but a system of which she was a part. The truth formed a silent wedge between them, shattered finally by a call from the hospital.

"Sabrina!"

Lon. He had said he would return for her. How could she have forgotten?

"Sabrina!" came the call again.

Reality hit home. She was about to be discovered in the dark, alone with a man, a savage. The thought left her weak.

"That's Lon. I . . . uh, I must go. I—"

"Jasper? You said he wasn't your man."

"He isn't." But there he was, on the other side of this building, calling her back to the world, as from a dream.

And hadn't it been a dream? For a moment she wasn't even sure *she* was real. She certainly hadn't acted herself. She had shouted and kicked and argued with a man she called savage. She, the most weak-kneed person on this post. The only thing she could not find the courage to do, he had done for her.

He touched her.

She wished she had been as bold, just this once. It seemed the only thing lacking on this night filled with pain and, yes, with fantasy. Prodded by a sudden and fierce need to complete the image and by every past opportunity

lost to timidity and submissivness, Sabrina reached a tentative hand and placed four trembling fingers on his face.
It was the boldest action she had ever taken, and she
savored every electrifying sensation with heightened aware-
ness.

She heard his intake of breath. Or was it her own? Felt
the hum of his thrumming pulse. Or was it hers?

For a moment caught in time they stood, as close as
they could ever be, bound by a hundred and one erotic
sensations of skin touching skin.

Too soon he broke the spell with that deep and sad and
beautiful voice. "Watch over her, Sabrina."

Sabrina. The sound of him speaking her name played
along her frayed senses and gave substance to the fantasy.
Spoken softly in his full-bodied voice, it went straight to
her heart, like music.

Heart music. *Watch over her, Sabrina.*

Sabrina. Her name. When she didn't know his.

But he was gone. Vanished. Like before.

She closed her hand, the hand that had touched his
face, around the memory and held it to her breast, while
an irrational panic engulfed her. She glanced from side
to side, peering into the shadows, eyes searching.

Nothing. No sound. No sight. No sign of him.

She slumped against the wall of the steward's house.
Her heart thrashed and her breath came short. A mass of
insidious yearning fluttered in the pit of her stomach, a
yearning she could neither identify nor understand.

"Sabrina, where . . ." Lon's words trailed off when he
rounded the building and saw her leaning against the wall.
"Are you ill?"

"No." Strength returned with her need to protect the
precious moments she had just experienced, but when
Lon tried to guide her away from the building, she resisted.

To move would be to lose the vision. To leave would be to abandon the fantasy.

"I promised your mother I would see you home."

"My mother?" Anger brought her down to earth. "When did you see my mother?"

"Ah, Sabrina. Don't go getting pushed out of shape. I stopped by to give my regards. She was glad to see me."

She, as opposed to me? Sabrina wondered.

"I saw the gown, or what was left of it." Talking, he moved her off toward Officer's Row.

"Left of it?" It took every ounce of determination Sabrina could muster not to look back. Was he there, hidden among the red rock columns of Sleeping Lion Mountain, watching her walk away with Lon Jasper's arm around her shoulders?

And why did it matter? Regardless what she told the savage, Lon was, to all intents and purposes, her intended.

"You shouldn't have been out here in the dark by yourself," Lon scolded. They crossed the moonlit clearing. Sabrina felt the soft pad of spring grass beneath her feet. She wondered if the Apache were watching her. That was ridiculous. He got what he came for—information about his niece. She hadn't heard a horse's hooves, but that didn't mean anything.

Yet, the memory of his presence followed, enveloping her even as she walked away. That didn't mean anything, either, except that she was given to flights of fantasy.

"I was worried about you," Lon said. "There's a savage roaming around somewhere and—"

Sabrina came to a halt.

"You didn't see him, did you? He didn't . . ." Lon stopped to peruse her. "If that bastard hurt you—"

"He didn't."

"But you saw him?"

Sabrina fought for a lucid response. "Do you mean the Apache you were arguing with this afternoon?"

"That's the bast—You haven't seen him since?"

"I've been at the hospital, Lon. Apaches aren't usually numbered among our patients."

Leading her on through the gathering shadows, he seemed to relax. "He told me he had come to find a child. It wasn't until later I remembered it. Then I thought of the half-breed Harry Applebee brought in."

"The little girl with Major Applebee is full Apache."

"In that case she can't be Tremayne's."

"Tremayne?" The name practically slid down a rainbow and off her tongue.

"That's his name, the renegade squaw man you saw arguing with me. Said he'd come after a child. I figured it was one of his own."

Sabrina stumbled over a clump of grass. Lon's grip tightened on her arm.

"A squaw man?" she asked when she trusted her voice not to tremble. "What do you mean?"

"You know what a squaw man is. A white man who takes up with an Indian woman."

"Marries her?"

"They aren't that civilized. They're heathens. That's why I told him to stay out of sight. I didn't want him frightening our women."

Sabrina was stunned. She excused herself as soon as they arrived home, claiming it was her turn to prepare supper. . . .

"You're awful quiet tonight, sugar," Papa said once during the meal. Mama didn't notice. She was busy sewing gold bows. Sabrina refused to consider what the green gown would look like this time.

It didn't really matter. She had lived her fantasy. Now she would try to live her mother's.

After the dishes were done and the fire banked in the stove in their detached cook shack, she retired to her small room at the back of the main house. But sleep eluded her.

In bed she relived the events of the day, from the ludicrous way she stumbled around in the road to her final exhilarating act of courage—touching the man's face.

Lon called him a squaw man, which seemed an insulting term, considering that he obviously cared deeply for those he loved.

Why else would he have come to this post? He had taken his life in his hands coming here to determine the welfare of a child. Now he was gone, and she felt inexplicably alone.

Crossing her arms about her chest, she held them where he had held them. Myriad emotions assailed her. An improbable combination of concern and an all-encompassing sadness mingled inside her with a compelling new yearning that was innately sensual.

She had never imagined meeting such a man. The romances she read seemed suddenly juvenile, their heroes insipid compared to this wild and forbidden savage—a man who had displayed the highest of human qualities, compassion and courage and a strange sort of vulnerability.

That he had a wife was of no consequence. He had come to her out of nowhere, like in a dream, and he vanished back into nowhere. The fantasy was hers.

Tremayne.

She fell asleep with his name on her lips.

Chapter Four

Sabrina awoke the next morning feeling bereft, as if she had turned the last page of one of *Godey's* romances only to learn that the hero abandoned the heroine. She knew this was somehow connected to the renegade Tremayne.

She knew, too, that her mother was being proved right once again. Martha continually harangued Sabrina for reading the romances in the monthly magazine she ordered for fashion news.

"They're fantasy, child. Rubbish. Work that tatting pattern on page twenty. Your hope chest isn't half full." Martha was afraid Sabrina would confuse fantasy and reality.

Sabrina knew the difference.

Tremayne was fantasy.

Lon Jasper was reality. *Her* reality.

By the time Lon called that evening, she had made a couple of important decisions. First, she would give up reading romantic stories. Truthfully, that wasn't much of a sacrifice. After her real-life encounter with the renegade, she couldn't imagine mere stories being exciting.

Second, she would encourage Lon Jasper's suit. Her mother was right. Marriage was a woman's duty and her only security. It was high time Sabrina set about securing her future.

"Thought I might sneak another peek at that gown you'll wear tomorrow night," Lon suggested good-naturedly. "See how many ribbons I'll have to wear to outrank you."

Which was not the reason he had come to call, Sabrina learned after Martha refused to undrape the newly redesigned gown, calling it "my little surprise." Sabrina was just as glad. She wasn't eager to confront her fate any sooner than necessary. Lon seemed to forget he had asked.

In fact, he was so distracted, she began to worry that he'd come to propose. *Not tonight,* she prayed. *Wait for the soiree. At least that long.* Her anxiety proved unfounded.

"Lieutenant Young was up at the hospital this afternoon," he began after they were seated in wicker chairs on the front porch, facing the violet-hued evening sky. "He overheard something distressing."

"Carrie's husband?" Sabrina knew who he meant. She also knew what he overheard. Her resolve to encourage Lon's suit wavered as he continued to probe.

"I doubted his claim, of course. You didn't really help Major Henry amputate that orderly's leg. Not after I—"

"Doc Henry amputated Jedediah's leg, Lon."

"Did you help him?"

She stewed silently.

"Did you?"

"Of course I helped. He needed me."

"Why, Sabrina? You aren't a surgeon. Why would he—?"

"He was not inebriated, if that's what you're asking. Every doctor needs help. When we get a hospital steward, well, maybe . . ." She stopped short of making a promise she might be called upon to honor at a later date.

"Jones claimed your stitches were the neatest he'd ever seen."

"I must remember to thank him," she answered dryly. While seconds ticked by and she awaited the inevitable reprimand, a lone bugler blew Tattoo from the center of the parade ground.

Lon jumped to his feet on the first note. "Fifteen minutes till Extinguish Lights. I'd better head back to quarters. Can't set a bad example for the men."

Lon was like that. Dependable. Always conscious of duty. Admirable traits. Except when he expected her to follow his own rigid rules.

He took her in his arms, as expected, but instead of the goodnight kiss she was prepared to endure, he returned to their previous conversation. It was a trick he used on occasion, pretending to drop a subject only to bring it up later, after she had let down her guard. She had long ago decided the tactic might work well in leading troops but was definitely less effective as a wooing technique.

"Exceptionally fine stitches, Jones claimed," he scolded softly. "See, if you'd set your mind to it, you could have sewn your own gown for the soiree and saved yourself from your mother's creations. Next time you'll know." The words whispered against her lips, but he wasn't speaking of love. He was issuing an order.

Do not ruin your reputation at that hospital. That's what he was saying. *A woman belongs in the home.* She had heard these admonitions a million times from her mother. She purposely missed the point. "Are you getting cold feet about tomorrow night?"

"I'm getting cold feet right now, Sabrina."

When he kissed her, she almost welcomed the change of subject. His lips opened over hers in a warm and wet kiss she was certain would have produced a swarm of fluttering butterflies in the most staid matron. He drew her close and pressed her body to his, and she felt his heart beat against her chest, decidedly faster than her own. Guilt squirmed inside her.

"Lon, it isn't even dark yet."

He lifted his face, leaving her wet lips to cool in the night air. She resisted the impulse to wipe them dry. "I'm a patient man, Sabrina. Wait till you see how patient."

She watched him go, feeling miserable and guilty for disappointing him. What he saw in her, an obvious misfit, she couldn't fathom. He deserved better. But he walked up the path that followed the parade ground with no hint of disillusionment, military sharp to the nth degree.

Only when he was out of sight did she dry her lips with the back of her hand and slump against the door and at last allow latent thoughts of the renegade Tremayne to surface.

How would she have reacted to his kiss? Even knowing he was married, she wished she could have kissed him to see if there was a difference. Just thinking about it set her insides to humming.

The following evening Sabrina's resolve suffered another blow. With a mere half hour before the soiree was to begin, Martha unveiled the gown she had redesigned for the second time. The creation was wilder than anything Sabrina could have imagined.

It had taken an hour by the mantel clock for Martha to curl Sabrina's straight auburn hair and force it into a cluster of curls on top of her head. In the end, a large gold bow was required to hold it all in place.

More suitable for First Communion than for accepting a marriage proposal, Sabrina thought. But she said nothing. Experience had taught her well. If she complained, Papa would come to her aid, and Mama would stay home with a sick headache.

Next came the corset. Tonight Martha seemed intent on squeezing not only the breath, but the life out of her. The truth dawned slowly.

"You didn't let out the bodice?"

"It would have ruined the lines, dear." Tug. Tug. "Such lovely lines." Tug. "Mr. Worth certainly knows how to cut and drape for the best effect."

In truth the lines of the Worth original were completely obscured by bows—dozens, perhaps hundreds, of gold silk bows. Large bows ringed the hem of the garment and the neckline, concealing what Martha considered an immodestly low décolletage. In between, scores of bows literally covered the green silk.

To give due credit, Mama was an artful seamstress in her own right. She sewed for many of the officers' wives. At some post functions every gown in the room had been made from scratch or redesigned from something old by Martha Bolton. With piece goods scarce as hen's teeth, ladies often exchanged gowns after a couple of wearings; Martha remade these hand-me-downs so the original owners recognized nothing except the fabric, if that. Never what one would call conservative, Martha reserved her creative experiments for Sabrina's gowns.

If Lon Jasper's imminent proposal was the major topic of post gossip these days, Sabrina's gown for the soiree ran it a close second. One look at the undraped gown and Sabrina knew the ladies would not be disappointed by the latter.

"Maybe a few . . . fewer . . ." she mumbled weakly.

"You don't like it?" Martha's plump hand fluttered to her black-faille draped bosom. "I knew you wouldn't. I work so hard to please you, but how can I? I'm only your mother. I don't know what you like. I work so hard, but there's no pleasing . . .''

Without a glance to the portrait hanging above the mantel in the parlor beyond, Sabrina experienced the familiar swelling of guilt. It rose in a sour mass from her stomach and filled her chest and paralyzed her from the neck up. She wanted to cry, *Then stop trying. If I'm so miserable, so terrible a daughter, leave me alone. Abandon me.* But of course she didn't say any of that.

Instead, tears rushed to her eyes. Her head swam. And the voice in her head chastised, *Now look what you've done.*

Her sister's voice had been an integral part of Sabrina's consciousness since just past her fifth birthday. The portrait told the story. Two little girls, captured for all time at three years of age. Twins.

Sabrina and Serena.

One was alive and one was not.

Subdued by the intimate reminder, Sabrina stepped dutifully into the gown her mother had removed from the dress form and held for her. Doing so, she experienced the familiar, if irrational, sensation that she was dressing for two. That she had always dressed for two. Lived for two. If her sister had lived, she would have had to endure half as many flowers for May Day; if her sister were alive now, she would have to wear half as many bows to the commander's soiree.

If her sister were alive, she would live with half as much guilt. Or none at all. She would not have been trapped in a time warp since five years of age, and her mother would not be caught in an eternal web of depression.

How different their lives would surely be! It didn't bear considering. The fact was, Sabrina wanted to share her mother's burden. Her patience returned. "It's lovely, Mama."

"Do you think so? Truly? Look in the cheval."

But Sabrina wasn't quite ready to view herself in full-length bows. Desperate to gather her wits before she hurt her mother's feelings, she mumbled something about shoes and dashed from the room.

"Wait, child. Let me see how you look."

Crossing the porch that separated her bedroom from the main house, Sabrina spied her father's shaving tools. A hand mirror. A straight-edge razor. A wild idea half-formed. She snatched them up, caught her father watching from the doorway, then heard her mother fast behind her.

"Give her a minute, Martha," Edward called into the house. *Bless Papa.* "She can't go dancing without shoes."

Sabrina closed her bedroom door and leaned against it, catching her breath. Which was worse, she wondered, not being able to breathe, or looking like a Christmas tree in May?

"Captain Jasper will arrive any minute," Martha lamented from the porch. "Let me see how you look, child."

Sabrina knew how she looked—frightful! Wielding the straight-edge as though it were a scalpel, she severed a bow here, another there, in places she thought her mother might not notice.

"Martha," came Papa's voice. "Catch the door, would you? That must be Jasper."

Sabrina stuffed the few bows she had been brave enough to remove into her rag sack. Eyeing herself in her father's small shaving mirror, portion by portion, she shuddered. She could never remove enough bows to make a difference.

Worse yet, she was girted so tightly she could hardly draw a shallow breath. Tonight she might very well swoon before Lon proposed, saying he intended to propose at all, which at the moment seemed unlikely. He would probably take one look at her and think she belonged in pigtails.

"Sugar?" Papa's voice came low at the door. "Jasper's

here. Don't make him late. You know he won't want to
walk in behind the lieutenants.''

Grim-faced, Sabrina opened the door and stood before
her father. Attired for the soiree in his dress-blue Quarter-
master uniform, resplendent with gleaming brass and rows
of service ribbons, Edward Bolton looked every inch the
role he played in Sabrina's life: He was her hero.

Tall and broad, his auburn hair now sandy with the
advent of gray, Papa was more handsome than any fictional
hero she had ever read about. Her hero. And so much
more.

Papa was her ally. He never failed to come to her aid
when Mama made unfair demands.

''She means well, sugar,'' he would say. ''She's had a
rough time of it, but she'll be well one day. You'll see. We
just have to be patient with her until then. She'll get over
it.''

Sabrina never doubted that her father had loved Serena
as dearly as her mother had. But the past fourteen years
taught her that a man's role in the family was to be strong
and to give comfort.

*Like the savage drying her tears with tender hands to her face,
turning her flesh to quicksilver by his simple touch?* Coming out
of the blue, the thought shocked her.

''Jasper's here,'' Edward said again.

She snapped back to reality. How could she think about
a renegade at a time like this? ''Oh, Papa. It's awful!''

''No, sugar.'' His brown eyes grew dewy. ''You're pretty
as a picture.''

A picture? Only one picture mattered in the Bolton
household. The one hanging above the mantel. Two little
girls. Twins. But not identical.

One had a full head of auburn ringlets and a sweet,
lovely smile. She would never have needed a giant bow to

hold her curls in place; they sprang like springs without any coaxing.

The other child wore a grimace, for her plank-straight hair was pulled back from her forehead in tight French braids, which Sabrina to this day credited with creating the arch in her eyebrows.

Two little girls. One serene, as her name suggested. The other a flurry of provocation. If Serena were alive there would be swags instead of bows. For Serena would surely have been the lady their mother so desperately wanted. Serena would never have dashed into the road half-dressed and ruined the gown their mother worked her fingers to the bone—

She fought tears. "I'm sorry, Papa. She tries so hard."

Edward took the straight-edge from her hand. While Martha cooed to Lon Jasper in the parlor, he discreetly sliced away another handful of bows, then kissed Sabrina on the forehead.

"Chin up, sugar. You'll still be the belle of the ball."

She smiled, rueful. "I'm just worried about how I'll make it through the soiree without breathing." In the parlor she kissed her mother on the cheek and thanked her for the gown.

"Trust me, child," Martha whispered. "Tonight will be the night. For you and your handsome captain. And for all of us."

The latter reference was to the other announcement Martha had her heart set on hearing tonight—that Fort Davis was being closed and its soldiers marched home to civilization. Rumors of the fort's closing had been rampant of late, exacerbated by the visit of Senator Carmichael.

Outside Lon gave Sabrina a quick once-over. "Yep. I should have worn more ribbons."

Grateful for his good-natured response, she squeezed her hand in the crook of his arm. "You're just what I needed tonight, Lon. A good sport. I'm sure there isn't another captain in our entire army who would attend a commander's party with a Christmas tree on his arm."

The church, which served as social hall and schoolhouse in addition to its primary function, was full by the time they arrived. Lively strains of "Under the Double Eagle" drifted through open windows.

Carrie Young and her lieutenant husband Neil fell in line behind Sabrina and Lon. The strawberry blonde skipped up the steps in a cloud-pink gown of a new fabric *Godey's* called dotted swiss. On the porch she stopped and pressed a hand to her chest. "I haven't drawn an easy breath since I arrived in this place."

"It's the altitude." Sabrina tried to inhale. "For you."

Carrie tiptoed to whisper in Sabrina's ear. "I know I was wrong, but I bet your mama will be right. Tonight's the night."

"The night I expire," Sabrina returned. "Mama didn't let out this bodice. How does she expect me to accept a marriage proposal if I can't draw a breath?"

Carrie eyed Sabrina's waist. "It's your corset." To prove the point, she pinched an inch of green silk at Sabrina's waist. "She laced it too tight. We can go over to my house and fix it."

Tempted, Sabrina glanced to Lon, whose attention was already on the receiving line. "Later, maybe. Lon's almost as anxious as Mama to meet Senator Carmichael. Colonel Merritt assigned him to the senator's temporary staff."

"My, my, aren't we important," Carrie teased, obviously not as impressed as Mama had been. "Well, tell me when you're ready to loosen your stays." Before Sabrina turned away, the newlywed patted her tummy, pantomiming a question that needed no words.

"As tightly as I'm girted, Carrie, any butterflies in my stomach are already smothered."

"Your bows are coming off, too." Carrie fingered a small gold bow that hung from a thread. It fell off in her palm.

Sabrina grimaced. "Keep it. I have a few hundred to spare."

Then Lon was tugging her away, guiding her through the receiving line, past Mrs. Merritt, the colonel's wife, who welcomed them politely with never a wayward peek at the atrocious gown; to the post commander, Lieutenant Colonel Wesley Merritt, who introduced Senator J. J. Carmichael.

After all the build up, the senator wasn't nearly as impressive as his reputation—not to Sabrina. A stout man, he looked a good decade older than Papa. Muttonchop side whiskers accentuated his round face which, stained red, bespoke intemperance, as did his rotund belly. When his glassy eyes blatantly dropped from Sabrina's face to her chest, she whispered a silent prayer of thanks for her mother's staid sense of modesty. A mammoth gold bow hid any hint of a bosom.

Anxious to meet his own destiny, Lon didn't appear to notice the senator's lascivious inspection of her person. The moment the colonel introduced them, Lon reached for Carmichael's hand. "Colonel Merritt assigned me to your staff, sir."

"Ah, yes, Captain Jasper." Carmichael's amorous twinkle vanished in an instant, replaced by a lusty welcome and vigorous handshake, both of which appeared feigned to Sabrina. Of course, she probably judged the man unfairly. He was all Mama had talked about lately, and Mama tended to run any subject to ground.

Fortunately the senator seemed genuinely interested in Lon, for Lon, like Martha, had enthused for days.

"It's my chance of a lifetime, Sabrina." Lon had picked

up Mama's favorite term. After which, he recounted—and recounted—in glowing detail how Carmichael's prestige in governmental circles would be a godsend to his own career.

Carmichael continued to pump Lon's hand. "Merritt says you'll be a big help in treating with the Apache. Says you know more about those red devils than any man around."

Red devils? Sabrina's head snapped up. Two days ago she wouldn't have noticed the slur, but now, after meeting—

"Thank you, sir. I've seen my share of the savages."

Stifling an uncharacteristic rise of anger, Sabrina made her way through the rest of the line, leaving Lon to gush over the senator. Alone in the middle of the floor, she searched the room for friends, admired the decorations— festive bouquets of spring wildflowers graced the mantel and tables, red and blue ribbons draped lamp fixtures and the bandstand—and stewed.

Within moments Lon joined her. "If we hurry we can get behind Senator Carmichael and Mrs. Merritt for the Grand—"

"Senator Carmichael!" Mama's animated voice rose above the din. "A privilege and an honor, sir."

Sabrina turned in time to see her mother vigorously pump the senator's hand.

"Do tell me you've brought orders for us to return east. That *is* why you've come. I just know it." The black ostrich feathers on Martha's moire bonnet bobbled in rhythm to her enthusiasm. When one inadvertently brushed the senator across the nose, he swatted it away.

"East, madam?" His voice reverberated through the room with the percussion of a cannon shot. "I should say not. We haven't finished cleaning house out here, yet. Trust me, Mrs. Bolton, once we rid this place of those red devil Apaches, you won't want to leave. This land will be as civilized as the East ever was."

"But I so hoped . . ." Martha's countenance had fallen flat.

"No, no, my dear lady. We are here to stay. The railroad's next. Then the settlers. This land is our destiny."

Her mother's crestfallen expression tore straight to Sabrina's heart. Despite hers and Papa's warnings, Mama had once again placed all her hopes and dreams in one basket. Returning east ranked right up there with securing Sabrina a suitable husband.

This certainly wasn't Martha's first disappointment. Nor, Sabrina knew, would it be her last. Mama had a knack for setting herself up for one emotional fall after another, as though she dared fate to hurt her again and again. As though she were crying, "You took my daughter—see what else you can do to destroy me."

Papa believed Mama would heal, given time. After fourteen years Sabrina didn't know what to believe, except that she must always be there to pick her mother up when life knocked her down. That was the least a lone remaining twin daughter could do.

Anxiously, now, she watched Papa usher Mama through the remainder of the receiving line. When they came close enough, Sabrina reached a hand.

"Get in line with us, Mama."

But Martha already had her handkerchief to her face. "I'm not up to it, child." Glancing left to right and back, she waved a limp-wristed hand. "I feel a bit of a . . . headache."

"Help her find a chair, sugar." Edward sounded tired, yet resigned. "Jasper and I will fetch some punch."

Obligingly, Sabrina guided Martha toward a row of chairs banked along the far wall. She paid scant heed to greetings called from either side, until a man materialized out of the crowd.

"Need a hand? Let me help."

"Nick!" Relief swept through her at the appearance of Nick Bourbon. Handsome and articulate, Nick owned a hunting lodge in the mountains. Not much else was known about him, except that he came from somewhere in Europe and was liked and respected by all. If Lon Jasper was a gentleman, Nick Bourbon was one in capital letters. Along with a number of other civilians, Nick attended post social functions when he was in the area.

"Don't tell me my two favorite ladies intend to sit out the Grand March."

Sabrina raised her eyebrows, while Martha complained, "I'm not up to dancing, Nick. I had so hoped ... I just knew the senator had come to—"

"Over here," Sabrina broke in. "Papa will be back in a minute. He and Lon have gone for punch." While Nick assisted Martha into a chair, Sabrina glanced around for sight of her father. Martha's "spells," as the family called them, were bad enough at home. Sabrina always hated for them to occur in public. Even though her mother was well liked on the post, the sharp-tongued gossips used anything for fodder—

When Sabrina's eyes fell on the man who stood still as a statue to Nick's left, her thoughts came to a jarring, jolting halt. All sound stilled. Every concern melted under the scrutiny of those intense green eyes.

Tremayne.

Chapter Five

Tremayne.

She recognized him by his eyes—only his eyes. For in that initial moment he in no way resembled the savage who had flung her against the wall of the steward's house, then dried her tears with his thumbs.

Searching his face for confirmation, she found it aplenty. Broad planes, narrow angles. Handsome. Oh, yes, he was as handsome as she recalled, in that dark, rugged way. Again she felt his strength and sensed that it emanated from something deep within him, from some profound human tragedy, perhaps, that reached out and grabbed her heart, like he had grabbed her arm that night. Who was this man? This renegade whose presence dried her skin and whose lips beckoned hers? Seeing him left her breathless, feeling wild and reckless.

"Sabrina, let me introduce . . ." Nick's voice filtered through the hum in her head, but she paid it little heed.

Momentarily stunned, she felt that her senses were impaired. Unable to either speak or hear properly, she could only lift her face and take the assault of those intense green eyes head-on. For an uncomfortable minute, the floor seemed to give way beneath her feet. The walls began to spin. When things steadied she felt lighter, as if a heavy coat had slipped from her shoulders, leaving her both lighthearted and light-headed. She felt as though she were drifting.

"I forgot," Nick was saying. "You've already met."

Met? Her gaze swung to Nick. The room still spun, a vibrant mix of colors—blue uniforms and multicolored dresses. Nick was in black. His face seemed to peer at her from close range, which distorted his cheeks, his Romanesque nose, his huge black eyes. Beside him . . .

"No." Her breath caught and she was suddenly angry that her mother hadn't let out the bodice. If she ever needed to draw a decent breath, this was the time. Boldly she found Tremayne's gaze and her voice. "Mr. Tremayne and I have not been introduced."

Something light and airy fluttered inside her at his look of surprise when she spoke his name. He took her offered hand. His was large and hot, familiarly so. The room shrank around them. Her lungs strained against the corset. She drew a tremulous breath.

"I thought you said you'd met," Nick was saying.

"I said we talked." That same deep, rich voice. Those same intense green eyes. They never left Sabrina's face. She knew she was trembling. Seeing the man she called savage standing in the midst of her own very civilized life was an astonishing thing. More astonishing still, he looked for all the world as if he belonged.

Not that he blended in. This man would never blend in. Not even dressed as now in a tailored black suit, dark hair pulled straight back from his face, caught at the nape by something or other. No red headband in sight.

Except in her mind's eye.

"Miss Bolton." Even that wild, down-from-the-hills voice sounded civilized.

"We're here to meet with the senator," Nick explained. "Tremayne has agreed to work on the peace negotiations."

"Peace?"

Nick chuckled. "You sound as skeptical as my friend. Oh, here comes Edward now."

Until Nick glanced to the row of chairs behind her, Sabrina had forgotten her mother. When her father approached, she somehow managed to draw her attention from Tremayne and take the cup of punch. As she turned toward her mother, she was gripped by the strange sensation of turning away from the light, of reaching into the dark. She aided her mother by rote.

Behind her in the light, the men busily greeted one another.

"Nick Bourbon!" her father exclaimed. "Long time no see. Where you been keeping yourself?"

Edward was easily the friendliest man on the post. Martha often chided him for being overly boisterous: "It isn't proper, Edward. Officers and gentlemen contain themselves."

Sabrina listened now, while Edward continued as gregariously as ever. "Tremayne! You old son of a gun! Good to see you."

Papa knows Tremayne? Fascination fluttered inside her. By the time she turned back to the men, the scene had become bizarre. Senator Carmichael strode toward them with a lumbering, bear-like gait, followed by two men who had been introduced as his aides.

Then came Lon. Not until he stood toe-to-toe with Tremayne did she recall the animosity each man had expressed toward the other. She hadn't considered that they might actually have met.

"See you aren't particular who you keep company with,

Nick," Lon charged. Dismayed, Sabrina searched Lon's face for signs he was joking but found none.

Nor was there any hint of amusement in Tremayne's expression. His features were tight, fierce. He might be dressed in civilized, white man's clothing, but at this moment he appeared pure savage. His eyes glowered; his lips were pursed; a muscle in his jaw twitched.

"He on the guest list?" Lon prompted when Nick failed to respond to his earlier barb.

"Tremayne and I are here at the behest of Colonel Merritt," Nick explained in even tones. "For the peace process."

"I doubt there'll be talk of peace tonight," Lon returned. "Tonight is for revelry. The *civilized* kind."

Sabrina could practically hear war drums, so palpable was the sense of loathing in the air. She would never have believed Lon capable of such an unabashed affront. Less offensive remarks had started brawls—or wars. In two steps she reached him. Placing a hand on his arm, she drew his startled attention.

His blond eyebrows popped up. "Sorry, Sabrina. You weren't meant to hear that."

Fury vied with acute embarrassment. She wanted to berate him for saying such disgusting things in the first place, but she didn't know how. She wanted to apologize to Tremayne, but she didn't know how to do that, either. Anger continued to simmer in his green eyes, which were fixed on Lon.

Yes, these two men must know each other. And hate each other. Desperate to avoid a confrontation, she tugged Lon toward the dance floor. But once in his arms, she became even more discomfited, for Tremayne followed her with a steady gaze.

He had accused her of belonging to Lon. Now he knew she did. Not that it mattered. It couldn't matter. He was married. She pursed her lips, recalling how she had fantasized about kissing him. With his eyes following her around the brightly lit ballroom, the idea flustered her. Breathing became painful.

"Do you know Mr. Tremayne?" she asked when they were safely out of earshot.

"I wouldn't call him mister," Lon retorted. "Man's a troublemaker, that's what he is. But yes, I know him. Dealt with him out at Bliss, or tried to." Gracefully, he swung her in a wide arc. Lon was easily the best dancer on the post. They glided past Tremayne with her back to him. She felt, or imagined she felt, his unwavering gaze burn into her from behind.

Gathering her wits, she chanced another question. "Who is he?"

"I told you who he is, Sabrina. A renegade white man. The West is full of them. Men who shirk responsibility. Who abandon the civilized world for what they consider freedom. They should know there is no freedom without responsibility."

Having lived her entire life on army posts, Sabrina was familiar with that claim. She had always agreed with it, and thought now that Tremayne must, too. Wasn't he working for peace? She resisted coming to his defense.

"Without order," Lon continued, "society would fall apart. All men must obey the laws or pay the penalty. That's what we've come west to create, an ordered society. No savage is going to stand in our way, red man or white."

Lon, the soldier. He followed rules in a rigid, uncompromising fashion. He was destined to go far. Everyone said so.

"Tremayne fancies himself a warrior," Lon startled her by saying. "A savage. He's wild and undisciplined, Sabrina. A scourge to our race."

By now they had rounded the far end of the dance floor.

Inadvertently her eyes sought Tremayne. His were already fixed on her. The jolt of meeting his gaze left her weak in the stomach. A savage? No.

Wild and undisciplined? Undeniably. For while Lon led her toward him in the waltz, Tremayne watched her every step with undisguised absorption. What was he thinking?

Why did it matter? she demanded silently, desperately. Why had the sight of him set the room to spinning? Why did his gaze fire her skin? How would she make it through this night when her shallow breath choked in her throat every time she looked at him? And even when she didn't, she *felt* his eyes on her. It was astonishing, this rapt attention, as if she were the only other person in the room.

By the time the music stopped, Sabrina's composure was as hard-won as her breath. "I'm afraid I won't be much of a dancing partner tonight," she told Lon. He didn't seem to care. He and the senator had taken a liking to each other.

Across the room Nick and Papa and several of the Chihuahua crowd had claimed Tremayne's attention, to both her chagrin and her relief. This might be a perfect time to loosen her corset. But when she spied Carrie, the newlywed danced in her husband's arms, her pink froth of a gown floating around them like a private cloud. The sight tugged poignantly at Sabrina's heart. And lower, where an insistent gnawing left her with a strange sense of urgency . . . or expectancy. She wasn't sure what it meant, but she sensed this was not the time to disturb Carrie.

When Harry Applebee requested a dance, she welcomed the distraction. On the floor he immediately launched a discussion of little Emily. Reba had stayed home, he said, with the child.

"Maybe you could drop around tomorrow, Sabrina."

His tone alarmed her. "What's wrong?"

"It isn't working. The poor little thing is withering away.

She never makes a sound. She won't eat. She's terrified of everything, even my uniform. I've taken to dressing out back in the room attached to the cook shack. We keep the curtains drawn in the house, and Reba holds her at every bugle call."

"I'll be there first thing tomorrow," Sabrina promised. "Right after Sick Call." Guilt nudged her. *Why hadn't she kept an eye on the situation?* She had intended to but demurred for personal reasons. Relegating the reality of that day to fantasy had proved a difficult task. She didn't need anything to remind her of its reality. Now she was sorry for being so selfish.

Watch over her, Sabrina, Tremayne had asked.

She hadn't. How fickle she had been. How . . . Inspiration struck suddenly. She stopped in the middle of the dance floor, prompting Harry to stop, too.

"What is it?"

Quickly, before sanity returned to temper her impetuousness, she took his arm. "Let me introduce you to someone who might be able to help." With a rapidly beating pulse, fluttering insides, and waning courage, she led him off the dance floor and toward the group of men in the far corner. As commonly happened with impromptu decisions, sanity soon kicked in.

This isn't about little Emily, Sabrina.

Of course, it is.

It is not. You don't have a lick of sense.

Harry needs—

Harry, my foot. It's Tremayne. With or without that red headband and flowing hair, he's wild.

Wild and undisciplined?

You're the one who is wild and undisciplined, Sabrina. Will you never learn?

As alert as a predator, Tremayne lifted his head at their approach and found her eyes. His face remained a mask, implacable, unreadable. But his gaze. . . . oh, his gaze. Like a tether on a young colt, his unwavering gaze drew her to him, even as she fought the compelling urge to retreat. Her indecision must have showed, for when they came closer he excused himself from the group and stepped toward them.

"Mr. Tremayne." Her gaze skimmed his face, while her heart skittered in her chest. Its erratic cadence beat at odds with the music from the regimental band, making her feel uncertain and slightly off balance. "This is Major Harry Applebee."

Tremayne recognized the name. She saw that in a heart-beat. Green eyes grew dark. Jaws clenched beneath swarthy cheeks. Tight-lipped, he cut a narrowed gaze her way.

Was she betraying his trust? She saw the question form.

"Harry and his wife need help with an Apache child they have taken to raise," she explained quickly.

"We're doing our damnedest with her," Harry added, "but she isn't responding. Any advice you can give will be . . ."

Tremayne stood tense, as though poised to strike, and intimidatingly silent. Harry's words drifted off. At length, he tried again. "We want her to be happy."

"She'll come around," Tremayne finally offered. His words sounded as brittle as limbs snapped from a dead tree. "Give her time."

"Perhaps you could look in on her?" Sabrina's request was met by a glare of stony accusation. Nothing undisciplined about him now. Only wild. Wildness, coupled with a sense of imminent, controlled disaster.

The major must have sensed it, too, or at least the futility of further conversation, for he offered his hand. "If time is what it takes, time is what we have. We are determined to make this work."

Still Tremayne remained unmoving. Finally Harry

dropped his hand to Sabrina's shoulder. "Reba is following your suggestion," he told her. "She constantly sings to our little Emily, every song she knows, some she just makes up."

"Wonderful." Sabrina's response came in broken syllables, which seemed to add to Harry's discomfiture. He glanced from Sabrina to Tremayne and back.

"I'd better get going. May I return you to Captain Jasper?"

Determined to make amends for a situation she had created, Sabrina drew as deep a breath as her girted state allowed and plunged dauntlessly ahead with the only excuse that came to mind. "Thank you, Harry, but this dance is promised to Mr. Tremayne."

"Certainly, my dear." Obviously confused but hiding it well, as befitted a major and a gentleman, Harry offered his open palm, in which rested a small gold bow.

A feeble laugh strained through her throat. "Take it home to Reba. I have bows to spare tonight."

After Harry left, the awkwardness became a physical thing between them. Tremayne remained silent, arms crossed rigidly over his chest. Sabrina stewed in her own juice, as Papa often said, having compounded her original error of expecting Tremayne to talk freely with Harry, the white man who would raise his niece, by shamelessly asking him to dance. But she wasn't the only one at fault here.

She wanted to berate him for his callousness to Harry. She should return to Lon. Across the room she spied him, still in conversation with the lecherous Senator Carmichael. Every time she had looked tonight, Carmichael had been leering at one officer's wife or another. He made her skin crawl.

Beside her stood Tremayne. She felt him. *Felt him,* when they stood a good foot apart. Yes, she should return to

Lon. But . . . After Lon's rudeness, perhaps she should stay
and . . .

You're rationalizing, Sabrina.

Before she talked herself out of it, Sabrina sucked in
enough breath to carry a sentence. The least she could do
was apologize. "Mr. Tremayne, I—"

"It's Tremayne."

His abrupt response took her aback. When she chanced
a look, he was staring at her with a hint of amusement.
The bottom fell completely out of her stomach this time.
How on earth would a real smile from this man affect her?
"Tremayne what?" she quizzed over the clamor in her
head.

Not a lick of sense.

"Just Tremayne, to you white people." His scornful
retort belied the intensity in his eyes, which bore into her,
shutting out everything around them—music, laughter,
people. "Apaches don't generally use names," he
explained, quieter now.

Her skittishness settled into a hum of fascination. "How
do they address one another without names?"

He studied her face with absorption, as though he had
never seen it before. And she soaked up his attention as
if he had every right to give it.

"We describe the person," he said after a while, empha-
sis on *we*. "Take me. I could be described as the man who
ran down the woman with hair like a red fox."

He took her completely by surprise. She touched her
hair beneath the large gold bow. "Red fox?"

"The pelt is highly prized by my people."

The air around them teemed with something tangible,
something that separated them, even as it drew them
together. When she trusted her voice, she returned, "Then
I should fear for my scalp?"

"I'm a renegade, Miss Bolton. I rarely collect scalps."

What about hearts?
Not a lick of sense!

"I never called you a renegade." Breathing inflicted welcome pain. It told her this encounter was real, not fantasy.

Reality. This man was as near a savage as anyone she had ever met. He was forbidden to her. Even if he weren't married, he would be forbidden to her. Why, if they weren't so preoccupied with their own lives, Mama or Lon or even Papa might have already witnessed this runaway fascination, which must be obvious to the most impartial bystander. Any moment they could drag her away. . . .

Yet, he was a friend of Nick's. No friend of Nick's could be savage or even truly forbidden. What harm could it do to be nice? Here in a crowded room, for heaven's sake. His friend was dead. He lost his niece. Lon insulted him. . . .

Not a lick of sense.

Recklessly, she forged ahead. "Now that I've asked, would you mind if we danced?"

Before the words were half out of her mouth, he had swept her gown with a perusal that left her heated and flushed. "The last time I got too close to you in a fancy gown, the gown lost." His gaze found hers. Held hers.

Time seemed marked by the beat of her heart.

Desperately she ducked her head, feigning interest in the hideous gown. "Mama sewed everything down good and tight this time." But the gown belied her claim. In numerous places bows had either fallen off or were hanging by a thread. She plucked one and held it in her palm.

"Some of it," she added wryly. "This is embarrassing. Mama has probably swooned by now."

But thoughts of her mother didn't have a chance when she stood this close to Tremayne. She warmed beneath his inspection as he studied her, head cocked, that hint of amusement on lips she had dreamed about far too often lately. She felt heady with some burgeoning new power. Fleeting thoughts of kissing him were not so fleeting any more.

Then, without warning, his expression changed. Spying something over her shoulder, his mercurial disposition turned contemptuous. "Find another partner, Miss Bolton. I'm not much for dancing. Not the *civilized* kind."

"Sabrina."

Lon!

Coming up behind her, he took her arm, but his attention was on Tremayne. "What are you—"

Like earlier, Sabrina felt caught in a stranglehold of contention between these two men. She resented Lon's intrusion. She resented his very being. . . .

Yet, Lon wasn't the outsider here. Tremayne was. Quickly she extended an open palm, not so much a peace offering as a plea for him to leave Tremayne alone.

Lon snatched the little bow. "What do you know? I rate one, too."

His sarcasm stung, but Sabrina held her tongue. Two reels and a waltz later he had "simmered down," as Mama would have said; he hadn't mentioned Tremayne, and Sabrina had resisted so much as a peek at the man.

Not that he wasn't on her mind. She knew she had flirted with him. Her boldness surprised and embarrassed her.

But she wasn't sorry. She would do it again in a minute, should the chance arise. That didn't seem likely, given the fact that Tremayne was on everyone's mind.

Especially the ladies—at the punch table, along the edge of the dance floor. Her atrocious gown hadn't caused a ripple tonight, for Tremayne had captured the attention of every female in the room. She longed to look at him, to see where *his* attention was.

But if it happened to be on her, she could find herself

in trouble. Post gossip would sink to new depths with rumors of an illicit love affair.

Love affair, Sabrina? Hasn't this fantasy gone a bit far?

Once Lon stopped in the middle of the dance floor and had her fasten the gold bow to his jacket, using one of his service medals.

"I can't be the only man in the room not wearing one." This time he said it with a smile.

"There." She patted the bow in place.

Lon was right. Practically every man in the room wore one of her gold bows on his jacket. Every man but one.

Tremayne's black suit remained unadorned.

When Senator Carmichael hailed Lon, Sabrina was relieved. "I'll sit with Mama awhile."

"Fine. We've neglected her tonight."

If he was trying to pique her guilty conscience, he didn't succeed, for Sabrina had far more urgent things to worry about—namely breathing. With the senator keeping Lon occupied, this might be the perfect time to slip away to Carrie's house and loosen her stays. But Carrie and Neil were dancing again. She hated to disturb them. Perhaps . . .

Sabrina checked the whereabouts of anyone who might miss her. Thelma McCandless was sitting with Mama, Lon was with the senator, and Papa . . .

Allowing herself a brief glance across the room, she located Papa in the crowd of Chihuahua businessmen. Lingering a moment, she found Tremayne in the center of the group. His attention was on the men, his back to the dance floor.

In the space of a split second she experienced a surge of sheer joy at seeing him, followed by a sharp pain of abandonment to find his attention elsewhere.

Abandonment? This fantasy has definitely gone too far.

Indeed. Relinquishing fantasy to reality, Sabrina stole behind the senator's group and out the back door. Her plan was simple. While everyone's attention was occupied, she would slip out behind the building where there were plenty of boulders to hide behind, loosen her stays, and return before anyone noticed.

Guided by an inky sky studded with millions of stars, she headed for the nearest cluster of boulders. Once out of sight, she groped hurriedly with the buttons at the back of her gown, easing them one by one from their loops. In no time she had unbuttoned her dress and three petticoats and reached beneath her corset cover. Locating her laces, she quickly worked the bow loose. Elated, she knew her plan would work. Just a few more . . .

"Sabrina?" The call came from beyond the boulders. She froze.

Tremayne! His low, deep voice shocked her. Panicked, she gaped dumbstruck, as though she could see through the stone to the man himself. "Stop right there," she ordered.

"I have to talk to you," he said.

The three-quarter moon was high and bright, and lit the clearing like a bonfire would have done. "Don't come any closer."

How could this happen? How could one man find her with her dress undone, not once, but twice? She, who never . . .

"It's about . . . Emily." The name strangled out.

Her heart thrashed against her stays.

"I couldn't talk in there," he continued. "I don't tolerate white soldiers very well."

"So I noticed. It was a toss-up whose manners were worse, yours or Lon's." *Concentrate,* she ordered. *Concentrate.* With the bow untied, she worked her fingers through the laces from her waist as far up her back as she could reach.

When he didn't respond, she made conversation, desperate to finish with her dress, to keep him here. "Harry isn't like Lon." Still he didn't answer, and she came up with something else to worry about. Had he gone? If she could keep him from leaving until she finished loosening her stays, she could talk to him face-to-face.

Face-to-face in the moonlight, Sabrina? You really don't have a lick of sense.

"Harry is different," she tried.

"How? Will he allow us to live in peace?"

Sabrina savored the first good breath she had drawn all evening. Not even Tremayne's cynicism could deny her the pleasure. "Harry and Reba will love the child," she insisted.

No response, only night sounds—crickets, a far-off rock dislodged from the hillside by a passing animal, the wind playing cool and soft around the boulders. Tremayne said nothing, while Sabrina searched for a way to extend the contact.

Her fingers were cold and fumbling. She forced them to stuff the loosened laces beneath her corset cover, eager, so eager, to step around the boulder and see him. In her mind's eye moonlight glinted from his wavy hair, loose and flowing beneath the red headband.

Wild and undisciplined, that's you, Sabrina. Or could it be his wildness that made her so?

"Tell the major's wife not to sing to her."

"Not to . . . ? You said to sing." One after the other, Sabrina buttoned her petticoats.

"I was wrong. Tell her not to sing in English. To hum."

"She'll hear English in other ways. They can't stop talking."

"In time she'll get used to it. It'll be natural. But not so soon, not in a lullaby."

"Oh." Spoken aloud in his deep, sad voice, the truth was sickening. *Her mother sang to her,* he had said. "Take her home, Tremayne."

"This way is best."

"It can't be. Take her home. There must be some-one—"

"I know what's best, Sabrina."

Didn't men always? She recalled Lon's rigid adherence to rules. But this was different. "She's frightened. Harry said his uniform frightens her, and bugle calls."

From the foothills came the cry of a coyote. From beyond the boulder came a quieter sound. Short and guttural, it shattered her senses. She remembered thinking she would always share his pain. She felt it now.

"Blue uniforms and bugle calls frighten us all," he said at length.

Us. Did he do that intentionally? Did he relish reminding her of the vast differences between them. Loop by loop she buttoned her dress. "All soldiers are not bad soldiers."

"All Apaches are not wild savages."

His rage refuted any claim that she could share his pain. No one who hadn't experienced such a life could share it. Strangely, this left her feeling abandoned again.

And frightened. Lord in heaven! She had buttoned her dress wrong. Unfastening it, she started over.

"Obviously, you are civilized," she tried to placate. Still she searched for ways to keep the conversation alive. He couldn't leave before she finished. "Tonight you fit right in—"

"That's what's wrong with you people. Your idea of civilization applies only to your own ways."

"But you aren't Apache," she argued weakly.

"Tell that to the Apache woman who took me in and raised me."

How did she always manage to say the wrong thing? "I'm sorry." She had never issued a more heartfelt apology, but it was met by silence.

Sabrina had other worries, however. Panicked that she

could not button her gown in time to return to the soirée without being found out, she fumbled with the buttons. Failed again. What was wrong? She ran her fingers up and down the placket, inside the gown and out, but she couldn't isolate the problem. The truth was undeniable, and terrible in its implication—she needed help.

"Tremayne?" When he didn't immediately respond, she almost died. Was she out here alone? "Tremayne, if you're still there, help me. Please."

Before her plea faded into the cool night, he had rounded the boulder. She glanced up. He stopped short. Her heart stopped along with him.

Sight of him benumbed her. Like the wicked wife of Lot had turned to a pillar of salt, Sabrina gazed upon the forbidden and was turned to stone. His hair was still tied back, no headband in sight. Moonlight glinted from the dark depths of his feral eyes. She remembered that first evening alone with him. Slowly her heart resumed beating, but not in her chest. It throbbed heavily in her throat.

"Are you ill?"

She felt as if the sky had fallen and now lay over them, a blanket of black velvet, cross-stitched in silver, smothering, even as it drew them together. "My dress. I can't . . ." How could she tell him? With time slipping away, how could she not? Turning, she presented her back. "The buttons . . ."

He stepped near, so near it became his presence that threatened to smother her. She heard his labored breathing. Heat emanated from his body and warmed her. Again she imagined a bonfire, this one encircled by wildly dancing men with painted torsos and flowing hair.

"At the waist," she said, and felt his strong rough hands touch hers. "I had to loosen it. Mama didn't let it out and I couldn't breathe, it was choking me, I—"

"So that's why you were so short of breath tonight. A few times I thought you might fall on your face again."

And might still, she thought. His nearness left her weak.

"Bend over so I can see."

She bent and his hands moved with her. Repercussions of his touch sped along her arms.

"What is this string?"

"String?" She felt totally ignorant, as if her brain were devoid of any thought that wasn't explicitly of him. Then he tugged on her corset laces.

"Oh." How could she have gotten so flustered? "Stuff everything back inside. Button the outside buttons." *That's what was wrong,* she thought. *The laces were in the way.*

While he worked on her gown, she relaxed. The noises in her head settled down to a steady hum, a new song with new words, one word: *Tremayne, Tremayne, Tremayne.* The blanket changed from velvet to a shimmering web of starlight, a net cast around them.

"Hmm . . ." His fingers lingered inside her gown, where he traced the whalebone up and down.

The hum inside her shimmered, grew more tantalizing with each stroke of his fingers.

"Here's a curiosity," he murmured, his voice deep and low.

The shimmer burst into flame and sizzled up her spine.

"White women are made differently."

With the greatest of difficulty she resisted the compelling temptation—it felt more like a necessity—to lean against him. "Those aren't my ribs. They're stays. A . . . a corset." Wildly she thought how moonlight did unsettling things to a girl's composure. Things she would never say in the clear light of day seemed to slip out in the night.

Or was it with this man? For a moment longer, his fingers explored the corset stays, tracing them, spanning her waist, while her weakness centralized into a writhing mass in her belly. Then she heard a low, deep chuckle.

"This you call *civilized?*"

When she found her voice, she answered on a breath. "Mama insists."

His large fingers fumbled with the tiny buttons. Lightness consumed her, fluttered inside her, leaving her trembling and unsteady on her feet.

"There," he said finally. "The white lady is dressed."

Now she held her breath for a different reason—to savor the moment, the fantasy. But rather than release her he turned her by the waist, held her at arm's length, and stared solemnly into her eyes. The distance between them seemed a chasm. She couldn't read his thoughts here in the darkness. She doubted she would have been able to in broad daylight.

She wondered whether she would ever have the chance to try. Suddenly she knew she wanted another chance. He was engaged in the peace negotiations. He would be coming to the post—

He's a renegade, Sabrina. A married renegade. Mama would die.

Oh, but to kiss him. Once. Tonight.

It seemed so possible. So necessary. So . . .

Into the stillness, the back door slammed. Tremayne's hands tightened on her waist.

"Sabrina?" came a call.

Lon. Panic and anger struggled for her attention. Although she knew Tremayne recognized Lon's voice, he made no attempt to release her.

"Wait a minute, Lon," she called.

"Are you all right?" The voice was closer.

"Yes . . . but wait. I'm not . . ." She felt bound to Tremayne, his hands to her waist, his gaze to hers. A thrill sizzled through her, as though by his look, his touch, he transmitted his wildness to her. She was about to be found out, yet—

"You shouldn't have come outside alone," Lon called from across the boulder. "That damned renegade is out here somewhere. I saw him leave. No telling what a squaw man like that would do to a white woman."

Sabrina flinched at the slur. She watched Tremayne's jaw clench, felt his hands squeeze her waist. She had yet to touch him. Now she lifted a hand. Tempted to touch his face, she stopped on his arm. "Go," she whispered. "Please, go."

His gaze deepened. His stature challenged. It was a disaster in the making. For even as they stood trapped in a private aura of sensuality, sounds of running feet and worried voices joined Lon's. She envisioned an army of nosy, well-meaning people discovering them. They would string Tremayne up without question.

"Please, go."

Still he stared. Lifting a hand he stroked the back of his fingers across her cheek, lingered tantalizingly on her lips. Then she knew.

He wanted to kiss her, too. Now it was too late. He was gone. Vanished. He was good at that. And at so many other things. Like causing her heart to throb and leaving her dizzy and wanting to hold him and kiss him.

A married man. What did that say about her? About him?

Her freed lungs filled with air. She inhaled a mixture of sweet desert scents, scents irrevocably linked with this man who was infinitely more civilized than he wanted to be, and far wilder than anyone Sabrina had ever expected to encounter.

This man who pushed the limits of reality and led her into a world of fantasy, a world to which she could never truly go, nor, she sensed, ever forget.

"Sabrina," Lon called.

Gathering resolve like a coarse shawl around her shoulders, she stepped from behind the boulder.

Lon reached for her. "You had us worried."

"I'm sorry."

Martha pushed through the crowd and threw her arms around Sabrina's neck. "Let me look at you, child."

Benumbed, Sabrina braced herself against the lies that must follow. "I'm fine, Mama."

"We were worried," Lon said again. She felt his hand on her back. It felt foreign. Wrong. With rare courage, she stood her ground.

"You should have worried alone, Lon. You had no business involving Mama."

"Your mother is the one who saw you leave."

"Then she knew I left alone."

"We aren't accusing you of anything, Sabrina. Mrs. Bolton said you had gone out back just before I saw that squaw man—"

"Lon Jasper, whatever you think of Tremayne, or of anyone else, refrain from using such derogatory language in my presence."

He stiffened. "I was worried," he argued defensively. "No telling what a man like that would do to—"

"He didn't."

Sniffling, Martha stepped away and clutched a white handkerchief to her mouth. "Thank heaven for that. You shouldn't have come out alone. What were you thinking, child? Thank heaven that awful savage didn't hurt my baby."

"I'm sorry, Mama." And she was. "I didn't mean to worry you." It was one of the things Sabrina lived with— her mother's terror of losing her only remaining daughter. It wasn't a burden. Sabrina was certain she would feel the same way if she had witnessed the violent death of a child.

"I came out to loosen my stays," she whispered in Martha's ear. "Let's go inside." With an arm around her mother's shoulders, she guided her toward the building. But even after everyone returned to the festivities, the voice in Sabrina's head reviled, *Now look what you've done. You'd better make it up to her.*

She danced with Lon, while Martha moved her chair closer to the dance floor and watched from the sideline. Her loosened stays helped, or they would have if she hadn't been in such a dither.

Tremayne had almost kissed her. Even the mushrooming guilt over worrying her mother couldn't extinguish the fiery flames ignited by his touch.

Near the end of the dance, Lon questioned gently, "Still mad at me?"

"Mad at you?" How could she be mad at him for something she had done? On the other hand . . . "I didn't know you tonight. You were so rude, so . . ." She stopped short of calling him cruel.

"Maybe I was jealous."

"Then you should have taken it out on me."

"Nick shouldn't have brought that renegade here. I don't know what he was thinking."

"They came for the peace talks."

"Tremayne should have stayed outside. He doesn't belong in a room of civilized folk."

"You're the one who acted uncivilized, Lon. He didn't do a single thing, yet you attacked him."

He seemed to stare through her. "You don't know the whole of it."

She didn't want to know. She didn't want to know anything that would deny the fantasy. Not until she'd had a chance to cherish it. "No reason justifies name calling in a public place," she argued. "If you have a fight with Tremayne, settle it in private."

Lon stopped in the middle of the dance floor. Suddenly

she realized that whatever memory had flashed through his mind was gone. Now he focused on her with single-minded intent. The bottom fell out of her stomach, but it had nothing to do with her fantasy.

This was reality.

Don't let him propose, she prayed. She couldn't accept a marriage proposal as mad as she was. She wouldn't.

"Do you realize we've just had our first argument?"

First? No, Lon. Please.

"No renegade squa—" He stumbled over the word, then rephrased. "That renegade isn't worth it."

Disconcerted, Sabrina glanced to the sideline, where her mother watched with rapt attention. Seeing Sabrina, she waved her handkerchief gaily. *Gaily?* Yes. A rare smile shone on Martha's somber face.

Don't ruin this, Sabrina, the voice in her heart warned.

"I suppose you're right, Lon." She tried to smile for her mother's sake, but tears stung her eyes. Inside her the fantasy began to die.

Tremayne. She squeezed back tears. If only she had kissed him.

Chapter Six

Convinced that the fiasco with the bows had kept Lon Jasper from proposing to Sabrina, Martha Bolton set out to redesign the Worth original for the third time. Creative work, as always, revived her spirits. By the end of the week following the soiree, she even acquiesced to Sabrina's accompanying Edward to the trading post, although not without her usual reservations.

Edward had owned the trading post, located in the little town of Chihuahua just outside the post boundary, for a couple of years. He and several other officers bought businesses in Chihuahua, as a means of livelihood if and when the rumored fort closing became reality. A constant source of contention between Edward and Martha, who was determined to move back east at the earliest opportunity, the trading post provided a much needed escape for Sabrina. Even though both she and her father pampered Mama at every turn, Papa stood up for himself and for Sabrina when it came to the trading post. At least once a week he insisted that he needed Sabrina's help in town.

"Promise you will keep an eye on her, Edward," Martha fretted. "That wild man at the soiree was proof women are not safe in this barbaric land. When a savage masquerades as one of us and invades our—"

"Martha," Edward cautioned, "that's enough. I know the man Tremayne. Granted, he's a far cry from a son we would have raised, but he was well within his rights to attend the soiree. In my books the welcome mat is out for any man who can help us reach a peaceful settlement with the Apache. It isn't like he's petitioning to join post society."

Sabrina held her tongue until she and her father had set out for Chihuahua. It was dusk. The air was soft and cool, fragrant with the smells of early spring; the sky was pink, and the mountains a rich purple. Walking through the twilight to Chihuahua with Papa had always been a special time, a time for the two of them to share things they kept from Martha, by mutual consent.

Sabrina had anxiously awaited this opportunity to discuss Tremayne, but now she tried to mask her eagerness with a casual comment. "You never mentioned knowing Tremayne, Papa."

Edward didn't respond for several minutes. They crossed Limpia Creek down by the post gardens, walked through the grove of cottonwoods, and rounded the east end of Sleeping Lion Mountain.

"Never considered it important," he replied at length. "Like I told your mama, he's a different breed from a man raised in a civilized home."

Sabrina was stunned. Papa was the one person in her life who never looked down on people, never made judgments.

"I like the man," he added. "But he harbors some deep-seated hatred for whites. Raised by Apaches like he was, I reckon that's understandable."

Deep-seated hatred?

Wild and undisciplined?

And Papa knew him. A thousand questions presented themselves, but Sabrina resisted asking them lest she arouse Papa's curiosity about a situation that did not exist, could not exist.

Even if Tremayne weren't married.

Which he was.

Meanwhile, Papa's mind skipped to another, equally frustrating topic. "How're things coming along with you and Jasper?" He asked the question without so much as a cough by way of introduction.

"He hasn't proposed, if that's what you mean."

"Your mama has a keen sense about these things, sugar."

When he glanced at her askance, Sabrina laughed. "I know that, Papa. She chose you."

"That she did, over twenty years ago, and I can't say I've been sorry a day in my life."

A bold statement, Sabrina thought, considering Mama's fourteen-year state of depression.

"You won't be sorry, either."

"Me?"

When he continued, she realized that everything he said before had been prelude. "I know you're having a spell of cold feet, Sabrina, but look at it from your mama's point of view. She's almost forty. That's old for a woman of her generation. Being half that age, you might not realize, but—"

"I'm middle-aged at nineteen? Is that what you're saying, Papa?"

He draped an arm around her shoulder companionably, as if they were talking about the weather instead of about the most important choice of her life. What he said next could be interpreted to mean several things, she decided, but whichever way she looked at it, one thing was clear: She had no choice.

"I knew you would understand, sugar. Your mama's spent almost twenty years worrying about you, and she'll continue to worry until you're settled down. That's just the way of a mother. Don't you think it's time to let her rest up for those grandchildren you're going to give her one day soon?

No choice at all.

Sabrina said no more. What was left to say? Papa was right, of course. Coming from him, it carried more weight, for he never lectured or gave advice. Coming from him, it was serious. She was grown up now; it was time she settled down.

No choice. The words tolled in her heart with the ominous ring of a funeral bell.

By the time they arrived in Chihuahua, a pale, round moon had risen above the trading post, illuminating the dusky adobe building. Yellow lamplight glowed from a row of tall windows that opened onto the long front porch. Rosa Raméríz stood beneath the deep overhang.

Rosa knew all Sabrina's secrets, what few there were. At thirty she was full of vim and vigor, with a round, youthful face, long black hair, and a curvaceous figure revealed by attire Martha Bolton would find scandalous, should Martha ever meet the woman. Rosa's low-cut white blouse and flirty calico skirt made Sabrina feel downright old-womanish in her staid brown percale with high banded collar and wrist-length sleeves.

Rosa and her sheepherder husband Manuel married early. Although they had a sixteen-year-old son and another twelve, to hear Rosa tell it, she and Manuel were still wildly in love. Rosa claimed butterflies were not a true judge of love; that butterflies died early. It took something more substantial to keep the flame burning. Perhaps that was what Papa meant when he said he had never regretted marrying Mama.

Until lately, Sabrina had never wondered about such things. But since her first meeting with Tremayne, she had impatiently awaited an opportunity to confide in Rosa.

"*Hola*, Sabrina! I'm watching for Manuel's fire." Rosa's explanation was needless. Every night while Manuel was away tending his flocks, he lit a bonfire in the hills as a signal that he was safe. Rosa swore she wouldn't be able to rest without that reassurance.

Sabrina often wished her own parents could enjoy such warm companionship. From what Papa said tonight, perhaps they did. Were they as happily married as Rosa and Manuel? Could they have concealed their happiness from her?

Papa's lecture had left her confused more than anything else. Yes, it was time she settled down, but every time she imagined marriage, it was Lon Jasper's face that rose in her mind. And she hadn't even missed him very much while he was out on patrol.

Joining Rosa's search of the distant hillside, she saw a tiny fire flicker against the purple mountain.

"He's safe." Rosa returned Sabrina's embrace. "I'm glad to see you, *chica*. It's been a long time."

"We've been busy at the hospital since the troops returned."

Rosa laughed. "Here, too. The cantina is full again tonight."

Since the day it opened, Edward's trading post, half cantina/half mercantile, had been the favorite gathering place for ranchers, settlers, and off-duty troopers—a place to buy supplies, swap gossip, catch up on news, and wet one's whistle, as the saying went.

Martha knew about both establishments, but considered the cantina a separate entity, else she would never have agreed to Sabrina working in the mercantile. Tonight, true to Rosa's claim, every table was full—a few townsfolk, but mostly troopers. Floor-to-ceiling windows along the front and one side were propped open with long poles to provide ventilation for the cigar and cigarette smoke.

"*Hola,* Sabrina." José Garcia managed the cantina. He hailed her with his chin, since his hands were full of beer mugs, held three each by the handles. "Long time no see."

"I've been busy. Looks like you have, too."

"Every night since the troops returned. I'm glad you're here. Nick Bourbon is over in the mercantile waiting for Rosa to cut him some calico. Why don't you help him and let Rosa serve the senator? Not that Carmichael needs another drink. He's been bending his elbow steadily."

Sabrina had stopped listening at the mention of Nick, whose presence here was certainly not unusual. Nevertheless, since the soiree, he seemed permanently linked to Tremayne in her mind. Seeing Nick now, her limbs went weak. She lifted a leaden arm.

Then she saw Tremayne. It took a moment for him to come into focus through the haze of smoke and dim lamplight. Like at the soiree, he stood beside Nick. And, like at the soiree, the sight of him set the room to spinning.

She wondered for the hundredth time what could be so wrong with him if Nick befriended him. Nick, who was respected by all. She wondered what he was doing here. She had never seen him in Chihuahua before, had never seen him anywhere until a little over a week ago. Now he turned up everywhere she went. Why? And why had the bottom fallen out of her stomach? His mere presence took her breath.

His red headband and flowing hair were no more than treasured memories. Tonight he was again dressed in white man's clothing—fitted duckins and a chambray shirt that snugged over his shoulders. No headband—his hair was tied back like at the soiree.

"Go ahead," Rosa encouraged. "Cut Nick's calico. I'll call if I need help."

Truthfully, a herd of stampeding buffalo couldn't have held her back, and she wove her way through the tables on wobbly legs. Customers greeted her here and there, but she barely heard her name called above the thundering of her heart. Strains of Tollivar's guitar twanged faintly against the background of harsh laughter and an occasional sharp retort. She prayed her legs would hold, and her movements would not betray her. How foolish. She lost all control over her body and her brain in this man's presence.

Not a lick of sense, her conscience accused again.

When she came close, Nick, ever the gentleman, pulled out a chair at a nearby table. "Join us, Sabrina. We were just—"

"No. I can't." She avoided Tremayne's eyes; to look at him would be to lose complete control. She tried to laugh and knew it sounded weak. "This place is bursting at the seams. I have to help Rosa. José said you wanted some calico."

"For Lena. But hold on a minute. I'm going after beer for Tremayne and me. You want something?"

"No. I'll cut the fabric while you're gone."

"Give me a minute. I'll show you what I want." Then he was gone, and she was left standing dumbstruck in front of Tremayne.

Not a lick of sense.

Alone with him, while shyness overcame her, she was unable to keep from looking at his face. Pray God her trembling was all inside.

The silence between them became palpable. Aggravated by the profound effect he had on her, she blurted out the first thing that came to mind. "What are you doing here?"

He didn't respond, except to stare at her with that unwavering intensity that seemed so much a part of him. It spoke of tragedy and suffering, and set her skin afire even as it generated a legion of questions she knew she could never voice. He addressed one of them.

"Her name was Nakia."

Spoken urgently in that rich, down-from-the-hills voice, his statement socked Sabrina in the stomach.

"I called her Woman Who Captured My Heart."

It took her half a second to realize who he meant. She sucked in a breath.

"Your wife?"

"She died four years ago."

Sabrina slipped to the chair Nick had pulled out for her. All control gone, she stared up at Tremayne. His intense gaze seemed her only tether in an out-of-control world.

He isn't married.

Stop this, Sabrina.

Before she could think of a suitable reply, he added, "She was killed by soldiers."

"Soldiers?" The word blew from her lips on a weak breath. "I'm so sorry. I . . . I don't know what to say."

Seating himself opposite her, he seemed to relax, as though he had accomplished what he came here to do.

"There's nothing to say. I wanted you to know the truth. Not some lie concocted by that man of yours."

"Lon?" She fought for sensibility. All week she had struggled to deny the attraction she felt for Tremayne. For it was true. She had never felt the things she felt in his presence.

He isn't married.

His wife was killed by soldiers. Soldiers . . .

"Why would Lon lie?"

"You'll have to ask him that. I'm not exactly on speaking terms with the man."

She had sensed he had known tragedy. Now she knew part of it. Was there more? She recalled his concern for little Emily. His grief over the loss of his friend. His compassion for her own tears. This man had known suffering and anguish. He didn't deserve the vilification of small-minded men.

"I apologize for Lon's outburst at the soiree. He isn't usually like that. He never insults people. I—"

"Think what you will. I'm not here to change your mind." When he diverted his gaze to the crowd beyond them, she thought for a moment the music had stopped. But no. Tollivar still strummed. A slow tune, made poignant by the newness of what she had learned. His wife was dead.

He isn't married.

It doesn't matter.

It can't matter.

Oh, but it did. "Why *are* you here?"

"Where I don't belong?"

"Where I haven't seen you before." Her mouth was dry. She wished she had asked Nick to bring her something to drink. "I work for Papa at least once a week. I've never seen you here."

"I come into this world as little as possible. Tonight Nick and I were supposed to meet with the senator."

Sabrina followed his gaze to Senator Carmichael, who sat at a table near the bar. The table faced the door, and the senator sat in the position of power, where he could see everyone who came and went. He was surrounded by his aides, the same men who hovered around him at the soiree. She wondered suddenly where Lon was. Wasn't he on the senator's staff? Pray God he didn't walk in now.

"Not that we'll get any negotiating done tonight," Tremayne said. "Carmichael was already drunk when we arrived. That's what I like about this Washington of yours. They send us men who are as weak as their treaties.''

She didn't try to defend her world to him. Where Senator Carmichael was concerned, she tended to agree. ''A cantina isn't exactly the place for serious negotiations. Carmichael must have thought—''

''It was my idea.''

Surprised, she turned back to him. A mistake, for her stomach took another tumble. ''Yours?'' Her eyes roamed his face, the planes, the angles, the strength, skimmed his lips, the lips she still dreamed of kissing, and came to rest on his startling green eyes. Tonight, as so often before, his thoughts were unreadable.

''After your fancy party last week I told Nick I would help only if I never had to set foot on that post again.''

''Never set foot on the post?'' She felt condemned along with all the narrow-minded people who considered themselves better than buffalo soldiers and Apaches, and yes, a white man who did not follow the strict rules of their white fraternity. She wanted to defend herself, to say, ''I'm not like that.'' Discomfited, she glanced down, studied the scarred plank table. ''If you feel that way, why do you bother?''

''With peace talks?''

She nodded. Not trusting herself to look at him, she stared out the narrow window. All she saw was blackness.

''If there's a slight chance a treaty might be honored for a few years, I have to try.''

''A few years? Why not forever?''

''If you are half as bright as Nick claims, you know what forever means for my people.''

There it was again. *His people.* She felt his eyes on her.

He had talked to Nick about her.

He wasn't married. That one simple fact toppled a crucial barrier. The implication of it left her vulnerable and determined to hide it. The flutter inside her became intense. She felt light-headed. She must gather her wits. Married or single, Tremayne was not the man for her. He was the antithesis of everything she was expected to look for in a mate. Yet, wasn't that exactly what she had been thinking?

Comparing him with Lon Jasper? From the very first day she had compared him with Lon, and Lon always came out the loser. Lon, the soldier, rigid and uncompromising. Tremayne, the warrior, wild and undisciplined.

She tried to argue that it was that very wildness that attracted her to him. But was he really wild? She knew him as a quiet man. She valued quietness. As a compassionate man, in an open way that defied one to call him weak.

But in the final analysis only one thing mattered—he was totally and completely forbidden to her. Even her father, who never made judgments, said as much. She couldn't imagine her mother's reaction should he come to call—Martha, who considered him a savage.

But he wasn't. Hadn't Nick befriended him? "How long have you known Nick?"

"Four years."

Since his wife died?

"I started scouting for him. We became friends."

"You must know Lena, then," she said, searching for some safe way to keep the conversation going. Lena Saucedo was Nick's housekeeper and, many claimed, much more.

"Lena and Nick helped me get back into the white man's world."

When he didn't elaborate, she asked, "How?"

"The usual. Reading, writing." He glanced down at his attire. "Clothes."

She thought of the first time she had seen him. The image of that red headband seemed permanently etched in her memory. Wildness. Yes, that must be the attraction. And Papa considered her sensible. But what harm could it do to be nice? Here they were in a room full of people. She chanced a smile.

"They didn't teach you to dance?"

She saw again that hint of amusement. Not quite a grin, it nevertheless set her afire.

Moments passed in silence so intense it shimmered around them, like the air during a thunderstorm. Finally he changed the subject. "Nick says you're a rebel."

"A rebel? Me? I should say not. I'm the most weak-kneed person on the post." Even now she was so nervous her heart pounded in her throat. "Maybe in the whole world."

"Nick said you work at the hospital despite disapproval from all sides."

"Yes, well, I don't do all that much."

He cocked his head, studying her more candidly than ever before. "Nick says you do."

He talked to Nick about her.

Giddiness played havoc with her inhibitions and loosened her tongue. "I don't usually admit this, mind you, but some of the things I do, even you would find reprehensible."

His eyebrows quirked. "Even me?"

Lord in heaven, how did she always manage to put him on the defensive? "I didn't mean it that way."

Again moments went by in silence while he studied her, deep, probing, intense, leaving her as short of breath as at the soiree. This time she knew it wasn't her corset. She had laced it herself. Finally he nodded for her to continue. "What is it you do?"

"My latest offense was to sew up an orderly whose leg had been amputated."

"Did he survive?"

"Of course he survived."

"Then who was offended?"

Sabrina pursed her lips over the name and turned her head. She might be attracted to this man, but that was as far as it went. She could not, would not, disparage Lon to him.

"Never mind," he said, his tone a combination of nonchalance and rebuke. "I can guess."

"You don't understand. We live in totally different worlds. We have rigid rules of society, propriety that must be—" Sabrina's tirade was interrupted by a sudden escalation of noise. The room seemed to explode with it.

"By God, Carmichael!" Edward's angry voice rose above the others. "I don't care if you're the President himself, I won't stand for such behavior in my establishment."

Sabrina's attention flew to the far end of the room, where her father confronted Senator Carmichael. Edward Bolton might be taller and younger, but the senator outranked him enough to repudiate any physical consideration.

Instead of backing off, however, Edward stepped toward the belligerent man, revealing Rosa, who cowered against the bar, gripping her bodice in tight fists.

Sabrina jumped to her feet. Tremayne rose beside her.

"Edward's handling it," he said quietly.

"Is he ever!" Together they watched her father lean into the senator's face.

"The ladies in this establishment are off-limits." Edward's warning was issued loudly enough for every person in Chihuahua to hear. "Even, by God, to a United States Senator."

Carmichael glowered. The tip of his cigar glowed red as he drew on it, then arrogantly rolled it between his teeth. "Since when are barroom wenches considered ladies?"

"Since I said so, damn you."

Carmichael's flushed face went dark. Even from the distance Sabrina could tell the man had been gravely offended. Alarmed, she pushed into the crowd, only to have Tremayne catch her by the shoulders, stopping her in her tracks.

"Hold on."

"He can't do this." Panic rose inside her. "Look at Carmichael. He's furious. Papa's putting himself in a terrible position. The senator could have his job, his—"

"Let him handle it," Tremayne urged, again quietly. His hands remained on her shoulders, one each, large and hot.

Sabrina glanced back to Rosa; her panic turned to fury. The woman's hair flew about her face; torn ends of her blouse hung from her fists. In a room full of drunken men, the sight was like a lighted match tossed into the post magazine.

"Rosa Ramériz ain't nobody's whore!" came a shout from the crowd, after which a clamor erupted. A chair flew from somewhere off to the side, crashed over the head of one of the senator's aides, and the brawl commenced. The room became a melee of flying mugs, chairs, and oaths. And there was Rosa, wedged between two men.

Desperate to reach her, Sabrina tore free and plunged into the ruckus. Eyes only for Rosa, she pressed through the angry crowd. "Rosa! I'm coming!"

Tremayne caught her around the waist this time. One minute she was running, the next her feet treaded air. She glared over her shoulder.

"Put me down." Thrashing wildly, she struggled for freedom.

"Ouch! Stop kicking," was his only reply, before he pinned her arms to her chest and turned his back to the room, shielding her from the frenzied mob. Furniture crashed around them. Something careened off his shoulders. He moved.

"Put me down, Tremayne. Rosa . . . I must help her."

"Nick's closer." With that he hauled her bodily toward the nearest window.

He stumbled through the window, caught his footing, and fell against the adobe wall, pulling her with him, sheltering her in strong arms against the uproar inside, which by now sounded like all-out war.

But Tremayne held her safe from harm, her face pressed to his chest. She felt his heart throb against her. When he finally relaxed his grip, she lifted her head and stared at him. The crowd noise faded beneath the hum and flutter inside her. The world fell away from them, and they were alone. Staring fate in the eye suddenly took on a whole new meaning.

"That's weak-kneed?" he questioned.

"Where's Rosa?"

"Nick has her." His arms tightened in a proprietary way that seemed to add, *And I have you.*

Did he ever! She felt lost in him. Safe with him. Right with him. Her giddiness increased. As light as goose down, it floated inside her. Fluttered . . .

Lord in heaven! Could it be?

Butterflies?

Butterflies. She had been feeling them for days. Ever since she met him. Every time she was around him. And she hadn't known until now.

Butterflies. She strained to read his expression in the darkness. "Tremayne, I . . ." Her brain would not work; she seemed unable to speak.

Tongue-tied, that's what she was. Tongue-tied by something soft and sensual and right.

But it wasn't right. Nothing about this was right. It just felt that way.

"Isn't this where Jasper usually comes to your rescue?"

The reminder brought every swirling, fluttering sensation inside her to a standstill. Like on a teeter-totter when one child jumps off and the other falls to the ground, all movement came to a jarring halt. The earth could have stopped spinning.

For the longest time she leaned against him, suspended in time and thought, caught in a web of attraction, on the verge of stepping over a threshold into a new world, on an uncharted and certainly turbulent course.

Weak-kneed? No, she was eager. Her lips trembled with the image she had held for days. Kissing him.

I don't care, she wanted to say. *Let Lon come. Let Papa . . .*

Even as she thought it, Tremayne cupped her head in the center of a large palm and guided her face gently, slowly, toward his. Lips toward lips . . .

Her breath choked in her throat. Anticipation fogged her vision. He was going to kiss her. Like she had dreamed. Like she wanted.

He isn't married.

In the night air their breath mingled. Their lips almost touched. She trembled with a thousand prickly sensations—anticipation, fascination, expectancy—yet she possessed a startling clarity of mind and heart and desire. A touch, a brush, soft, hot, sensual . . . Heart thrashing. Pulse racing. Lips open. Wet. Wet . . .

Then everything went still.

He had twined his fingers in her hair and pulled her head to a stop. Wide-eyed they stared at each other. She felt abandoned. Butterflies fluttered anxiously, aimlessly filling her mind with a kaleidoscope of swirling colors.

What had happened?

After an eternity, or so it seemed, he shoved her face into the crook of his shoulder. "This won't work, Sabrina." His breath whispered against her temple, tingled down her body.

CHANCE OF A LIFETIME

Hope sank like lead. Despair filled the void. Tears stung her eyes, but she blinked them back.

She felt his heart beat against her and hers throb painfully in her chest. She felt the crisp fabric of his shirt and thought that it was probably new.

She wondered what that calico shirt would have felt like. The one he wore the first time she saw him. Soft, she decided. Soft and right.

But it wasn't right. Nothing about this was right. She had felt butterflies for the first time in her life, and for the wrong man. Butterflies, which in her fantasy world should have been a beginning.

In reality, they were the end. Butterflies, after all, were short-lived. Carrie was the lucky one. Rosa was right. And Mama . . .

Get hold of yourself, Sabrina. Mama deserves better from you. You are all she has left. You can't let her down again.

Tremayne rode up the corridor of red hills and entered the high mountain valley, pressing hard. Rays of the rising sun shone through breaks in the columns of red rocks, but he was aware only of the anger that burned hot and bright inside him.

Leaving Chihuahua, he headed for Apache Wells, hounded by a thousand warring emotions, trailed by an insidious attraction to a woman with white skin and flaming hair and uncommon compassion.

He had made a grave mistake returning there while Lon Jasper's slurs still rang in his ears. He had thought his conditions for continuing with the negotiating team would solve the problem: No Lon Jasper. No negotiations at the fort.

Chihuahua should have been safe. White women of Sabrina's station didn't frequent cantinas. Nick, damn his hide, should have warned him.

Reaching the ancient well he drew rein so sharply the black reared on his haunches. Tremayne slid to the ground. Apache Wells. The only place on earth he could call home. He had returned to live here only recently, after Nakia's death. Nakia's senseless death. Like Chi's senseless death. And so many others before and since and yet to come.

In despair Tremayne rested both hands on the rock well and peered into its depths. "Guide me now!" he shouted. The only answer was the echo of his own voice. He hadn't heard the laughter in years.

He had never believed in it. In twenty-odd years with the Apache, he had never been able to fully accept their belief in spiritual guardians. Why bother? What good were guardians if they didn't protect those who believed in them from white bastards like Jasper?

Dropping the ancient wooden bucket into the blackness, Tremayne held the rope as it sped through his hands. When the bucket splashed into water far below, he began to draw it to the surface, his mind on other things.

Yes, going back had been one mistake. There had been others. He should never have touched her. Not in the road, not at the hospital, not at that fancy white man's social, not tonight. Especially not tonight.

When the slight breeze blew ends of his headband against his cheek, Tremayne batted them away absently, only to realize with a jolt that he was not wearing a headband. *She had touched him there.* That night beside the steward's house, with four small pads of her fingers. He felt them still.

And he had never felt so alone. Apache Wells with its legendary well and crumbling rock dwelling might be his home, but there was no place on earth where he truly belonged.

He gripped the wooden bucket as tightly as he had

gripped the hackamore on his wild ride through the night, and stared sightlessly into the red water he had drawn. The water was just short of boiling. Steam heated his face. But instead of water he saw hair—red hair, the color of the red fox.

The color of *her* hair. A witless white man's woman who couldn't stand on her own two feet or get out of the way of a charging horse or keep her dresses fastened—or her hands to herself.

He should never have touched her. While steam bathed his face Tremayne felt the heat of that soft hot skin. He had not felt such softness in a long time. A feminine thing, that softness, it evoked memories and needs he could not dwell on—had not dwelt on since the death of his wife. Yet from her first touch, Sabrina had rendered him senseless.

And he remained so, yet. Drawn to her against his will, he could not stop thinking about her. Sabrina. The sound of her name danced upon his tongue.

She felt the attraction, too. He could tell by the way her eyes sought his. By her eagerness to touch him, by the tremor in her voice, the way her pulse throbbed in her throat.

He should have kissed her when he had the chance. She had wanted him to. Not even his mention of Lon Jasper dimmed her craving. Or his.

And he had known Jasper would not appear at the trading post. Hell, he'd arranged Jasper's absence himself. He should have kissed her.

He almost had. Only at the last minute had he regained enough of his wits to keep from making that one final mistake.

For she belonged to Lon Jasper, whether she was ready to admit it or not. Jasper, a soldier who wore the hated blue uniform to mask his true character. The uniform with yellow stripes down the legs; yellow stripes to match the

yellow stripe down his back. Even Jasper belonged somewhere—with someone.

Driven by a surge of rage and despair, Tremayne hurled
the bucket against the base of the towering mountain. Hot
red water sloshed over his *civilized* clothing, burned his
face and stained his white man's shirt and britches, but all
he felt was Sabrina's heart beating against him.

Sabrina, who in a cruel stroke of fate turned out to
be Lon Jasper's woman—which was best for her, a white
woman reared in *civilized* society. He had nothing to give
a white woman. Certainly not love. Except for Ket, he loved
no one. The soldier who murdered Nakia destroyed his
ability to love, and not even the guardian of the well could
restore it.

Not even if he believed.

When he turned from the well, they stood before him—
three Apaches pulling a travois. The youngest spoke.

"The old one among us who knows all things cannot
heal her."

Tremayne rushed to the travois. Keturah lay motionless,
lids closed over her green eyes, which were all she inherited
from him. Her beauty came from her mother. And he
loved her twice as much now that Nakia was gone.

"Ket, darling." He fell to his knees, touched her brow.
She was burning up. He stripped back the deerhide robe
and looked for a wound.

"She fell into the great bonfire three moons ago."

"Three moons ago? Why was I not told?" Fear immobilized him. He saw her leg, wrapped from the knee down
in cloth that had been soaked in some kind of foul-smelling
ointment. Witch's brew! Fear exploded into anger.

"What do you mean, the shaman cannot heal her? It is
his business."

"He has tried. He said to bring her here. Maybe the
guardian of the well—"

"The guardian of the well be damned." Tremayne scooped Ket in his arms. "This is my daughter. She cannot die." Cradling the heated body to his chest, he lay his face close to hers and carried her to the stone dwelling he had begun to rebuild. Even as his heart wept, his brain sought solutions.

Chapter Seven

"Captain Jasper stopped by while you were in Chihuahua last night." Martha's voice filtered through the closed bedroom door, startling Sabrina fully awake.

Following a sleepless night, she had intended to arise early and escape to the hospital without seeing her mother. She needed time to think. The events of the evening before and their aftermath had left her confused and lethargic, so much so that she lacked sensibility to face the coming day. It was as if all her hopes and dreams had died in Tremayne's arms, along with the butterflies.

Now, in the clear light of day, she knew her mother had been right—she was definitely given to flights of fantasy.

During the night her imagination had sprouted like windblown seeds. She and Tremayne flirted through her dreams; he lay with her in her small bed and held her in his arms. When his lips touched hers, he did not pull away. He kissed her until she was dizzy and she kissed him back, recapturing the magic, conjuring the butterflies, feeling their flutter and lightness, this time in her imagination.

"Captain Jasper was disappointed to find you gone," Martha called again.

A reply lodged in Sabrina's throat, held there by remnants of the fantasy.

Not a lick of sense.

"He expected you to be home."

The fantasy began to die. Arising, she dressed, while dead butterfly wings drifted to the pit of her stomach. She was cold and lonely. Empty. She'd felt butterflies, yet . . .

For the wrong man, her conscience accused.

He isn't married.

Married or not, he is forbidden to you, Sabrina.

Don't say that!

He knows it if you don't. Even Papa said so.

"Captain Jasper expected . . ."

Futility seeped into the hollows vacated by hope. Dismally, Sabrina jerked her corset laces, trying to ignore the chastisement in her mother's tone. This morning it wasn't hard. With the fantasy so fresh she barely heard her mother's voice. Lacing her corset reminded her of Tremayne, of his hands on her stays. Of his dismay. He charmed her. And more. So much more.

It wasn't his wildness. After last night she could no longer make that claim. When the fight broke out he was the most civilized man in the room.

Entirely too civilized, she thought, wishing for the hundredth time he had kissed her. It seemed the only thing missing now that she'd felt butterflies.

"He expected to see you, child."

"Then he should have come to the trading post, Mama." Again she wondered why he hadn't, since he was a member of Senator Carmichael's temporary staff. She wondered how he would have reacted to Carmichael's treatment of Rosa.

"Colonel Merritt assigned him to guard duty last night,"

Martha explained proudly. "The Officer of the Day took ill and Colonel Merritt called in Captain Jasper. He's a dependable man, Sabrina. Dependable and . . ."

Despair flooded Sabrina's small room. She was glad Lon had been absent from the trading post last night, for whatever reason. Glad he hadn't been there for her to witness his reaction to Carmichael's maltreatment of Rosa.

The despair thickened like fog and she thought she might suffocate on it. How could she judge Lon so harshly? So unfairly? She was selfish, nothing less. She hadn't wanted Lon around when she kissed another man. It was that pure and simple. How could she face him after last night? Last night, when she'd felt so right in another man's arms.

"I invited him to supper tonight, Sabrina. Come out so we can discuss the menu."

"The menu?" How could she think of food when her head was filled with despair?

"You must come home early to help prepare," Martha continued. "I'm planning a candlelight supper."

"A candlelight . . . ?" When she opened the door, Martha stood with polishing cloth in one hand, a silver candelabra in the other. "Mama, I . . ." Sabrina's despair settled into the nest of dead butterfly wings in the pit of her stomach. A cold premonition swept her, leaving her with the sickest feeling. Was this to be her fate? Was she even now staring it in the eye?

No, she prayed. But the fantasy was already dying inside her. Her conscience was right. Not even Tremayne believed it could work, else he would have kissed her. That was the only explanation for why he hadn't. What harm could one kiss in the dark have done?

More mysterious was her profound disappointment that he hadn't. Why had she wanted him to kiss her? Why did she want it still? She hated kissing. She avoided kissing

Lon at every opportunity. So, why did she long to kiss Tremayne?

It made no sense. Certainly not in the clear light of day. Her conscience was right. Even Papa disapproved of Tremayne.

As if he hadn't made it clear enough on the way to Chihuahua the evening before, on their way home, he reiterated his concern.

"We'll hope no one noticed you sitting at the table with Tremayne, sugar. I realize you're too sensible to let a thing like that get out of hand, but you know how the gossip would distress your mama."

Sabrina knew, all right. By now she also knew that Papa would be as stunned as Mama if he learned the truth. Fortunately Tremayne had vanished into the night as soon as the fight was quelled. She was confident Papa hadn't seen what transpired on the porch. She hoped no one else had.

"I'll be home after Sick Call," she promised now.

Sick Call seemed to last forever. By the time she arrived at the dispensary, the line of troopers stretched through the breezeway and wrapped around the south side of the veranda. Fallout from the fight at the trading post, she discovered.

The senator was on every bruised lip. Few of the men even remembered Sabrina had been in the room; none gave her the slightest indication they had seen her engaged in anything untoward. To a man, they praised Papa and condemned the senator.

Not that the opinions of a dozen, or even a hundred, troopers would carry weight with someone of Senator Carmichael's stature. Papa had placed his career in jeopardy without a moment's hesitation to protect Rosa from the man's assault. Sabrina would have expected no less from her father.

He was her hero. He always had been.

And Mama was her responsibility. Mindful of her promise to return home after Sick Call, as soon as the last trooper
departed she took up her shawl and went in search of Doc
Henry to advise him that she was leaving for the day. But
when she stepped into the surgeon's office, he extended
palsied hands. No explanation was needed.

"I was on my way to seek your help, my dear. Jedediah's
dressing needs changing, and these danged ol' hands have
failed me again."

Major Gerald Henry, the post surgeon, was somewhere
around Edward Bolton's age. Of medium stature, he was
the most carefully groomed officer on the post. His head
of thick salt-and-pepper hair was always slicked back in the
fashion of the day. His beard was always trimmed and
combed; his uniform, so crisp he might have changed it
at every bugle call.

In the beginning Sabrina had thought him merely fastid-
ious. Lately, she had begun to see it as part of his overall
scheme—a charade to draw attention away from his infir-
mity. Weren't sick people known to forgo personal hygiene
and attention to grooming?

"I hate to ask it of you, my dear, but these hands wouldn't
be much use in changing that bandage."

"Of course. I'll help." More and more often lately she
performed tasks Doc Henry, with his palsied hands, could
not. Sabrina and Jedediah were the only two people at the
hospital who knew the truth, although Sabrina sometimes
wondered if anyone knew the whole of it. In the last few
months she had begun to peruse medical journals in
search of answers.

She suspected the diagnosis might be easier come by if
he could be more open, not to mention putting to rest

the gossip that he overimbibed. On the other hand, she understood the necessity for pretense, for in the peacetime army officers were being decommissioned at the drop of a hat. Doc Henry was far too good a surgeon to lose when she could lend her hands.

Which was something she would have to work out if and when Lon proposed. But that was then, and this was now. Right now, Doc Henry needed her help. With barely a thought of Lon's chastisement earlier in the week, she followed him down the hall.

Maybe she didn't have anything to worry about, she argued. Maybe Lon didn't intend to propose; or maybe he would propose, and she wouldn't accept.

What do you mean, you wouldn't accept?

I . . .

Mama would die if you refuse Lon Jasper.

But what if he proposes tonight? At the candlelight supper? That's too soon. Too—

You owe Mama, Sabrina.

"I was certainly wrong about Carmichael." Doc Henry's comment startled Sabrina out of her reverie.

"Wrong?"

"Edward showed uncommon courage standing up to the man."

"Or stupidity," she worried.

"It was courage, all right. Edward had no choice. Until last night I'd decided it was in the nation's best interest for that dad-blasted senator to spend so much time out here where he couldn't do all that much harm. At least he wasn't in Washington messing up the government."

"That's one way to look at it."

"I'm sure Señora Ramériz wouldn't agree this morning."

"Like you always say, everything good has a price."

"There's nothing good about a man like that. He won't last long in the West, treating womenfolk that way."

When they arrived at the small room where Privates Jones and Hedgewick had deposited Jedediah before vanishing to perform other duties, Doc Henry changed the subject.

"I told Jedediah you would continue his lessons up here at the hospital until he's able to get around enough to go down to the church house to that school your friend Carrie is fixing to start."

Approaching the table, Sabrina smiled broadly at Jedediah. "We'll start tomorrow. First thing after Sick Call." Methodically, she set about the task of unwrapping his stump and cleansing the wound with clear, warm water. Doc Henry watched from across the table.

"Looking good." At his approval, Sabrina reached for the antiseptic.

"I expect you to study hard," the surgeon continued. "You're still going to be our next steward."

"Withouta leg?" the orderly questioned.

"You've got a leg," Doc Henry snapped.

Sabrina applied carbolic acid and began to rewrap the stump with a length of clean sacking. "You'll make a wonderful steward," she complimented.

"What'll I do for me a leg?"

"I'm working on that." The surgeon glanced up, winked at Sabrina, then froze. She watched his jaw tighten. His attention focused on the doorway behind her. She went cold.

If Lon Jasper had caught her holding Jedediah's leg again . . .

With rare defiance, she shook off the nagging trepidation and continued to wrap the wound, taking her time, focusing on her work, making certain each turn lapped the previous. By the time she split and tied the ends of the bandage, she was furious. How dare he treat her like a child, sneaking up, checking up? Turning, she cast a withering—

It wasn't Lon.

Tremayne. Her mind leapt from anger to dismay, while her body flushed. She felt that fluttering, again, as the butterflies came alive. Butterflies? Carrie's term didn't begin to describe the insidious craving that surged through her. Her first lucid thought was that he wasn't supposed to be here. Hadn't he said he would never set foot on the post again?

"Something I can do for you?" Doc Henry had stepped around Sabrina and headed for the door, while she stood glued to the spot, absorbing Tremayne's unwavering gaze.

His intensity reminded her of Lon's reaction when he burst into the ward and caught her cutting away Jedediah's trousers. But Tremayne wouldn't condemn her for treating Jedediah. Something was wrong.

"I'll take care of him, sir," she mumbled, or thought she did. The hum in her head was so loud she wasn't sure whether she had actually spoken or not.

By the time she reached the door, Tremayne had backed into the hallway. When he indicated she should follow him to the back gallery, she guided him instead to the dispensary and closed the door behind them.

Only then did she noticed his clothing. He hadn't changed since last night. Something red was splattered over his shirt, liquid, dried now. Her world stopped spinning.

"What happened?" The question stuck in her throat.

He followed her gaze, absently inspected his shirt, then found her eyes again. She could tell he was distracted.

"All that blood," she prompted. Reaching a hand, she touched his shirt, felt his heart hammer beneath her palm. Reverberations resounded through her like a thousand trampling horses. "Where are you wounded? How badly . . . ?"

Understanding flashed in his eyes. "It isn't me."

"Not you?" Air escaped her lungs. Her eyesight blurred and she felt dizzy. But relief was brief, for something was terribly wrong. She stroked the dried stains. "Who?"

"That's not blood, Sabrina. I . . . I need your help."

"Not blood?" Sanity seemed a thing foreign.

"For a child . . . burned . . . three days ago, four. She's hot with fever. Nick said you know medicine. Will you come?"

"I don't know much about burns. Let me get Doc Henry."

Tremayne seized her arm. "You. No one else." His breath came heavy. She watched his chest rise and fall in rapid succession. "Will you come?"

"Of course, but—"

"Damn it, Sabrina, trust me. I need your help. You. Alone."

His anguish fueled her fear. "Let me get some medicine. I'll be right back."

Before releasing her, he added, "I brought horses. Meet me out back, behind the magazine." His eyes were dense, black not green, and desperate. "Hurry." He swallowed convulsively. "Please."

Doc Henry met her at the medicine closet. "Isn't that the scout Tremayne? What does he want?"

"A child has been burned." She stuffed bandages into a sack. "I have to go with . . . uh, to her."

"I'll go. You hold down—"

"No. He said . . . I mean, Nick said I should go." The lie weighed like a stone in Sabrina's heart.

"Nick Bourbon?"

Nick, respected and trusted by all.

"Where is this child?" Doc Henry wanted to know.

"I didn't ask. Not far." She turned to him, pleading. "Tell me what medicine to take. I don't know anything about burns. Or fever or anything."

He stared at her until it was all she could do not to squirm. Could he see the truth? She wasn't good at lying or misleading or whatever she was doing. And Doc Henry of all people didn't deserve to be deceived. On the other hand, she had protected his secret without once asking or receiving an explanation. Couldn't she request a favor of her own?

"I don't like this, Sabrina."

"There's nothing to worry about. Really. I . . . I must go."

"Then let me send Jones along or Hedgewick."

"No." She struggled to lighten her tone. "Really. Everyone trusts Nick. I wouldn't go if I didn't know it would be all right." Turning back to the closet she scanned the contents. "Tell me what to take."

"Quinine for the fever." He reached around her, picked a bottle off the shelf, then another, and dropped them on top of the bandages. "Carbolic acid to clean the area."

Two more bottles went into the sack. "Here's some lime. Mix it with water and add linseed oil for a poultice. Did you get some of those strips of sheeting Jones ironed?"

"Yes, sir." When she allowed herself a brief glance at his face, she read his questions. *Where are you going with that renegade? And why?* Questions for which she had no answers, even if she had been free to give them.

"I won't be late." The assurance was as weak as watered-down tea. In truth, she had no idea where she was going, or how long she would be gone.

He kissed her on the forehead. "Don't be. Your mother wouldn't like this very much."

"Mama!" *The candlelight supper.* "She's planning a . . . uh, she's invited Lon for supper. Will you . . . ? I hate to ask it, but Mama would die if she knew I'd gone . . . and Lon . . ."

Her words stumbled over the request. She was unable to come right out and ask him to lie for her, but he knew. With bated breath and wildly thrashing heart, she watched him surrender.

"How can I refuse, my dear? It is no more than you do for me on a daily basis."

She hugged him, relieved, and hurried down the hall.

"You will be careful," he called after her.

"Yes, sir."

The words had barely faded in the clear mountain air when she rounded the corner of the magazine and came face-to-face with Tremayne. Storm clouds brewed in his intense green eyes, and she wondered at her sanity. What in the world was she thinking?

You don't have a lick of sense, Sabrina, her conscience accused. *Mama will die.*

Mama will never know. The claim was as feeble as her badly quaking knees.

Tremayne seemed oblivious to her turmoil. Without speaking a word he led her fifty yards or so up Hospital Canyon, where two horses were ground hitched behind an outcropping. The black was barebacked. The pinto, fortunately, wore a saddle, and Sabrina climbed astride as if she rode without a sidesaddle every day of the week. At the moment unladylike deportment was the least of her transgressions.

Not a lick of sense!

I have to go. A child . . .

A child, my foot. It's Tremayne. He's wild, Sabrina.

I have to go. What if Lon proposes tonight? This could be my last chance. . . .

If Lon proposes, you'd better be there to accept.

I will. I will.

Not a lick of sense.

The assessment was confirmed during the next two hours, while Tremayne set a breakneck pace and Sabrina struggled to stay aright, holding to both reins and saddle-horn. Riding up a narrow canyon, they followed Limpia Creek farther north than she had ever been from the post. When the sun reached its zenith in a cloudless blue sky, he cut back into the mountains, finally drawing rein at the edge of a cliff that overlooked a high mountain valley.

Sabrina glanced down into what folks called a box canyon, only there didn't appear to be even one entrance to this one. After two hours in the saddle, her inner thighs ached and burned by turn.

"Where are we?"

They had ridden the distance without speaking. Indeed, Tremayne seemed unaware of her presence except for an occasional glance back, presumably to assure himself she followed.

"Apache Wells," he responded now, surprising her.

"Apache Wells?" The valley was small and looked peaceful, belying the terror usually associated with the mere speaking of the name. *Apache Wells.* A spring burbled out of tall red cliffs, only to reenter the earth several yards distant. A few trees stood amid rocks and scant grass. One, an ancient cottonwood, grew beside a rock cabin that looked as old as the hills themselves. "Isn't it haunted, or . . . ?"

The expression he turned on her was one of pure scorn. Her words faded. *Lord in heaven, what had she said wrong this time?*

But Tremayne was already urging his stallion down the

steep, rocky incline, and she followed as best she could. Reaching bottom he galloped across the valley without slowing, then slid to the ground in front of an ancient hitching post.

His hostility had taken her aback, for in it she saw nothing of the man with whom she had flirted the night before, nothing of the man she had dreamed of kissing, indeed, longed to kiss. She tried to convince herself it had nothing to do with her; she had done nothing to offend him this time. A child was sick. He was frightened for a child.

Chilled by growing trepidation, she reached the hitching post moments behind him and dismounted at his silent command. Unable to resist, she glanced around the valley, viewing it from closer range. Rimmed by steep red cliffs, it was ethereal, unexpectedly so, for Apache Wells was a place few dared come. Indeed, she had heard many tales of this valley but had never met a soul who had ventured here.

She felt as though she had ridden into another world, led there by a man who remained an enigma to her. Strangely, she wasn't afraid.

"Bring the medicine," he ordered curtly before entering the stone cabin.

She retrieved the sack and followed on his heels. The one-room rock building had definitely seen better days. A shaft of light poured through the open door and slashed a pallet of animal pelts in the far corner. It was the only source of light, other than the small fire in the fireplace. In the dimness the room resembled less a home than a storehouse, a sparsely filled one at that.

She saw no furniture. Squinting into the darkness, she made out a human form on the pallet. Small—it would be the child.

Movement from a shadowed corner turned out to be a person who sat on something, a stump perhaps. No chair or table in sight. The hunched form snapped up at their entry. A woman. Her sewing fell to her lap. Sabrina gaped, shocked that she recognized the old lady. Her relief, too, came as a surprise. She hadn't realized she had been so tense.

"*Señora Ramériz. Hola.*" Rosa's mother-in-law. She lived in Chihuahua.

"*Hola,*" the señora returned, a bony finger to her lips. "The child is finally asleep."

Sabrina shifted her attention to the opposite corner, where Tremayne knelt beside the pallet. With halting steps, she left the door and went to him, although he gave no indication he remembered she was there.

"Ket, darling, I'm back." The tenderness in his deep, rock-solid voice brought fear to Sabrina's heart.

Coming closer she saw a girl of ten or so, covered to the neck by a heavy buffalo robe. Only her head and long black braids were visible.

Lon's claim came back to her. He had called Tremayne "squaw man," had thought little Emily was one of Tremayne's children. She wasn't.

Was this his daughter? If so, no wonder she had seen terror in his eyes. No wonder he had been distracted, sharp, angry, impatient. If this were his daughter . . .

Why hadn't he said so?

Dropping her sack of medicines to the buffalo robe, Sabrina knelt beside him. Lit by the shaft of sunlight, the child's face looked brown as an acorn, oval shaped with high cheekbones and delicately rounded chin. Her brows were straight and thick, as were the black eyelashes that rested on her cheeks, her eyes being closed. She seemed asleep, but the skin was stretched taut and her lips were dry and chapped.

Tremayne's daughter? Emotion clogged Sabrina's throat.

She rested a gentle hand on the girl's forehead. "She's burning up, poor child."

Tremayne's hand partially covered hers. "The fever is the same, I think."

"It's way too high." Fear dominated all other concerns. "We must get it down." Her mind awhirl, she turned to the señora, who hadn't moved except to glance up from her lap. "Will you draw water from the well, señora, while I—?"

Before Sabrina finished the question, Señora Ramériz had shrunk so far back into the corner, she almost toppled off her perch. Her sewing scissors clattered to the hearth. The whites of her eyes glowed in the firelight. As though she had been assaulted, the old woman swung a terrified expression to Tremayne.

Sabrina felt him sigh. "No one drinks from the well. I'll fetch water from the spring." Rising, he lighted a lantern and placed it on the sod floor at the head of the pallet. Taking up a pail, he closed the door behind him.

When he was gone Sabrina considered enlisting the señora's help, but decided she would do better alone. She got a dose of quinine down the child, then unwrapped the wounded leg. The odor almost gagged her. Extending from knee to ankle, the wound had been smeared with a thick application of something black and gooey. What wasn't black was red; streaks radiated from the wound like rays from a setting sun.

Dear God, this injury was far beyond her meager skills. Sick at heart, she lifted the girl's head and shoulders and cradled her in quivering arms. With lips to the feverish forehead, she began to sing. "Hush little baby, don't say a word. Mama's gonna buy you a mockingbird. And if that mockingbird don't sing . . ."

When the door opened, splaying the shaft of light across the pallet, Sabrina glanced up to find Tremayne standing in the portal, still as death. Her arms tightened around the child at the anguished expression on his face. Her words drifted slowly into a muted hum.

"Where do you want the water?" His voice was low, charged with pain, the pain of recognition.

This was his daughter. He knew she was dying.

"By the fire." Calling on her depleted store of strength, Sabrina issued quick instructions to the señora in Spanish. "Reserve a portion of water for a poultice. Use the rest for tea—you'll find sage leaves in my sack. We'll bathe her with it to bring down the fever."

While she spoke, Tremayne lit a second lantern and carried it to the opposite side of the pallet. She followed his movements, distracted by the formidable task that lay ahead. Absently, she watched him set the lamp on a stump that served as a small table. The circle of yellow light fell across the rough surface, illuminated an object.

Her breath caught. Her heart skittered against Ket's head.

A gold bow.

He had taken one of her gold bows, and she hadn't even known it, taken it and kept it. The idea stunned her. Heat burned her cheeks, swept down her neck, sizzled inside her. The flames simmered with a nameless, insidious yearning, as though fanned by a mass of tiny fluttering butterfly wings.

She looked up. Tremayne glanced away, but not before she saw acknowledgment in his eyes. He had seen her recognize the bow. Inadvertently she glanced down, only to focus on the lush pallet of furs. His bed?

Could it be? Could this be his home? She found his gaze again, but by now the old barrier had fallen into place. She couldn't read his thoughts. When had she ever been able to? Only once, when he came to seek her help for his daughter.

His daughter. Tears brimmed in Sabrina's eyes when she studied the dangerously ill child. "She needs a doctor."

"You can treat her."

"I'm not a doctor." She tried to temper her own fear, lest she frighten him more. "I may not be able to . . . This is serious. Extremely serious."

"You can do it." The pain in his voice cried out to her, but the truth was undeniable. She shook her head. He remained adamant.

"Try," he said.

She held his tormented gaze, bound to him, as she had thought before, by his pain. Her mind raced back to that first night outside the vacant steward's house. She had suspected it then. She knew it now. Incredibly the question she must ask today was the same torturous question she had asked then. It stuck in her throat twice before she got the words out. "Is she your daughter?"

Moments passed in silence, while she watched the truth struggle to escape. At length, he nodded.

Her hand went to his forearm. Tenderly she fingered the shirt he had worn two days now. It no longer felt crisp. "You are frightened for her."

Not a lick of sense, she denounced. A woman never accused a man of being afraid. Was she losing her wits?

"Damn right, I'm afraid," he admitted without shame. "Keturah is all I have left. She's—"

"Then we must take her to the hospital."

His response was quick. And brusque. "Never."

"I'm not qualified to treat her, Tremayne. I don't know what I'm doing. She could . . . she could die."

"Nick said—"

"What is this?" she demanded angrily. "No matter what Nick says, I am not a physician. I can't . . . I'm not skilled enough . . ." Heaving a sigh, she continued in a quieter tone. "I understand why you hate soldiers. I'd probably hate them, too. But you can't let your hatred stand in the way of your daughter's life. If you love her, you want the best treatment that's available for her. Doc Henry—" He cut her off with a scathing denouncement.

"My daughter will not die in fear. She watched white soldiers kill her mother. I will not take her to a post full of the bastards."

Chapter Eight

She watched white soldiers kill . . . ? Reflexively Sabrina lifted a hand to the child's head, a whisper-stroke, no more, as though she expunged a curse, when in fact, the horror of Tremayne's words could never be erased.

Her eyes sought his. His despair cried out to her. Reflexively she touched his arm, clutched it. His pain seemed transmitted to her. It engulfed her. Suddenly the most important thing in the world, the only thing in the world was him, this man, Tremayne.

"I'm not a physician," she said. "I—"

"I'll help."

"You don't understand. I . . ." But his plea was palpable, as was his faith in her, misplaced though it was. He expected her to heal his child.

"Tell me what to do."

Anguish choked her. She had thought earlier that this valley was another world. Now she knew it was—another world from which there was no escape and certain ruin.

It had nothing to do with the towering cliffs that enclosed this small valley.

Nothing, yet at the same time everything, for the natural barrier held back not only civilization, but reality. Within these red rock walls time stood still, and with it life.

Premonitions spun like dark-hued tops in her head, propelled by a strange new fervency. It hummed in her ears, obscuring all but her immediate circle of concern. which in itself contained every imagined and unimagined aspect of her life. With his dying daughter in her arms and her gold bow on the table beside his bed, she strove to focus not on this man who had turned her ordered and civilized world upside down, but on the only thing that mattered in this moment caught in time—saving the life of his precious daughter.

"I gave her some quinine while you were gone," she said, as if the matter were settled. Moving aside, she motioned Tremayne to take her place. "Hold her in your lap while I bathe her with this tea. Maybe she won't be so anxious that way."

"Why sage?" he asked after a while. Sabrina had bathed the child's heated limbs, one by one, then her chest and shoulders, carefully recovering each portion to prevent chills.

"Mama used sage tea. Doc Henry says it's as good as anything. The water's the main thing. Her temperature will go down as her body struggles to dry the water."

"Nick was right," Tremayne observed.

"No, he wasn't. I don't know the first thing about treating something this serious." A sudden thought brought her head up. "Does she understand?"

"English? Yes, if she hears us."

"What should I call her?"

"Her name is Keturah. Off the Apachería I call her Ket."

"Keturah," Sabrina murmured, continuing to bathe the

child. "I've never heard that name. It's lovely. As lovely as she is."

"It isn't Apache," Tremayne observed with a trace of scorn. After a short silence, he added, "Keturah was my mother's name."

His mother? Sabrina's breath caught. New and bewildering questions formed. With difficulty she focused on the child and not the father.

The bathing finished, she turned reluctantly to the burned leg. She wished she could put it off forever. She wished Doc Henry were here. "What is this ointment?"

Tremayne scoffed. "Witch's brew."

"Don't condemn field medicines. Doc Henry says remedies made from natural herbs often work better than chemists' concoctions."

When she chanced a glance, he wore a strangely bemused expression. *Lord in heaven, he believes in me. Too much. Far too much.* Desperately she turned her attention to the patient, keeping her voice low and soft. "This will hurt, Keturah, but your daddy is holding you. He won't let anything happen to you."

When she touched the wound with a rag she had wrung out in fresh water, Ket writhed and cried out.

"Ket, darling, hold still. Sabrina will make you well." His voice was strong, confident, and it accelerated her growing feeling of inadequacy.

I can't make her well, she wanted to cry. *She's dying, and I can't save her.* But his faith swelled inside her. It strengthened her determination and helped alleviate the vile odor that rose from the wound or from the concoction or from both. She inhaled shallow gasps of air to keep from gagging. When the wound was clean the sight was worse.

"Maybe you'd better leave," she told Tremayne. "This won't be pleasant, seeing your daughter—"

"Finish," he ordered.

So she did. First she smeared the area generously with carbolic acid, which brought more writhing from Ket, along with cries not unlike those of a small cat. Tremayne stilled her with soothing words, causing Sabrina to wonder whether he had held Nakia while she died. Or Chi Caliente.

The way Martha Bolton had held Serena.

By the time she tied the lime and linseed poultice in place, Sabrina's eyes brimmed with tears. She kept her head down and her face turned from Tremayne, hoping her weakness wouldn't show.

She shouldn't have worried. When she chanced a look, he was gone. Quieter than a leaf falling on water, he had placed Ket's head on a pillow of furs and vanished.

He was good at that.

Guide me now! Show me how to save my daughter; then get this witless white woman the hell out of my life!

Tremayne braced his arms on the ancient well and peered into its depths, praying to a god, to a spirit, a guardian in whom he could not believe. He believed only what he saw—and felt.

What he saw had been enough to break his warrior's heart. His daughter was dying, yet he could not bring himself to put her through the horror of waking up in a hospital staffed by people who had murdered her mother.

What he felt had sent him racing for fresh air. The white woman he called witless had proved yet again that she was not. She was compassionate and courageous. She would do all she could to save Keturah.

But the cost to him was steep. The price was his heart. His cold, unloving and unlovable warrior's heart. He heard her footsteps behind him but he did not turn from the well.

"She's resting," she called softly.

He nodded that he heard but otherwise ignored her presence.

"You're tired," she said, softly again. Too softly. "You look like you haven't slept in a week."

"They were here with Ket when I returned from Chihuahua last night."

"She doesn't live here?"

"She lives at the Apachería with her grandmother."

"Poor sick child." Sabrina stood beside him. Close to his shoulder. "She's lost so much. And you—"

Don't say it, he thought. *Just heal her and get the hell out of here.* "Thank you for coming. I should get you back to the post now."

"I left instructions with Señora Ramériz. She's to administer quinine every three hours and bathe Ket with sage tea. When I return I'll bring something more tasty."

"You don't have to come back."

"I want to come back, to help—"

"Tell me what to do, what signs to look for. Now that you've seen her, you can tell the señora and me how to take care of her. If she gets worse, I'll come for you."

An uncomfortable silence filled the small valley. With difficulty he remained stiff and stoic, when what he really wanted to do was turn to her, take her in his arms, take comfort from her compassion, comfort and more. . . .

He could kiss her at last, like he should have done at the trading post, like he had wanted to ever since that first night beside the hospital when he dried her tears, tears she shed over the death of his friend. Her tears today were for his daughter.

"How did the accident happen?"

Again he felt she had read his thoughts and diverted them to safer territory. "She fell into a ceremonial bonfire," he said, grateful that she had drawn him out of his stupor.

"The kind they dance around?" Her voice was soft, the question innocent, but softness and innocence were not emotions Tremayne could handle, not with his daughter at death's door, not with Sabrina so close he could reach out and . . .

He turned to her in anger. "The kind *we* dance around." Avoiding those enchanting brown eyes, he stared at the top of her head of fiery red hair. He had been right to compare it with the pelt of the red fox. In a contest, Sabrina's hair would win, hands down. He had never been so drawn to someone, so captivated by a woman.

When she reached toward him, he stood his ground, feigning imperviousness. But her hand on his shirt opened a floodgate of raw need. His eyes flew to hers. He saw her own shock, felt her fingers lift mere inches, as though she, too, had been taken by surprise. For a brief but desperate moment all he could think was, *Don't. Don't move your hand.*

She didn't. Settling her palm tentatively over his thrashing heart she smiled at him, and he was lost in her.

"If this isn't blood, what in the world is it?"

Her tone was light, and he was tempted to relent. To relax and converse with her. He enjoyed conversing with her. But that was a luxury he couldn't afford, for even now he was hard-pressed not to follow her lead, to touch her, hold her. . . .

"It's well water."

"From here?" Her voice was thick. He knew it echoed his. He nodded stiffly.

"No wonder you don't drink it."

"It's also hot enough to come from the depths of Hades, which many believe it does."

"Oh, it's the well that's haunted?" When she smiled, his insides went queasy. She was good at that—smiling and sending him sailing off on the wings of fantasy. He dragged himself back.

He wasn't the man for her, and that was, of course, what she was thinking. Then it came to him, the way to prove to her how different their worlds were.

"Haunted?" He searched for scorn. "Only to witless whites."

He watched her fight to conceal a reaction to his harshness. In the end she lost, because her hurt was too strong to hide. He felt it as surely as if she had backhanded him across the face.

"I'll see to Ket, then be on my way."

Before she'd taken two steps he grabbed her arm, bringing her up short.

"You're right," he said, brusquely. "It's the well. Whites and Indians alike are afraid to come here."

"Señora Ramériz came."

"She won't get out of the cabin. You saw her terror when you asked her to draw water from the well."

"What good is she to Ket if she's afraid to leave the cabin?"

"I'll bring her what she needs. At least she would come. Few people will, besides Nick and Lena."

"And me."

Her glorious hair shone like a red halo in the afternoon sun. The red accented her white skin, on which he tried to focus. *Don't look into those doe eyes again,* he cautioned. *You'll never drive her off if you lose your way in her eyes.*

"After you hear the truth you might not be so quick to return," he challenged.

She didn't speak for several heartbeats. Then she changed the topic. "Why didn't you tell me I would be treating your daughter?"

She might as well have socked him in the gullet. To hide the fact, his response was curt, sharp. "Would it have made a difference?"

Color bloomed on her cheeks, but he realized in an

instant that she, too, could play the game. "I came, didn't I?"

He felt like an everlasting heel. He never intentionally hurt a person. But he pressed on, for his salvation lay in driving her away. Their salvation. "Why did you come?"

"You said a child was ill." She sounded angry, but she was still more hurt than angry. He regretted that, deeply.

"If you think there was any other reason, you're as much of a bastard as . . . some others—"

"Others?" he challenged deliberately.

She turned away, stared down into the well. The silence lengthened and became a thing tangible, heated, as hot as the afternoon sun reflected off the cliffs. As hot as the red water at the bottom of this well. As hot as he felt staring into her fiery red hair.

"Tell me about the well," she said at length.

"Truth or legend?"

When she glanced up, he saw a determination that had not been there before. She was strong, this white woman, even while she sapped his own strength. Standing beside her was a lesson in self-discipline such as he hadn't experienced since his days as a novitiate.

"Take your choice." She smiled a tight sort of smile. "But be forewarned, you will not frighten me away. I won't leave Ket without medical attention. I may not be able to save her life, but I will continue to come. Nothing you say will prevent that."

She had seen right through him. Seen, and challenged him in return. He almost lost the will for what he was about to do. Certainly he lost the stomach for it. But what else could he do? Was it more cruel to hurt her now, or to wait until later?

If the attraction that sizzled between them continued to grow, would he be able to stop it later? No. Now was the time, perhaps the only time.

"The word haunted is a white man's term," he said, cutting her no slack. "Much of what you whites call haunted is considered spiritual by the Apache. There's a difference." He paused, watched her struggle to conceal the raw emotion that was stronger than either of them. He steeled himself to continue this fool's task.

"This well, this valley, is sacred to us. Anyone who defiles it will die."

"That's the legend of Apache Wells?"

"Part of it."

"What else?"

"Anyone who drinks the water and lives will become the chief of . . ." He glanced around, motioning to the encircling red walls.

She followed his gaze, then grinned. "It isn't a very large kingdom."

"My mother called it—" He stopped abruptly, for she had caught him off guard, and he had spoken without thinking.

"A what?"

"A teacup." He diverted his gaze, furious with himself for allowing this woman into his life.

"What a delightful—"

"Delightful? She and my father were murdered here. Right here in this delightful teacup valley. They were simple folks. Came here from Tennessee, wanting only peace and a chance to start a new life. I was six when they died."

"Oh, dear Lord!" Sympathy, in the form of tears, sprang to her eyes. "Apaches?"

"Apaches? Those red devils who are trying to steal the white man's destiny? We're blamed for everything these days. No, Apaches did not kill my parents and enslave me."

"Then who?" she shot back.

"I don't know." The admission was a relief. "Comancheros, I was told. We never found them."

"You lived here alone after that?"

"A couple of days after the raid Apaches came, took me with them, and raised me as one of their own."

"But you live here, now?"

Keep this impersonal, his better sense cautioned, although he had a feeling his better sense had deserted him some-time back—probably on the day he met this woman. "I returned after Nakia was murdered," he explained to the well.

"Oh." A few moments later she asked lightly, "And did you drink from the well?"

Back to the legend. Yes. Keep it there. On the legend, away from personal experiences, personal lives, personalities.

He nodded.

"Obviously you didn't die. Tell me about it."

"By the time I turned sixteen, I realized I could never really belong to the tribe. Oh, I had learned the skills. I could perform any task my friends could, but my skin would never be the right color. My hair . . . isn't Apache hair." Reaching back, he lifted a wavy skein. "Nor are my eyes Apache eyes. At sixteen it was important to earn my place in the tribe, so I came here in search of my spiritual guardian, knowing they would follow."

"Your spiritual guardian?"

Her expression was open again, unguarded and mesmer-izing, even as he enthralled her with the tale. She wouldn't believe it, of course. He had lured her into his wickiup; now he was about to show her, a cultured, white Christian woman, how barbaric his parlor, his world, really was.

"We Apaches," he said, driving home the difference, "believe that every person has a spiritual guardian in nature. Before a young man can become a warrior, he must go alone to fast and pray until his guardian comes to him."

"You returned here to find yours?"

He grunted.

"Of course," she mused. "Your home. The perfect place."

The legend, he reminded himself. *Stick to the legend.* "My father had once given me a drink of this water, so I knew I could drink it and not die." He stared into the well, shaking his head at the memory, momentarily lost in the recollection. "Lord, it was bitter stuff. But back to the story. My fellow novitiates didn't know I had lived here. Only the older people knew where I came from. In fact, it was the shaman's idea that I come to Apache Wells to seek counsel from my guardian. So I came, spent three days without food or clothes or weapons. On the third day, when I knew they had gathered in the rocks—"

"They?"

"My fellow novitiates."

"Chi Caliente?"

"And others—Flies with the Wind, Sleeps in the Clouds, Feet like Water, and yes, Chi. We called him Waits for the Sun. . . ." Tremayne's words drifted off as thoughts he had avoided returned.

"What were you called?"

He stared at her, sightless for a moment. "I had yet to earn my name."

"These friends," she asked quietly, "where are they now?"

Unable to resist, his gaze found hers. He knew what she was thinking. With startling clarity he felt the tug of a bond that linked them. Was it too late to drive her away? Regardless, he had to try. It became more necessary with each moment that passed between them. "You mean are they all dead like Chi?"

"Are they?"

"Sleeps in the Clouds died at Cañada Alamosa. Only he and Chi are dead. That I know."

She glanced around the valley, then back to him. Her eyes glistened with unshed tears. "I never realized—"

"What? That Apaches were dying?"

"Any of it. I never understood—"

"I'm getting away from the story," he interrupted abruptly. "As soon as I knew they were watching from the cover of boulders, I drew water and drank it." Again the memory took over and before he realized it, he added, "Being a typical youth of sixteen, I decided to test the rest of the legend. I lifted the bucket over my head and poured the hot red water over my naked body." Inadvertently, he rubbed a hand over his chest, remembering. "That's how I know exactly how hot it is."

Her eyes were large and round; her cheeks flamed. He couldn't have stopped himself reading her mind if he had tried.

"Ah," he said, hoping to cover his own discomposure, "I have shocked the civilized white lady."

She didn't answer right away, and for that he was grateful. For her eyes told him more than he ever wanted to hear in words. "Was that your intent?" she asked finally, quietly.

He was the first to avert his gaze. Why had he thought to frighten her off? Standing beside her, speaking into her open and receptive face, each word had become a caress. The need to hold her, to kiss her consumed him.

She recovered first. "What does that mean? Pouring the water over your . . . uh, body?"

He watched a blue jay take flight and thought perhaps his sanity had, too. "According to legend, if the chief pours the water over his body he will find love everlasting."

"Love everlasting?" Her words came quick and soft, on

a gasp, leaving her mouth open, her lips parted and moist, as though waiting for him.

For a moment he was lost in the spell of this white woman who was neither witless nor weak nor any of the other things he had been reared to believe. He shook off the drugging effect she had on him.

"Damn it, Sabrina, it's a legend. I was sixteen."

"Had you already found Nakia?"

Nakia? He hadn't been thinking about Nakia. Fortunately Sabrina had. "Later," he mumbled, knowing he hadn't succeeded in establishing the limits of their relationship. How could he, when she twisted everything he said into a jumble of personal innuendoes?

"No," he said definitively. "We had not yet looked at each other."

"Looked at each other? But if she was Chi's sister . . . ?"

"I didn't mean I hadn't seen her. I meant we were not yet . . ." He gave up and barked, "To look at each other is an expression, the way Apaches describe the attraction between a man and a woman."

Watching her swallow convulsively, he resisted the need to do the same. His mouth was so dry even a swallow of bitter well water would be welcome.

"What else does the legend say?" she asked, although he had trouble hearing her through the turmoil that roiled between them. He was the one who had fallen under her spell, into her heart, against his will and despite his best efforts not to.

"Nothing much," he brushed off, taking refuge in the legend for his own sake, now. "Except a warning: If anyone harms the chief, the water will turn to fire and consume the bastard."

"Whew! I'll bet you don't have many enemies."

"Except for Lon Jasper," he quipped, smiling in spite of his disillusionment, for his plan had obviously not worked. Her eyes glowed with interest, not disgust. Well, he wasn't finished with this tale of spirits and demon wells.

"Something else happened that day when I was sixteen. To Apaches it was sensible, logical. To you, a civilized, white Christian lady, it may sound like sacrilege. I hate to disgust you, but since I've begun the tale I should finish it."

He watched her cock her head, assessing his statement. It didn't take her half a minute to get his meaning. "Go ahead, Tremayne, see how much it will take to disgust me."

He shook his head in wonder and continued, knowing beforehand it was a long shot. She was determined, and he had never seen a determined woman yet who didn't stick like a turtle. "You recall that I was here to search for my spiritual guardian. Well, while I drank from the bucket, a sound came out of the old house over there. It drifted across the clearing and floated down into the well."

"A sound?" She canted her head, ear to the well, as though listening. "What kind of sound?"

"Laughter."

"Laughter?"

"The shaman later explained that it was my spiritual guardian. He said it would remain with me forever. That anytime I needed an affirmation, I should return to this valley for guidance. Needless to say, I haven't heard any laughter since."

"That's why they brought Ket here," she mused, eyes wide with wonder. "If only we could hear it now. For her."

"If only that pinto over there could sprout wings," he retorted, "you could fly back to the post."

"Scoff if you like. Your cynicism is probably what keeps you from hearing the laughter again." She peered intently into the well, and he took the opportunity to study her. He was surprised at her unaffected ways. Not once during this full day of riding through the mountains and tending Ket in that smoky cabin had she complained. Red hair straggled from her bun all around and lay in long sheaves over her shoulders and down her back. He had yet to see her fret over how she looked.

And how she looked tempted him as no woman ever had.

She glanced up and found him watching her. With a fair hand she swept the hair back from her eyes, the better to see him. He could tell she was deep in thought. When she spoke, she took him by complete surprise.

"It would be your mother's."

"What?"

"The laughter would be your mother's. Don't you think so?"

"My . . . ? No, I do not think so. That's crazy."

"It isn't." She caught his arm. Her hand might as well have been a branding iron. Her touch seared the length of his body. While he stood there wondering how he could have misjudged this woman so miserably, she continued in earnest.

"It's your mother's laughter, Tremayne. I know it."

"How would you know that?" he retorted.

"I hear a voice, too."

He caught himself gaping at her. "You what?"

"I hear a voice—my sister's. I've never told anyone, but ever since she died fourteen years ago I've heard her voice. She chides me to behave, to treat Mama right." When she looked up, Tremayne's heart caught in his throat.

"My twin sister, Serena, was run over by a wagon when we were five. Mama has never been the same since. It's no wonder. Serena was like her name, sweet and serene. She was the little lady Mama wanted us both to be. I'm not, you see. Fortunately, I have Serena's voice to keep me from hurting Mama more."

Tremayne listened, stunned. He had tried to run her off, and she had drawn herself closer.

"I'll never understand you people. Why would anyone expect a little girl of five to be a perfect anything?"

"Oh, Mama did. Does," she corrected. "That's why she designs those dreadful dresses with swags and bows—"

Everything inside Tremayne went still. *That damned bow!* He'd been a fool for keeping it. But who would have thought she would ever see it?

"That's why we must save Keturah. I know what it would do to you if she died. Your life would be ruined."

His mouth was dry. His heart was breaking for his daughter. His body ached for this woman who stood so close all he had to do was move a couple of inches and she would be in his arms.

"You'll save her," he said witlessly.

"No, but maybe the legend can."

"Damn, Sabrina, don't get caught up in that nonsense. That isn't why I told you."

"I know why you told me."

He didn't want to hear her response, but the only way to prevent it would be to stuff something in her mouth. He pursed his lips against the carnal suggestion that popped to mind.

"You wanted to scare me off," she was saying, "to make me think you're heathen. You can thank your lucky stars it served a better purpose."

"I don't have any lucky stars," he muttered, thoroughly disgusted with himself.

"I can't heal Ket, Tremayne. I'm not skilled enough. But with the guardian—"

"First you have to believe. I don't believe."

"You believed in me."

That shocked him. Not the claim, but the truth of it.

"Isn't believing that I could heal your daughter more

farfetched than the laughter? I know nothing about medicine. I can talk to Doc Henry, but unless he sees her he won't know what I mean. The legend of the well and your mother's spirit may be our only hope.''

"You believe that?"

"I don't disbelieve. Do you?"

"Put that way . . . I don't know."

"Can you stand there and tell me you did not hear your mother's laughter once?"

"You're the one who said it was my mother's."

"The shaman said it was your spiritual guardian," she argued. "Who could be a better spiritual guardian than a mother?"

He couldn't believe the turn of this conversation. "Doesn't anything faze you?"

Without warning her sweet, lovely face contorted into a mask of horror. Her eyes filled with tears; her voice could only have come from a bottomless pit of despair. "Yes. I caused my sister's death."

"Sabrina . . ." Without another word, he drew her to his chest. His arms curled around her, shielding, protecting. "Not you," he soothed. "You couldn't cause anyone's death."

A sigh escaped his lungs as she settled against him. She felt so good there, so right. But it wasn't right.

"I'll do anything I can to save Ket," she mumbled against his chest. "Even turn to spirits."

Threading fingers through her hair, he pulled her face back and was tempted. Oh, so tempted. "Then you'll have to believe for me."

"I will," she promised. "Until you can believe for yourself."

Damn. Why did she have to be this way? So compassionate, so understanding.

So tempting, so willing. All he had to do was kiss her

and she would be his. But he couldn't have her. And she shouldn't have him.

Pushing her away took every ounce of training he had received as a novitiate—all the self-discipline, all the self-denial. He held her at arm's length, recalling how proud he had been when as a young warrior he had exercised such control over an enemy or a situation.

He didn't feel proud now. He felt lonely. As lonely as he had ever felt in his life. But he didn't have to be. She was here, in his arms, waiting, willing—

Suddenly she moved. One minute she was lost in his gaze, the next she pulled away. How many times today had he felt she could read his mind?

"I'd better get back to the post." She tidied her hair with hands that gave no indication of stress. Her expression had gone from soft and sensual to unreadable.

"I'll take the pinto," she said. "You stay here with Ket."

"The señora is with Ket."

She ignored him. "I'll talk with Doc Henry before I come back, see what else he suggests."

"Sabrina." He reached for her shoulder, but let his hand fall limp before he touched her. "I didn't mean to involve you in this. Your parents won't understand. Hell, no one at the post will understand. I don't want to make your life harder—"*I don't want you to leave.* That's what he almost said. God, he'd almost said it. This time she didn't read his thoughts.

Or had she simply chosen not to let him know?

"Worry about something important," she replied, "like taking care of Keturah." When she tossed her head, his heart rate skyrocketed. Then she hit him the most unexpected blow yet.

"I really must get back to town. Lon is coming for supper."

"Jasper?"

She smiled as sweet as you please and walked off toward the horses. "I won't keep your horse," she called over her shoulder.

"Damn it, Sabrina, that isn't the point." Bewildered, he wondered what was. "You'll get lost," he argued feebly.

"Don't worry. If I do, Lon will send a search party."

He shook his head in wonder at his own stupidity. This witless white woman had as many hues as a rainbow, and every one of them baffled him.

Chapter Nine

The man was infuriating. From the moment he began the story of the legend, she had known what he was up to. Hadn't he forewarned her at the trading post?

This will never work, Sabrina.

He didn't need to tell her that. Spiritual guardians and sacred wells aside, Apache Wells was still farther from her own world than the moon. The fantasy might hold her in its grip, but the reality was equally strong.

Life with Tremayne was fantasy, pure and simple. So many changes would be needed for their worlds to mesh that were she the Lord in heaven she wouldn't know where to begin.

So many changes it didn't bear considering.

Apache Wells was a land of fantasy.

Reality, Sabrina's reality, was the post, civilization, Lon Jasper.

Reality—her only business with Tremayne must be to save his daughter. Keturah must not die. He had already lost so much. Losing Ket would ruin his life.

Like Martha Bolton's life had been ruined. Sabrina knew what losing a child did to a parent. And Tremayne had no one left with whom to share the devastating loss. Not that she and Papa had been much help to Mama.

Tremayne accompanied her back to the post. He wouldn't hear of her making the trip alone. But he was distant, quieter than usual, if that was possible. And he remained adamant about not bringing Ket to the hospital or allowing Doc Henry to come to Apache Wells, even if she persuaded him to wear civilian clothes.

"Ket's very sick," Sabrina argued once more, as Hospital Canyon opened up to reveal the post magazine not fifty rods distant. Tremayne drew rein. She did, too. Neither made a move. Evening shadows had lengthened. The setting sun was a mere sliver; it slipped slowly but irrevocably behind the sawtooth ridges above them. Emotions warred inside her—contentment at being with him, anxiety that the time had come to part, and disgust that she could not suppress her attraction to this man. Hopelessness settled over her, prompted in part by his words.

They had looked at each other. Did that mean the fantasy would never die?

"I could bring Doc Henry—"

"He's a white man, Sabrina. If you think he knows more than you, talk to him. But I'm not taking Ket there, and he's not coming to her. If she has to die, I want it to be . . ." His voice broke. After a while he added so quietly his words faded into the evening air, "I don't want her to die afraid."

Like so many others, he might have said. Or *like she has lived so much of her life.* He didn't add either. With what Sabrina knew now, he didn't have to.

"I'll talk with him, find out everything he knows. In the meantime, be sure Señora Ramériz bathes her every few hours."

He nodded.

"All through the night. Be sure she has enough water."

"I will."

"In three days I'll return, unless . . . if there's a change, come immediately."

He nodded. "Three days. I'll be here."

Still she hesitated to leave him. "Señora Raméríz knows what to do."

"Go ahead on, Sabrina." His eyes found hers, but his emotions were indiscernible. As was the man, she thought. But that was no longer entirely true.

She knew him now, better than she had ever dreamed she would. Better than most people, she suspected. And knowing him this way, how could she keep from falling in love with him?

"Mustn't keep the captain waiting." His quip was designed to send her off, as if he, too, had difficulty with this parting.

She grimaced. Mama was probably having a conniption. Still she couldn't bear to leave. She didn't want to have supper with Lon Jasper. She wanted to stay with Tremayne, to return to Apache Wells with him. She wanted it desperately. But of course she couldn't. Dismounting, she handed him the pinto's reins.

Cloaked by the dusky evening his gaze held hers, and for once she knew every thought in his head—or believed she did, every wish, every desire, every regret, for they were her wishes and desires and regrets, as well.

"Maybe the bastard'll choke," he said finally. It wasn't a joke. It didn't sound the least bit jovial. Nor did it sound like jealousy. She wasn't sure what he meant.

"On Mama's cooking?"

She watched him consider this. His expression swung from whatever personal reason he had for wishing Lon ill to the situation at hand. She knew his question.

"Mama's the one who invited him," she explained. Then

before she realized what she was doing, she blurted out the truth. "She's looking for a husband for me."

Even one so stoic as Tremayne couldn't conceal his surprise. The setting sun played off his startled expression. She almost laughed, but this was no laughing matter. At least not for her. And Tremayne never laughed.

Wavy hair hung loose about his shoulders. She experienced a mad desire to touch it. She guessed he could tell what she was thinking. It made her reckless. Reckless and for a moment a little wild. She felt a surge of power, as though living life for herself were possible, for herself instead of for her mother or for her long-dead sister.

But that was fantasy. Pure fantasy to think she would ever be able to follow her heart. Her heart rode with a man her family called savage.

At length Tremayne grunted and tugged on the reins of the two horses. "Your mama, huh? She sure picked you a doozy."

A light was burning in the dispensary when Sabrina passed, so she stuck her head in the door. Doc Henry sat at her desk. Hearing her, he glanced up from one of several medical journals that lay open before him.

"How's the child?"

"Dying." The word choked out, and she realized it was the first time she had spoken the truth aloud.

"Bring her to the hospital."

Sabrina swiped at a sudden flow of tears. Suddenly she was tired beyond all reason. "Soldiers killed her mother."

The surgeon's jaws clenched.

"She saw it."

"She's Apache?"

Sabrina nodded, unable to reveal the whole truth.

"You saw her at the Apachería?"

"No."

Lamplight played off the surgeon's shoulders. He sat patiently, waiting, she knew, for an explanation. When it wasn't forthcoming, he shrugged as if to say they were even. She didn't ask about his secret, and he wouldn't inquire about hers.

"I trust you were not in danger, my dear."

"I wasn't." Then she realized what time it was. "But I will be when I get home. Mama invited Lon for supper."

"You don't need to tell me. Your mama's been up three times, Edward twice, and Captain Jasper once."

"What did you tell them?"

"That you were on a mission of mercy. That you were safe and would be home in good time. I've worried ever since."

"You needn't have. I was fine. But Mama must be fit to be tied."

"And Jasper. Edward took the news in stride."

"Papa would." Unless he discovered she'd been with Tremayne. But even the reminder of her father's disapproval couldn't quiet the anxiety that simmered inside her. She should have stayed with Ket. She should be with Tremayne. Yet her sense of duty was strong, and she turned to go.

Doc Henry stopped her. "Before you head home, my dear, something's come up, you should know about."

His ominous tone alerted her.

"That damn Carmichael, if you'll pardon my language, has threatened to call Edward before a court-martial."

"Sabrina, is everything all right?"

It was Papa. He stood beside the cook shack, watching her come up the path from the hospital.

"I'm sorry to be so late, Papa." She fell into his arms. "I didn't know."

Edward smoothed his hand over her crown, a loving gesture she remembered from childhood. She rarely thought about the comfort she took from her father; too rarely did she think to give comfort in return. "That despicable old senator."

"Don't worry about it, sugar. Every officer there stood firmly on my side. Carmichael can't court-martial all of us. The truth would certainly get back to Washington."

"Will they stand by you?"

"The officers? If it comes to that, I reckon we'll see."

"How's Mama?"

Edward's flippancy faded. In the hush that fell between them, Sabrina heard a rare sound coming from the house. The piano. Chopin, it sounded like. Strange. The only tunes Mama played were the hymns sung at Serena's funeral. No one ever played their piano for pleasure.

"Let's just say disgrace isn't her preferred vehicle for returning east. Be sweet to her tonight, sugar."

"I didn't help matters, did I?" Arm in arm, they headed for the house. He squeezed her shoulders for response.

"How's the young patient?"

"Dying." When he flinched, she knew he was thinking of Serena.

"We won't mention that to your mama. She's already in a state. Hurry now. She laid out your clothes, so get dressed and come on in. Jasper's been here over an hour."

Sabrina made it to her room before her tears fell. She closed the door, leaned against it, and cried tears she had held back for hours. Ket was dying. Why hadn't she stayed with Tremayne? Why had she left him?

How could she think of Tremayne and Ket when Papa was in such trouble?

The doorknob rattled. "Sabrina, child. Open up. Let

me see you. You know how disasters run in our family. Anything could have happened to you, child. I've been sick with worry. Sick."

"I'm sorry, Mama." Sabrina pushed her concern for Tremayne and Ket into a back corner of her mind and prayed they remained there, at least until after Mama's candlelight supper. "Let me dress. I'll be quick."

On the bed lay Sabrina's clothes where Martha had placed them, as one would for a child. And wasn't she? She allowed her mother to drag her around on her apron strings. She allowed—

She wondered suddenly whether *she* wasn't the one who held on. Could it be? If so, she would have to be the one to let go. Someday. When, like Papa predicted, Mama was strong again.

But tonight was not that time. Certainly not after the trouble Senator Carmichael had stirred up. Dutifully Sabrina washed her face and hands in water from the pitcher Martha had filled and left on her dressing table. Then she stepped into the green sprigged muslin Mama had ironed after she finished polishing silver and cleaning and cooking. *Working her fingers to the bone,* Martha called it.

Sabrina brushed her hair, caught its long straight length at her nape with the green bow Martha had left for that purpose, and went out to please her mother. It was the least she could do.

Supper came off better than Sabrina could have dreamed it would, thanks to Lon Jasper's good nature. Entering the dining room, she discovered the origin of the piano music. In the parlor beyond, Lon sat at the piano, in full dress uniform. Mama stood nearby, hands clasped to her black-clad bosom, face lifted to heaven, eyes closed. Absorbed in the music, she looked enthralled, as if she had never before heard such divine sounds.

A sudden crescendo alerted Sabrina that her presence had been noted. When Lon met her startled gaze, pride glowed in his eyes. She felt sick. He jumped to his feet.

"The prodigal daughter has returned." Unfairly she thought how his joviality was at her expense. She glanced to Papa, who had never taken a liking to Lon Jasper.

"Nothing I can put my finger on," Papa had replied when Sabrina quizzed him about Lon once. "Your mama's right, of course. He'll make a girl a good catch."

"But not me?" she'd prodded.

"I'm your papa, sugar. No man will ever be good enough for you in my eyes."

She had hugged him then, and she wanted to now. He was the one who needed their consolation tonight. But even tonight Mama needed comforting worse, and Sabrina knew she must provide what support she could.

Martha's rapture had faded at the sight of Sabrina. Pain tightened the worry lines around her eyes. "I've been so frightened, child." She rushed across the parlor, but Lon reached Sabrina first.

"You know how to torture a fellow, don't you? I've been smelling that roast antelope so long my stomach thinks my mouth has gone on strike."

Papa laughed and Mama chided, "Shame on you, Captain Jasper." But Martha was obviously so charmed that Lon's unmannerly mention of body parts didn't disconcert her. Her brow began to unfurrow. Almost coquettishly she glanced up at him.

Scanning the table, Sabrina felt duly chastened, for the candles had burned three-quarters down and the flowers were wilted. The food, left to heat in a plate warmer beside the dining room fireplace, had probably cooled. If so, it was the only thing in this house that was cool, Sabrina thought uncharitably, and felt the familiar pang of guilt. She recalled with longing the cool breeze at Apache Wells. It took her a moment to pull herself back from the memory.

"I'm sorry to be late, Mama. You should have started without me."

Martha was busy with the food. "I don't know what that doctor was thinking, child, sending you off—"

"Mrs. Bolton," Lon chided, "don't tell me you found the wait unbearable."

"Oh, my dear, Captain Jasper! My apologies. I didn't mean to imply . . ." Flustered, Martha set a platter of duchess potatoes beside the roast. "Your playing was my salvation tonight."

"I don't have many opportunities out here," Lon was saying. "Perhaps we could do it again sometime."

The creases in Martha's brow relaxed a bit more. "You are invited to play our piano any time. It's a bit off key, I'm afraid."

"Off key? To my deprived ear it couldn't have sounded more harmonious."

By now they were seated and Papa had opened the wine. When he lifted his glass in a toast, the others followed. "To friends."

"Friends." Lon extended his glass across the table, touching Sabrina's. Martha's glass clinked against them.

"To family." She sighed, a contented sound, which to Sabrina's ear was rarer and more melodious than any musical instrument could ever be. Lon had certainly done wonders for Mama's morale.

So it went throughout the meal. With the skill of a band of sorcerers the group evaded the major concern of the day—Carmichael's threat against Papa. The other issue, Sabrina's tardiness, seemed an appropriate substitute. But every time Martha broached the topic, Lon changed the subject with a smile, a compliment, light teasing. Sabrina knew she should be grateful to him for forestalling the inquisition she had in store. So why did she read censure in the glances he cast her? He seemed intent on making up to Martha for the worry Sabrina had caused. Was that her imagination?

Or her guilty conscience? She would not be easily cheered tonight, for the tone of this evening had been set for her even before she heard the dreadful news about Papa. As if for reinforcement she glanced through the parlor door to the mantel and above, to the portrait.

You're right to feel guilty, Sabrina. At least you have that much sense.

I did nothing wrong.

Nothing? You call flirting with a renegade nothing? Slipping away with a renegade nothing?

But Ket—

Will you never learn to face reality? Don't mess this up, Sabrina. Look how happy Mama is. Listen to her.

"I've just had the most fabulous idea!" Martha had risen to clear the table. Now she set her plate back in its place. "We'll leave everything right here and take dessert into the parlor. It's only macaroons and coffee." She smiled effusively at Lon. "You will entertain us with more Chopin, won't you, Captain Jasper? Oh, it does my heart good."

If Mama was playing the coquette, it was to Lon's coy flirtations. "Turnabout is fair play, Mrs. Bolton. Isn't it your time to play for us? Sabrina has told me what an accomplished pianist you are."

"Me? Oh, my dear . . ." Martha cast a tentative glance to Sabrina, then straightened her shoulders slightly, lifted her chin, and turned a brilliant smile on their guest.

On *Mama's* guest, Sabrina thought.

"If you insist," Martha demurred. "I mean, you being Sabrina's guest and all. We should accommodate . . ."

Sabrina knew what to expect even before Martha

reached the piano. "Amazing Grace" or "Shall We Gather at the River?" or "Abide with Me". She watched her mother slide across the bench and strike a heavy discordant chord with uncustomary flourish. Sabrina hadn't realized how out of tune their piano was. When escape was possible, neither she nor Papa remained in the house when Mama took to the keyboard.

"She doesn't need us around to drum up heavy memories, sugar," Papa always said.

"How about a duet?" Lon was asking now.

While Sabrina and Edward approached dutifully, Lon slipped onto the bench beside Martha.

She cast him a tentative, doubtful glance. Her hands stilled. Her gaze darted from Edward to Sabrina to the portrait hanging above the mantel.

Sabrina tried to recall what she might have told Lon about Mama's distaste for popular music. "The devil's music," Martha called it. She didn't mind secular tunes outside the home, but here, where they were engaged in endless mourning, where the piano faced the hearth and portrait of her deceased daughter, Martha allowed nothing but songs that evoked pain and misery. Chopin had been an exception. Sabrina doubted there would be others.

"You know 'Amazing Grace?' " Martha quizzed now.

"No, ma'am." His hands struck a series of lively chords. " 'Turkey in the Straw.' You know it?"

"No, I—"

"It's easy. I'll teach you."

Martha cast a silent plea to Edward, but Lon was firmly in control. "Play the chords," he encouraged in his best commanding officer impersonation. "I'll take the melody."

Martha was caught. Sabrina watched her panic. Then, as only Martha Bolton could when realizing that in order to save face and secure her goals, there was but one way out, she took it. The resulting duet rattled the lamp chimneys.

Martha's pale face flushed. Startled eyes betold her misgivings. As though oblivious to his hostess's distress, Lon beamed. Again his eyes found Sabrina's. Again she imagined, or hoped she imagined, his censure. *See how I make your mother happy? Why don't you do it?*

He did make Martha happy. The following half hour proved that beyond a doubt. One tune followed another, each one lighter and livelier. Martha's inhibitions, already lowered by Lon's attentiveness, evaporated. The evening ended with a songfest.

Lon and Mama at the piano, Papa and Sabrina leaning against the satin-draped back. Singing. Laughing.

Happy.

At least, Martha was happy. Although some of her glow could be perspiration, her joy filled them all. Lon's controlled tenor led them, while Edward's robust baritone lifted the rafters, and Martha's soprano was none the less sweet for its lack of use. Only Sabrina remained subdued, and she had long years of practice disguising the fact. With Serena's admonition ringing in her head and Lon's eyes on her face, she felt trapped and resentful by turn.

She was here, where she had always wanted to be, in her home singing and laughing with her mother, but something was wrong, missing.

Tremayne. The reminder took her breath. She couldn't imagine him spending so much time and effort to make her mother laugh.

Tremayne. She heard the fear in his voice when he called his daughter from her pain-induced sleep, felt the tenderness in the kiss he placed on Ket's burning forehead.

She still ached with guilt for leaving him to return alone to his dying daughter. But she had a bereaved parent here before her, one who, if this night were a prelude, might

finally emerge from years of depression. Tonight Mama
had played the piano and sung and laughed.

Laughed.

Even as Papa's future was being threatened by the despicable senator, Martha had begun to awaken from her nightmare. There was no doubt in Sabrina's mind that the true
cause of Martha's happiness lay not so much in Lon's
attention, as in what that attention represented—the fulfillment of her goal—securing Sabrina's future.

Or sealing it, she thought uncharitably.

Don't mess this up, Sabrina. You owe Mama.

Later, when she and Lon strolled along the parade
ground, she thanked him.

"Don't thank me. I enjoyed it. Your mother is
delightful."

"Tonight, she was. Amazing as it seems to admit it."

"All it took was a little effort."

Sabrina held her pique in check. In truth, she was too
tired to take offense. "For years Papa and I have tried to
make her happy, Lon. Papa never gave up, but until tonight
I didn't believe she would ever be well. I'd never heard
her laugh before. Isn't that amazing? Until tonight I had
never heard my mother laugh. You gave her joy, Lon. So
much joy. Thank you."

They had reached the road that ran alongside the post
boundary between the Bolton's house and Sleeping Lion
Mountain. Lon turned west and guided Sabrina up a sel-
dom used trail. The spring evening was still cool. Dust
hung in the air. Somewhere on the mountain a coyote
called his mate. Out of sight of the house, Lon stopped
and took her in his arms.

"I could be said to have an ulterior motive."

He caught her off guard. With so much else happening,
she had forgotten about Lon's long-expected marriage
proposal. *Lord in heaven! Not tonight.*

"Ulterior? What could possibly be ulterior about bringing joy and—"

"Make no mistake, Sabrina." His head dipped. "I have a purpose." He kissed her. Full on the mouth, lips open, wet and passionate.

She obliged him. Truthfully, she owed him something. With the parlor scene reverberating through her mind, she opened her lips to his probing and allowed intimacies she had not considered before. She owed him. But it felt so wrong.

When she failed to return his embrace, he tugged her arms around his neck, then swept her corseted back with an open palm. She tried not to think about Tremayne, but only hours ago she had stood in his arms and willed him to kiss her. He hadn't, and it angered her now. Why hadn't he kissed her? Then she would know.

You already know too much about that man, Sabrina.

No, she thought, she could never know enough about him.

Would never know enough about him. Standing in the same road where she had first encountered him, with another man's arms around her, another man's lips on hers, the only thing she could give thanks for was that she was fully clothed and buttoned.

"Come on, Sabrina," Lon encouraged. "Loosen up. Give a bit . . ." He moved a hand around her waist, between their bodies. When he cupped her breast, she gasped.

"Hmm . . ." Ignoring her protest, his fingers found her nipple, teased it against the taut fabric of her gown. "You don't know how I long to feel your skin, really feel it. Taste it—"

She squirmed, struggled, but he held her firmly in place by a free arm to her back.

"Lon!" Disgusted, she tried to laugh it off, to disguise her outrage. "Lon, this . . . this isn't proper."

"Not proper? Oh, yes, Sabrina, this is very proper." He kissed her hard on the lips. "As long as I'm the only man who does it." With his arm still holding her in place, he dipped his head, kissed her chest through the muslin, then found her breast.

"Lon, please." She struggled in vain. Anger rose fast and white hot.

"Hold still. No one can see."

His words washed her with fear. "That doesn't make it right, Lon. Stop. Please stop."

His lips closed over her muslin-clad breast. His teeth found her nipple. When she gasped, it only encouraged him.

"Lon, stop right this minute. If Mama could see you now, she wouldn't be laughing. She would—"

"Ah, so resistant." Lifting his face, he covered her breast in his palm, rubbing the nipple he had bitten through the fabric. "I'm a patient man, Sabrina. Haven't I told you that before?"

She jerked again. This time he loosened his grasp without freeing her. "Patience won't do you any good." Her anger built. "Hell will freeze over before you do that to me again."

He laughed softly. "Such an innocent. It makes you even more desirable. Did you know that? Wait until you see how much more there is to enjoy."

"Enjoy?" Even as she asked the question, she knew the word was right. Or would be. With the right person.

"Wait and see. One of these days I'll show you what true joy is." Laughing good-naturedly, he turned her toward home.

Taps had long since played; the moon was high overhead; a few troopers who had the night off could be seen in the distance, returning from Chihuahua.

When they reached the gravel path that ran alongside

the parade ground, Lon asked casually, "What time did you leave the hospital?"

"Tonight?"

"Earlier. To tend to that child?"

"Oh." Wary, she dreaded facing the inquisition Lon had so successfully evaded during supper. Yet wouldn't this be good practice for what she surely faced at home? "Why?"

"Just wondered. Private Jones said that renegade came in."

"What?"

"That renegade Tremayne. Jones said he came to the hospital."

Jones again. How deeply had Jones implicated her?

"Did you see him?" Lon prodded.

"Jones?"

"The renegade, Sabrina."

Sabrina took her time answering. "I don't think so," she hedged, feeling both criminal and stupid. "I treated a sick child all afternoon, Lon. My father is threatened with a court-martial. Anything that happened earlier pales by comparison. Right now, I'm so tired I'm having trouble remembering my name."

That much, at least, was not a lie. But her life had suddenly become a briar patch of falsehoods, either outright untruths or lies by deception or omission.

Lon continued relentlessly. "Jones said that Indian-lover looked like the red devils were after him this time."

Sabrina stopped in her tracks. Anger exploded inside her. She strove to keep it there. "Have you forgotten your promise so quickly?"

"I didn't say that word." Beneath his breath, he added, "True though it is."

But it wasn't true. Tremayne wasn't married.

And that made her life more complicated than she could

ever have believed. Complicated and hopeless. For beside
her was a man who made her mother laugh, not by accident, but by design, because he wanted to win her hand
in marriage. She no longer questioned his intent.

I have a purpose, he had said. His actions tonight proved
the point as nothing else could have. Glancing up, she
found him grinning down at her.

"Relax, Sabrina. I was merely inquiring about your day."

That she doubted. She knew her behavior was not above
suspicion. If she had spent an innocent day treating an ill
child, she would be gushing details. Lon knew her well
enough to expect it. So did Papa and Mama. They would
all be suspicious, and for good reason.

"I apologized for being late for supper," she snapped.
"Should I apologize for trying to keep a child from dying?"

At the door he took her in his arms again, and she
suppressed the urge to fight him. This time his kiss was
chaste and to the point.

"This courtship may be backwards," he observed, his
breath blowing against her face, "but don't expect me to
give up."

"Backwards?"

"Usually a couple fall in love and then the poor fellow
has to convince her parents to accept him. In our case it's
you who must be convinced. Your mother is on my side.
Your father . . . I suspect Edward may come around before
you do."

She didn't know how to respond, so she demurely hung
her head. He tipped her chin with a forefinger.

"I'll say it again. I'm a patient man. You'll see."

Later in bed her mind returned to the pallet of soft furs
in Tremayne's cabin, and the room began to spin around
her. How would she ever find her way out of this bramble
patch?

Her heart was with Tremayne. If she had doubted that,

today convinced her. Seeing him with Ket had been wrenching. She had never felt so close to another person, and only part of it could be explained by her own experience with Serena.

She felt bound to Tremayne, tethered to him by some invisible force. By a spirit, maybe. Even if he didn't believe in spiritual guardians, she knew she could believe enough for two.

Stop this, Sabrina. You can never leave Mama.

How can I not?

How can you even think of it? You owe her, and you know it.

She had never been able to quiet her sister's voice of reason. Now she knew why. She believed in it. She hadn't realized how much she believed until she tried to persuade Tremayne that the laughter he heard at sixteen was his mother's.

Of all the lessons she had learned this day, the most powerful of all was that—the voice was real. She could never discredit it.

She knew with no past experience or prescience that her feelings for Tremayne would also last forever. Even though she couldn't fathom what she could do about it.

Nothing, came the voice. *You must make Mama happy*.

Make Mama happy. A small price, insignificant when weighed against the life lost so long ago. Make Mama happy. That was all she had to do.

Lon Jasper had done it for her tonight. Hadn't he, though!

Sabrina fell asleep with her mother's laughter singing in her ears.

Chapter Ten

By morning Sabrina knew what her mother meant when she talked about there being too many demons in the night. For as long as Sabrina could remember, Martha had wandered the house at night, sometimes sewing, sometimes cleaning, always busy. Come morning she was tired, but relieved.

"Daylight scares the demons away," she would say.

Now Sabrina welcomed daylight, too, for the problems that presented themselves during the long night had no solutions, none that she could dwell on. She recalled thinking, mere weeks ago, that she had lived her fantasy and was ready to live the life her mother chose for her.

How naive she had been to think her chance encounter with Tremayne behind the steward's house could have been enough. How foolish.

How wrong.

But what to do about the situation was a different matter altogether. If she acted on her own impulses she would hurt too many people. And the time was definitely not right.

Papa was in trouble. He needed her attention, especially since he wasn't getting Mama's. As if to confirm that assessment, when she entered the kitchen, Martha greeted her exuberantly.

"What a lovely night! Wasn't it, Sabrina? I can't remember another so perfect."

Joy competed with guilt and lost.

She's happy like we always wanted. Don't hurt her again.

"I'm already planning our next dinner party," Martha was saying. "We'll have truffles and smoked salmon. Edward, you could get—"

"Summer's coming, Mama. It may be too hot for another dinner party." Or Papa may be court-martialed, or Tremayne's daughter may have—

"Then we'll take it outside. A picnic in the mountains."

"Mountains?" In one day's time Sabrina's concept of the mountains had been irrevocably altered. The mountains meant only one place to her now—Apache Wells.

Martha laughed. *Laughed.* "The foothills, I meant. Gracious, we couldn't climb a mountain. Our champagne corks would pop."

"Champagne?"

For the celebration, Sabrina.

"I suppose we couldn't." Unable to come up with the slightest bit of enthusiasm, Sabrina's one thought was to escape the house before she hurt Mama's feelings. Papa picked up his hat and followed her out the door. His step was decidedly lighter than Sabrina's.

"Didn't I tell you, sugar? Didn't I say one day she would snap out of the depression that's dogged her for so long? I never gave up, and it's happened. Finally." He gestured broadly around the wide open spaces. "Thank God!"

"And Lon Jasper," Sabrina added.

Moments later, without conscious design, she found herself standing in the middle of the Applebee's parlor, which had been turned into a playroom for every child under eight years of age on the post.

Quilts thrown over chairs formed tents for crawlers to swarm in and out of. In one corner little girls struggled with floppy brimmed hats and oversized shoes, beaded bags and boas of ostrich feathers; across the room little boys banged cooking utensils against pots and pans from Reba's kitchen as they marched around the room in imitation of their fathers on parade. The glued-together china was nowhere in sight, but Sabrina had no doubt Reba would take it down in a minute for impromptu tea parties.

"This is a brilliant idea, Reba."

"It seems to be working." Reba remained cautious. "Our little Emily is beginning to interact." The object of their attention hid behind Reba's skirts; only a tiny hand and a small crown of black hair were visible.

The sight was enough to set Sabrina's stomach to fluttering. Emily and Ket were cousins. Wouldn't they be friends, too? The idea had come to her during the night. Farfetched though it was, it was nevertheless the most workable solution to one of her major concerns—how to get Ket the medical care she so desperately needed.

"Emily, darling." Kneeling, Reba coaxed the child to greet their guest. "Look, darling. This is Sabrina, the lady who brought you to us."

A gift, Reba had called the child. A disaster, Sabrina thought at the time. She knelt for a better view, but Emily turned her face into Reba's shoulder. Reaching a hand, Sabrina capped the child's head and was stunned by a sudden numbing sensation that rushed straight to her heart.

It was physical and emotional and deeply personal. She blinked back tears and hoped Reba hadn't noticed.

She hadn't. Reba was absorbed in her precious gift. "She loves the children. It won't be long until she's right there in the thick of things."

Sabrina removed her hand from the child's silky smooth hair. Smooth, unlike the road ahead, which was certain to be rocky for them all.

Tremayne's way was harsh, but wasn't that the way of life? During the night Sabrina had thought of one possible way to persuade him to bring Ket to the post. Ket could stay with the Applebees—and Emily. Sabrina recalled Major Applebee telling her that he changed into and out of his uniforms in the cook shack back of their house to keep from frightening Emily. He could continue to do so until both girls adjusted. The cousins would be a source of comfort for each other. Ket's life might be saved.

If you believe you dreamed this up for Ket you really don't have a lick of sense, the voice accused.

Her thoughts on Emily and Ket, Sabrina returned to the dispensary after lunch, where she tackled a different but equally important task.

She'd found the medical journals Doc Henry was examining the night before open on her desk this morning, contrary to the surgeon's meticulous nature. A cry for help? Surely.

"Everything has a place and belongs in it," Doc Henry claimed at least a dozen times a week. The only time he ever lost his temper was when an orderly left instruments or supplies out of place.

Discovering the open books before Sick Call, she had marked the places and set them aside for later examination.

Returning to them now, the first thing that struck her was that Doc Henry didn't seem to know much more about what ailed him than she did. Several places were marked, discussions on diseases that could cause palsy.

Some were grievous, such as Parkinson's Disease. Some less serious, like low blood pressure. She soon realized she had far too little information to narrow the field. The best she could hope for would be to identify the most promising causes, then confront him with the evidence.

But what if he didn't want to discuss his illness? What if he had accidentally left the books? He hadn't pried into her—

Startled by a sound outside the door, she snapped the journal closed. Guilt stung her cheeks when she glanced up, expecting Doc Henry.

It was Tremayne. Her breath caught at the sight of him. The room spun, like it always did. Dismally, she knew it always would. But his presence here was ominous.

She was out of her chair before she realized it, crossing the room. "Ket?" The word was a mere whisper. She felt as if his intense gaze had sucked the sound from her throat.

"No," he said quickly. "She's about the same."

"The fever?" She had reached him, taken his arm without thinking. But thinking, she didn't release it.

"Some better, Señora Ramériz thinks."

"Is she conscious?"

He nodded, stiffly, like she felt. He neither moved nor touched her in any way except with his eyes which probed. Strangely, as if peripherally, she noticed he had changed clothes. Clean shirt and duckins. Hair tied back.

"She's taken a little broth," he said, then added again, his voice tight, "The señora thinks she's better."

"Thank goodness." Forcefully taking charge of her senses, Sabrina dropped her hand. "Let me get my things. Doc Henry told me about some new—"

"I didn't come for you."

She swung back to face him.

"The negotiations," he said thickly. "We're meeting over at Headquarters."

She wasn't surprised. Hadn't Lon said as much? "You agreed?"

"How could I not?"

How could he not, indeed. "I understand now." Peace was important to him. Ket hung in the balance. A few years, he had said. Until Ket grew up. It made perfect sense.

"Well," she said, an idea half-forming. "By the time you finish, I'll be ready—"

"No, Sabrina." Adding insult to injury, he turned to go without a further word. She followed him into the hallway; her stomach tumbled with the rejection.

She should have seen it coming. He had asked her to treat his daughter, not barge into his life. But she couldn't help herself.

"I should see her again. Doc Henry said—"

"Don't worry. The señora will follow your instructions."

Don't worry? She stormed after him, following him out onto the veranda, to the wide entrance steps.

"How can you say 'don't worry'? I saw how bad she is. I can't get her out of my mind. I have to go back, make sure . . . Don't you understand? She might be better, but she is far from out of danger. Her fever hasn't broken, has it?"

He stopped with his back to her. She watched his shoulders heave with a heavy sigh. Her stomach felt suddenly hollow. Except for the fluttering.

The butterflies.

"The señora can handle it now." He spoke to the clearing that stretched before them.

She reached him, stopped close, close enough to touch him. Not touching him became an issue she tried to ignore.

"If the señora knows so much, why did you come for me in the first place?"

When he turned, her words faded. He looked tired and worried. "Thank you for coming yesterday."

"Thank me?" She struggled for sensibility against anger and fear. The fear inside her had nothing to do with Ket. He was rejecting her, that's what he was doing. *It's over,* he was saying. Before it ever began, it was over. When she grabbed his arm, she felt his muscles bunch.

"Thank me?" she said again, a whispered plea. "Is that all you have to say? Thank you? Well, I haven't finished. She isn't well. She might—"

"Sabrina. We're being watched."

She felt like the life had been knocked out of her. *Watched?* By whom? Doc Henry? Lon?

"Don't turn around," Tremayne warned under his breath.

Her breathing came hard, heavy. She stood as in a trance while he turned and took the steps. Without a backward glance, he strode off toward Headquarters. To negotiations, where he and Lon would sit down together and . . .

Gradually, her breathing steadied, and she gathered her wits and turned around. All she saw were a pair of polished boots retreating into the hospital mess hall. In two strides she reached the door. Jones was busily polishing a table.

It obviously didn't need it. He glanced up. Held her gaze.

And she held her tongue. For any reproach would be reported to Lon along with the overheard conversation, which, after all, was hardly damning in itself.

"Jones, would you find Doc Henry for me, please? I need to talk to him about that child who was burned."

* * *

The first thing Sabrina noticed when she stepped into Tremayne's cabin two weeks later was that Keturah's eyes were open. They were Tremayne-green and as defiant as her father's. Sabrina thought strangely that that was the first lucid thought she had entertained in weeks.

During that time Tremayne had returned twice to the fort, and she had watched helplessly from the dispensary window. With difficulty she had restrained herself from rushing to Headquarters to see him.

She could ask about Ket; she should ask about Ket.

If he needs you for Ket, he will come, Sabrina.

Each time she saw him ride in on the big black stallion she slipped into the canyon back of the hospital, hoping against hope to find the pinto tethered and waiting for her.

Foolish though it was, she seemed possessed. She couldn't let Ket go unattended, she reasoned, knowing all the while that Ket's welfare, important as it was, was not the point at issue.

Foolish, indeed, given her run-in with Lon the day after Jones saw her talking with Tremayne on the hospital steps.

"Anyone who would malign my concern for a sick child doesn't have enough to worry about," she defended when Lon walked her home from the trading post the evening after Tremayne came to the hospital.

She still couldn't decide why Tremayne had come by. He hadn't made the effort since. She had accompanied her father to the trading post that night, hoping against hope that he would be there. He wasn't.

But Lon was, and his presence thwarted her other plans for the evening. She was desperate to talk with Rosa, maybe come away with some of Rosa's commonsense approach to life and love. But Rosa was home ill, and Sabrina dared not slip away to Rosa's house, for Lon sat at the bar and watched her every move.

"I just wanted to spend some time with you," he explained. "Thought I could walk you home." He waited until they were out of earshot of the trading post to reveal his true concern.

"Why didn't you tell me it was that renegade's child you went to treat?"

"You didn't ask." *Not in so many words,* she thought, irritated with Lon, with herself, with the situation. With the approach of summer, evenings were the only cool part of the day. She wished she were walking home with Papa. That way she could at least enjoy the evening with its night sounds and fresh smells.

"Now I understand why you were so quiet that night," Lon persisted. "You didn't want us to know where you had been."

"Lon, this is what you need to know—I couldn't discuss a dying child in front of my mother."

"Later, after dinner, when we walked outside. You could have told me then."

"Why? We had other things to discuss." For the life of her she couldn't recall what they had talked about. The only thing she recalled about that walk with any clarity was the way Lon had pawed her in the dark, and him asking whether she had seen Tremayne at the hospital. She remembered feeling trapped in the bramble of her own lies, knowing that one day she would trip in them. This turned out to be the day. Or night. Guilty, she turned her ire on him.

"Why don't we discuss why you engaged Jones to spy on me?"

"Private Jones wasn't spying."

"What do you call it, then?"

When he remained silent, she asked, "Am I that untrustworthy?" It was a rhetorical question, one to which she knew the answer better than Lon. The answer crawled inside her, increasing her guilt tenfold. "What is he supposed to report? If I touch a patient's leg or . . . ?"

Or Tremayne's arm? Jones surely saw that.

"Sabrina, be fair. Trust has nothing to do with it. Sometimes your judgment is . . . uh, limited."

"My judgment is limited? And yours is not? Doesn't engaging one of my colleagues to spy on me imply limited trust?"

"He isn't spying," Lon repeated. "Although I can't see the harm, if you have nothing to hide."

"You wouldn't!" But she wondered whether she would see things differently if she didn't have something to hide—something deep and serious and growing insidiously day by day.

"You were forewarned," he said, lightly. "I told you I would do whatever it takes to win you, and I will. Even if you do seem to be changing your attitudes daily."

"Changing my attitudes?"

"What's happened to that sweet, agreeable young lady?"

"Agreeable? Don't you mean pliable?"

He shrugged. And she resisted responding. For she was changing. She was always irritable, always anxious, always ready to jump down someone's throat, as Papa had accused recently. The only time she felt any peace was when she was with Tremayne.

Now, as she stood in his cabin looking into Ket's Tremayne-green eyes, Sabrina felt strangely that she had come home, even though the child made no effort to conceal her dislike.

Perhaps she shouldn't have come to Apache Wells, after all.

Perhaps, Sabrina? This is a fool's mission. Didn't I warn you? You don't have a lick of sense.

After biding her time for a second week, hoping Tremayne would come for her, she had taken matters into

her own hands. To give herself credit, she had tried everything she could think of to dispel the urgency she felt to
be with him, even drawing the drapes in the dispensary so
she couldn't see him arrive at Headquarters every day.
Nothing worked.

So shortly after Sick Call one morning, she gathered the
medicines Doc Henry had suggested and went to the stable
where she engaged a mild-mannered horse, one she had
ridden from time to time. Never alone, of course. Either
Lon or Papa always accompanied her.

She added another tangled lie to the briar patch. "I'm
riding into Chihuahua," she told the private in charge of
the stable. "Rosa Ramériz hasn't come to work for a while.
I'm worried about her." Which was true, albeit a truth
unassociated with her present mission. She must see about
Ket.

Ket, my foot, Sabrina.

*Why else would I go to her while Tremayne is at the post? I
can ride to Apache Wells and return before the negotiators finish
for the day.*

Not a lick of sense.

Not a lick of sense, she now concurred, looking into
Ket's defiant, Tremayne-green eyes. For the startling truth
had struck her the moment she entered the cabin.

She loved Tremayne. Even though she had never experienced anything close to the phenomenon before, she knew
without a doubt this was love. Something so powerful could
be nothing less.

She loved Tremayne. Loved him in ways she could never
have imagined possible. In physical ways that left her limbs
trembling, her stomach queasy, and her head spinning.

In emotional ways that made it hard not to look at him
touch him, and want him.

Want him in ways she had never known existed.

"How are you feeling, Keturah?" she asked when the

child remained stoically silent. *Like father, like daughter,* Sabrina thought fondly.

It was the last fond moment she was to experience with Ket, for the girl immediately turned her head away.

"I came to look at your leg," Sabrina coaxed. "We must be sure it isn't infected." But when she reached to remove the robe, Ket jerked away.

"Infections can be dangerous." Sabrina reached again. This time the girl flung herself off the pallet, screaming.

"Please, Ket. I won't hurt you. I want to help you get well. Your father—"

Ket interrupted her with a guttural scream that sent chills up Sabrina's spine.

"My father hates white-eyes, and I do, too."

"I understand, Ket."

"Get out! I hate you. I hate you. Get out." Switching from English to Apache, the child emitted a long, trebling shriek. It slashed through Sabrina and continued without cease, until the cabin reverberated with high-pitched shrillness.

Sabrina glanced to Señora Ramériz, who had greeted her when she arrived, then retreated to her corner. Now the señora's eyes were round with terror. At Sabrina's glance, the old woman leaped to her feet and dashed for the door.

"Stay where you are." Tremayne's harsh voice boomed into the room, silencing Ket's eerie chant. All movement and sound stopped.

Ket was the first to move. She hopped from foot to foot; then she started jumping. Wildly, she bounded about the small cabin.

Sabrina knew each step should cause the child excruciating pain, but Ket was beyond pain. The poor child was terrified.

And Tremayne was furious. Sabrina tried to steady her

mind, to think. But the shock of being attacked by a child for whom she had only moments earlier felt such love and tenderness overwhelmed her.

The situation became suddenly clear. Understanding dawned. For weeks she had believed Tremayne was rejecting her, when in fact he must have known how Keturah would react to her now that she was conscious.

"Are you satisfied?" Tremayne was enraged. Haggard from too little sleep and too much worry, his most difficult task the last few weeks had been staying away from the hospital. Now he knew why.

Sabrina set his blood to boiling. Riding up to the cabin, he had been wary of the strange horse hitched at the rail. That it wore a US Army brand was even more bewildering. Then he heard Ket's scream. Primordial in tone, it was a sound made by trilling the tongue against the roof of the mouth. No more shrill and piercing sound could be heard on this earth. Apache women used the wail to show grief.

Hearing it, his bewilderment turned to fear, which he had yet to shake. He had dragged Sabrina as far as the well before he came to his senses. Dropping her arms as if they were hot from the fire, he struggled to suppress the anger that was his way of dealing with fear.

"You knew she would . . . ?" she stammered, leaving the sentence unfinished. But he understood.

"Not that it would be this bad," he admitted.

"Why didn't you—?"

"Tell you my daughter would do everything but attack you at dawn? How would that have made you feel?"

"I'm not the one who matters!"

The claim was preposterous. Of course, she mattered. He stopped short of telling her that, but he knew she saw it written on his face. Where had his senses gone? He glanced away, lest she read the answer in his eyes.

"I'm sorry she was so hard on you."

"I understand. I mean, I understand the reason. I could never begin to understand the hurt."

"My daughter attacks you, and you understand?" No white woman could ever understand an Apache's fear. And Ket's was worse. She wasn't even full Apache. She was a poor little half-breed who would never be accepted anywhere.

"She has your eyes," Sabrina said softly.

He shrugged, but didn't look at her. He didn't dare look at her. "How is her leg?"

"I didn't get a chance to examine it. I had barely arrived when you came—"

"Just in time," he said. "For you."

"She wouldn't have hurt me." He could tell she wasn't convinced of that. "I'm sorry to have frightened her."

"It isn't the first time."

"It is for me. I don't usually go places where I'm not—"

"Then why did you come?"

"To see Ket."

Like hell, he thought.

"If you think it was for any reason other than to examine Keturah's leg, you're wrong. You were at the post when I left."

"You knew I would return."

"Not until I had come and gone."

If that were true, why was she so angry? He resisted pursuing the topic, for he was leading her down a path he couldn't follow, a path to certain pain and rejection. But she continued, as courageous as any person he had ever met.

"Until the wound is healed," Sabrina was saying,

"there's danger of infection. She must remain inside, in bed as much as she will."

"She hasn't wanted to get up."

"Until today. That must have caused her enormous pain. I brought morphine for the pain. Doc Henry said to expect a rough time."

"She's used to rough times."

"I mean walking. She'll have scar tissue. Maybe a lot. She may need crutches. Hopefully, for just a while."

The thought brought instant and intense pain. "Something else to make her different from the others."

"Different?"

"She isn't full Apache," he pointed out. "They accept her, but only on the surface. They never let her forget that she isn't really one of them."

"I didn't realize. I mean ... those who are only half-white are not accepted in Chihuahua, but I never realized it worked both ways."

"A lot of things work both ways," he commented, half-aware of the double meaning of what he expressed. But when he turned to her, Sabrina was looking up at the cliffs. He studied the back of her head, her fiery red hair that at once blended and clashed with the surrounding red earth.

He had lifted a hand to her head when it struck him. *He loved her.* As terrible as that fact was, he loved her.

He'd been trying to put the burden on her, accusing her of using Ket's injury as an excuse to come here, when all the while it had been he who was lost.

He loved her. How had such a dreadful thing happened? He was in love with a white woman. His hand hovered for seconds mere inches above her head before he was able to drop his arm. If he touched her it would not be the end. And the end was far too terrible and too wonderful to contemplate.

She turned and caught him staring at her. Her brown eyes were large and luminous. Unshed tears sparkled on their surface. If he never did another right thing, he vowed, he would not cause those tears to fall.

"Tremayne, if . . ."

He stopped her words with a shake of his head. This moment caught in time was all he had, and he intended to savor it as long as he could without her growing suspicious.

As if she understood, she continued where he had interrupted her. "If you'll measure Ket's legs I'll have crutches made for her at the post. As soon as she's healed enough, we'll work with her. Before she goes back to the Apachería, we'll have her walking on her own."

We? Oh, no, Sabrina, not we. He couldn't draw his gaze away, although he knew she would be misled.

When he broke the silence it was to change the topic. "What happened the other day?" He watched her try to make the leap from crutches for Ket to whatever his runaway mind had conjured.

"That trooper who saw us at the hospital," he prompted, knowing full well that it would be safer to discuss crutches or morphine or damn well anything else.

"Oh, well . . ." She shrugged, attempted a smile, but it was stiff. "Nothing, really."

"Jasper heard about it?"

She nodded. "It doesn't matter."

"It matters. I don't want you hurt by . . ." He swept his hand toward the cabin as if to include Ket, but the truth was between them. He saw in a flash she knew it, too.

"Don't worry about me. If they . . . he . . . doesn't understand my treating a friend's daughter, then . . ." She left the sentenced unfinished, but Tremayne hardly noticed.

His mind had stopped on the word *friend*. Was that what she thought this was? *Friendship?* Couldn't she feel the tension? He felt wrapped in it, like in a vine. Bitterweed, that's what it was. Right now it was so tight it strangled him.

"This *friendship* could ruin your reputation."

"Not with the right people."

"The right people?" he scoffed. "Who the hell are the right people? Who at that post would understand you going off into the mountains with a squaw man?"

She looked away. "Don't use that word," she said through clenched teeth.

Roughly he grabbed her shoulder and jerked her around to face him. "Why? Because it reminds you of the truth?"

"What truth?" she demanded.

"Who I am. Who you are."

"Who am I?"

"The daughter of a soldier who should watch her reputation so she can grow up to marry some high-ranking officer in the damned US Army."

Before his very eyes, she fell to pieces. By the time she reached for him, she was shaking so hard he could not deny her need to be held. For he was consumed by the same need, the same fierceness, the same hopelessness. He drew her close, held her fast, and prayed she couldn't feel the thrashing of his heart. "I should never have involved you. Never."

"Ket might have died," she argued feebly against his chest. "You needed me."

Like lightning his hands caught her hair, pulled her head back. He stared hauntingly into her wet face. "Needed you? You don't know how . . ." The words had escaped on a breath, and he regretted them the moment he realized.

For it was a moment of mutual understanding. They stood still, as if life had drained from their limbs, caught in the grip of something so strong, wrestling with emotions so strained, the earth seemed to vibrate beneath their feet.

He watched her tongue dart out and lick her lips and he felt the same need, the same dryness of mouth and shortness of breath. The same thrashing heart, the same desperate, desperate longing.

Then as suddenly as insanity had struck, sanity returned. He shoved her away, dropped his arms. "I didn't say that."

He watched her absorb his bitterness, saw the stunned look on her face. "How dare you deny it?"

"You aren't thinking straight, Sabrina. I had no right to bring you here, to involve you—"

"I came on my own. You didn't force me."

"Didn't I?"

"I haven't seen you in over a week."

"Two." *God, was he condemned to play the everlasting fool?* She recovered first, but not before he saw the truth—his slip had revealed the only thing she needed to hang onto the slight, gossamer thread of hope. "And you don't need me," he added more softly.

Her face crumpled. "How dare you make judgments for me! You sound like Lon Jasper. But you aren't like him. You couldn't be like him in a million years. So stop trying to drive me away."

Without warning she flung herself against him again, giving him no choice but to hold her. That's what he told himself. Their hearts throbbed heavily in unison.

"What are we going to do?" she whispered against him.

"Nothing."

She went stiff in his arms.

"Sabrina, be reasonable. Your world is different."

"All worlds are different."

"Maybe. But I'm living proof that crossing from one to another never works. I have no life. I belong nowhere. Thanks to me, neither does Ket. I've condemned her along with myself. I won't do the same to you."

"What about Emily?"

"Emily." Yes, there was Emily. Chi's child. "For her, maybe . . . She's still so young."

"She'll always be Apache. How can it be right for her and wrong—"

"There is no right," he admitted. "Only wrongs. Listen to me, Sabrina. You can't throw away the life you were born to. If you won't think of yourself, think of those who would be hurt. Think of your mother."

"My mother? How could you bring up my mother?"

"Someone has to."

She drew away, as in a trance. Backed off, two steps, bumped into the well. Turning, she stared down into dark depths. "Where is the laughter when we need it?"

He steeled himself. "It doesn't exist."

Mad as a hornet, she turned on him. God, but she was beautiful. Beautiful and courageous and compassionate . . . and the wrong woman for him. Not that he had succeeded in convincing her of that, yet.

"Then don't believe," she persisted. "I told you I would believe for you, and I will. A chance, Tremayne. That's all we need. It may not work—who are we to say? We haven't given it a chance. Please, let us give it a chance."

His heart lodged so firmly in his throat, it cut off all air. And sense. Yet from somewhere deep inside, where he stored experiences too painful and personal to ever bring to consciousness, he dredged up the courage to shake his head.

"I'll believe for you," she pled. "You'll see. When Ket is well—"

"I mean it this time, Sabrina. You can't come back to Apache Wells."

Chapter Eleven

That she managed to reach a compromise with Tremayne would, she often thought, be etched on her tombstone as her life's greatest accomplishment. From the depths of desperation, she had persuaded him that she could and would keep their relationship purely platonic if he would promise to inform her of Ket's condition.

As she'd known he would, Tremayne honored her request. Twice a week when he and Nick arrived for negotiations, he stopped by the hospital first.

Although their conversations were limited to impersonal topics and carried out in full view of anyone who happened to be at the hospital, she lived for his visits. Tremayne seemed to enjoy them, too, as if the unspoken but strictly adhered to limits satisfied his need for emotional distance. He became, if not easy-going, at least relaxed in her presence. She knew better than to cross the tacit line. After asking and receiving an update on Ket, she would inquire about the negotiations. His response was invariably a variation of the cynicism they both felt.

"No better than you would expect," he would reply. "They're trying to agree on a proposal for me to take to Mangas and the other chiefs. That'll likely take the rest of my lifetime."

"But summer's here," Sabrina protested once. "Isn't that the time for . . . uh . . ."

"For the red devils to go on the warpath?"

She held his defiant gaze, returning it with a noncommittal shrug. "Something like that."

He grunted, shook his head, and almost grinned. "You don't make a very convincing adversary."

"I'm not your adversary." In the moment of stillness, while her words rang in the charged air between them, she saw in his eyes that he knew exactly what she was to him.

"No. Well, I'd best get going. See what plagues the estimable senator can propose today."

It was the closest she had come to making a personal statement, and oblique though it was it sent him away. But not before the gossip mill had begun to churn.

Later Sabrina realized she should have seen it coming. She had awaited Tremayne's regular arrival so eagerly, however, that she'd given little thought to her reputation. She had restrained herself, for heaven's sake. She never touched him, when every moment by his side was sheer torture—not being able to touch him, to wrap her arms around him, to feel his arms around her.

She lost count of the number of times and people to whom she explained, "His daughter was badly burned. He comes to check with Doc Henry about her treatment."

Then one day Nick came alone. Until then she hadn't questioned why Nick never came to the hospital with Tremayne. But when Nick stepped into the dispensary alone late one June morning, the bottom fell out of her stomach.

Her fear must have been obvious, for Nick hurried to explain.

"He's all right, Sabrina. He's taking the proposed treaty around to the chiefs. He'll be gone awhile."

"Oh." Sabrina strove to conceal her disappointment.

"I didn't want you to worry."

Nick knows, she thought.

Knows what, Sabrina? There's nothing to know.

"I should check on Keturah."

Nick shook his head. "He asked Lena and me to watch out for her. I'm to report to you if we see anything amiss."

"I really should go—"

"No, Sabrina. I'm to make it clear that you are not to go out there while Tremayne's away. Ket's grandmother has come from the Apachería to care for her."

During the long summer that followed Tremayne was away for weeks at a time, taking the treaty to the various Apacherías. Although she hadn't missed Lon Jasper during his twenty-four day patrol, the weeks without seeing Tremayne were the longest and most unbearable of her life. His absence confirmed the truth.

She loved him.

Adding to her confusion and guilt, her mother's spirits actually rose following Tremayne's departure. Sabrina didn't make the connection until her mother broached the topic one day while they were in the kitchen preparing for the picnic.

The picnic had turned into quite a project. Martha invited Carrie and Neil Young, the Applebees, and Sabrina wasn't sure how many others. Lon was scheduled for Officer of the Day duty on Martha's first date, so she had changed it.

"We'll take a gallon of pickled eggs and several tins of paté and smoked salmon," Martha was saying. Sabrina prepared the pickling spices. With Martha's emotional recovery had come an unexpected camaraderie between them. Sabrina enjoyed her mother's company now, more and more.

On this day Martha began innocently enough, even though she raised a topic Sabrina had done her utmost to avoid.

"How is the child you've been tending, dear?"

"Better." Sabrina still didn't suspect. Then Martha dropped the bombshell.

"The ladies at bridge said she belongs to that renegade who invaded the soiree."

Caught unprepared, Sabrina answered without thinking. "His name is Tremayne, Mama."

Martha continued to peel eggs, speaking casually. "Why didn't you tell me about the child?"

"There wasn't any need. It would have upset you, and—"

"I'm not as fragile as you and Edward think, Sabrina. I know children die. I'm glad you are saving one. I'm proud of you. I don't think I've ever told you that. But I am."

"Oh, Mama." Sabrina held her mother's gaze until Martha looked away, disconcerted.

"I do worry, though."

"I know."

"You mustn't ruin . . . I mean you can't go off with that man alone. The ladies are talking."

"Then they're foolish," she finally managed. "There's nothing to talk about." But wasn't there? She dared not ask exactly what the ladies were saying.

"Edward says the man has gone now. That he won't return for some time."

Sabrina shrugged, noncommittal.

"I'm so relieved. I've lived in fear of Captain Jasper hearing the gossip. What on earth would he think?"

Sabrina learned the answer to that question the following evening after the picnic. At Lon's insistence they had invited Senator Carmichael and his aides, but not without an argument.

"He has threatened to court-martial Papa, Lon. How can you suggest we entertain the man?"

"You've blown this out of proportion, Sabrina. Carmichael won't pursue a court-martial. Haven't I told you that?"

"Yes, but—"

"It's time Edward made up with him."

"Papa won't agree, and frankly, neither do I."

Lon turned conspiratorial. "I could tell you something about the senator that would change your mind."

Sabrina doubted that.

"But you'd have to keep it under your hat."

"He's a secret admirer of the Apache?" she responded sarcastically.

"I'm not teasing."

Neither was she, but she dared not say such a thing to Lon.

They were on the porch at the time. It was midday, and Lon had come during the noon hour for the express purpose of obtaining an invitation for the senator. In spite of the hour, he took one of her hands and placed it over her heart. He kept his hand there, too. Somehow, she resisted pulling away.

"Cross your heart?"

"Cross my heart." She was unable to muster the proper enthusiasm.

"You may think you won't be impressed, but you will be. Carmichael owns half this damned country."

"What?" Before he could repeat the statement, she added, "What does that matter? A lot of people own land out here."

"Not as much as Carmichael. He and his brothers have

been buying up land for years. They're fixing to be rich men.''

"I don't see the relevance, Lon. He could own *all* this country and I wouldn't want to invite him to our picnic.''

"Listen, Sabrina. Just listen. The senator is working with very powerful men. You know what that means?''

"Of course. Carmichael is a senator. He should work with powerful men.''

"This is different, special. Truly special. They've almost finalized the deal. That's why Carmichael has stayed out here so long.''

Too long, she thought, but resisted saying it. Both Lon and her mother had pointed out how argumentative she had become of late.

"It doesn't befit a lady," Martha had chided softly.

"What deal, Lon?'' she asked now in a dutiful attempt to curb her contentiousness.

"The southern route of the Second Transcontinental Railroad. That's what deal. They're building it right through here.'' Speaking, he turned to sweep a hand across the landscape. "Right here, Sabrina. Like he told your mother, businesses will come, towns will spring up, people will come, families, children, the whole shootin' match. Carmichael is fixing to be a rich man.''

"Then he will certainly have the power to ruin Papa.''

"Sabrina, give the man credit.''

For what? she wanted to ask. Again she let better sense prevail. "You still haven't explained why we should invite him to the picnic.''

"For me, Sabrina. For us.''

Dear God, what now?

"Carmichael has taken a liking to me. I like him, too.''

"Oh, Lon, he's a—''

"A what?''

"For one thing, he should confine his attention to single women."

"His attention? Sabrina, Senator Carmichael is a married man. He isn't interested in any of these ladies. He has a wife and son back in Washington. He means absolutely no harm. The women who complain wouldn't know lechery if it slapped them in the face."

Sabrina hid her irritation.

"I'm asking you again. Will you invite him to the picnic?"

"Why?" she persisted.

Lon sighed. "I thought your mother talked to you about this argumentative stage you're going through."

The reprimand didn't faze her. She wondered whether that meant she was losing her wits. If Mama were eavesdropping she would already have swooned. "I asked why we should be required to entertain Senator Carmichael."

"Because he is the best thing that has ever happened to my career, that's why," Lon snapped. "He's going all the way to the top, Sabrina, and he's promised to take me with him."

She didn't ask to the top of what. She didn't ask anything more. She acquiesced to inviting Senator J. J. Carmichael to the picnic, if her parents agreed, which Martha did. At the last minute, Papa begged off, claiming work at the warehouses.

As expected, the senator made the usual spectacle of himself, but Lon Jasper was too enamored of the man to take note.

In other ways the picnic, held at a favorite spot at the base of Sleeping Lion Mountain, was a rousing success. For proof, one had only to witness Martha's broad smile at the end of the day. Even Edward's absence hadn't dampened her joy. When Lon asked permission to walk Sabrina once around the parade ground before full dark, Martha's beaming rivaled the sunset.

Sabrina had never expected to see her mother so happy. It was almost enough to convince her that Lon Jasper was her chance of a lifetime. Certainly he was her chance to make her mother happy.

Lon, the good sport, filled in for the absent Edward without missing a step. Only later did he lament the fact that Edward hadn't attended.

"He was foolish to have stayed away on the senator's account," Lon complained on the way home.

"He had work to do," Sabrina excused. She didn't argue, for her head still spun with Reba Applebee's earlier observation.

It followed a major accomplishment for Sabrina. For weeks she had visited the Applebee's, hoping to hold little Emily. Even at the picnic when Sabrina sat on the pallet with Reba, the child hid in Reba's lap. Guiltily Sabrina wondered whether somewhere deep in her consciousness, Emily held her responsible for the loss of her family.

Guilty or not, Sabrina found comfort with the child, comfort she knew she shouldn't need or seek. She should be using this time to forget Tremayne, for more than ever she realized how much he meant to her. Even though they never spoke of personal things, seeing him regularly twice a week had made their relationship, fantasy though it was, seem normal, possible.

In reality, it was neither normal nor possible. The more human he became, the more forbidden he was to her, for nothing about him would meet the approval of her parents.

Nothing. Which always brought to mind the white Spode china with pink roses Mama had painstakingly packed piece by piece in lamb's wool on their moves from post to post.

"It belonged to your Grandmother Bolton, Sabrina. She wanted you and Serena to share it. Now, of course, it will all be yours."

All twenty-five place settings. The boxes they were packed in wouldn't fit in Tremayne's cabin. He didn't have a table, for heaven's sake.

He hadn't even kissed her, and here she was thinking of weddings and china. And of Tremayne, the man, of the way he made her body sing and her heart skip every time she saw him approach.

He hadn't even kissed her! Lon would probably propose marriage before Tremayne allowed himself to kiss her.

Distracted, Sabrina started when little Emily stumbled across the picnic blanket and landed in her lap. For a moment she could only stare as though dumbstruck. Tears rushed to her eyes. She clasped the child to her bosom and buried her face in the silky soft black hair and hoped Reba hadn't noticed. But this time Reba had.

Leaning over, she whispered in Sabrina's ear. "Has Lon proposed?"

"What?" Lon Jasper had been the furthest thing from Sabrina's mind.

"I'd be willing to bet he proposed today. At long last."

Sabrina glanced around to see who might have overheard. "Why would you think that?"

"You can always tell when a woman has marriage on her mind. She starts cuddling babies."

"Marriage . . . ? Babies . . . ?" Before Sabrina could come up with an acceptable response, Carrie diverted her attention by whispering in her other ear.

"We're leaving. I have to get Neil away before he slugs that lecherous old senator." Several other wives had done the same thing.

But not even thoughts of the lecherous old senator could dispel the sheer joy Sabrina felt holding little Emily or the dismay that lingered from Reba's observation.

Yes, she had been thinking about marriage.

But not to Lon Jasper.

"Thanks for inviting Senator Carmichael," Lon said now. They walked side by side up the road where Sabrina first met Tremayne. She suppressed the memory as best she could.

"I told you he would behave himself."

She stifled a retort. The senator had not behaved himself in the eyes of most of the ladies or their husbands. Lon was surely only one of two people in attendance who hadn't noticed—Lon and Mama.

By the time they reached the foot of Sleeping Lion, the sun had settled behind the mountains to the west, and the air was becoming cooler, a respite from the stifling summer heat. No sooner were they out of sight of the lingering picnickers than Lon stopped beside an overhang formed by a rocky ledge high above them.

Taken by surprise, she glanced around. "What are you—?"

"This." Drawing her back into the hollowed niche, he took her in his arms and kissed her.

"Lon, don't. I . . ." Would she ever become accustomed to his kisses?

"Shh. Let's not argue. There are plenty of more thrilling things to . . . explore." His hands trailed a path to her breasts.

She writhed and wriggled, trying to get away, but he seemed to have a dozen hands. No matter which way she moved, they were there.

"Lon, don't."

He paid no heed. His lips found her neck, and she wished she had worn a banded collar instead of a flat one which allowed his tongue access to her skin.

But it was his hands on her breasts that inflamed her. When a shudder tripped down her spine, he laughed against her skin.

"I told you you'd learn to like this."

But she didn't like it. "Lon, please." She hated it. Now she knew why women were admonished to wait until after marriage to allow men such privileges. Then they would be trapped.

But she hadn't felt trapped in Tremayne's arms. She had felt wonderful. She longed to feel them around her again. Overwrought at the comparison, she suddenly realized that Lon had lifted her skirts on one side. His hand moved up her thigh.

"What do you think you're doing?" She jerked her leg away and fought off his hand with her own. "I said stop. Please. Don't make me scream."

"Scream?" He backed off a bit. Then his features relaxed in a knowing expression. "Ah, so modest. I like that in a woman. But you don't have to be modest with me." Again he gathered her skirts in his hand, moving ever closer to her thigh.

"Lon, please. I've never—"

"Of course you haven't. But we're alone now. Let me show you how . . ." He pressed his body against hers, forcing her back against the hard rock wall. Flush against her, his body suddenly . . . She felt something hard, probing. When he nuzzled her with it, shock and terror competed. She tried to break free, but he had pinned her against the hard red rock. So intent was she on escape that she didn't realize he had reached beneath her skirts until she felt his hand high on her thigh.

"I'll scream," she mumbled, but the sound was muffled by his mouth. His kiss was harsh and hard, like the rest of him. When she fought with her hands, he reached between them and gathered her wrists in one fist.

"Lon, please stop." She rocked her head from side to side. "Please!"

"Hold still, Sabrina." His tone had lowered, was urgent,

breathless. "Give me a chance. You'll like this. If you'll just hold still."

Panic took on a new meaning when she felt his hand at the opening of her pantaloons. His fingers reached for the most private, intimate part of her. Ruled by a fear so great it stung her eyes, she fought with the only means left to her, her feet.

"Lon Jasper, stop this. Stop." She kicked and kicked, again and again. Finally he dropped his hand and stood back, but not far enough away for her to escape.

Her heart thrashed wildly. Tears brimmed. "Don't ever . . . ever do that . . . again. Never."

"Never's a long time, Sabrina. Sure you mean it?" He sounded wounded, as if she had been the one at fault.

Panicked, she slipped free, but had only gained the road before he caught her arm, jerking her around in her tracks. Her heart thrashed a warning in her ears.

"This how you treat that renegade Tremayne when he gets fresh with you?"

She slapped him. It was an involuntary reaction, one she knew immediately she wouldn't have had the nerve to perform had she thought it through. Stunned by her behavior and his, she stood immobilized, heaving for breath.

Lon rubbed his cheek, clearly taken by surprise. Then he began to laugh, low in his throat, but the sound was ugly, horrible. "Whoa, there, Sabrina, you're becoming a feisty little filly. Didn't know you had such spirit."

She wasn't sure what he meant, but she had no intention of hanging around to find out. Again she started for home. This time he let her take a couple of steps before catching up. They walked in silence, Sabrina steaming, Lon with his hands clasped behind his back, as if he were in the best of humor.

"Righteous indignation. Is that what it's called?"

She refused to answer. Truthfully, she was afraid what

would come out were she to open her mouth. Would she berate Lon? And would it ring false? Voiced, would her true feelings sound as loud as they did ringing through her body?

The clamor inside her now had nothing to do with butterflies. All she wanted was to be away from this man.

To not be touched by him again.

To not be found out for the awful secrets in her heart, the awful longing that sang through her veins, that cried for Tremayne, for his touch, for his kiss.

"If I thought there was an inkling of truth to the rumors," Lon said beside her, "I'd be the one righteous with indignation."

Sabrina's feet came to an involuntary halt at his claim. "I don't know what you're talking about." She tried to sound offhanded, but knew she failed. She started up the road again. He fell in step.

"Ah, so innocent." He laughed softly. "I believe you, Sabrina. You wouldn't go off into the mountains alone with a man like that. Not like they're saying."

Fear filled her head with mush. She concentrated on the magenta-streaked sky.

"Jones said you had a good cause. Said that half-breed kid of his isn't well yet."

"His daughter," she said quietly. "Her name is Keturah. Her burns were severe. She could have died. She isn't out of the woods, yet. Doc Henry is having a pair of crutches made for her." She had been speaking into the night air. Now she turned to him. "Convict me for that, if you will. Surely you understand why keeping a child from dying is a vital concern for me. If you don't, then you don't know me very well. Certainly not well enough to try what you just tried."

She outdistanced him this time, keeping her eye on the black outline of her parents' house in the distance. She didn't hear Lon behind her until she reached home. Suddenly he leaped into the path behind her.

"If I said I'm sorry, would it make a difference?"

Angrily she almost shouted the truth—no, it would not make a difference. "Would you mean it?" she asked, her back to him.

"I'm not in the habit of apologizing. If I were to, it would be sincere." He took her shoulders, turning her to face him. Blond hair fell over his brow and grazed her face. It reminded her of Tremayne's red headband.

Lord in heaven! Would she spend the rest of her life being reminded of that man? Then her heart stopped for a completely different reason. Lon Jasper had gone down on his knees. His hands found hers.

"Sabrina . . ."

No. Dear God, please not now.

"I apologize for being such a boor, Sabrina. I know you value your reputation as much as I do, and that you would never tarnish it."

What did that mean? She didn't want to know.

"I told you before that I'm jealous. I shouldn't have listened to the gossip. I should never have accused you of consorting with the enemy."

"The enemy?"

"Another man. Any other man."

She stared beyond him, into shadows that gathered along the parade ground. Her mind focused, not on the terrible events of this night, but on Tremayne. A sense of peace returned to her as she thought of him, of being in his arms, of his compassion. He would never have treated her the way Lon did tonight. She knew that. Felt it. And she felt so alone.

"I'm an officer on the way to the top," Lon was saying. "That's not bragging. It's the truth. I've worked hard for it. Any luck I need, Carmichael will furnish."

"Fine," she commented.

"And you are . . . I've always considered you the perfect example of what an officer's wife should be."

"Me?" Her brain spun into focus. Was this a proposal?

He rose to his feet and pulled her into a light embrace. "That gossip served a good purpose. Guess I'd better get serious before some renegade turns your head, huh?"

She didn't know what to say. Had he proposed? Was he building up to a proposal? Suddenly she spied a figure walking toward them across the parade ground.

Papa. He was returning from the warehouses. He wouldn't reach them in time to prevent Lon from proposing, if that was his intention. But . . .

"Papa's coming, Lon." She stood aside, climbed a step.

"Well?" he queried.

It had been a proposal. Or had it? She huffed indignantly. "If that was a proposal of marriage, Lon Jasper, it certainly lacked proper sentiment."

Before he could respond, she lifted her hand and called to Edward. . . .

A few days later Sabrina walked in on Martha while she was ironing small strips of gold cloth. The green gown hung on the dress form denuded, the elegance of the Worth design as obvious as Martha had claimed. Martha had untied all the bows, and for a moment their absence weighed heavily on Sabrina. She wondered whether Tremayne had thrown his away after she found it.

"What are you doing?" She watched her mother iron what had been another gold bow. "There are no more soirees planned until fall."

Martha fairly beamed. "You must have a suitable gown for your betrothal party."

"My what?"

"My dear child. Captain Jasper is going to propose. It's just a matter of time."

Time? How much did she have? Or how little? Had Lon really tried to propose the other night? Or had she imagined it? She longed to talk to Rosa, but Rosa had been ill much of the time lately. She had never been able to confide in her mother, but now Mama had softened. Perhaps . . .

"Was Papa the only man you ever loved, Mama?" She blurted out the question without preamble, and Martha glanced up from her work, obviously scandalized.

"Of course, child. Certainly." She ironed another ribbon flat, laid it aside, and picked up another. "That I remember."

"You mean you forgot . . . someone?"

Martha stared in the general direction of the dress form. Sabrina wondered what vision swam in her mind's eye. "One must, child. One must."

Sabrina was shocked. She had asked the question expecting, indeed hoping for, a denial, for something that would persuade her to give up the fantasy. She had received the opposite.

Yet, if her mother was right, didn't that mean she might someday forget?

Then Tremayne returned. She had finished Sick Call and had gone to the window to stare dismally toward Headquarters when he rode into view. He came straight to the hospital.

He was back. He was coming to see her. Washed by weakness, she caught the window ledge for support. From there she watched him dismount and hitch the black at the rail. She barely restrained herself from racing to meet him. He stepped up on the porch. She savored the sight of him. Lean and tall, hair tied back, white man's clothes. Crisp shirt, duckins. Clean, like Lon had been the day he rode in from patrol and found her holding Jedediah's leg, when he had cleaned up for her.

Had Tremayne? Fascination buzzed in her head. Anticipation stirred her heart, but she held her ground.

The dispensary offered a measure of privacy, however
small. As she awaited him, her arms trembled, and enough
butterflies fluttered in her stomach to churn butter. She
stared at the open doorway.

Then he stepped into view and, forewarned though she
was, the jolt took her breath. In his eyes she read the same.

*Looked at each other. Oh my yes, they had looked at each
other.* And nothing would ever be the same again. She
remembered the night at the trading post when neither
of them could speak. For a while she savored the moment.

Finally, for want of another thing in this world to say,
she blurted out, "Emily let me hold her."

"Good." He held her gaze. "That's real good." His
voice was thick, strained, like her own.

"Come in." She watched his eyes smolder. She knew
the feeling. She smoldered, too. It was all she could do
not to throw herself in his arms here in the middle of the
hospital where anyone could see, even Jones, Lon's spy.

"I came to say . . . hello."

"Hello."

With a finger he tipped his hat. "Hello." It sounded
more like good-bye. Was he leaving? She called him back.

"Have you seen Ket?"

He nodded.

"How is she?"

She watched him consider, what she couldn't tell, then
settle for a noncommittal, "Good."

A great gnawing took hold of her. She needed more.
Another word, another look. A touch. It had been so long
since she'd touched him.

"Better get on over to Headquarters."

He couldn't leave! She followed him onto the veranda.
"How did your trip go?"

He shrugged. "Not well."

"I'm sorry."

"No more than I expected."

"What'll you do now?"

"Try again."

Try again. Here. He would be back. Relief left her weak.

He reached the steps but did not stop. Without breaking stride he headed for the hitching rail where the black was tied. She followed him.

"Ket's crutches are almost ready."

He worked at untying the reins. "Good."

Good? Was that all he could say? *Look at me,* she wanted to cry, *hold me. Can't you see how much I missed you? How much I need you?* Lifting her skirts, she hurried down the steps and placed herself between the hitching rail and his horse. "I'll bring them out when they're done."

He looked up. At her, into her, with those intense green eyes. Her breath caught. Today his eyes were the only giveaway that he had ever met her before. His eyes and his voice.

"To be sure they fit," she explained. "They might be too short. Or too long. Or—"

"When is it you're going to marry Jasper?"

The question knocked the wind out of her. She staggered, felt the black's heated breath on her shoulder. How could he ask such a thing? Suggest it, as if it were a certainty? A reality?

"You hate Lon Jasper." It was the only thing she could think of to say.

"I hate what he stands for," Tremayne acknowledged. "But he's right for you."

"Right for me? What are you saying?"

"He is."

She pursed her lips in a useless attempt to still her trembling. She knew what he was saying. Good-bye. Telling her this was it, the end. It was over. He was leaving. Going somewhere she couldn't follow, somewhere she didn't belong, would never belong.

In the two long months while she waited and longed for him, he had forgotten her. Or he was pretending awfully hard to have.

Desperation blurred her vision. If the hitching rail hadn't been between them she would have flung herself in his arms. But it was between them. A bar between them, it represented so much more.

His reins were untied. He held them loosely, looking past her down the clearing. Suddenly she realized he was waiting for her to move. He didn't trust himself, either. If he came around to step into the saddle, he would be too close.

Hope stirred.

Not a lick of sense.

Too close? Impossible. She could never be too close to him. In that moment of torture, when he looked back to her, she saw it in his eyes. Nor could he ever be too close to her.

That was the hardest blow of all. Knowing he cared but still expected her to marry Lon Jasper.

It meant only one thing. He didn't really *love* her. He might be attracted to her, but he didn't *love* her. Not like she loved him.

"You know," she said, shaking her head, trying to smile but falling short. "You're the second person lately who has asked me about that damned wedding. Maybe I'll just set the date."

She watched him go. Sick to the soul. Was Mama right? Was it possible to forget? In her heart of hearts she knew she would never forget this man. A hundred years from now she would recognize his particular walk, his bucolic scent. His intense green eyes. His deep, soft voice, his wavy black hair.

A hundred years from now when she was married to another man?

The crutches.

A solution?

A chance. She raced to find Doc Henry.

Chapter Twelve

The morning sun had barely topped the distant horizon when Tremayne drew rein in Hospital Canyon behind the post magazine. His initial reaction to the message, which he still carried in his shirt pocket two days after receiving it, lingered in his mind like a flower wilted on the vine.

> *Mister Tremayne. Doc Henry asked me to inform you that the crutches for your daughter will be ready in two days, as we discussed.*
> *The date has been set.*

The date has been set. Damn! Sleeping Lion Mountain might as well have fallen full-weight on top of him. That was how smothered he felt, reading those words.

But hadn't he the same as told her to set the damned date? The fact that it was as far from what either of them wanted as these mountains were from the moon didn't count. The truth was, it was best for Sabrina. Best for both of them.

Still, he hadn't expected her to act so soon. Or to make it a point to tell him about it. He didn't want to know. If it weren't for the negotiations and what peace could mean for Keturah, he would leave and never look back.

That thought, leaving Sabrina, never again to see her, left him physically weak. Witless, like he had called her.

And hadn't she proved that! Not only had she sent him the message, but she had it delivered in full view of Jasper.

The woman baffled and bewildered him. In that order, and reversed. Hell, any way he looked at it, Sabrina Bolton was trying her best to tree him, even though she hadn't the slightest idea what kind of wildcat she'd set her sights on.

Two months away from her had been both curse and blessing. Every minute he had longed for her, ached for her in more ways than the mere physical. But two months' absence had shown him the truth. Making a clean break now would serve them both.

He shouldn't have stopped by the hospital again. He'd thought it best, more honorable, to see her one last time, to tell her good-bye in person.

But he hadn't said good-bye.

He had said hello.

And what were her first words? She'd held Chi's daughter. Tremayne's arms still trembled, recalling the effort it had taken him not to grab her and hold her and kiss her. *Kiss her.* He never had. Now he never would.

But he had certainly thought about it. Kissing her and a whole lot more. Visions of her holding Chi's little girl ran amuck in his brain. The child became a baby, his baby.

Fortunately, that image broke the spell. He had come to end things with her, and he had. Or he thought he had. Then, not two hours after he left her fuming on the hospital steps, he walked out of Headquarters and into trouble.

The negotiations had gotten nowhere. Carmichael was as bullheaded as ever; Jasper ran him a close second. Negotiation was a poor term for the concessions they expected from the Apache. By noon the stalemate appeared unbreachable, but Colonel Merritt insisted they break for a couple of hours and return to try again.

"There's common ground somewhere, men. We just have to roll up our sleeves and find it."

Tremayne doubted both—first, that one inch of common ground existed between the two factions; second, that if some miracle did unearth a grain of common soil, the two sides could agree on how to deal with it.

Leaving the building behind Carmichael and Jasper, he and Nick discussed the situation. At first he hadn't noticed the orderly who raced across the road and skidded to a halt in front of the captain.

"Jones, that for me?" Jasper reached for the message.

"Ah . . . uh . . . no, sir. Miz Breena said . . . uh, it's for *him.*"

Lon Jasper popped his brows.

Jones? Tremayne recognized the orderly then—the one who eavesdropped on his conversation with Sabrina. That witless white woman! What was she thinking? Had she sent him a note by the very man who . . . ?

"Miz Breena said to bring you this message."

Jasper's hand shot out, but with a shrug that fell somewhere between penitence and terror, the orderly handed the message to Tremayne, who avoided both the paper and Jasper's eyes.

"She said the doc asked her to write it."

Tremayne relaxed slightly. Only slightly. He stuffed the message in his pocket.

"That witless white woman," he hissed after he and Nick mounted and rode off toward Chihuahua. "What the hell does she think she's doing?"

"Why don't you read it and find out?" Nick queried in a calm voice that multiplied Tremayne's temper.

"Delivered it in front of Jasper, for God's sake. Doesn't she have a lick of sense?"

"She has a lot of sense. Read it."

Although he was reluctant to read a message from Sabrina in front of anyone, even Nick, Tremayne figured Nick was right. It might be urgent. So he pulled it out of his pocket and read. A formal message. It could have been from a stranger.

Except it wasn't. Her handwriting curled on the page like her memory curled through his mind, a stream snaking down from the mountains, seemingly placid, but with a treacherous undercurrent. Nick was too much of a gentleman to ask the message's contents, but Tremayne decided he had best satisfy his friend's curiosity, nonetheless.

"Says the doc asked her to inform me that Ket's crutches will be ready day after tomorrow." He reread the last sentence, letting it sink like a boulder to the bottom of his heart. After a while he added, "She and Jasper have set the date."

"Date?"

"Wedding." It was the only word Tremayne felt sure of getting out. A complete sentence would have tumbled through the air like clouds in a thunderstorm.

"You sure about that?"

Tremayne shrugged. "Nothing unexpected."

Nick gave him one of those looks that said who the hell was he trying to fool?

"Hell, Nick, don't look at me that way. You knew it was coming. It's the talk of the post. Every damned time we come up here someone mentions it."

"I hadn't realized it was *every* time." A moment later, he asked, "Why's she telling you? Inviting you to the ceremony?"

Nick was baiting him, trying to get him to admit what was on his mind. This wasn't new, either. Nick had been trying to get him and Sabrina together since Tremayne first mentioned meeting the woman. Nick didn't have the sense the Great Spirit gave a tree frog. He'd told him so more than once.

Now he handed the letter to his friend. "Read it yourself, if you don't believe me."

Nick read. Afterward he stared out at the mountains, chewing his bottom lip. "How do you know that's what she means?"

"Nosy, aren't you?"

"Maybe. I don't usually pry, but I think I know women a little better than you—"

"That's a laugh. When are you and Lena tying the knot?"

Nick's face went lax. For a long time he neither moved nor spoke. Tremayne knew he had crossed the line.

"Hey, friend. I'm sorry."

"It's all right. It's a fair question. I've been meaning to ask you to stand up with me."

"Ah?"

"Don't go mentioning it to Lena. I've got a few problems to work out back home before I pop the question."

Tremayne grinned. "That's damn fine news, Nick. I've been hoping you'd hang around for good."

"I intend to. One day soon." They rode in companionable silence for a while. Then Nick asked, "Friend to friend, how do you know Sabrina meant her wedding date? Maybe she means the date the crutches will be ready."

"Trust me. I know." When Nick's brows remained arched, Tremayne added, "I asked her. Now are you satisfied?"

"You asked her what? When?"

"This morning before the negotiations. I asked when she and Jasper were setting the date."

"Whew! That's a hell of a way to greet a woman after two months' absence." He shook his head. "You don't know a hill of beans about courting a woman."

"I'm not courting a woman, Nick. Don't take me wrong, I appreciate all you've taught me about this damned ol' world I'm trapped in, but I will decide when, where, who, and how to conduct the personal side of my life."

"Fair enough. I just hate to see you . . ."

Nick didn't finish the sentence, and Tremayne was glad for it. He didn't like discussing his life, the futility of trying to adapt to the white man's ways, the hopelessness of trying to be Apache. So life had dealt him a bum hand. So what? Others had it a lot worse.

At the negotiating session that afternoon, Tremayne steered clear of Jasper. He wasn't avoiding a fight over the message Sabrina had witlessly had delivered to him in front of Jasper, but the man himself. It was the best thing for her, marrying Jasper. But he didn't have to discuss it with the bastard.

Nick felt no such compunction. Never one to meddle in another's affairs, that he did so now was added proof how much he valued their friendship. Nick wanted him to have a normal life, whatever the hell that was. An impossible dream if ever there was one.

"Hear the wedding date's been set," Nick said to Jasper after Colonel Merritt called an end to the day's discussion. Tremayne hung back, ostensibly to discuss the new terms he was to deliver to the Apachería. In truth, he didn't need to discuss anything. He knew his role. But he didn't want to be within shouting distance when that damned wedding was discussed.

"It's like I said," Nick told him later, leaving the post. "There isn't any wedding."

"What?"

"Not yet. Jasper seemed genuinely surprised I would ask. Said he's been trying to find the right way to propose."

While Tremayne struggled to digest that piece of news, Nick went on. "So you'd better put on your thinking cap and decide what she meant. Appears to be a coded message."

"Nick Bourbon. You're a dang fine friend, but don't ever try detective work. The Pinkertons wouldn't hire you in a pinch."

Tremayne didn't tell Nick, but he knew exactly what Sabrina meant. At least he feared he did. She intended to return to Apache Wells on the date the crutches were ready and stir up the anthill one more time. And he couldn't let her do that.

Waiting for her now back of the magazine with dew still fresh on the bear grass, Tremayne rehearsed what he would say, how he would talk her out of returning with him. He could take the crutches. Ket would offend her. Hell, he'd tell her anything that would work.

It was true. He couldn't bear to see Ket hurt Sabrina again. But it was also true that he had another, equally desperate reason for not allowing her to return to Apache Wells. He couldn't trust himself alone with her again.

He, who excelled in the art of self-denial, had none with her. His feelings for Sabrina, his longings for her were too strong to be denied. No, he couldn't let her return to Apache Wells.

Then he saw her coming, and his best laid plans fluttered like fall leaves before a determined wind. The morning suddenly seemed brighter, as if the sun had burst from behind a cloud—in the cloudless blue sky.

Seeing him, she gathered her skirts and ran toward him. She was laughing.

Laughing. The sound reached him on a breeze that played through the canyon; it lifted him like a soaring eagle on wing, transported him to Apache Wells, back to when he was sixteen and trying to earn the respect of the tribe.

To the well . . . to the laughter. In all the years since, he had tried to deny that laughter. It was a figment of his imagination, the wind rustling new leaves, nothing more.

Now he knew why denial had been futile. It wasn't his imagination. It was something more real and more deeply embedded in his soul than mere flights of fantasy could ever be.

He knew that now. For Sabrina's laughter trilled through the dew-laden morning air and filled him with an insidious yearning, a sense of giddy expectation, like on that long ago day, yet as far from it as mother love is from lusty passion. Hearing it, he felt renewed, exhilarated. Against all his efforts not to, he felt it again, like on that long ago day.

Hope. He watched her approach, desperate to banish this weakness before she came too close. There was no hope. There never had been, never could be. Not for him. Not for anyone in his life.

Didn't she know that? He was no good for her. He could never offer her anything, least of all, hope.

But she didn't know it. Her laughter, so unaffected and contagious, made him want to laugh in return. He, who never laughed.

Coming closer, she called, "You understood. I knew you would."

"That was a damn stupid thing to do, Sabrina. That orderly you sent is the one who was eavesdropping on us."

"Jones? I know. That was the plan's beauty. Lon had already admitted to having Jones spy on me."

"God, Sabrina!" Witless didn't begin to define this woman.

"Don't worry. I let him overhear me asking when the

crutches would be ready. Then I suggested sending you a message before you left the post, and Doc Henry agreed."

Tremayne shook his head, bewildered, as always. "And I suppose you instructed him exactly when to deliver this message so Jasper would witness it?"

"Not in so many words, but that was the idea. If Lon hadn't seen, he would have been suspicious."

"He wasn't?"

"A little," she admitted. "He came up that afternoon and asked Doc Henry what he meant sending messages to the enemy."

"The enemy?"

She grinned. "That's what he calls you."

Little the man knew. Or maybe he did, since he was having Sabrina spied on. That thought fired the warrior instinct in Tremayne.

"Hand me those crutches," he instructed. "And thank you."

"I'm going with you, Tremayne. They won't do Ket any good unless they fit."

"I can see to their fit."

It was a standoff, albeit a one-sided one. She stood her ground, firm, determined, while he tottered on quicksand.

"You know how Ket would treat you."

"She has good reason to be wary."

"Not wary. Hostile. She's filled with hatred. You top her list right now."

Sabrina wasn't listening, of course. He could see that. She intended to come along, and nothing he said would stop her. But he had to try. It was the only honorable thing to do.

Then she snared him with, "If you didn't expect me to come, why did you bring the pinto?"

* * *

Watching her simple observation take Tremayne by surprise, Sabrina was suddenly struck by how well she knew this man. Only a few months ago she had been unable to read his expressions. Now she knew that stony facade to be only that: a mask that hid myriad emotions. He was as skittish about this undertaking as she. And she had been a worthless wreck for two full days. . . .

The moment she sent Jones off with the message, she had begun to doubt her sanity.

Not a lick of sense, the voice accused.

He won't figure out what I mean.

What if he does?

Then I'll take him the crutches.

You can't go with him, Sabrina.

I don't intend to. I only want to give him the crutches.

Then why the subterfuge?

Why, indeed? She wondered that with every step she took toward the canyon. The answer, of course, was simple. She simply and purely craved to be with him. Alone with him, where she didn't have to guard her every word, every gesture. Alone, where she might be able to touch him. Touching him became a goal comparable to fighting disease or winning a war.

Thoughts beyond touching him gnawed at her subconscious and were exacerbated every time Lon Jasper kissed her. She hated kissing.

Then why do you dream about kissing Tremayne? Why do you think about it every waking minute?

There was no answer to that, not one that she could fathom.

By the time they set out, the answer didn't seem important. They traveled up the canyon, like before, cut across Limpia Creek like before, then back into the mountains near Apache Wells.

Summer was waning now, but the weather was still hot. Unlike the last time they rode this trail together, the air had taken on the pungent aroma of early fall. But the season wasn't the only difference today. Everything was different, for now she knew she loved him, and she had no idea what to do about it.

"When did you realize what I meant by the date?" she asked. He had drawn rein on a hill, waiting for her to catch up. She could tell he was angry, but she chose to ignore it, since she was sure his anger was directed at himself, not at her.

"I didn't." He headed the black down the opposite hillside. "Watch where you're going."

"I'm following you," she said primly.

Not a lick of sense.

True. Not only was this man unacceptable to her family, forbidden to her as a suitor, at times he was downright disagreeable. Why was she so desperately drawn to him?

"If you didn't figure out the message, how did you know to meet me this morning?" she quizzed at the next opportunity.

"Nick," he said.

"You showed the message to Nick?" The idea unnerved her. "What if I'd written something . . . else?"

His gaze held hers, intense. Two months ago it would have been unreadable. Today she saw layers of emotion behind the carefully guarded exterior. Anger on the surface, which didn't begin to hide the passion beneath. Her stomach took a tumble and she glanced away, lest he realize what she had seen.

Coming away with him today had not been wise. Simply being alone with him wasn't enough. She craved more.

"I read it first, Sabrina."

When he started to ride off again, she stopped him with, "You're right. I couldn't very well have said, 'Meet me in the canyon,' could I have? So how did Nick know?"

"I thought you meant the wedding date. Nick didn't buy that, so he asked Jasper."

"Nick asked Lon? What did Lon say?"

He narrowed a frown her way. "Why so interested?"

"Why are you so mad?"

"I'm not mad."

"You couldn't prove that by me."

"Why should I be mad? If you want to ruin your reputation by going off to see a child who will probably thank you by biting off your head, who am I to be mad about it?"

She was furious and elated by turn. He wasn't mad about those things, he was mad—totally and completely angry—about being this near her and not touching her, this near and not holding her. She knew. She saw it all. In his eyes, in his awkwardness, in his distaste for conversation. She knew, because she felt the same way.

Again when he shifted the reins, she stopped him.

"If you're not mad, then tell me what Nick asked Lon. I really need to know. For . . . later."

"Nick congratulated Jasper on the wedding and Jasper said he hadn't proposed yet."

"He hasn't?"

Tremayne's astonishment stopped just short of a gaping mouth. She tried not to let on that she understood.

"I thought he proposed the other night, but I guess—"

"Sabrina. This isn't a teasing matter. You could have gotten yourself in real trouble. Your reputation—"

"I'm not teasing. He said something about he guessed he'd better get serious before I let some renegade . . ." She paused when Tremayne's expression froze over. Had she pushed the matter too far? Should she continue?

While she contemplated taking the sensible approach and dropping the entire subject, he took her by complete surprise.

"Cornered yourself, huh?"

"It was after I objected to the way he . . . uh, hand . . . uh, kissed me, and he asked if I let you do those things—"

"What the hell did that bastard . . . ? I mean . . . me? Hell, I've never even kissed you."

Silence sizzled in the heat generated by that statement. The distance between their two mounts became a hated barrier.

"I know," she managed.

Both of them knew. The truth of it, and how hard-wrought that truth had been.

And was, still today.

"Don't worry," she said finally, returning to the original topic. "It's just gossip."

"What's gossip?"

"Nothing. Don't worry. Post gossip comes easy. It's a form of entertainment. The ladies talk about everything. Mostly, they make it up. I don't care. This isn't what they think."

The passion that roiled inside her and burned in his eyes belied her statement. Merely looking at him sparked a charge that zinged her to her toes. But living with those feelings and voicing them were two different things. If neither of them spoke them aloud, perhaps they would go away.

He just shook his head. "You charge headlong into trouble, don't you?"

"Not me. I'm afraid of my shadow."

"Don't give me that. I've seen you in action, remember?"

"Well, it's true. I give in to everyone. I can't stand up for myself with Mama or Lon, or anyone. I always give in, even when I don't really have to. Except with you. You're the only person I've ever gotten mad at.''

''Mad? When did you get mad at me?''

She loved taking him by surprise. ''When you wouldn't dance with me.''

They arrived at Apache Wells in a much better humor than when they set out. Tremayne carried the crutches in, for they had decided ahead of time that he should give them to Ket without mentioning Sabrina's hand in the matter. Sabrina was there to check Ket's leg one more time before she returned to the Apachería. That was all.

In the long run, it didn't make all that much difference.

The cabin was hot when they entered. An old woman stirred something over the fire. She turned at their entrance; her eyes narrowed on Sabrina. Dark eyes in a dark, weathered face. *Expressionless,* Sabrina thought. A curious thing, that a face which looked to have the world etched into it could remain so devoid of emotion.

"La madre de mi esposa," Tremayne introduced.

His wife's mother? The description unnerved her, yet hadn't Nick told her the woman was here? *"Hola, señora."*

The old woman nodded once, stoically, after which she returned to her cooking. Wielding a bone-handled knife, she peeled something . . . some kind of root. Keturah lay on the pallet.

''Ket, darling, look what I've brought.''

Sabrina hung back, reluctant to intrude too soon.

''With these you'll soon learn to walk,'' Tremayne claimed.

Ket possessed none of her grandmother's stoicism, at least not where Sabrina was concerned. She eyed the crutches briefly, then looked past her father, to the shadows where Sabrina waited. Her green eyes were dark and angry.

''What is she doing here?''

"She's come to look at your leg so you can go home."

"I can't go home. Not ever. She ruined my leg."

Sabrina gasped.

"Shh, Keturah. As soon as you learn to use these crutches—"

Ket was having none of it. Considering the circumstances, Sabrina made a snap decision. Wouldn't it be best for all concerned if she got her business with Ket out of the way? She stepped around Tremayne.

"Hello, Ket. Let me fit the crutches. You'll be on your feet in no time with—"

In a frenzied move, Ket jumped from under the cover and thrust her wounded leg at them, revealing a deep scar that resembled a gash in the red earth. The surrounding tissue furrowed into it like erosion on a hillside. "Look what she did to me, Papa!"

"Ket, please, Sabrina wants—"

Ket's scream caught even Tremayne off-guard. It was keen, like before, eerie and shrill and loud. Silently berating herself for bringing the girl such anguish, Sabrina shrank back into the shadows.

Ket leaped from the pallet and bounded to the hearth.

"Keturah," Tremayne tried. "You'll hurt your—"

But Ket would not be hushed. Nor stilled. Sabrina had just gathered her wits enough to know she should leave when the child grabbed the knife from her grandmother's hand.

"Ket . . ." Tremayne reached for his daughter, but she darted away, pulled out one of her braids, and cut it off. "Look what she did to me!" The angry girl hurled the braid in Sabrina's face.

Horrified, Sabrina watched the frantic child dance out of her father's grasp. While in full movement she chopped off her second braid. "She ruined my leg, Papa. I can't walk. I can't go home. I hate her." The words faded into

another bout of that bloodcurdling keen. Then, as suddenly as it had begun, the fight left her; she fell against
her father.

Muffled by his shoulder her keen came softer, but was
every bit as unearthly. Cradling her, Tremayne went down
on his knees. His voice was low, but earnest. "You know
how you hurt your leg, Ketur—"

"No, Papa. She did it. Make her go away, please! Look
what she did to me."

The cabin was close, confined, and hot. Like a top out
of control on a dirt field, it began to spin. Sabrina's eyes
filled with dust; her senses with the debris of a lifetime of
guilt. She held onto her balance by sheer force of will.

Over Ket's head, Tremayne's eyes found Sabrina's. His
face said it all. He had known so much tragedy. Wanting
to help, she had only brought him more.

"Look what she did to me, Papa! Look what she did!"

Tremayne tried to stifle the terrible shrill keen by pressing Ket's face back into his shoulder, but between trills,
she continued to accuse. "Look what she did to me! Look
what she did!"

Now look what you've done!

While her limbs would still carry her, Sabrina fled.

She raced from the cabin. Behind her she heard Tremayne croon to Ket. "Sabrina didn't do this, darling. You
fell in the fire all by yourself. Sabrina brought medicine
and . . ."

Look what you did!

Sabrina gulped fresh air. Keturah's screams echoed
around the small canyon.

Keturah's?

"Look what she did to me!"

Or Serena's?

Suddenly Sabrina was back in the old nightmare.

Look what you've done, child. Look what you've done.

Sobs wracked Sabrina's chest. She stared blindly into the well, but its rim looked like a wagon wheel. Beneath it lay her sister.

Look what you've done.

Sabrina didn't do it, Martha. She didn't do it.

Oh, my baby. Oh, my baby.

From the cabin behind Sabrina the screams continued. They rose from the well, from the center of the wagon wheel, and Sabrina ran again, stumbling blindly, while her thoughts raced. Old thoughts. Old fears.

Old guilt.

She reached the pinto and had begun to tear frantically at the reins when Tremayne took her by the shoulders. His gentle touch shattered everything inside her.

"Let me go. Please . . ." Tears burst from her eyes. She fought him, tried to get away, but ended up in his arms.

"I'm sorry, Sabrina. She knows better." Threading his fingers along her scalp, he lifted her face, kissed her once, softly, on the nose. "She doesn't really blame you for the accident."

She didn't do it, Martha.

"I know." As hard as she tried, she couldn't stop shaking. "That sound, it's . . . and her hair . . ."

He kissed her cheeks. "That's the sound Apache women make when they mourn. They also chop off their hair. It's an expression of pain and loss."

"When she grabbed the knife, I thought—"

"Shh, it's all right now."

She squeezed her lids. It wasn't all right, of course, but then he kissed the corners of her eyes, one by other.

"Shh," he whispered again, kissing her face, kissing away her tears. Her fears. "Shh."

"It isn't just Ket." The words tumbled out. Her tears continued. She wished she could dissolve and flow away.

His hands slipped to her face. He kissed her lips, softly, gently. "I didn't want her to hurt you," he whispered. "I don't want anyone to hurt you."

Now look what you've done.

He kissed her lips again, lingering now; his lips lay softly upon hers, upon her wet skin, upon her heated skin.

And in that moment when their defenses were down, when all he thought was to console, to comfort, and when all she sought was peace, passion sneaked in.

Her hands crept to his chest. His arms went around her. He drew her close; her lips opened and his kiss deepened.

Nothing tentative or preliminary now. They hadn't the mind for it. The kiss began full-blown and escalated quickly. Born of despair, he kissed her with a fierceness that was at once earthy and innately spiritual. And she responded in kind. Desperately holding him, lips meshing, bodies pressing, they became one, inseparable.

Even when he lifted his face, it was as if they were still one. His eyes delved into hers with pure, undiluted passion, passion too long denied. With no conscious thought she lifted her lips and he took them, covering, exploring, delving.

Gradually sensibility returned and with it a wild kind of joy. She opened her eyes and found his open, too. The world and its problems whirled away and left her here in his arms, alone, holding, kissing, like she had craved. Like she had dreamed. And oh how wonderful it was.

"God, Sabrina . . . I didn't mean to do this . . ." But even as he spoke his lips sought hers again.

"If you hadn't I think I would have died."

Relief filled his gaze, what room was left there amidst all the passion. "About time?"

"Don't talk." She pulled his face down to hers. Not

about time, she thought, forcing hopelessness away again. But even as passion swirled around them, despair returned.

His beloved, precious daughter hated her, blamed her for a deformity that would never heal. Ket's scar would remain with her the rest of her life, disfiguring not only her leg, but her outlook on the white world. Sabrina's world.

The world that killed her mother. Despair became so ponderous, even her tears could not flow.

"Sabrina? What is it?" Tremayne's lips hovered; his eyes sought hers. "I'm so sorry," he whispered.

"It isn't Ket," she felt obliged to say. "Not wholly."

He brushed back her hair. His face lingered close.

"Memories are like monsters," she whispered. "They never leave you. They never die."

"Your sister?"

She nodded.

Silently he settled back against the tree to which the pinto was hitched, propped a foot on the trunk, and drew her into him. She rested her arms on his chest and felt safe and secure.

"Tell me about it," he encouraged.

She spoke, staring at his shirt so intently she could see the weave of the fabric. "We were chasing a cardinal. It was my idea, of course. I was always the one who thought up the things that got us in trouble."

He shifted, kissed the top of her head, and absently caressed her breast. Nothing in her life had ever felt so exquisite. She thought of when Lon Jasper tried the same thing and how offended she had been. She wasn't offended now.

It was as if this were Tremayne's right, his and only his.

"Go ahead," he encouraged. "You were chasing a cardinal."

"Papa had come home the night before with some story,

and Mama replied that it would be like salting a bird's tail. It seemed like an interesting thing to try."

His eyes grew dim with something that looked like fondness. The runaway emotions he evoked inside her were much more earthy.

She found her voice and continued. "Anyway, the bird flew across a road, I followed, and Serena followed me. Neither of us saw the wagon until it hit her. I can still hear her screams. I turned, but it was too late. Mama came running out. I'll never forget her face. She's never been the same."

"Neither have you."

"Or Papa, I guess. I didn't look where I was going, and it changed all our lives."

"*She* didn't look where *she* was going."

"She was following me."

"You weren't leading her."

"I always led her."

"And Ket's outburst brought it all back?" Dipping his head he took her lips, kissed them, caressed them, showering her with fiery sensations that burned her painful memories to ash.

It was fleeting. For the truth was there between them. Ket's rejection was only part of the problem. As Sabrina's memories were only part of it.

The major problem was between them—between her and Tremayne. Her pain was for them, for their anguish, for their longings that could never be satisfied, for their love that could never be shared . . . or even admitted.

Here in his arms, where she had longed to be, she felt consumed by the hopelessness of it all. Their worlds were too different. She could never understand his, and he hated hers.

"Sabrina?" Tremayne kissed her eyes, her tears. It reminded her of the first time they met. It was dusk when he wiped tears from the corners of her eyes with his thumbs. Now it was broad daylight and she could see his eyes, his beautiful, intense, worried eyes. "What's wrong now?"

"Everything."

He stared at her, into her, with that intensity that set her afire. "I know," he admitted at length. "God, how I know."

This time when he kissed her they took their time, molding raw emotion into a rare and beautiful mass of exquisite longing. She never wanted it to end. She wanted to remain right here forever, in his arms, lips touching lips. Driven by some deep and sensual longing, she raced toward a light that shone brighter and brighter, even as it retreated farther and father from reach.

"You don't know how long I've wanted to kiss you," she said.

"I have a pretty good idea." The passion in his eyes clouded. "I should be shot for this." He kissed her forehead and held her tightly, protectively against him. "We've crossed a line we should never have even approached."

"We tried not to."

But there was no placating him now. He held her so tight, she thought he might never let her go, prayed he would never let her go.

"We should have tried harder." Then he kissed her again.

Chapter Thirteen

Once when Papa was stationed at Fort Concho, Mrs. Matrice McIntyre visited one of her officer sons. While on the post she spoke to the Ladies' Sewing Circle about her experiences on the Overland Trail. Young Sabrina accompanied her mother to the lecture, expecting an exciting tale of exploration and adventure.

"The journey mirrored life," a grave Mrs. McIntyre claimed. "No sooner had we crossed one mountain range than another, larger, loomed in the distance. Like life, the journey traversed from obstacle to obstacle, from dream to shattered dream and, ultimately for many, to an unsought destination, the jaws of death."

In the days following her trip to Apache Wells and what she had thought would be the fulfillment of her most cherished dream, kissing Tremayne, Sabrina recalled Mrs. McIntyre's lecture and came to the terrible realization that the woman had been right. Life was no more than a series of mountains to climb, barriers to overcome.

Every time she thought she had broken down the last

barrier with Tremayne, another one loomed ahead. This final hurdle, his daughter's fear and hatred, was the most formidable of all.

For fourteen years she had tried and failed to win her mother's acceptance of who she was. How could she hope to win the trust of a child who, with good cause, hated her for the color of her skin? It would tear Tremayne apart to be placed in the middle of a such a battle. Loving him as she did, she couldn't burden him with more tragedy.

But neither could she forget him. On those days when she allowed herself to gaze out the dispensary window in time to see him arrive or leave Headquarters, her fantasy swirled like a dervish in her head. And, yes, fluttered wildly in her stomach.

Instinctively she knew she would never feel this wildness for Lon or for any other man. But a civilized life required more than butterflies and passion. Soon she must learn to accept the life set out for her. Soon.

But she had first to conquer her penchant for fantasy. One afternoon as she finished tutoring Jedediah, the dispensary door burst open. Aquiver with expectancy, she glanced up, only to see Lon stride through the door at a military-sharp pace.

Her disappointment was palpable. She prayed it didn't show. Instead of intense green eyes, her gaze met a steady, pale blue gaze. *Disappointment.* Lon would never fill the room the way Tremayne did. Nor her heart.

How quickly one adjusts, she thought. Only months before she had cringed any time someone walked in on her, thinking it Lon, come to rebuke. Tremayne had cured her of that. Lately it was he she expected with every shadow that fell across an open door.

"I've brought good news, Sabrina." Lon stood aside while Jedediah picked up his books and hurried off.

"Thank you kindly, Miz Breena."

"Same time tomorrow." When he was out of earshot, she added, "He's learning fast."

Lon paid no heed. He crossed the room, took her shoulders, and beamed. Her heart sank.

Had the time come? Even the thought of Lon proposing marriage was no longer terrifying. Resigned to the inevitable, she hadn't yet decided how she would respond. Only time would tell. Since that terrible, wonderful, frightening day in Tremayne's arms, life seemed out of her control.

What would happen would happen. When it did she would deal with it. Life was so much simpler now. Lonely, but simple.

"Senator Carmichael has agreed to drop his plans to court-martial Edward."

"Truly?"

"Didn't I tell you to trust me?"

"What do you mean?"

He popped his blond brows. "You never give me credit, do you? Soon you'll learn the error of your ways."

The error of her ways? Pray God he never learned that.

"He's throwing a little celebration tonight, and he specifically wants you there."

"A celebration? Papa?"

"Senator Carmichael," Lon explained patiently. "At the trading post. I'll come for you. Why don't you find a little gift for him? A pipe from Edward's collection would be suitable."

"You're asking me to bring a gift to thank that disreputable man for not calling Papa before a court-martial?"

"Sabrina . . ." The warning fell on deaf ears.

"He was the one at fault, Lon. Papa had just cause for kicking him out of the cantina. The senator was offensively drunk. He accosted Rosa. He—"

"Sabrina, forget it. It's over."

"Over? This one incident, perhaps. I doubt Carmichael—"

"What's gotten into you? You never used to hold such liberal opinions."

"I never used to express them." She heaved a heavy sigh and turned aside. He took it for submission.

"There now, I knew you'd come around. Cut the senator some slack. He carries a heavy load on his shoulders."

"A heavy load? What's that, Lon? Exterminating the red devil Apaches?"

"Call it what you will, the senator is a dedicated citizen and a tireless worker for this great country of ours. I told you he's taken a shine to me."

"A shine?"

"I promised not to say anything yet, but believe me, his plans are big. Only a United States Senator could pull off something so big." He straightened a bit, as though to validate the added stature. "He's taking me to the top with him, Sabrina."

"Wonderful."

Lon either ignored or didn't sense her sarcasm. "For my plans to work, though, you have to play your part. I was able to get Edward off the hook for one simple reason. Carmichael doesn't want a court-martial to mar my future."

Your future? Her breath caught. Was this another offhanded marriage proposal? If so, she was grateful it had been vague enough to ignore.

"I'll come for you after supper," he said upon leaving. "And, Sabrina, be careful about this newfound rebelliousness. It could hurt . . . a lot of things."

Rebelliousness? From the window she watched him stride with a brusque military gait off toward Headquarters. Tremayne hadn't come today, nor Nick. Indeed, she hadn't seen Tremayne's horse in several weeks; she surmised he had returned to the Apacherías with the new proposal.

She always stopped there, for to allow herself to think about him further was an exercise in futility.

At home she broke the good news to her parents. Of the two of them, Martha was the one to rejoice.

"Oh, thank heavens, Edward. Thank heavens the senator came to his senses."

"That dad-blasted senator," Edward fumed. "Throws his weight around like he rules from the top of Mount Olympus." He looked from Martha to Sabrina. "Sounds to me like Jasper might be learning the senator's bad habits."

"For shame, Edward."

"What's this about you playing your part, sugar? If he's proposing marriage in return for getting me off the hook with Carmichael, I'd as soon be booted out of the army."

"Edward!"

"If I thought Jasper was that devious, I wouldn't tolerate your mama's interest in the man."

"Edward!"

Sabrina sighed. Mama was about to swoon. "Lon isn't devious," she offered.

Edward wasn't convinced. "He and Carmichael are thick as thieves."

Sabrina hoped the description wouldn't prove prophetic but resisted saying so. It would only upset Mama. What would happen, would happen. She was rather pleased with herself, though, for the way she had spoken out to Lon.

Was that what she learned from Tremayne, to stand her ground? Had that been the purpose of their meeting? The caldron of heat burbling inside her warned that she had gained far more from their brief relationship than she allowed herself to admit.

Later, when Lon arrived to walk with them to Chihuahua, both she and Edward were on their best behavior. Sabrina didn't bring a gift for the senator, and Lon did not ask again.

Rosa stood on the porch as they approached.

"She must be feeling better," Edward said. Rosa had worked only sporadically all summer.

"She doesn't look better." Sabrina hurried ahead.

"Hola, chica." Rose kept her eyes on the far hillside. "Manuel returned to the flocks today."

"I've been worried about you."

"No need, *chica.* I'm fine."

"You don't look it." Sabrina stopped short of mentioning Rosa's shapeless black dress with its high collar, long sleeves, and cuffs. Appropriate attire with the senator expected.

Inside, Lon ushered her straight to Carmichael's table—the seat of power, she recalled thinking the night of the brawl. She scanned the men assembled—the senator, his two aides, and, sitting with his back to her, Nick Bourbon.

Her heart skipped a beat. Her head buzzed, and when she dared, she looked for Tremayne. Her eyes came to rest on the far table where she had sat with him that fateful night, the table where she learned that his wife was dead.

Tonight he wasn't there. Disappointment laved her like a cold dew; the strength of it surprised her. Even after Lon dropped her elbow, she had trouble shaking it off.

At their approach the men had risen. Senator Carmichael greeted her enthusiastically. She smiled in return—Yes, a pleasure to see him again.

"Hold your tongue," Lon warned, a whisper in her ear. "The kind of lady a man chooses says a lot about the man himself. I want the senator to get to know you, the real you."

"The real me?" He had no idea what he was saying. Edward came up behind them. Nick greeted him.

"Long time no see," Papa returned, a subdued version of his boisterous self. He sounded as self-conscious as Sabrina felt.

Her discomposure increased when Nick, ever the gentleman, offered her his chair. A cohort in a sea of sharks, she suddenly felt him. Their shared friendship with Tremayne formed a bond between them. She resisted meeting his eye for fear of giving away her burning secret.

But she knew she couldn't sit at this table. She would ruin the festivities. At best she was certain to disappoint Lon.

As if he read her thoughts—did all guilty people feel that way?—he squeezed her shoulder. "Go ahead, Sabrina. Sit down."

"No, I couldn't. I . . ." She searched for a reasonable excuse. "This looks like the negotiating team. I shouldn't—"

"We don't negotiate without Tremayne." Nick's firm reply hinted at previous contention. But it was the name he spoke that left her so weak she thought for a moment she would have to sit after all.

"I should get to work." She nodded respectfully to the senator. If Lon wanted more from her he could just want.

But the senator had turned his attention to her father. "Join us, Edward. We've come to your fine establishment to celebrate our reconciliation." His muttonchop side whiskers bracketed florid cheeks, rendering his rotund face a grotesque caricature. "Drinks are on me."

"Like you said, Senator." Edward's tone was carefully restrained. "This is my establishment, which means I'd better get busy. Drinks on the house," he called to José.

"I insist." Before anyone moved, the senator's gaze shifted to the side. *"Mujer!"* he called to Rosa. "Drinks all around." To Edward, "Sit with us, Major Bolton."

Papa glared at his adversary, face flushed, jaws clenched.

He was seething. "Off base I go by Edward." Tight-lipped, he indicated Rosa. "The lady is Señora Ramériz."

Carmichael's eyes glinted a warning, but Edward refused to relent. "Rosa, my dear, I will serve this table."

"Sit here, Sabrina." Lon nudged her toward the chair.

"No, I . . ."

As though born to mediate, Nick edged smoothly into the troubled water. "Let me be your first customer, Sabrina. I came for the calico we didn't get a chance to cut that night. I'd hoped you would be here to help me choose."

"Sabrina?" Lon challenged.

She flashed him a smile. "I'll be back." But it was Papa who worried her now.

"Edward will be fine," Nick allowed after they'd left the table.

"Like last time?"

"We'll keep watch."

After failing to persuade her to, Nick chose the fabric. Three bolts, she wasn't even sure of the colors. She hoped she measured it right, cut it straight, for her mind was awhirl.

Dared she ask about Tremayne? Suddenly she missed him with all her heart and soul—and body. But what would Nick think if she asked? Would her voice hold steady, or would it give away her true feelings? Finally she settled for asking about Keturah.

"Poor child," Nick said. "Tremayne doesn't talk much about her. He did say she blamed you for her injury."

"She didn't mean it. She's angry at the world. With just cause."

"She isn't the only one angry at the world."

Sabrina couldn't turn away from his knowing gaze. Her skin burned. Her heart throbbed, and those damned insidious butterflies fluttered hopelessly in her stomach.

She wanted to talk about Tremayne, wanted it so badly tears stung her eyes. But the words stuck in her throat. She ducked her head, concentrated on cutting the blue fabric.

"He's one crazy hombre," Nick said lightly.

"Tremayne?" Like the first time she ever spoke it, his name slid off her tongue in a flash of light.

"Don't tell me you hadn't noticed?"

She felt herself blush. "I don't guess I . . ." She shrugged and tried to grin. "I don't guess I'd recognize a crazy hombre."

Nick studied her for a moment. "He told you about the guardian of the well?"

"He says he doesn't believe in it."

"He's afraid to, would be my guess."

She tried to focus on folding the cloth but had trouble steadying her hand. "He's had a lot of heartache," she tried, reluctant to let the topic drop, even though she knew it would be best. "More than most folks."

"True. It'll take persistence to get through to him. But he needs someone, Sabrina. Someone to love him."

She handed Nick the cloth, hardly daring to take his meaning.

"Tremayne's a fine man," Nick continued, pressing a case that was nonexistent. "I've never known a finer man, this side of the Atlantic or across it."

Again she couldn't draw her eyes from his, while inside she melted. Anticipation stirred insidiously. She tried to quell it but couldn't. Girded by the strength of Nick's trust, she asked the question she'd been so eager to ask.

"I haven't seen him lately," she said quietly. Then she added in her own defense, "I've wondered how Ket is."

"He's making the rounds of the Apacherías. Should be back in another week or so."

She nodded.

"Tremayne has a highly developed sense of honor, Sabrina. He's not about to hurt someone he cares about. If you want to know how Ket is, you'll have to find a way to ask him yourself."

Someone he cares about? What did that mean? Was it the same thing as love? He didn't want to hurt someone he cared about. Neither did she. She had been determined not to hurt him; he was determined not to hurt her.

Nick's warning was clear. She could not expect Tremayne to make the first move. She would have to do it herself.

That encouragement was all she needed to play the fool. Although she consciously fought it for the next couple of weeks, her subconscious sought a solution to the puzzle Nick had posed.

How could she talk to Tremayne? Unwittingly, Doc Henry provided the opportunity.

Jedediah's recovery was nothing short of miraculous, and Doc Henry was jubilant. The orderly had become adept, some claimed dangerous, at using his crutches. When the doctor suggested it might be good for him to join the classes Carrie Young had started down at the church house, Sabrina agreed.

"I'll walk with him the first couple of times."

"Fine. You're closer to him than anyone, my dear. You choose the time."

In the days that followed, while Sabrina laid her plans, her innate sense of self-discipline battled with her new wild recklessness until she was certain insanity would lose, reason would win, and she would never see Tremayne again.

But on the morning he rode up to Headquarters on his big black stallion recklessness won. The wildness she had fought so hard to suppress exploded in her veins. She alerted Jedediah that this would be the day. Then, as soon as Sick Call was over, she dashed home to change clothes.

She brushed her plank-straight hair, twisted and secured it with pins.

"What on earth has gotten into you, child?" Martha came upon her in the pantry, where she searched for the bottle of olive oil Papa brought home the week before. "You never change clothes in the middle of the day."

"I, uh, needed to." She was back in that bramble patch, and it didn't even bother her.

"Let me look at you. That's your new fall gingham. Don't go staining those white cuffs with something that won't come out."

Sabrina pecked a kiss to her mother's cheek. "I won't, Mama. It's a beautiful dress. Thank you."

It was a beautiful dress. And she felt beautiful wearing it. Beautiful and wild and reckless and scared to death.

"You're jittery as a June bug on the Fourth of July, Miz Breena. No use worryin' yourself 'bout me."

Lord in heaven. She was walking too fast. She had practically dragged Jedediah across the clearing. She slowed down and tried to calm the clamoring inside her.

"I'm not worrying about you, Jedediah. I know you'll do fine."

But would *she* do fine? The meeting was still in progress next door, when she assisted Jedediah up the church steps and into the makeshift schoolroom, the same room where the soiree had been held, where she had twirled in a green dress with gold bows and flirted with a renegade called Tremayne.

She felt giddy, like a schoolgirl herself, when her thoughts skipped to the gold bow he had taken—and placed beside his bed.

Now he was here, next door, closer than he had been

in months. And now a new fear reared its head. She had arrived too early. How could she bide her time? She talked to Carrie. Settled Jedediah at a desk. Opened his books. Glanced out the window.

"Run along, Miz Breena."

"He'll do fine, Sabrina. I'll walk him back to the hospital when we finish," Carrie offered.

"Thanks. I'll . . . uh, I could wait a while."

"You already offered that once," Carrie admonished. "Don't worry about him. He survived the amputation. He'll survive my class."

"Of course. I didn't mean . . ." Through the window she saw men emerge from Headquarters. "I'll leave you to your class."

The door banged behind her; the porch seemed like a mile in width; the steps were so steep she knew she would trip. Every muscle in her body had begun to tremble at once, to disparate rhythms. Her breath came short; she feared she might choke.

Get hold of yourself, she admonished. *If you're determined to carry this through, don't make a complete fool of yourself.*

Then she saw him and the world spun around her, out of control. He and Nick walked to their horses. He wore duckins and a crisp shirt. She called to him.

"Tremayne?" Her voice sounded like a brass bugle, loud enough to wake sleeping troopers, but he didn't hear. She swallowed convulsively and called again. "Tremayne?"

This time she knew he heard, because she saw his shoulders bunch. Still he didn't turn around. For one miserable moment he continued walking. She watched, scarcely able to breathe.

Not a lick of sense. She should never had tried something so reckless, so wild, so undisciplined.

He turned. With an almost imperceptible sweep of his

eyes, he took her in. And that one look made it all worth-
while.

She knew why she had taken this terrible chance.
Because she had to. Seeing him again was the only thing
that mattered in the whole wide world. She stood as still
as she could while the wildness inside her became a crea-
ture and clawed for freedom.

She chanced a step. Then another. Above the pounding
of her heart she heard Nick's voice.

"Hold on a minute. I forgot to ask Colonel . . ."

Tremayne held her in the grip of that intense green
gaze. He didn't move toward her. He didn't move at all.

When she'd come as near as she dared, she asked,
"How's Ket?"

"At the Apachería." His answer wasn't an answer at all,
but hearing his voice was all that mattered. That deep
down-from-the-hills voice brought tears to her eyes. She
squeezed them back.

"Did the crutches fit?"

He nodded.

Finally she remembered the bottle of olive oil, and
extended it to him. Try as she did, she couldn't keep her
arms from quivering. "I brought this."

When he made no move, she stepped closer. "It's for
Ket. For the scar. Rub it with this every day and maybe it
won't . . ." Her breath played out.

At long last he reached for the bottle. She held it in a
death grip and his hands grazed hers. Lingered.

"I should see her . . . I'd like . . ."

His steady gaze drew the life from her.

"Could we talk?" she managed. "Walk around the
parade ground or . . ."

"No." Without warning he pulled the bottle free and
stepped back. "Move away, Sabrina. Jasper's watching from
the porch."

"I don't care. I—"

"You have to care. It's the only way."

"Please, just can't we talk?" She grabbed her throat where the wildness clawed to get out. "It hurts."

He caught his bottom lip between his teeth. "It won't always."

She knew he didn't mean it. He felt the same way she did. They had looked at each other, and that made the hopelessness they shared even more devastating, certainly more lasting.

With one final lingering gaze, he turned on his heel and headed for the black.

"Sabrina." Lon caught her by the shoulder, spun her around. She didn't try to hide the tears in her eyes—she didn't realize they were there until later.

"What's he done—?"

"Nothing." She tore free and raced for the hospital, coming to a stop at length behind the vacant steward's house, where she leaned against the wall, the same wall Tremayne had thrown her against so long ago, and she wept. Lon didn't come after her. For that she was grateful, even though she realized it probably meant he knew what was going on in her heart.

At least she wouldn't have to explain—or lie. She was tired of lying. Sick to death of lying. Perhaps it was best, after all. A relationship built on lies wasn't a good one. Theirs had never even developed into a relationship.

Except deep inside her heart, where it would always remain.

Expecting a reprimand from Lon, she was ill prepared for one from her father. It came later that evening when she walked home from the hospital. He met her halfway.

"What on earth were you thinking, sugar?"

Already the nights were becoming cooler. She crossed her arms, clasped them, and felt the new dress. A new dress that belonged to her civilized life. Inside her the wildness persisted.

"You know how tongues wag on this post," Papa continued.

She knew.

"Your mama's sure to hear what you did."

Again she nodded, for she didn't trust her voice. Her newfound courage was of no use now.

"What's going on between you and Tremayne?"

For once she could tell the truth. "Nothing."

"That's sure not what it looked like."

"I asked about Ket."

"His daughter?"

"Her scar is terrible. It could keep her from walking properly. I took him some of that olive oil to rub on it."

Edward sighed. "You know, sugar, we can have the purest intentions in our hearts, but it won't matter if our actions don't bear them out. What you did in front of Headquarters confirmed the sordid gossip that's been making the rounds. It might have died out if you hadn't thrown yourself at Tremayne today."

"I didn't throw myself at anyone, Papa." *I just wanted to. I would have,* she amended, *if Tremayne had allowed it.*

"What is it you see in the man?" Papa wanted to know. "What does he have that Jasper doesn't?"

"Lon? You've never liked Lon Jasper."

"I've been thinking about that. Maybe my judgment was . . . well, maybe I've been thinking like a papa. I probably won't be fond of any man who wants to take you away."

"The last time we discussed Lon Jasper, you called him devious. You said he and Carmichael are thick as thieves."

"He's young, Jasper is. A good woman could likely bring him around. He may be exactly what your mama claims."

"You're taking Mama's side?" Sabrina couldn't hide her dismay. *Not you, Papa!* she wanted to cry. Papa, her staunch ally through thick and thin. "Maybe I don't have a chance of a lifetime. Maybe I don't want one."

"Sabrina, I've always given you credit for having a level head. It's time you put some of that good sense to work. There're far and away too many differences between you and Tremayne for—"

"Stop, Papa. Please, stop. There's nothing between Tremayne and me. Nothing. So stop . . ." *Stop reminding me.*

"Well, you've sure got yourself in a pickle, then. When your mama hears about your escapade, and there's no way on earth she can keep from hearing this, she'll be madder than an ol' wet hen. Be careful you don't make her sick."

Mama had already heard. But she wasn't sick or even mad. It was worse—she was hurt. She stood in her spot beneath the portrait and began to voice her disappointment the moment Sabrina and Edward stepped through the door.

"I have never, never, never been as humiliated in my life, child. Not in my life. What on earth possessed you to throw yourself at that savage with Captain Jasper and the entire post looking on? Tell me that? What were you thinking? Have you completely lost your mind?"

A sudden image of telling her mother the truth flashed through Sabrina's brain. The truth, that she suffered from a love so wild and undisciplined she would have thrown herself at the man she loved if he had allowed her to. That it wasn't Tremayne who was a savage, but she herself.

"I didn't throw myself at anyone, Mama." She repeated the words by rote.

"Don't take that attitude with me, child. Thelma said it was simply awful. Awful. To think, Captain Jasper saw the whole thing. Now he'll never propose marriage."

"Thelma McCandless saw what happened?"

"Well, maybe it was Elmina. What matters is that you threw your body at a savage."

Furious at her mother and the world in general, still Sabrina held her tongue. This was not the time to test her newfound courage. With anyone else, she might have defended Tremayne. She hated hearing him called a savage. But this was her mother. She deserved better.

"It wasn't only your body, child. You might well have thrown away your whole future, your chance of a lifetime, your—"

"Martha, Martha, calm down." Edward took his wife by the shoulders, but she shrugged him away.

"A savage, child. For the life of me, I can't understand—"

"Mama, I'm sorry. I didn't mean to hurt you. But I did nothing wrong."

"Captain Jasper saw it all," Martha wailed. "Captain Jasper, of all people. You've thrown away—"

"I did nothing wrong." One more minute and Sabrina knew she would rebel against her mother, who had suffered so much.

Turning suddenly on her heel, she fled. The front door slammed behind her with the repercussion of cymbals in the regimental band.

"You've thrown it away, child!" Martha wailed from inside. "Thrown it . . ."

Now look what you've done! Haven't you hurt her enough?

As she raced down the steps it occurred to Sabrina that she, too, had suffered. But she was young, she reasoned— a fourteen-year-old argument. She had the future ahead of her, time to recover. Mama didn't. Today, the old reasoning fell flat.

What future awaited her? Certainly not one she had the courage to take. Even if Tremayne were willing to pursue a relationship, she doubted she would have the courage. Certainly not if it involved a nightly clash with her mother.

Tonight was hard enough. And look how she'd handled it. Desperate to escape, she had dashed off without offering the least bit of appeasement. She had never left like that . . .

Never . . . Rounding the corner she ran headlong into a body turning into their path. Lon Jasper!

He caught her by the shoulders.

Lon Jasper. Of all the people on the post, he was the one she least wanted to see right now. "If you've come for a pound of flesh, you're too late."

He laughed. *Laughed.* It startled her back to reality. Then he surprised her further by kissing her on the forehead.

"Rough, huh?"

She inhaled a trembling draft of evening breeze, scented by the parade ground grass. Fall was in the air, now. The grass was dying. Like the butterflies. Like the fantasy.

"I take it your mother heard the gossip."

She nodded, head hung, willing her heart to stop thrashing. She wondered what he had in mind, why he had come.

"Let's go inside and assure your mother of the truth."

Sabrina's head snapped up.

"The truth," he repeated. "That you didn't throw yourself at anyone, including me." He turned her toward the house. "I witnessed the whole thing, remember?"

What was he saying? Tremayne had warned her, but only after she begged and pled and babbled. Or had she merely wanted to do all that? Had Tremayne stopped her before she made a spectacle of herself?

"I couldn't hear what bone you had to pick with that renegade," Lon was saying, "but I have a pretty good idea."

Sour fear coated her throat. She pursed her lips against

an outburst that would surely condemn her more than she already was.

"As much as Major Henry means to you, you have a right to be furious with Tremayne."

"What are you talking about?"

"Doc Henry. That is what you . . . you haven't heard?"

Sabrina felt dimwitted. "I don't know what you're talking about."

"Senator Carmichael is pushing for a court-martial."

"I thought Papa—"

"Edward's off the hook, yes. The senator has found another target." He shook his head. "That man. He's so far from the seat of power, he's just itching for a contest. It's understandable. And with the doc, he has a case. With Edward, since the altercation took place off the post—"

"Lon, tell me what's going on."

He hesitated. "I hate to be the one to break the news. Promise you won't shoot the messenger?"

"Of course I won't. Tell me."

"Carmichael has submitted papers for the court-martial of Major Henry."

"Doc Henry? Lord in heaven. He's the fairest, most honest, most skilled—"

"He endangered the life of one of the post's civilian dependents."

As hard as she listened, the words didn't make sense.

"Yours, Sabrina."

"Mine? He didn't endanger my life. Why, that's absurd—"

"It's true. He sent you off alone with Tremayne."

"He did not."

Now it was Lon's turn to frown.

"I went, Lon. Doc Henry did not *send* me."

"Then he allowed you, as a representative of the hospi-

tal, a civilian dependent, to go into the hills with a known
. . . uh, renegade, to a destination he refuses to reveal.''

"He refuses? Why didn't you ask me?"

"Not me, Sabrina. I'm not doing the asking."

"Well, no one consulted me. I'm the one who went *into
the hills*. I made the decision to go. I will swear to that in
court. Doc Henry did not send me anywhere. Tremayne
came to ask me . . ." Her self-incriminating words drifted
off. She regrouped, rephrased. "Nick had told him that I
knew a lot about medicine. He came for my help to save
his daughter's life. Doc Henry couldn't go, because . . ."
The truth made the gossip look small by comparison. "The
child's mother was killed by soldiers. Doc Henry would
have frightened her."

When Lon continued to frown, as stoic as Tremayne
had ever been, she added, "That's the truth, Lon. Plain
and simple. Believe it or not."

He bobbed his head, nodding slightly, as though
absorbing her statement. Finally he guided her toward the
porch. "I believe you, Sabrina." Before they reached the
door, he stopped again. "I admire your tenacity, your loy-
alty, your compassion. Before we go inside and clear things
up with your mother . . ." He paused and used two fingers
to innocently tip her face to his.

"I'm asking you to be my wife." Taking her hand, he
went down on one knee there on the porch.

All life seemed to drain out of her when she realized
what he was doing. It was happening. The thing she had
dreaded and feared for months. Dazed, she glanced
around. Darkness had fallen; the air was chilled. Sleeping
Lion Mountain was a mere inkspot against a black sky,
brightened by a million stars. She picked one out, stared
at it. It seemed her only tether to Tremayne.

Where was he? At Apache Wells? Was he standing by
the well, looking at the sky? Did he see this star? Was he

watching it even now, while she stood with another man kneeling before her, asking her to . . .

"Will you marry me, Sabrina?"

She wondered what she had expected. Lightning to flash? Heavenly trumpets to sound? She had built herself up to expect this moment, and now that it had come, it was just like any other—except that she was faced with the need to respond.

Lon Jasper always picked the worst times.

Or was Lon himself the worst possible choice?

Or was Mama right? *Was* he her chance of a lifetime?

"Well?"

She gathered her wits. "What a time you've picked. I mean . . . everything around us is out of control."

"Nothing is out of control." Rising, he held her hands between them, as if they were standing before a preacher and he was about to put a wedding band on her finger.

A wedding band. A bond. She felt like she might choke.

"But Doc Henry?"

"Ah, Sabrina, I hope one day you will use that pretty head of yours to worry about me . . . and our children."

Our children?

"Will you marry me, Sabrina? We can announce our betrothal immediately. It will save your reputation."

"You're proposing to save my reputation?"

"I'm proposing because I want you to be my wife. I want to spend the rest of my life with you. What do you say?"

"I . . ." She drew an unsteady breath. Withdrawing one hand, she pressed it to her heart. *Stall for time,* she thought. *And for a lucid response, a proper way to decline.*

"I can't help it," she finally managed. "I'm so worried about Doc Henry. If I caused his discharge—a dishonorable discharge . . . I mean, let me get that off my mind. Then we can talk about marriage."

"I can take care of Major Henry."

"You—"

"You still don't understand, do you?"

"Understand what?"

"My influence with the senator. I told you, Sabrina, Carmichael has big plans for me. In turn, he demands a lot from me. That gives me license to make a few requests of my own."

"You mean you—"

"Didn't I tell you I was responsible for Carmichael dropping his plans to pursue a court-martial for Edward?"

"Yes, but . . . how?"

"I asked."

Stunned, she couldn't decide whether to believe him or not. "And if you *asked* him to drop his plans for Doc Henry, he would?"

"Yes."

The full implication of Lon's confession didn't dawn on Sabrina until much later that night, after she had retired and lay in bed taking the events of the day apart, piecemeal. She hadn't actually accepted his proposal. It was more like a compromise.

They wouldn't announce it to the post, but they told Martha. The news, as Lon suggested it would, erased every trace of the hurt Sabrina had caused by her reckless behavior outside Headquarters.

"The gown is almost finished." Martha beamed, more radiant than the shimmering gold ruffles she'd been sewing for weeks. "As soon as Edward gets home, we will set a date for the announcement party." Sabrina watched wheels turn in her mother's head. "Oh, my dear!" Martha clasped her cheeks. "I've just had the most marvelous idea! Christmas isn't far off. I'll order red velvet, a red velvet cloak will be perfect with that green gown. And red bows . . ."

That Sabrina hadn't accepted the proposal didn't seem to register with Martha. Lon came to the rescue.

He laughed. He was doing a lot of that today. And why not, Sabrina wondered. He had gotten his way at every turn. She recalled her father saying how the senator threw his weight around. Lon had learned that lesson well.

"Hadn't we better wait to plan the party until Sabrina accepts?" he queried lightly, giving a squeeze to Sabrina's hand that sent Martha dabbing her eyes with an already wet hanky.

"Oh, she will accept." Martha turned pleading eyes on Sabrina. "You will hurry, won't you, child?"

"Now, Mama, shouldn't my acceptance be as perfect as the gown will be?"

Lon grinned, but she didn't.

It occurred to her that she might have smiled her last smile, although she couldn't remember when. For her mind busily reconstructed everything Lon had said. Papa's court-martial had been dropped at Lon's request. She hadn't paid much attention to that at the time, but now Doc Henry was being court-martialed for something she had done. She spent a good part of the night worrying about how she would greet him in the morning. What would she say?

Guilt engulfed her. He faced court-martial, possible dishonorable discharge, for her actions. But why? What she did, whom she treated, was none of the senator's business.

Near morning the answer came to her, and she prayed it was but a figment of the long, sleepless night. She must be delirious to think such . . .

But the logic was inescapable. If a word from Lon could stop a court-martial, could a word from Lon start one? The question kept her awake until dawn. Could Lon Jasper, the man her mother considered her chance of a lifetime, have instigated such a horrendous thing?

She felt guilty having thought it. But having thought it, she couldn't erase the thought. Was Lon so devious?

Papa had believed that. Once. Before he thought she was involved with Tremayne. Was a devious Lon Jasper a more desirable mate for his daughter than a renegade white man?

Chapter Fourteen

"Senator Carmichael has an advanced case of court-martial on the brain, my dear."

Plagued by guilt for involving her friend and mentor in her sordid life, Sabrina arrived early at the hospital, where she immediately apologized to Doc Henry.

"I made my own decision to go with Tremayne," she argued. "You tried to discourage me, or to send Jones or Hedgewick along. I made my own bed, and I won't stand by and allow that despicable senator to take it out on you."

"No, my dear. The blame is entirely mine. I didn't try hard enough to dissuade you. I should have considered the consequences to your reputation."

"Don't worry about that. Lon proposed last night."

The physician looked genuinely perplexed. "Magnanimous of him, stepping up in time to save you from post gossip. Or did he offer a more viable reason for asking you to share his life?"

She had long suspected that Doc Henry was aware of her feelings for Tremayne. Taking her time, she folded another bandage from the stack Hedgewick ironed the night before. "It's been expected."

"Indeed." Under his continued scrutiny, she began to squirm. "You accepted?"

"Not yet. Of course I will . . . eventually. Even Papa is on Lon's side, now."

"Sabrina, my dear. I couldn't feel closer to you if you were my own daughter. Still . . ." He paused, as though hesitant to continue. "I have no right—"

"You have every right. Say what you think." Lately, she felt closer to Doc Henry than to Papa. She knew why. Doc Henry had never once spoken ill of Tremayne or judged him, while Papa was so against Tremayne that he wanted her to marry Lon Jasper.

"Will you make me a promise?" Doc Henry requested at length.

Her hands stilled. When she looked up at him, he continued.

"Don't let yourself be railroaded into marriage until you are certain. It isn't Martha or even Edward who will live in the same house with your husband."

"I know." But the reality of Mama's laughter echoed guiltily through Sabrina's fantasy. "Lon makes her laugh. That's something Papa and I have tried to do for fourteen years. Tried and failed."

After a moment of silence, the physician added, "Whatever your decision, you know I will support you."

"Thank you. Your support means—" A call from across the clearing claimed their attention. "It's Papa!"

"Doc, are you there?" came Edward's frantic call.

Sabrina led the way to the veranda, where they watched Edward run toward them, a woman in his arms.

Sabrina went weak in the instant before she realized it wasn't her mother. Then Edward arrived, carrying Rosa.

He took the steps two at a time, followed by Felipe, the

younger of Rosa's two sons. "She came just after you left, Sabrina. She and the boys. Manuel hasn't lighted his fire for three nights. The boys went into the hills but couldn't find him. She came for help."

Rosa hadn't said a word. She looked unconscious. "What's wrong with her?"

"Collapsed. Right in the middle of our parlor."

"This way." Doc Henry led them to one of the two rooms reserved for civilians.

"I sent Diego for the colonel." Edward spoke of the Raméríz's older son.

By now Jedediah had hobbled in on his crutches, Jones behind him. Troopers were lining up for Sick Call.

"She needs a sedative," Doc Henry was saying.

Rosa opened her eyes, found Sabrina. *"Chica,"* she mouthed.

As soon as Edward put her down, Sabrina threw her arms around her.

"Manuel," Rosa moaned. Tears trickled from her eyes. *"Mi esposo."*

"Shh, Colonel Merritt is on his way. They'll mount a search party. They'll find him. They'll . . ." Feeling something wet against her arm, she realized it was blood.

Edward stood in the doorway, flanked by several troopers. "Get Mama," she requested. "Tell her to bring one of her nightgowns."

"I'll prepare the sedative." Doc Henry steered everyone out of the room. "Call if you need me, Sabrina. Come, son." With an arm around Felipe's shoulders, he guided the boy into the hallway, then closed the door.

Rosa continued to cry quietly.

"They'll find him," Sabrina repeated.

"Send Felipe for the priest."

"The priest? Of course. But you aren't dying, Rosa."

"The *bebé*. I will lose the *bebé*."

"Baby?" That's what the blood was. She had thought it Rosa's monthly. Lord in heaven! A miscarriage. "I'll get Doc Henry."

"No." Rosa clamped fingers around Sabrina's wrist, restraining her. *"Por favor, chica.* I will lose the *bebé."*

"No, you won't. Lie still. We'll keep you in bed. You won't lose your baby."

"Manuel . . ." Her words drifted on a tired breath. She closed her eyes and lay quietly awaiting fate's decision.

"They'll find Manuel. Don't you worry. They'll find him." Sabrina murmured soft words, while tears stung her eyes. Rosa was pregnant; Manuel was missing.

"Count your blessings," Mama had chided most of Sabrina's life. "There's always someone worse off than you." The fact that Martha hadn't applied the admonition to her own life didn't make it less true.

By the time Papa returned with Mama and the requested gown, Colonel Merritt and several others had arrived. Through the closed door to Rosa's room, Sabrina heard the senator's voice. And Lon's.

"We can't waste time waiting for a scout." It was Lon, uncharacteristically arguing with Colonel Merritt. Sabrina's eyes found her mother's. Even Martha looked stunned. Sabrina's chance of a lifetime continued in a peppery tone.

"If I can't find my way around these hills after all this time, I'm not fit to command. I didn't get us lost last time out."

He had a valid point. The last patrol had been out twenty-four days and Lon led them every step of the way.

"We'll wait," the colonel responded. "Nick Bourbon and Tremayne are due in for negotiations. You may have learned your way around these hills, Captain Jasper, but Tremayne was born in them. He'll cut down the time by half. Ramériz's life may depend on how quickly we find him. You will lead the search and rescue mission. Tremayne will scout. He will serve you well.''

Like oil and water, Sabrina thought. No wonder Lon stood up to the commanding officer. She heard boots clomp across the veranda floor boards, as the men left the hospital. A soft knock came at the door.

"Sabrina?"

Opening it she found a compassionate expression on Lon's sharp-featured face. "How is she?"

Leaving Rosa to her mother, Sabrina stepped into the hallway. "Find him, Lon, please. Alive."

"We're going to try."

"She's with child."

"I'll do my best."

She knew he would. Lon was a good soldier. Even before Papa came around to approving of him as a prospective son-in-law, he agreed that Lon was an exemplary soldier.

But when his fingers touched her chin, she flinched. He appeared not to notice. "Think you'll have my answer by the time I get back?"

At first she didn't take his meaning. At Rosa's plight, marrying Lon had fled her mind. Irritated by the guilt he piqued in her, she wondered why he always picked the wrong time to court her. And why she expected him to be perfect.

Contritely she followed him to the front steps, where she dutifully watched him cross the clearing. Even then, however, she was more aware of activity in the distance than of the man who had only the night before proposed marriage.

She stood thus until she saw Tremayne ride up to Headquarters. He didn't glance toward the hospital and she returned to Rosa, feeling guilty for putting her own hopeless fantasies ahead of her friend's very real anguish.

* * *

"I'd as soon ride with a pack of wolves," Tremayne hissed to Nick, then corrected, "Sooner. Wolves follow the laws of nature."

"I'll watch your back," Nick quipped. The two men had ridden into the fort ready for negotiations, only to be drafted for search and rescue.

It was a top-heavy detail, destined from its inception to failure, to Tremayne's way of thinking. If the senator didn't usurp Jasper's power, together they would certainly undermine Tremayne's role as scout.

Rosa's sons, Diego and Felipe, rode with them into the hills, pointing out the various places they had searched for their father.

"Gather your flocks," Tremayne suggested to the boys, finally. "We'll find your papa." He led the detail through the deep, brush-filled ravines that slashed the land between Apache Wells to the west and Nick's hunting lodge further north.

From the outset he ignored Jasper and hoped only that Jasper would return the favor. By the first noon camp, however, Tremayne learned that was not to be. Mounting up, he instructed the twenty men how to split up for best advantage. Jasper didn't speak until everyone had swung into their saddles.

"Get on up there ahead of me, Tremayne," he called just loud enough to be heard by the nearest men, including Nick and the senator. "Don't want to risk a bullet in my back, now that I'm to be a married man."

Tremayne's mouth fell open. His first conscious thought was to knock the captain out of his saddle for insinuating that he would shoot him, in the back or otherwise. But the shock of Jasper's latter claim offset his offense at the former. Pain stabbed through him. Reflexively he grabbed the black's mane.

So Sabrina had agreed to marry the bastard? He should have known she would.

"What's the matter, renegade?" Jasper's rasping jeer thrust him through a second time. Forcefully Tremayne remained on his horse, but Jasper hadn't finished searching for his jugular. Couldn't the man see he'd hit it the first time?

"You didn't really think you ever stood a chance with her?"

After a tense moment in which he struggled to control every savage impulse in his nature, Tremayne replied, "I wish your wife a longer life than mine had."

Lon Jasper's pale blue eyes turned to ice. "What's that supposed to mean?"

Tremayne shrugged. "You tell me."

They found Manuel near sundown that same day, and the sight raised the hair on the back of Tremayne's neck. Lon Jasper was forgotten, and for a brief moment in time so was Sabrina. The sheepherder's body lay draped across the well outside Tremayne's cabin at Apache Wells, in exactly the same position Tremayne's father had been left so many years before. Manuel, too, had been burned.

"What the hell?" Jasper's voice rose on a note of alarm.

Tremayne stared at the ghastly sight, praying for life to flow back into his cold body. Nick sat stiffly by his side. Behind them gathered the few troopers who dared come into the valley to water their mounts. Most remained on top of the hill with the senator.

"I don't like the looks of this," came a high-pitched whisper from behind.

"Me, neither."

Tremayne turned to see the men backing their horses out of the clearing. Scanning right and left, he inspected the fold in the cliff that led down to the creek, peered into the shadowed spaces between the red rock columns. Nothing out of the ordinary. He dismounted. "Let's get him off here." Nick came forward. No one else.

Tremayne turned a scathing glare on Jasper, whose sharp features were virtually colorless. "What's the matter, Jasper? Legend getting to you?"

The captain jerked in a spasmodic attempt to straighten his shoulders. "Get on with it, renegade."

"You know the legend?" Tremayne taunted. "If any man brings harm to the People, the water will become fire and he will be consumed by it."

The blue of Jasper's eyes had turned white. He exuded hatred and defiance by turn, finally glancing away to the hilltop.

Tremayne laughed harshly. "You and Carmichael make a team. Running scared from a tall tale."

"Tall tale, hell," Jasper rasped. "You're the one who found him. Rode right to him. Straight as an arrow. That's the tale I hear."

With no help from the skittish troopers or disdainful captain, Nick and Tremayne removed Manuel's body, wrapped it in a deerskin robe Tremayne retrieved from the cabin, and headed back to town.

"You know the hell of it?" Tremayne and Nick rode at the rear of the column now. Tremayne led the mule laden with Manuel's body. He spoke low, his words for no one but Nick. "That's exactly the way they left my pa."

"Whoa, there." Nick frowned into the night sky. "Thirty years ago, wasn't it?"

"Near enough."

"Who was responsible?"

"Comancheros, everyone figured. Reckon they could still be around?"

The question was rhetorical, and Nick didn't bother to

answer. "Why leave Manuel's body on your well? What did he ever do to you?"

"This wasn't against me," Tremayne argued. "The legend of Apache Wells is fair game for anyone wanting to make a point. But like you asked, why Manuel? He never hurt a soul that I heard of. What the hell does it mean?"

"The question you'd better be studying is how to tell Sabrina. She thinks the world of Rosa."

"Let Jasper tell her. He's the one fixing to marry her."

Manuel's funeral was held two days later in a little cemetery located on a barren plain outside Chihuahua. Rosa's bleeding had stopped, but Sabrina knew she wasn't safely beyond miscarrying the baby.

"Take care of your mother," she told Felipe after the short service. It had been agreed that for the time being the boys would take turns tending the flocks and caring for their mother. "Come for me if she doesn't stay in bed and eat what I send."

"*Sí, señorita.*"

Sabrina had begged Rosa to remain in the hospital a few days longer. Failing that, she tried to persuade Rosa to let her come home with her.

"No, *chica*. This is my life now. I must get used to it."

"We will take care of her," Diego assured Sabrina. "Papa would bar the gates to heaven if we did not."

They were good boys, both of them. At sixteen, Diego was already a man in most ways. And Felipe, twelve, was maturing fast. "I know you will, but remember, I'm your friend. I want to help. Don't be afraid to ask."

Edward came around and helped Rosa into the wagon. Martha scooted over to make room on the seat. Martha had surprised everyone except Sabrina and Edward by taking a firm hand in Rosa's recovery. She prepared broth and other nourishing foods and sat long hours beside the sick bed.

Lon, too, had been stalwart. Now he took Sabrina's elbow, but before he could lift her onto the wagon seat Carrie Young arrived.

"Have they arrested Tremayne yet?"

Lon's hand tightened on Sabrina's arm. She felt like he had squeezed the air out of her lungs, instead. "What?" she asked Carrie.

"Haven't you heard? Tremayne killed Manuel."

"No." Sabrina wasn't sure she had spoken the word. It felt lodged in her heart, fighting its way out.

"We don't know that for sure, Carrie," Lon was saying.

"For sure?" Sabrina glanced from Carrie to Lon. "What do you mean? Tremayne didn't murder Manuel."

"You wouldn't want him to have," Lon corrected. "You're like a mother hen, Sabrina. You'd take up for a black widow spider until it bit you. Then it would be too late."

"You're serious." Confused, she tried to clear her mind. "You're serious?"

Carrie shrugged. "Everyone says so." When Sabrina continued to stare at her, Carrie added, "Well, someone killed him."

"Not Tremayne." Sabrina gathered her shawl to ward off the chill. Her breath was as scarce as a breeze on a still day. "What proof—?"

"No proof," Lon admitted. "Not that would hold up in court. Manuel's body was draped over Tremayne's well."

"So?" She felt dumb and wished for a moment she were deaf and couldn't hear these groundless, impossible accusations. Her stomach tumbled as rapidly as it had when she heard about the gruesome discovery. Tremayne's well, where he heard his mother's laughter. It made her sick. Tremayne's well, beside which he had kissed her.

She closed her eyes and saw again the dried red water on his shirt that morning when he came about Ket. Her heart thrashed, like it had on that morning, when she thought it was his blood.

"That well's haunted," Carrie explained.

"Haunted?" Sabrina snapped. "What does that mean?" *What do you know?* she wanted to scream. *You or Lon or anyone.* She fought for reason. "If Tremayne killed Manuel, he wouldn't have draped him over his own well. That doesn't make sense."

"Sense or not," Lon said, "it looks like the truth. He led us straight there. No one else would have found that body in a month of Sundays."

It was only later that Sabrina realized she had listened in such shock she had been unaware of those around her. Rosa, on the wagon seat beside Martha; her sons, standing shoulder to shoulder in rapt attention.

Diego and Felipe. Sabrina didn't recall their presence until Diego spoke.

"You shouldn't have come to Papa's funeral, Captain. You should be out arresting that murderer."

"The army's handling it, son."

Diego and Felipe exchanged glances.

"Not any more." Straightening his shoulders, Felipe moved closer to his older brother.

"We'll go after Tremayne ourselves." Diego obviously spoke for both boys. "Don't expect his body for burial."

"My brother speaks the truth," Felipe added. "There won't be enough left of him to bury."

Tremayne heard the horse and went out, only to stare in disbelief. It was dusk and an early white moon rode the top of the hill. Silhouetted against it was a form he would recognize in a dead sleep. *Especially in a dead sleep,* he thought, aggravated, since his dreams were all of her.

Immobilized by some irrational expectancy, he watched her guide the horse down the steep incline, cross the clearing, and come at last to a halt in front of him. He had called her witless; now he was the witless one. He'd lost his heart to her long ago. Tonight he couldn't even find his tongue.

He wondered what she wanted—regardless, he should send her away. Yet the thought was as foreign as the distant moon. Once she had baffled him. No longer. Now she intrigued him, beckoning even as she sat the saddle, motionless, as though uncertain whether to dismount.

Her eyes sought an answer in his, and he knew that what she read there was the opposite of what he should be thinking.

He should send her back to the post.

"Rosa's sons are coming," she said after neither of them had spoken for several heartbeats. Her words strained through a constricted throat. He didn't need a spiritual guardian to tell him why.

"They think you murdered their father." When her eyes filled with tears, his almost did, too. He could hardly consider her shocking statement for the even greater shock of seeing what he had done to her.

He had thought it was best for her, to cut off the relationship before it got out of hand. One look at her told him he had failed. It was already out of hand, had been since the moment he saw her in the road, wearing that ridiculous green gown, her hair glowing like a bonfire.

Her hair still shone as brilliantly as ever, but there was no life in her, no hint of that indomitable spirit he had always admired. All that was left was despair.

A despair he alone had inflicted upon her. With guilt snarling in his head, he stepped closer and compounded the issue by lifting his arms. She slid into them without hesitation.

For a moment all he could do was hold her. His arms trembled and his heart thrashed. Miraculously he felt the answering tremor in her arms, the echoing throb of her heart, her warmth, her softness.

Her hair had for the most part come loose from its moorings. He slipped his fingers through it, and it felt like cornsilk.

"Sabrina, Sabrina. I never meant to hurt you." When he drew her back, their lips met, slid apart, then readjusted. They kissed hungrily, starved by separation; greedily, as though this were the last morsel of nourishment left on earth. Their tongues searched and found, seeking and plunging on a quest for consummation that was at once physical and spiritual. Who needed the guardian of the well? He had Sabrina. She was his spirit, his soul, his everything.

And he was her downfall. But when he tried to set her free, loosening his hold was all he managed. She broke the kiss.

"They're coming."

"Rosa's sons?" He couldn't stop kissing her. Wet hot heat spiraled through him, washing away the last remnants of his resistance.

Again she broke the kiss. "They're coming."

Let them come, he wanted to say. He was already in heaven. "How far behind?"

"I don't know."

"Did they leave before you?" The serious nature of her mission tugged at his consciousness but didn't stand a chance against the raging passion he felt to hold her.

She shrugged, languidly. All her energy was in the embrace, an embrace they had each despaired of ever sharing again.

"They'd have to find horses," he argued.

"They will. I'm sure they have. They were determined—"

"And weapons," he added, speaking into her mouth. "I doubt they have weapons of their own." That broke the spell for her.

"Tremayne! Stop. This is serious. They're coming to kill you. They said so in front of—"

Jasper? he wondered when her words stopped abruptly. With her in his arms, he didn't want the bastard's name between them. "Why do they think I killed their father?"

"Rumor. It's all over the post."

"Whose rumor?"

"I don't know. But we have to do something. Do they know how to get here? They'll—"

"Wait a minute." He couldn't get enough. "Just another minute." Like a drunk man he craved one more kiss, one more touch, one more taste of the magic.

But she was serious. When she pulled away, he watched her demeanor change. Her eyes, those glorious eyes, fairly popped open. Nothing languid about her now. She cocked her head, flinging hair across his face. He captured a strand with his lips. Captivated. Call him a fool. Call him a fatalist. Life ended sometime. Where better than in her arms?

"Listen. It's them. Hear . . . ?"

He went still, senses alert. The night was chilly and silent. Even the crickets had gone to bed. He heard no one.

"Listen," she urged, strangely insistent.

He tried again, again shook his head. "Don't worry." He nipped her lips, but she pulled away.

"You don't hear it?"

Something in her tone made him look closer, not at the now black hills from where the Ramériz brothers would come, but at Sabrina. The moon had turned golden and shone on her face, which was contorted with intent.

"You don't hear it." A whisper, a statement. Not a question this time, but an affirmation.

Wary, although he wasn't sure of what, he watched her attention turn inward, watched her consider, evaluate. Then suddenly he knew what she was thinking, even before she said it, perhaps before she realized herself.

"I hear it." Her words were awe-filled and struck him in the gut.

A reply lodged in his throat. Drawing on years of training, he was able to maintain a stolid expression, but he didn't feel it, not inside. He tried to shrug off her claim, even as she spoke it. But her voice was steady and clear.

And certain. "It's the laughter, Tremayne. I hear the laughter."

Her assertion carried an undercurrent of desperation. Moonlight fell on her pale face. He watched her come to life, like an animal with the arrival of spring. The arrival of hope.

Alive—like a heart, hardened against the world, when love is suddenly forced into it.

She took his face in her hands, and he watched a miracle transform her. The rebirth of her spirit—that's what he saw, her glorious indomitable spirit, which he had all but killed.

"It's the laughter," she said again, as certain as before.

He tried to deny it. He didn't believe in the laughter. He didn't believe in anything.

Except in this woman who held his face and healed his heart. Damn! She thought she had the world figured out.

If she heard the laughter, she did.

"You don't hear it?" she asked, soft as a night breeze.

He shook his head. His voice seemed lodged somewhere between his heart and his throat.

"How can you not?"

"Easy. It doesn't exist."

But she would have none of his cynicism. "How can you not believe?"

"Easy," he lied again.

He believed in it. Now. Like she said, how could he not? It lit her eyes, brought back her glow, her fighting spirit.

He believed in it. Never as strongly as at this moment. But if he told her that, there would be no turning back. No reverting to where they had been before their worlds collided. No salvation, no deliverance of Sabrina from the tiger whose jaws she had so fearlessly opened, into whose mouth she had so eagerly stepped. He could not tell her, for she didn't belong in this land. She would never survive here. He knew that, even if his soul already cried for the loss of her. This land had killed his mother and his wife.

Mobilized by renewed energy, she took charge. "We have to get away from here. Those boys mean to kill you."

Tremayne studied her face to memorize it. As if he could ever forget it. "That may be the only way out of this, now."

She went stiff. "Out of what?"

He'd said the wrong thing. In an attempt to appease he landed a soft kiss to her nose. "Whatever the hell is going on between us."

She took her time answering. "I've gone to great lengths to save your life, and I intend to do it with or without your help."

"Hey, I didn't mean to rile you."

"Then don't ever say such a terrible thing again. Come on. We have to get away from here."

"We'll take a back way to the post."

"No. Everyone believes you—" Her words drifted off.

"The post," he repeated. "With luck they haven't missed you, yet."

"By now they will have." She didn't sound the least bit concerned. He was the one concerned.

"Jasper said the date's been set."

"What?"

"He made a point of telling me he was fixing to be a married man." He didn't add the rest.

"He proposed. I didn't accept."

"But you didn't reject him?"

"Not yet."

"Then I have to return you to the post. You understand—"

"I understand that my absence has surely been noted by now. The hostler will have told my father, or Lon, or whoever asked, that I took one of the horses. They'll put it all together and know where I came. They'll probably come after us. We have to get away."

"You're telling me the truth about Rosa's boys? You didn't just run away from Jasper?"

"Tremayne! How could you—?"

"I had to ask, that's all." For the life of him he couldn't insist on taking her back to Jasper. For the eternal damnation of his soul, he couldn't let her go. Not just yet.

Not until he had to. "Mount up," he said finally. "I'll be right back." While he fetched his hackamore from the cabin and whistled for the black, anticipation mushroomed inside him. They were together. For however short the time, they were together. He couldn't suppress the expectations, the desire.

The instant he leaped on the black a bullet whined through the still air. It ricocheted off the old well. Splintering stone showered them.

He reached for Sabrina. "Jump!" A split second later another shot spat dust at them. Grabbing her around the waist, he hauled her from her horse to his. As soon as he had a good hold on her, he urged the black around the corner of the cabin.

A third shot splintered rock on the corner of the building. A fourth struck the same spot.

"I told you they were coming."

"Maybe I should have listened harder. I hadn't expected the Raméríz boys to be accurate shots." An inch either way, and they'd have hit something. Or someone.

"You don't think it was them?"

No time to speculate. He swung Sabrina around in front of him. "We'll leave your horse, go to Nick's."

For answer she snuggled back against him. He imagined a smug smile on her lips. The taste of her was still in his mouth. It mingled with the bitter taste of fear. What kind of trouble had he gotten her into this time? He was no good for her. The black responded to the command of his heels, plunging headlong into the red rocks.

Hell, he knew what she was thinking. The same thing he'd been thinking. But she didn't know anything about him. Nothing except what Jasper told her. And that was pretty much all lies. He didn't know anything about her, either.

Except how she set him afire, how she filled the cold and lonely hole in his heart with something hot and sweet and very similar to love. With her in his arms, he felt whole again, complete. Like he belonged somewhere.

But he didn't belong. Not in her life. He couldn't do that to her. He wouldn't. He would get her to safety, then he'd send her back to the post with Nick.

Chapter Fifteen

They raced through the night on a horse that was black as Hades, and she knew she should be afraid but she wasn't. She had never felt more safe in her life. Even when the black plunged down a hillside so quickly her stomach fell; even when they drove into brush so thick she had to hunch forward, her face in the horse's mane, she wasn't afraid.

Tremayne sat behind her, cradling her in arms that brushed the sides of her breasts, against a chest as solid as a shield of armor, close to a heart that beat to the rapid rhythm of her own.

She wasn't afraid, for she had heard the laughter. And that, in the end, made all the difference. The sweet trilling melody drifted through her brain. Poignantly she realized it could be the laughter Tremayne heard as a child, his mother's laughter.

She had known instantly it was the laughter. Whether because she had lived with the voice in her head so long she was conditioned to accept such matters, she couldn't say, but hearing it set every discordant part of her right.

Everything inside her now played the same tune; every missing piece of the puzzle of her life fell into place.

She belonged with Tremayne. She couldn't marry Lon Jasper. She belonged to Tremayne. And he belonged to her, even though he firmly denied the existence of the guardian. She told him she would believe for him, and she would.

Not a lick of sense.

I heard the laughter.

Tremayne is right, Sabrina. The laughter doesn't exist.

Then neither do you!

It was well past midnight by the time they arrived at Nick's, or began to arrive. The black sky was studded with stars and accented by a golden moon that guided them through canyons, across a high valley, and into the distant Rattlesnake Mountains. Now the sky was brightening in the east. The stars began to fade. Shapes took form.

"We're almost there," Tremayne said against her temple. "How're you doing?"

Wonderful. Nestled against his warm chest, she had never felt so warm and secure. An hour or so before he'd told her to relax, that their pursuers would never find them now. He'd taken a short but dangerous path through the mountains. Now it was almost over, and she was already sorry. Several buildings lined the road, which was more distinct with the approaching dawn.

"What town is this?" she asked.

"This's Nick's place."

"All these buildings?"

"All of them. Barns, houses, employee cottages, guest houses, security . . ."

"Security?" Suddenly her breath caught. Ahead loomed an edifice that looked like a castle out of a book of fairy tales. "Even that?"

"And a whole lot more you can't see."

Sabrina was stunned and said so.

"Nick didn't design the layout," Tremayne explained. "His brother André is the pretentious one."

"You know Nick's brother?" She had never heard a word about Nick's family. "Who is he?"

"Nick? He's an aristocrat from some tiny country along the Mediterranean coast."

"An aristocrat?" The idea was astonishing but not preposterous. Nick gave definition to the word gentleman.

Tremayne sounded amused. "Nicholas Josef Christof de Bourbon."

Sabrina thought she should pinch herself to see if she hadn't ridden unaware into a real-life fantasy. "Our Nick?"

Tremayne's arms tightened around her, or perhaps she imagined they did, as he confirmed, *"Our* Nick."

"I didn't know."

"Only a few people do, and they know better than to talk."

"What's he doing here?"

"It's a hunting lodge."

"I know that, but it looks so . . . so permanent."

"It is, in a way. Nick doesn't get on too well with the folks back home. Having met André a time or two, I can see why. The man is a schemer from the word go. And pompous to boot. Reminds me a lot of Carmichael, come to think of it. He acts more like an emperor than the second son of aristocracy." Tremayne rubbed his face alongside hers. "Nick doesn't like his business known, so don't go running back to the post and telling that man of yours."

Thrown casually into the crisp new dawn, the statement was more chilling than the weather. The sun had yet to break the horizon, but its promise glowed red and gold around them. The courage Tremayne always inspired in her rose now through a strangled throat. She turned sideways in order to better see him.

"You still don't understand, do you?"

He didn't answer. Not in words. His gaze held hers and the inches between them seemed a mile.

"My *man* isn't at the post, Tremayne," she whispered. His heated gaze incinerated any attempt he might have made to deny her meaning.

With one hand he cupped her head at the nape. Anticipation shimmered through her. The contact seared her neck and was hot enough, she imagined, to curl straggling strands of her plank-straight hair. Her body flushed and she knew this must be reality. If a fantasy, they would be sailing over the Milky Way, and it had already faded into the graying light of day.

The kiss that followed took her breath and gave her life. It was full of promise and affirmation. When they parted, he stroked hair away from her forehead and planted a hot, wet kiss there, too.

Passion and compassion. This man felt both, intensely, and inspired both, intensely. She felt whole with him, more so at this moment than ever before. The feeling that her love for him would only grow stronger with time seemed at once impossible and inevitable. Butterflies had turned to flames. She was afire for him. Even her skin felt scorched. With difficulty she held her fervent impulses in check.

She could never leave Tremayne. She knew that now, beyond doubt. Not for her mother. Not for Lon Jasper. Not for the Lord in heaven.

More to the point, she could not allow him to leave her.

In the days that followed, Sabrina's sense of reality was turned topsy-turvy. Fantasy reigned, and anything that threatened the illusion was relegated to the back of her mind, where it festered unobserved.

Later she would face the formidable reality of confronting her parents. By now they would know their dreams for her had been destroyed; everything her mother had worked and lived for the last fourteen years, gone.

But here in the idyllic world of the lodge the only factor that seemed the slightest bit real was the danger to Tremayne. Neither he nor Nick appeared sufficiently concerned.

"Two little sheepherders will have their work cut out if they intend to get the best of Tremayne." Nick laughed. But that was the following day.

That first night when they awakened Nick and Lena, Nick had taken the situation seriously. He questioned first Tremayne, then Sabrina, and afterward roused vaqueros and sent them out to search for the Raméríz brothers.

"You'll be safe here," he had assured Sabrina before Lena led her off to bed.

"It isn't me I'm worried about."

"Get some rest," Nick advised. "I'll take care of this crazy hombre for you."

She had no reason to doubt that he could, for here in his own element Nick Bourbon seemed larger-than-life.

She had never been inside a house like his; indeed, the term inadequately described such castle-like proportions. A swarthy fellow had led them into the entrance hall and drawing room; he had stepped out of a small rock dwelling several rods from the lodge, blocking their way until he recognized Tremayne.

Even so, he accompanied them to the lodge, where he entered the massive iron-hinged doors as if he owned the place and guided them to a sitting room with a fireplace as large as her parents' entire parlor at the post.

"Who is he?" she whispered when the man left to awaken Nick.

Standing close, Tremayne squeezed her shoulder. "No need to whisper. I don't think there's a chance of being overheard in this cavern."

His observation delighted her. "I'm beginning to believe your outlandish tale about Nick's heritage."

"Believe it. That was Iago, his manservant."

"Shakespeare," she whispered.

"Othello," Tremayne agreed as though they discussed world literature every day of the week and Sunday, too. "Rest assured, he isn't as wicked."

She grinned, delighted, realizing too late that her surprise must have showed. His expression turned grim.

"Nick and Lena taught me to read, Sabrina. There aren't any *McGuffey Readers* in this library."

She grimaced. She'd done it again, said the wrong thing.

"I wish you wouldn't do that," he added, as though privy to her thoughts.

"What?"

"Remind me how far apart our worlds really are."

But they weren't. In this great rock castle Tremayne had taken on a different persona. Not that he was changed or diminished in any way. He was the same man who lived in the rock cabin beside the legendary well. The same man who heated her blood above the boiling point. The same man who had captured her heart whether he wanted it or not.

The same man. He fit in his cabin. He fit here. And more and more she began to understand how well he fit in her life.

And she in his.

Nick had raced barefoot down the broad stone staircase, stuffing shirttails into trousers as he came. He entered the room, black eyes flinty with apprehension. Behind him followed a woman with black hair flying about her shoulders, white nightgown blowing against her legs, and a bright red shawl clutched around her shoulders.

"Lena, this is Sabrina Bolton," Tremayne introduced once he assured Nick they were fine.

"Nothing fine about being shot at by two hotheaded kids who think you murdered their father." Nick turned Sabrina over to Lena. "Get some rest. I won't let anything happen to him."

Reluctantly she had followed Lena from the room. Tremayne caught up with them on the staircase.

"Your horse may have already made it back to the post. We'll send one of Nick's vaqueros to assure your parents that you're safe and will be home by tomorrow night."

Tomorrow? She resisted voicing the objection that came instantly to mind, but she knew he saw it in her eyes, for his gaze held hers in the flickering light of the dozen or so candles that burned in wall sconces to either side. Her insides fluttered. If this wasn't a fairy tale there never had been one and never would be.

While she contemplated kissing him in front of Nick and Lena, he kissed her. Softly, quickly, on the lips, hands burning into her arms. "Sleep well. You've earned it." One last kiss to her forehead. "You're safe here, Sabrina."

But it was he who wasn't safe. Fear beset her as she watched him return to Nick, waiting until he disappeared into the drawing room to turn and follow Lena, who waited on the landing where the staircase split into two arms, into the depths of the mammoth building.

Surprisingly, she slept. Her body took command, and she slept without dreaming. When she awoke, it was to a sunny sky and an insidious longing in the pit of her stomach. Why hadn't she accepted the first room Lena offered?

Not that the room she settled for was less luxurious. Large, with intricately carved walnut furniture and a mattress so deep and soft, not even a princess could feel a pea beneath it.

But it wasn't the first room Lena led her to the night before.

"This is Tremayne's usual room," Lena explained, opening the door to a large, well-furnished bedroom. "If it isn't suitable, I'm sure he wouldn't mind changing."

Oh, it was more than suitable. The extra-large bed invited; fluttering butterflies clamored for her to accept, to crawl into that big bed and wait for him to come to her. Only years of proper training gave her the resolve to ask for a separate room.

Lena was duly embarrassed. "I apologize! I didn't think twice, seeing you together ... I shouldn't have assumed—"

"It's all right. I'm not offended." *Far from it.*

Now, in the clear light of day, she felt herself blush, then blush again, when she realized her clothing had disappeared. In its place, a white peasant blouse, the kind Rosa had worn before Carmichael started tormenting her, a full, black cotton skirt, and a bright woolen rebozo for warmth. Underneath it all, a fresh pair of pantaloons and a chemise.

No corset! She had never been so bold. Except once, she realized, recalling her first encounter with Tremayne, his hot hand inside her unbuttoned dress. That insidious flutter set up a flurry of anticipation in her stomach again.

Not a lick of sense!

Let me have the fantasy, for a little while, please.

Downstairs, she found Lena alone in the kitchen. Nick and Tremayne were out searching for the Ramériz brothers. No fantasy now. Stark reality. Her disappointment, too, was real.

"Tremayne said to assure you he will take you back to the post the moment he returns."

She wasn't sure what to pray for—except, of course, his safety.

The day passed quickly. Lena was as easy to know as Rosa—more so, Sabrina decided, because she and Lena shared a vital concern—the men they loved were friends. At least, Sabrina liked to think of Tremayne that way. This formed a poignant bond, one Sabrina dared not discuss.

Lena, however, was not hesitant. During an extensive tour of the 'castle,' she spoke readily of Tremayne, of hers and Nick's respect for the man, of how lucky Sabrina was to have caught him.

"Caught him? Oh, no, Lena, you've misjudged the situation by a country mile. There's nothing between us."

"*¿Verdad?*" Lena's black eyes grew round and luminous. Sabrina cringed, for she could tell Lena was not convinced.

"Truly," she repeated. They were in the kitchen at the time, sharing preparation of the evening meal. Lena slathered antelope ribs with a sauce that smelled like it might have been made in the fires of hell.

"Chile pequins," she explained. "Nick and Tremayne like their meat hot."

The room was large enough to serve as the post mess kitchen, with enough work space for several chefs to prepare food side by side and never get in each other's way. Earlier in the day Lena had explained that with only her and Nick in residence they kept a couple to share the cleaning chores, but did their own cooking. When Sabrina inquired about Nick's brother André, Lena responded vaguely, then politely changed the subject.

"I left some of the ribs unbasted, in case you prefer a milder taste." She slid the pan in the oven.

Sabrina peeled potatoes, her mind miles away from basting sauces. Several times she had been tempted to tell Lena about the laughter. She was fairly bursting to talk about it. "Why did you think there was something romantic between Tremayne and me?" she asked instead.

"Think?" Standing, Lena pressed fingertips to the small of her back. "It's as plain as the sparkle in your eyes. As the tremor in your voice when talk about him."

Sabrina was stunned. "It can't show. I mean, there's nothing—"

"It isn't just you. Since the first day he met you, I doubt Tremayne has spoken a sentence without mentioning your name."

"My name?" Sabrina's mouth was dry. Her pulse skittered as erratically as if Tremayne himself had walked into the room.

"*Sí*, my dear lucky Sabrina, your name."

Sabrina held a tenuous breath. If only she could believe that. "It probably doesn't mean anything."

"It means something," Lena insisted. "It means everything."

When the men had not returned by suppertime, Lena urged Sabrina to eat.

"You, too," Sabrina insisted. "You haven't eaten all day."

Lena patted her tummy gingerly. "I'm not up to it."

"Eating sometimes helps a sick stomach."

"Not this one." When Lena smiled proudly, Sabrina knew.

"You're expecting a baby?"

"Shh."

"Nick doesn't know?"

Lena turned away, pensive. "He can't know. Not yet."

"But he's planning to leave as soon as the negotiations are finished. You must tell him soon."

Lena shook her head. "It's hard enough for Nick to return to Europe without an additional burden from me."

"But surely you want—"

"Of course, I want him to stay. I can't tell you how badly. But it must be his decision. If I tell him about the baby, he might stay out of duty. I don't want it to be that way. If he stays with me—with us—it must be his idea."

"Has he ever . . . I mean, forgive me, but have you ever considered going back with him?"

Lena was visibly shocked. "He has never spoken of it, and I wouldn't ask."

Sabrina wasn't sure she understood, but in the back of her mind—where she stored things too painful to think about until absolutely necessary—she knew her relationship with Tremayne could be as complicated. She, like Nick, had another life to live. Unless she had already burned every bridge between this fantasy and the reality that awaited her at the post, she too, would face tough choices.

No choice at all, Sabrina. You owe Mama.

I don't owe Mama. But didn't she?

Sadly, she had hoped to one day still the voice in her head. Now she knew that was impossible. She would always hear her sister's voice. And the laughter? Would she ever hear it again?

"After Nick leaves, you must come to the post and stay with me." When Lena objected, Sabrina pressed. "I insist. For your baby's sake. And for yours. You'll need the company." *And I will, too.*

Lena hugged her. "You're as good a person as Nick told Tremayne."

A good person? "Oh, no. You don't know me." A good person didn't hurt her mother. Mama had probably taken to her bed over this latest escapade. More distressing, Sabrina's mind was so full of Tremayne—worry that the Raméríz brothers might shoot him, eagerness to be in his arms again—that she couldn't even concentrate on the wrong she'd done her mother.

When again Lena insisted Sabrina eat, Sabrina agreed on one condition. "If you'll rest until they return, I'll eat."

After Lena went upstairs, Sabrina ate. More to the point, she nibbled, then wandered out on one of the several verandas that offered majestic views from the lodge from every direction. This one faced north, in the opposite direction from which they had come last night. Not far away the mountains parted, forming an ever widening canyon with a distant view of El Capitán. She recalled Lon saying it was the highest peak in Texas. She wondered whether he had seen it or was merely relating facts, which he was good at doing.

The remembrance startled her, for she hadn't thought about Lon Jasper once today. His image didn't belong here. Imbued with the grandeur that spread before her, she felt suddenly, peacefully, alone. Enjoying the moment, the sense of isolation, she wrapped the colorful rebozo more tightly against the evening cool and wished this were her home.

Not this particular house, but this place, this land. A smaller house would be fine. But this land . . .

She didn't hear Tremayne's footfall on the stone veranda. He came up behind her, taking her unawares, and turned her in his arms.

And this man, she finished her wish, washed by weakness at his touch. *Most of all, this man.*

Her heart skittered in her throat when his lips touched hers. Then she was in his arms, holding him, being held by him, kissing him, being kissed by him.

"I'm sorry it took so long." He lifted his lips a mere inch. "It's too late to return to the post tonight."

The post? She never wanted to return to the post. "Don't be sorry." He smelled of the earth and tasted like heaven. She savored the feel of his warm breath on her face. Here in the chill of early evening it felt as if a furnace had been lit. "You've brought me to heaven."

"Heaven?" Red and gold from the setting sun glittered in his intense green eyes. "There is no heaven on earth, Sabrina."

"This feels like it." She knew he agreed, for though they stood in silence, lips softly resting against lips, his pulse throbbed as laboriously as did her own.

"It's only a *tinaje*," he whispered at length.

"A water hole?" She smiled, thinking not of the depressions that centuries of rain and runoff had carved into the rock mountains, but of the eons ahead for them. She loved this man. Her arms trembled with it. Her stomach fluttered with it. Hot liquid flowed through her veins with it.

"It offers sustenance, but only while the water lasts. In this arid land, water evaporates—"

Despair threatened the fantasy. "Don't, Tremayne. Please, don't." They both knew the fantasy was about to end, but she couldn't hear him say it.

"I'm not good at dreaming." His deep, down-from-the-hills voice carried the weight of centuries. "Or pretending. Life is real."

"I heard the laughter," she declared, obstinately holding to the fantasy.

He just looked at her, shook his head, kissed her tenderly, then released her. "Lena sent me to bring you to supper."

They ate on the southern veranda at a small table that added to the intimacy. With torches flaming all around and a sky full of stars overhead, Sabrina felt sure this was heaven. Then she broke the spell by asking if they'd found the Ramériz brothers.

Nick and Tremayne exchanged glances. Nick obviously lost.

"More or less," he said.

Tremayne turned his eyes to his plate. "These ribs sure hit the spot, Lena. Been way too long since I've—"

"More or less what?" Sabrina challenged.

"We found their horses."

"Like I was saying," Tremayne continued, "Been way too long—"

"Tremayne," Sabrina interrupted. "You didn't find the boys? Just their horses? Where were their horses?"

Again, it was Nick who answered. "Carmichael and . . . uh, some others were camped above Apache Wells."

Tremayne cursed. "We agreed not to talk about this."

"Why?" she demanded.

"Why should we? It's over."

He sounded like Lon, but she didn't tell him that. Questions clamored to be asked. "What does the senator have to do with the boys?"

Exasperated, he answered, "Their horses were at his camp."

"Why? What was Carmichael—"

"Hunting, he said."

"You rode into the senator's camp?"

"Straight into the spider's web."

"This isn't a laughing matter."

"The colonel didn't think so, either," Nick allowed. "That's what took us so long. We rode into Fort Davis and straightened this mess out with Merritt."

She glanced to Tremayne, who studied his food. "Did Colonel Merritt believe you?"

"Merritt said except for Carmichael's talk, there's not one damned thing to tie me to Manuel's murder."

"Thank goodness. What about the boys? Were they convinced?"

"We don't know exactly where they are," Nick explained. "We took word back to Carmichael's camp." The irony seemed to register, for he stopped and shook his head. "Carmichael's camp, hell. That's Tremayne's land."

"No, it isn't."

"What?" Nick looked utterly astonished.

"It isn't my land," Tremayne repeated.

A memory flashed through Sabrina's mind. "Maybe it belongs to the senator. Lon said—"

Tremayne's head shot up. Her words stopped. Lon Jasper's name hung between them. Neither of them said another word.

Nick spoke into the tension, which was as thick as smoke from a dying campfire. "What's this about Carmichael?"

"He, uh," Sabrina dragged her attention back to the table. "Supposedly he owns a lot of land out here."

Nick doubted her claim. "I would have heard about the purchase. My family has owned this property for fifteen years, and hell, Tremayne, this is your home. I was certain that land belonged to you."

"It belonged to my pa. But that was a long time ago. I haven't checked it out, but I haven't been paying taxes, either."

"According to . . . uh . . ." Sabrina rephrased. "The senator is supposed to have grandiose plans for this area, something about bringing the railroad through."

"Railroad?"

During the debate that followed, while Nick and Tremayne argued the destruction a railroad would bring to these mountains, it occurred to Sabrina that she was more content here at this table, with these people, than she had ever been in her life. Even though the ordeal they faced was formidable, she was part of it. She belonged.

At a break in the conversation, she observed, "Your home is so grand, Nick. I never suspected. Now I know why you have such good manners."

"Why's that?"

"You were, how do they say it, to the manor born?"

"To the manor shackled is more like it," he mused. When Lena rose to clear the small table, he stopped her with a gentle hand to her wrist. "We can do that later, love. Why don't you play for us?"

"Nick," she chided softly, "our guests aren't likely to appreciate my playing as much as you do." To Sabrina, she explained, "Nick is biased. He thinks I'm talented."

"She is," Tremayne added. So Lena relented. Fetching a guitar, she played evocative Spanish tunes and sang in a whisper-like lullaby, or so Sabrina imagined.

The poignancy brought tears to her eyes. They would think her a ninny! Maybe if she . . .

Jumping to her feet, she caught Tremayne's hand. He was visibly startled. Before sanity kicked in, she tugged him to his feet.

"The only thing Nick and Lena haven't taught you is how to dance."

He balked, of course, but she refused to relent. "Don't you agree, Nick? What better time?"

"Wholeheartedly! Come, friend, show us some of that old warrior grace you're always bragging about."

Lena switched to a livelier tune. Still obviously reluctant, Tremayne studied Sabrina with that old hint of amusement that set her afire. "You sure about this?"

She nodded.

"How sure?"

The second time he asked, she experienced a tremor of expectancy. Too late she recognized it as a forewarning, for when he took her in his arms, she realized this was one impromptu decision that was about to backfire.

The moment his hand touched her back, a surge of sheer passion sizzled through her. Astonished, her eyes flew to his.

He acknowledged her plight with gleaming green eyes.

Against her temple, he whispered, "So the white lady out-smarted herself?"

Acutely aware of their audience, she felt her face flame.

"I'm a fast learner," he continued in a louder version of that deep, down-from-the hills voice. "Let me see if I remember how it's done."

"You said you'd never danced."

"I did plenty of watching at that fancy ball."

His hand burned into her, bringing back the memory of the first time he touched her there, in the road when his hand slipped inside her green gown. Now his hand was under the rebozo, separated from her skin by thin cotton. She felt consumed by the insidious yearning incredibly fostered by that one hand to her back.

Yes, she had definitely outsmarted herself. And she wouldn't have changed it for the world.

Lena's tune picked up tempo. Determined to at least pretend mastery over her impetuous nature, Sabrina instructed, "Here we go. Watch my feet."

"I'd rather watch your face. It's as red as your hair." Tremayne's cheek grazed hers, his breath whispered against her ear. Obviously, he didn't feel the same compulsion for pretense.

Discomfited, she glanced to see Nick sitting on the arm of Lena's chair, an arm draped intimately over her shoulders. In Sabrina's stomach, butterflies fluttered more insidiously than ever. But Tremayne hadn't finished teasing her.

"Let me see . . ." His hold tightened. "Is this the way Jasper does it?"

He might as well have slapped her face. Stiffly, she jerked away. "How dare you say that?"

The image of Lon Jasper rose like a specter between them.

Reality versus fantasy.

She wasn't ready to face reality.

"Come on, Lena," Nick was saying. "I think we can leave them to settle their own quarrels."

For long moments after Nick and Lena left them alone on the veranda, Sabrina stood in Tremayne's arms, his eyes burning into her face. When she'd about decided she would have to make the first move, he lowered his lips.

"I've thought about this all day."

"Me, too." Then every lucid thought left her, and into the void flowed passion as potent as wine, as wild as this land, and this man. But his mention of Lon exasperated her and finally she asked, "Why did you say that about Lon?"

He held her so tight and still, she could scarcely breathe. His voice was strained. "Because you're going to marry him."

"I'm not. How can you think so?"

He kissed her tenderly, one eyelid, then the other. "Ah, Sabrina. I didn't say you love him. I know you don't love him. But you will marry him. Mark my word. You will."

"How can you stand here and . . . and kiss me and . . . while you believe I could ever marry—"

"You didn't reject him, did you?"

"I will."

"I doubt it."

"The night he asked wasn't the right time to refuse. Mama was upset, and Doc Henry was being investigated."

"Investigated?"

"Senator Carmichael has called for a court-martial, claiming Doc Henry sent me into danger."

"He sent you . . . ?" Tremayne drew back, stiff with anger. "That son of a bitch! This is about me, isn't it? I took you to see Ket. So they're—"

"You didn't take me. I went. Freely." She brushed his

cheek with her fingers, then left them there, like that first time. How brave she had felt then.

How frightened she felt now. For him. For Doc Henry. For them.

"Wild horses couldn't have kept me from going to Ket." When she started to remove her hand, Tremayne held it in place.

A simple gesture, a hand covering fingers that rested on a cheek. Simple.

Stunning. He remembered.

"I went freely," she repeated, her voice strained, now, too. "Even before I heard the laughter."

He ignored her claim about the laughter. "How did you find this out?"

"About Doc Henry?"

He nodded.

"Lon told me." She sighed deeply. "Then he proposed marriage. The insinuation was clear."

"I should have known he was behind it. He'll never stop trying to get to me. One way or another, he's going to get me."

"You?" She recalled thinking the two men hated each other. "Why you?"

"Because he's a bastard."

"But he doesn't know about . . . us." She said it tentatively and watched passion flame in his eyes. "Not really."

"There's more to it than that, Sabrina. More than you . . . and me. He's hated me ever since Nakia. I was rash, maybe reckless. I condemned him for the way he botched the investigation of her death. He'll never forgive me that. But I wouldn't have thought he would take down every person my life touches."

"He won't hurt me."

"No? What will you do about Doc Henry?"

The question was rhetorical and unanswerable. Would

she abandon Doc Henry, her friend and mentor, for Tremayne, a renegade white man who was unacceptable to everyone in her life? More than unacceptable, he was forbidden.

Desperation burgeoned inside her. She thought she might choke on it. It lodged in her throat, and she saw in his face that he felt the same sense of impending doom. The same unacceptable but inevitable crashing down of the fantasy.

With the truth mounting around them, he scooped her in his arms and carried her into the house. She didn't speak, nor did he, until they reached her room, where he set her on her feet, then stepped back over the threshold.

She panicked. "Where are you going?"

"Somewhere safe."

"Safe?" She felt physically faint. "I won't bite you," she managed.

"Safe from myself." His words choked out.

He couldn't leave. She couldn't allow him to leave. Moving so close their bodies would have touched except for their clothing, she forced his arms around her waist. "I told you I would believe for both of us."

"Not this, Sabrina."

"This." When she guided his face to hers, the butterflies set up a clamor. Then she kissed him full on the mouth, lips open and questing. The result was riveting, spellbinding, magical. It was the second boldest act she had ever taken, this one out of sheer desperation. She loved this man. To tell him so would drive him away. So she would show him.

"We can't do this, Sabrina."

"Please don't make me beg." By now she had untied the band holding his hair back, and for a moment she thought perhaps she had unleashed the wildness in both of them. Slipping her fingers through the wavy length of it, she felt a shudder tremble down her arms. His echoing groan reverberated against her.

"You would, wouldn't you?" He caught her up, slid his hands beneath her blouse, and the wildness commenced. The kiss that followed was mutual and ravishing.

The next time she was aware of anything other than his lips, his hands, his body, and her spiraling desire, they had moved to the bed. He stripped the blouse over her head, tossed it aside, and followed it with her camisole. His rough hands gently spanned her ribcage; his thumbs rested beneath her breasts.

Her very nude breasts. Instead of embarrassment, she felt only the butterflies. Their urgent clamor vibrated through her, from her stomach to the lowest, most intimate part of her. Exactly what she wanted, she couldn't have described, but she wanted it with an urgency that escalated by the moment. It left her feeling wild and totally undisciplined.

She slipped her hands beneath his shirt when she felt his lips close over a breast and tug in exquisite accompaniment to the flutters in her stomach. The only time he dislodged his lips was for her to pull the shirt over his head, and by then he had succeeded in removing her skirt and bloomers.

They lay together in perfect complement. His chest was furry and she sifted her fingers through it and nestled her breasts into it. Only then did she realize he had moved his lips to her abdomen. His long hair hung around them, forming a curtain, closing out the world, closing out reality, bringing the immediate present into sharper focus.

She had loved this man for so long, loved him with her heart and with her soul. Tonight she would love him with her body. Overwhelmed, her body hummed with expectation. Cradled with his arms to either side of her, his hands found her breasts, his lips burrowed into the tight red curls below her abdomen, and she thought for one fiery moment she might expire from the sweetness that swept through her.

Gripped by a wild and fierce urgency to experience him to the fullest, she lifted her legs from the bed, reached for his head, slipped her fingers through his hair, drew him to her, desperate to fulfill, to reach . . . Involuntarily her body began to convulse, wracked by a series of fiery shudders.

"Tremayne, please, I . . ." Her mouth was so dry she could hardly form the words. She felt his forehead drop to her abdomen. His hands stilled on her breasts. Her heart hammered in her chest.

Then suddenly, before she realized what had happened, he had leaped from the bed. Dazed by the magic of the experience and his sudden abandonment, she looked to the window where he stood, nude to the waist, hands spanning hips, staring out into the star-studded blackness.

"Tremayne, what is it?"

In the ensuing silence, fear crept to the fringes of her consciousness. Was what she had allowed so wanton that he would abandon her? Slipping off the bed, she went to him, stood close behind him, her body to his body, her arms around his waist. She knew he could feel her heart thrash against him. She felt his, too.

"What did I do?" she asked quietly. "Was I wrong to . . . ?"

"Wrong?" Swiftly he turned and caught her to him. Their skin pressed together hotly, as though they were one. She felt his body probe against her through his trousers, felt him flinch when it did. But he didn't move away.

"I was the one who was wrong, sweetheart," he said. "My mother taught me better."

"Your mother?"

"My Apache mother. You people call us savages, but if an Apache woman sleeps with a man before marriage, her nose is mutilated. For the rest of her life, her disfigurement serves as a reminder of her indiscretion."

"I'm not an Apache woman," Sabrina said quietly. His only response was to bury his face in her hair. After a while, he added,

"That's the hell of it, isn't it?"

Panicked, she knew she would have to fight for this man. Nick had warned her of that.

"It'll take persistence," Nick said. Well, she was persistent—she had no intention of giving up—but what was she supposed to do? She felt so inadequate, so unschooled, with no one to ask. Again, she took the lead, reaching for his face, cradling it in her hands, lifting her lips to his. And once more he surrendered to the wildness.

The kiss was long and deep and wet, and she poured every ounce of love into it and he did, too. At least, she imagined he did. He cupped her face as she cupped his, covered her lips with his; he traced the profile of her lips, then the inner contours of her mouth. Then he allowed her the same freedom.

It was like every romance she had ever read and every dream she had ever dreamed rolled into one. It left her weak, yet eager, renewed for the quest ahead.

When at length he lifted his lips, she stood in his arms, trembling with desire and anticipation.

"Jasper's never kissed you like this?"

The question came out of the night and she suspected was designed to cool her passion, but thoughts of Lon Jasper didn't have a chance when she stood nude as the day she was born in the arms of the man she loved. "He tried," she said, playing his game. "It never worked."

"God, Sabrina, I don't know whether to be angry or relieved."

She almost smiled. She loved taking him by surprise. "He'll never get another chance."

"He will."

"I'm not going to marry him, Tremayne. How many ways do I have to tell you?"

"You will."

"You're the most aggravating man I've ever met. Lon Jasper doesn't belong here."

Tremayne cast a weary glance around the room, shaking his head. "I'm the one who doesn't belong here—not in your bed, not in your life."

Again she cursed her inexperience. How could she show him the truth? That he did belong in her life, and in her bed. That he was the only man who ever would.

"Come with me." Ruled by desperation, she grabbed his hand and tugged him toward the door. On the way she scooped up the first garment that came to hand—it turned out to be her skirt—and threw it over her shoulder, partially covering her nakedness.

Three doors down the long empty hall, she entered the door she hoped led to his room. His protestations assured her it was.

"Sabrina, not here. This room is—"

She silenced him with, "The one Lena wanted me to take last night." Leading him inside, she closed the door and leaned back against it, catching her breath. She had never been as frightened in her life.

Not of what could happen.

But of what might not happen.

"This isn't my room or my bed," she told him. "Lon Jasper can't follow us here."

As though dumbstruck, Tremayne stared at her, shaking his head. "Damn, Sabrina." Weakly he reached for her, tossed her skirt to the floor, and drew her full against him. It was the last weakness either of them exhibited for the next several hours. "You don't have a lick of sense."

"So I've been told." But the reminder did nothing to diminish the urgency of the moment.

The woman bewitched him. He tried to resist her, but she wouldn't hear no. At least, that's what he told himself when he submitted to her final assault on his power to reason.

"Come here," he said, tipping her chin. "Don't ever say you didn't ask for this."

She laughed—feebly, to be sure, weakened by the desire she had been so determined to see to a finish. Her laughter was one of the things he loved most about her. She was so full of the simple joy of life that he had begun to feel it, too, foolish though that was. Joy meant hope. Tremayne knew for a fact that there was no hope left on earth.

Except for tonight. Which, of course, was all anyone ever had, the present. Which, in itself, was reason enough to make the most of the next few hours.

Which he did. Sabrina, unclothed and in his bed, was the fulfillment of what he had believed an impossible dream. Since that first day in the road when his hand slipped inside her gown he had been offered tantalizing glimpses of her exquisite grace and beauty.

Nothing, he learned now, compared with the whole of her. Once pale skin had repulsed him—at least, he had fought to feel repulsed. Now it drew him, his mouth to her dewy fresh mouth, his lips to her porcelain breasts.

He fanned her fiery red hair across the white sheets and let it shimmer in the dim glow of the single candle, lit earlier to show him the way to bed.

Sabrina showed him the way to bed. No sooner had he removed his trousers and laid her down than he was lost in her. Lost in the wonder, lost in the love, lost in an ethereal, fiery passion that, although he had anticipated it for months, still left him breathless, stunned.

She met him measure for measure. When he ran his hands through her hair, she threaded her fingers through his; when he fondled her breasts, she caressed the hair on his chest, down his belly; and when he reached into her heated core, she caught him and stroked him until he had to tell her to stop.

"Whoa, sweetheart," he mumbled against her.

"Is this wrong?"

"No . . . it's . . . right, too right . . ."

"Then—"

"Wait. Wait a bit . . . It's your first time—"

"Our first time."

And our last, he thought, moved almost to tears by the hopelessness that momentarily gripped him. But the dominant emotion was unbridled desire, wild and unrequited passion.

He intended to warn her of the pain, but, caught up in the frenetic prelude, he thrust into the hot, wet soul of her only to stop at her reaction.

She didn't cry out. She merely blinked her eyes, surprised.

"I'm sorry. Is it bad?"

Her lips curled in a magnificent smile. "May I tell you something?" Her whispery voice told him she was as near her climax as he.

"What?" he said, breathless.

"I love you."

All he could do was stare at her. For one split second all else was forgotten, everything but her words. They spread like balm over his once-cold heart. With a start, he realized that his heart hadn't been cold in a long time.

Not since he met Sabrina—this "witless" white woman

who set him afire, who even now held his body in a tight-fisted grip, and his heart in her rose-soft hand.

Love him? Nobody loved him. Except maybe Ket. But that was different. . . .

"I just wanted you to know," she added softly, as though she sensed his discomfiture. It was his love he hoped she never sensed.

Wordlessly, his vision tethered to hers, he began to move inside her. In and out. Out and in. All heat, fiery heat, passion, hot and wet and bright, it exploded with the impact of two worlds colliding.

And wasn't that what had happened? He slumped to his side, drew her with him, savored the feel of her wet skin sticking to his, of her small but colossal heart thrashing against his. After a while he felt himself slip from her body, felt the flux of wetness on his thigh, as though she were emptying herself of all that was him, of all that could have been them.

He buried his face in her glorious hair and thought that this was the saddest lovemaking he had ever experienced. The saddest and the best.

"Was it bad for you?" he asked finally.

"Bad? How could you think that?" She lifted her face to his. "For you?"

"The best." At least he didn't have to lie about that.

"I shouldn't have said what I did earlier," she whispered, her lips to his. The next move was his. He knew the cue, what she wanted to hear. Damn his soul, he'd better say it right.

Supporting himself on an arm, with his free hand he drew strands of her hair through the light. "I love your hair."

"I suppose that's a start." Although she strove to conceal it, he could tell she was disappointed. Sabrina was good at hiding her hurt. And at so many other things. "Even if you did pick my worst feature to love first."

That surprised him. She was good at that, too. "Your worst feature? How do you figure?"

"For one thing, it's a horrible red."

"I told you what the color reminds me of—the red fox."

She nodded, obviously pleased.

"What I didn't tell you is that Apaches would believe it's a sign you possess supernatural powers."

Her eyes widened. He could tell she was delighted. "I do. I heard the laughter."

"Yeah. Well, now that I've dispelled your notion that your hair is your worst feature—"

"It's plank straight, that's the worst part. If it were curly, or wavy like yours, it might be nice. You should have seen Serena's. She had a head full of springy curls."

"You probably just remember it that way."

"No. We have a portrait of us. It was painted when we were three and has always hung over our mantel. Serena had beautiful curls. I had to have French braids."

"French?"

While she explained the technique of braiding in the French fashion and the pain inflicted on small girls, he sat her up. By the time she finished the tale, he had braided her hair.

"This is how you should wear it." He flung one long, thick red braid over her bare shoulder. "Hold on." With a length of rawhide retrieved from his trouser pocket, he bound the end.

Admiring his handiwork proved disastrous, however, for the braid hung to the tip of her nipple, and he reacted as though he hadn't just been inside her.

"Damn, Sabrina. How did this happen?" He pulled her roughly to his chest, intending only to hold her, but she sensed his dilemma even before she moved alongside him and felt the evidence of it.

"I must look like Lady Godiva."

"Who?"

She laughed. "And I thought your education was complete. Nick didn't teach you about the legendary lady who rode through the streets of Coventry to protest taxes?"

"Let me guess. She rode nude?"

"Except for her long, blond hair."

Absently he fingered the braid, while she pressed against him in a suggestive gesture that caused his body to probe. He watched her eyes simmer.

"This means you want me?"

"Umm."

"I'm glad."

He cuddled her closer, stifling his growing need.

"It's too soon."

"Why?"

"For you, sweetheart. You'll be sore and . . ."

While he spoke she aligned herself with his body, took him in hand, and as though she had done the same thing a hundred times before, she guided him to her. "Don't make me beg," she teased.

He needed no further coaxing, but this time he took it slow and lasted longer and hoped against hope this would be enough to last them both—for the rest of their lives.

Afterward she snuggled into his embrace, and he held her close, stroking her back, her hair, learning, memorizing.

"You said this could never work." She spoke into his chest. "Remember?"

"Hmm."

"It can."

"Maybe here, but we can't stay here."

"Apache Wells?"

He fingered the braid and wished for daylight so he could see her more clearly. He wanted visions to take with him, too. "I can't see you living at Apache Wells."

"You think I'm not strong enough? Smart enough? Brave enough?"

"No. You're the strongest and smartest and bravest woman I know. But no woman can survive out here, not even one born and raised to the land."

"There's Lena."

"No, *here's* Lena. This lodge is about as far from reality as a person can get. I'm not an aristocrat. I don't have a palace or a fortune to build you one."

"I don't want a palace."

"You saw that cabin. Hell, I don't even have a real job. I could never make you happy—or keep you safe."

She didn't answer for a while, leaving him to wonder what she was cooking up now. When finally she responded, it was with a noncommittal claim that gave him hope that she was beginning to see the truth of the matter. "I'm happy right now."

"So am I." He kissed her tenderly. "Go to sleep, sweetheart." She curled into him and her breathing steadied. Just when he decided she had drifted off, she lifted her face and kissed him softly.

"I will always love you, Tremayne."

And I will always love you, his heart whispered. Before full dawn, he rose, dressed, and left. It was the only kindness he had left to give her.

Chapter Sixteen

"Lord deliver me from honorable men!" Turning away from Doc Henry, Sabrina stood at the dispensary window, looking out, yet seeing nothing except the red glow of panic that had surrounded her like an aura since returning from the hunting lodge. "I can't let you be court-martialed for something I did."

Foolish, though it was.

Tending a sick child is not foolish.

You don't have a lick of sense, Sabrina.

In the two months since Nick and Lena returned Sabrina to the post, she hadn't so much as caught a glimpse of Tremayne. Day after day, she performed her duties by rote. With the setting of each sun, she was exhausted from the effort it had taken to deny the hope that refused to die inside her, the hope that this would be the day he came to her, this the day she saw the big black stallion gallop up to Headquarters, this the day he acknowledged his love for her.

It never happened, of course. Nick and Lena had explained.

"I told you he's one crazy hombre, Sabrina," Nick had said. "He thinks he's doing what's best for you. It's his own personal code of honor, and he won't break it."

"Men always think they know what's best," Sabrina retorted.

"He loves you," Lena insisted.

"I doubt that." She didn't really, especially not at night in her bed, alone, when she couldn't keep her mind from returning to the hunting lodge and the magnificence of the love she and Tremayne had shared, poignant with their imminent parting though it had been.

From the moment he surrendered to his wild desires, and to hers, she had known what was in his mind. He would love her once, once to last forever.

There was no doubt that he had succeeded in giving her an evening to savor for all time. Her pulse skittered at the memory of his wildness and hers, of his love and hers.

Love. No other word could define the way she felt about him, or for that matter the way he felt about her. Lena was right; he loved her. But love wasn't enough for him to risk ruining her life. Perhaps if it were stronger . . .

Perhaps if she were stronger, she would face the fact that Tremayne actually knew what was best for both of them . . . and for everyone else in their lives. For Ket, who hated Sabrina because she was white; for Mama, upon whose most fervent dream Sabrina had selfishly trod.

"Captain Jasper is an exceptional man," Martha enthused after it became clear that Lon would not withdraw his marriage proposal, even though Sabrina had virtually thrown her reputation to the wind. "This proves it, child, what I knew all along. Captain Jasper is your chance of a lifetime."

Sabrina wasn't sure she *had* a chance of a lifetime. Certainly, she didn't want the only one that was being offered.

"I'm a patient man," Lon kept saying. He never actually mentioned her foray into the mountains to warn Tremayne about the Raméríz brothers. His only comment had been something about black widow spiders. "I told you once, and I'll say it again, Sabrina, one day you're going to get bit."

The thing she was grateful for was that Lon ceased all romantic overtures. He still came to the house, although not as regularly, but he never made a move to touch her, not even to hold her hand. A blessing, certainly, for she recoiled at the thought of kissing him. Since that blissful night in Tremayne's bed, thoughts of Lon making the same advances were so abhorrent she became nauseated thinking of them. Feeling that way, she couldn't marry him. The distance he had assumed made it easier for her not to rush to reject his proposal, for he continued to bring Martha a small amount of pleasure, and the senator continued to threaten Doc Henry with a court-martial.

Lon's magnanimous pretense of ignoring her transgression did not extend to the physician. On the subject of Doc Henry, Lon was steadfast. "You can't trust Senator Carmichael to be as patient as I am. He's determined to drag the good doctor before the court."

Doc Henry remained adamant. "I will resign before I allow you to marry Lon Jasper," he said soon after she returned.

Not that he had any say in the matter, of course, but it added strength to Sabrina's other incentives to hold off rejecting Lon. But with the passage of time, guilt began to wear her down. Martha's depression returned full-blown; not even Lon's coaxing could gain a smile. He still played their piano, but Mama refused to join him.

"I'm sick to death at the thought of you ruining your life, child."

"I won't, Mama." Whether or not Martha understood the motive behind the senator's threat against Doc Henry, she never mentioned the poor man's plight. But Sabrina felt enough guilt for both of them.

"You are not responsible for Carmichael's red hot temper," Doc Henry allowed one evening before she left the hospital. "He got mad at Edward and threatened court-martial. He's mad at me and threatens the same thing."

"Only because he thinks I'm rejecting his protégé."

"That may be the root of his threat, but in order for the court-martial to succeed, he will have to prove that I endangered your life by sending you into the hills."

"You didn't send me into the hills."

"I know, my dear. I know."

"Then why did you say you would resign before you would allow me to marry Lon Jasper?"

"Jasper and Carmichael are birds of a feather. They're devious men, and I won't have you shackled to a devious man for the rest of your life."

"I couldn't let you resign your position in the army over me," she argued. "You love the army."

"To be quite frank, my dear, I've been thinking more and more about resigning. This country's settling up. I could find plenty of work to suit me right here in Chihuahua. More than enough, if the latest rumor proves true."

"You mean about Senator Carmichael and the railroad?"

"Man's got the clout. It could be true. Like Edward, I love this country, Sabrina. Nothing would please me more than to go to my Maker here in these mountains."

Sabrina's heart ached at the words, for they were true for her, too. She loved this country, more now than ever. She felt a part of it, of the hills, the valleys, the red earth.

She felt part of it, because Tremayne was part of it. Ruddy in color, rugged in nature, Tremayne and this land were part and parcel. The hills were rock-solid, like his voice; substantial, like Tremayne, the man.

And immovable, like his determination not to ruin her life.

He had ruined her life, though. By barreling down on her from the top of Sleeping Lion Mountain, he had become a part of her life for all time. Without him, she was no longer whole. She would exist, but not live.

Doc Henry cleared his throat. "Speaking of Edward brings up another little sermon I've been rehearsing. Care to hear it?"

She smiled, fond of her friend, but rueful. What could he say that would change things?

"You can't live your life for your mother, Sabrina. You are not a substitute for your sister. Not even if you were responsible for her death, which I'm thankful you now realize was not the case."

"Tremayne convinced me," she said half-aloud. "Or tried to."

"I figured as much. My dear, think long and hard about your future. I've never seen you as alive as when you returned from the mountains with him."

"Alive?" She felt dead to her core.

"Sad, sometimes, like now. Distressed. Unsure of what the future holds. But alive, Sabrina."

"I know," she managed. "But Mama would take to her bed and never get up if she so much as suspected."

"She may take to her bed, anyway."

"What do you mean?"

"You have no control over another person's happiness. Haven't you and Edward spent your lives trying to make her happy?"

"Pretty much."

"Has it worked?"

"No."

"Well, it won't. Not even if you marry Jasper. Nothing you can do will ever be enough. Every person is responsible for his own happiness, my dear. Martha for hers, Edward for his, you for yours." He glanced at his hands. "Me for mine."

"That sounds good, but Mama is frail. I don't mean physically, but emotionally. She couldn't make it alone."

Mama's emotional frailty vexed Sabrina more and more lately. Why couldn't Martha take charge of her own happiness? Sabrina's conscience had never been as clear, nor as adamant.

She's your mother, Sabrina. It's your duty to make her happy. Since Tremayne came into her life, the other phrase had stilled. No longer did her dead sister chastise her for causing her death.

That puzzled Sabrina. If one part of the voice could be silenced, could the rest of it? She regretted the thought the moment it popped to mind, for that voice had kept her safe and true for fourteen years.

And more. Didn't the fact that she heard it validate the laughter? How could she expect to hear one and not the other?

"I've always thought of the voice I hear as my guardian angel," she told Doc Henry now. "Serena keeps me on the right track. Or, she does when I listen to her."

"Rubbish. Guardian angels don't hold a person back. Your guardian angel would set you free, not bind you to the past."

"Free?" The concept intensified her despair. What good was freedom if she couldn't be with Tremayne? Why had she heard the laughter if she wasn't free to follow it?

She had told no one else about the laughter, not even Doc Henry, and she would not. It was her most intimate link with Tremayne, strangely more intimate than their lovemaking, as precious as that memory was.

"I'm too timid to be free," she admitted. "I've always thought Mama weak. Well, I'm weaker than she is. Perhaps it is I who need her, I who could not exist without her as my guide, my crutch."

Nick came again a few days after that conversation, as he had so often during the two months she had been back from the hunting lodge. Usually it was to assure Sabrina that Tremayne was well and safe. Once he reported that the Ramériz brothers had been persuaded to leave their father's murderer to the law. That didn't stop Sabrina from worrying, of course.

On this day Nick came with a question. "Can you get away in the morning? Early?"

"Lena?"

He shook his head. "Tremayne sent me to bring you to the Apachería."

She saw him before they had moved more than a few rods into the compound, which was virtually hidden in a small valley high in the Diablo Mountains. He stood straight and tall outside a wickiup halfway up the hill, hands on hips, watching their approach. The sight of him set her world to spinning, like it always did. Like it always would.

She had never been to an Apachería, had never seen the hide and brush wickiups that served as homes. Except for Ket and her grandmother, she had never seen an Apache.

Yet she rode beside Nick up the rocky trail that ran through the middle of the village hardly aware of the huts to either side. People had come out, old women mostly and a few children. They watched in silence while the two horses passed.

Sabrina's attention was on Tremayne. Her pulse skittered ahead of the plodding horse's hooves. She rode as though pulled to him by the intensity of his gaze, by the rock-solid strength of his stance.

He was dressed as on that first day—hair flowing from beneath the red headband she had but dreamed about during all these long months past, duckins stuffed into knee-high moccasins, low-belted calico shirt. Fear washed her with a cold premonition, a warning that rang through her soul. Every beginning has an end. She had heard that somewhere.

Don't let it end here, she cried. *Don't let it end now.*

They rode due west with the sun at their backs. It gilded her horse's ears and splashed over the brown and red leaves; it glanced off the rocks, which were more yellow and white than red. She felt as though they rode through the dawn toward a sunset. She knew the feeling came as much from within her as from the actual sun brightening the haze of this autumn day.

Try as she had to face reality, she had not been able to quell the hope that sprang to life when Nick said Tremayne had sent for her—hope which she knew, seeing him now, would surely die once and for all here in this Apache stronghold.

"I'll leave you now." Nick's voice brought her back to the moment at hand. Her gaze darted from Tremayne's. Fear again lathed her, washing away any trace of the fantasy. It left her chilled through.

"Where will you be?"

"I'll visit with old Anselmo. He's a friend. Ride ahead, Sabrina. Keep your chin up. You'll do fine."

If she had been called upon to describe the emotions that swirled inside her she would have been unable to, for they blurred in a kaleidoscope of joy and sadness, hope and despair, fear and only a smidgen of courage, just enough to carry her the rest of the way alone.

She drew rein directly in front of Tremayne and allowed her gaze to rest on his face. In truth, she couldn't have kept from absorbing the essence of him if she had tried. His magnificent features. Like on that first day, shadows from a nearby cottonwood slashed his face, leaving it broad and narrow, an enigma. Like the man himself.

Once she had thought she knew him. Did she? Or had she seen only fleeting glimpses of this simple, complex man?

When he stepped toward her in a formal way she recognized as an attempt to control his emotions, she knew she'd been right—the fantasy was ending.

Reality struck with the sizzle that spread through her when she took his offered hand. It threatened to undo any small sense of decorum she might find within herself. She clutched his strong, rough hand, the hand that had loved her, feeling that she might never let go. The vision of it, holding onto him this way for life, swept her with pleasure. And desire.

"You look like that first day . . ." Her words caught in her throat.

"I remember it well. You couldn't stand on your own two feet." As if to test her, as soon as she stood firmly on the ground, he tugged his hand free and stepped aside.

She searched his face for signs of the rejection that sounded in his voice and showed in his actions, but found none. His intense green eyes consumed her. She watched his gaze linger on the lone braid that fell across her shoulder. She had worn her hair thus since returning from the hunting lodge, but at the post she coiled the long braid at her nape. For this meeting she left it long, hanging above her right breast, as though he had only now placed it there.

It was an intimate reminder, and she knew he felt it, too, when he turned brusquely away.

"You must greet my family."

The old woman stood stoically in the entrance to the wickiup. Ket stood beside her grandmother, her hair falling in longer but still ragged patches about her scowling face. The crutches were nowhere in sight. Reaching, Tremayne drew his daughter to his side.

"You remember the mother of my wife?"

Your long dead wife, she wanted to cry, but settled for a defiant, "Ket's grandmother."

His gaze lingered on her a moment, then darted away, like a hummingbird seeking sustenance.

"Hola, señora." Sabrina greeted.

The old woman bobbed her head once. No welcome there, either.

"I wanted you to look at Ket's leg," Tremayne said by way of explaining her presence here.

Leery but ready to do whatever he asked, Sabrina bent forward only to have Ket set up a sudden, fearful howl.

"Don't let her touch me. She's evil. Look what she—"

"Ket—" Tremayne tried to restrain the angry girl, but she jerked free and began shouting again, this time to the crowd that had gathered at a safe distance around them. "Look at her hair," Ket cried. "It's evil. She is evil." Leaping toward Sabrina, she grabbed the braid and held it up, pulling hard, for all to see. "Evil! Evil! Evil!"

Sabrina wrenched her braid free and took a step backward. A rock rolled beneath her foot, but she held her balance.

Ket followed, leaned into her face. "Leave my father alone," she cried. "You can't take my father!"

The attack came without warning. One minute Sabrina

stared into green eyes that brimmed with hatred. The next Ket had spit into her face. Sabrina staggered back, too stunned to reply.

The entire exchange had taken only a matter of seconds. Tremayne stood firm, his eyes wide. He seemed genuinely shocked. By the time he reached for Ket, her grandmother had pulled the child to her chest.

Angry words flew from the old woman's mouth. They were as harsh as the spittle Sabrina wiped from her cheek. Later, she realized it must have been the surprise of the attack that benumbed her, for in that moment she felt nothing—not anger, or fear, or sadness.

Tremayne returned harsh word for harsh word with Ket's grandmother, speaking fluently in the guttural Apache tongue. After what seemed an eternity, the old woman shrieked a last mouthful of angry words, turned her back, and dragged Ket around the side of the hut.

Tremayne hadn't moved. "Are you all right?" His voice trembled. In the back of her mind, Sabrina realized she was trembling, too. Mutely, she stared at the retreating figures.

Then he reached for her, and her heart stood still. When he merely touched her shoulder, as one would a friend or acquaintance, she almost cried. She needed more than a mere touch. She needed his arms around her. She needed *him*. Her heart began to throb.

"Come inside, Sabrina, where we can talk." He guided her through the hide opening. Inside the dusty brush structure, she stood stupefied.

"I'm sorry," he said from behind her. "I didn't expect them to do that."

His voice was low and kind, and hope slipped in. She turned to find him closer than she had thought. The need to reach for him overwhelmed her. She clasped her arms with tight fists to keep them to herself. For the only thing worse than not touching him would be for him to pull away. "What did she say—Nakia's mother?"

"That I should not have brought you here." He studied her closely. "That you don't belong."

Moments passed, precious moments, while despair mingled with the smidgen of hope and soured inside her. "Ket's leg—?"

"It's all right."

"Then why . . . ?"

A deathly stillness fell between then. He hadn't brought her here to treat Ket? For what, then? The question sparked that smidgen of hope again—it had never taken very much, she realized. But it faded quickly when she looked him full in the face and saw nothing but rejection.

He studied her intently, as he had at the beginning, and like at the beginning she was unable to read his thoughts. Had they come so far, only to retreat, to become strangers again?

"Ever been inside a wickiup before?"

"No."

"Look around. It's a far cry from what you whites call civilized."

His cynicism hurt worse than Keturah's attack. She wanted to tell him they had traveled far beyond such remarks.

"Nick said you aren't well," he surprised her with.

"Not well?"

"What did he mean?"

"Mean?"

"I have to know." His gaze swept her again. "Are you . . . all right?"

"All right? Why shouldn't I be?" Anger surfaced, strangled by fear. "I've learned to stand on my own two feet." At least she thought she had, until this moment. Then he shocked her further.

"Nothing happened, that night at Nick's?"

"Nothing happened?" Everything had happened. The best. The worst. She had learned irrevocably that she could not live without this man. Not truly live. "How dare you belittle . . . ?"

Ignoring her implication, he came right out with the question. "Did you conceive my child?"

"Your child?" He might as well have slapped her in the face. To ask such about such an intimate, wonderful thing in that bitter tone. She turned away to hide her tears.

"Did you?"

She shook her head.

"Good."

Good? She felt like he had stabbed her in the heart. She actually felt the pain; it seared to her soul, white hot and vicious. Without thinking, she swirled to face him, demanding, "What are you trying to do? Make me hate you?"

When finally he spoke, his voice was heavy with longing. "It would be simpler, wouldn't it?"

"It's a little late for that. You should have tried being hard and cruel in the first place."

"We didn't know then . . ." His deep, rich, sad voice betrayed his emotions. Sabrina resisted taking heart. "Neither of us knew it would get out of hand," he was saying, "that it would hit us like this."

She swept him with contempt. "So the fierce Apache warrior dragged the helpless white maiden to his camp to prove to her that he's a savage?" Where once she might have seen a hint of amusement, she now saw the old emotional barrier.

"To show you the truth, Sabrina. Picture yourself here."

"You don't live here."

"This is my home. For as long as it stands and these people live, it will be my home. They took me in when I was orphaned and reared me as their son. I married one of their daughters. In the Apache custom, the man leaves his family and lives with his wife's. He is their keeper until they die . . . or he does."

She smiled wanly. "I can see you taking care of my mother."

"I can see her letting me." It was a fleeting cease-fire in the midst of battle. She seized the moment.

"I would never resent these people, Tremayne." Drained of strength, she almost whispered it. "You should know that by now. I would never object to your caring for them. I would never stop trying to win Ket."

"She wouldn't come around."

"With time—"

"Damn it, Sabrina, try to understand. Nakia's death at the hands of white soldiers bound me to these people the way your sister's death bound you to your mother."

The comparison, the truth of it, shocked her.

"We should never have met."

His claim staggered her. "How can you say that?"

"Not in this world. Not after all that has gone before us. We can never be together, Sabrina. Understand that. You have to believe it—in fact, and in your heart. We can never be together. I want you . . . God . . ." He turned away, tossed his head toward the rounded brush ceiling, hands to waist, loose but white-knuckled. "I want you to be happy."

"Happy?" She laughed bitterly.

When he didn't respond, she spoke to his back. "The first time I asked Lon about you, he called you a squaw man. When I asked about your wife, he said Apaches weren't civilized enough to believe in marriage. It's funny, isn't it? The Apache's strict sense of duty is what will keep us apart. In my world marriage is dissolved by death."

"Ours, too. We are free to remarry. We can take more than one wife, if we choose."

"If your former in-laws agree?"

"That isn't the point."

She challenged him with silent defiance. It worked, in part, for at length he turned to her.

"I brought you here to see my life for what it is. Look around this wickiup. Doesn't it tell you why our women are old and stooped by the time they reach your age? *If* they reach your age. Look at this firepit. Not only do you cook over it, stooped for long hours, but you have to dig the damned thing. You don't have a commissary to sell you food. You must go into the hills, these damned barren hills, Sabrina, and gather nuts and berries, grub for roots and preserve them and store them. You soak hides and scrape them and tan the leather to make clothes and even the wickiup to share with . . ." Like one possessed he raced from one thing to another. But Sabrina stood blindly.

"You haven't heard a word I've said." She was only half aware when he turned his head and followed her line of vision.

"Son of a bitch." The words were muttered under his breath and carried the weary sound of defeat. Reaching around her he snatched the golden bow from a stump, and in one swift move cupped her face tenderly, touching her intimately for the first time since her arrival.

She thought she might faint. His touch left her weak with want, weak with dread. Where before she had been chilled, hot, liquid love now flowed swiftly through her. She stood still, scarcely daring to breathe. He bent and kissed her. Lips to lips. Long and deep and desperately.

Reverently she returned the kiss, putting into it all her desire and longing, all her heart and soul, while his hands never left her face and her hands remained in fists at her side.

She didn't cry. Her eyes were bone dry. But her tears were not gone. They had collected in her heart, and it felt heavy with despair. Neither did she beg or plead or try to reason with him. She knew now it would do no good.

She simply returned his kiss, giving him the only thing she had, the only thing of value left inside her—all her love; taking away every ounce of his love, along with their mutual despair and pain and joy. She stored it in her tear-swollen heart like a squirrel stores nuts against the harsh winter of life that stretched endlessly ahead of them.

Too soon he moved back, lowered his hands, and looked at the bow that had been crushed between his palm and her cheek. She watched him squeeze his hand around it. She thought she might die at the tenderness in his expression.

His next move was to his forehead, where he untied the red headband, his eyes never leaving hers. She stood so still she felt encompassed by him. He was telling her good-bye, when she knew she could never leave him. But grief was suspended in the magic of this moment, a moment of acute desire and mutual recognition of that desire, a moment of belonging, completely and wholly belonging. Him to her, her to him. Forever. Belonging to each other, but worlds apart.

When he draped the red headband around her neck, necklace-fashion, she gathered it in her fists, buried her face in it, and inhaled the scent of him. In that moment her heart released her tears.

Ridiculously, she squeezed them back. She couldn't cry on his headband—it might wash away his scent.

She felt him take her shoulders, pull her to his chest. She felt his heart beat against her shoulder, and when she moved a smidgen, their lips met again.

It was the sweetest, most desperate kiss she had ever known. It engaged all her senses, and her body responded in disparate ways. Even as passion built, grief overwhelmed it. When he lifted his head, it was to wipe the tears from her face with the pads of his thumbs, like on that first day.

At the beginning.

Now at the end.

"We'll keep these, Sabrina, to remind us how different our worlds are. You would be as lost and lonely here, as out of place in this brush and hide wickiup as your shiny gold bow is."

Their gazes seemed tethered by a single thread of melancholy. "And that red headband could never attend a commander's soiree."

"A commander's soiree?" No longer could she hold her tongue. How could he believe such nonsense? "Is that what you think I want out of life? To attend soirees? To wear ridiculous gowns and . . . and—"

"Sabrina, don't. Please."

"Then you don't. You have no right to make assumptions about what I want to do with my life. About what is best for me, right for me. I know what I want. Whether it is right or best only time could tell. But you won't give us time, will you?"

"It wouldn't work. It would only hurt you more."

"Hurt me? Do you own the patent on being hurt? You and these people? Yes, you lost your wife and your friends, and Ket lost her mother. She's been hurt more than any child I know. Except her cousin Emily. At least Ket still has part of her family. Hurt? Don't you think I can take being hurt?"

"I don't *want* you to be hurt." It was a plea, a prayer, deep and compassionate.

"I heard the laughter, Tremayne. Doesn't that count—"

He stopped her with a kiss. A hard, rough, wild and passionate kiss. When he finished, he turned her toward the doorway and shoved her through it.

Outside, the cold air dried her wet lips. Through the dazzling sunlight, she saw Nick approach, leading their horses. Nakia's mother stood nearby, holding Ket by the shoulders. The din of barking dogs and yelling children came to her, but the sounds were far away.

Suddenly Sabrina knew that in reality it was she who was far away. So far she could never return. Rather, he would never allow her to return.

Nick helped her mount. She neither looked back nor spoke on the winding ride down the trail and out of the village. She felt Tremayne's eyes burn into her retreating form as hot as the noonday sun, as poignantly as when his gaze followed her around the dance floor at the commander's soiree. But she did not turn for one last look.

Numbed by her loss, she was barely conscious of the chant that began behind her and rose from either side. Harsh and ugly, she could not understand the words, yet she knew what they were. They served as her recessional.

Her senses shattered, she strove to recover by taking note of the mundane sights and smells of everyday life around her. The air was filled with a mixture of dust and cooking oils. No longer did the wickiups glow in the sunlight of fantasy. Now they looked like what they were, brush hovels, and the people who lined the trail looked old and tired and poor and downtrodden.

She had wanted to live among them. Would she have ever been able to? Who would have been proved right, she or Tremayne?

No one would ever know.

Dust swirled around the hooves of the retreating horses. Dogs nipped at their legs, performing the final act of driving Sabrina away from him. Tremayne stared after her, his heart heavier than it had ever been. Sabrina's going dimmed the sun and brought his soul into eternal night. But who was he to complain? Everyone here had lost loved ones. He glanced around at the People.

His people. That, he had fabricated to drive her away. He had no people. They might have raised him, but he didn't belong to them. He didn't belong here. He belonged no where.

Beside him his daughter began the chant. Soon others joined in. "Evil! Evil! Evil!"

He remembered telling Sabrina that the color of her hair would be considered a spiritual gift; Ket had turned it into a malediction.

Fighting to conceal his deep hurt, Tremayne knelt and drew his angry daughter to his aching, empty chest. "She isn't evil, Ket. Her red hair is beautiful, not—"

"I hate her, anyway. I'm glad she's gone."

Ket's hatred added to Tremayne's conviction that what he had done was right, but it also magnified his loss, and his grief. "All she wanted was to love you."

"I still hate her. I will always hate her."

"My darling, darling Keturah, you have learned too well how to hate. If you had let her, Sabrina could've taught you to love." *Like she taught me.*

Chapter Seventeen

Two nights later when Lon came to call, Sabrina met him on the porch. He mistook her intentions, of course. Didn't he always?

"Sabrina!" When he bounded up the steps in one giant leap, she feared he intended to take her in his arms. To prevent such an untenable debacle she stepped aside, leaving him to catch the porch rail for balance.

She had been unbalanced for two full days. The coldness that began to seep into her upon leaving the Apachería now benumbed her. Her skin felt dead. Her heart beat, but it dispersed anguish instead of blood. Despair clogged her throat and her mind and her vision.

And in the bottom of her stomach hope was smothered by dead butterfly wings. The only thing she knew for certain was that she must reject Lon Jasper's marriage proposal.

She could not marry him. The idea was repugnant. To not set him free was a disservice. Lon deserved better.

So does Mama, warned her conscience.

So did Doc Henry, of course. The only thing worse than

destroying Mama's dreams would be to knowingly subject Doc Henry to a court-martial. She had gone to him the first night back at the post.

"If I thought Lon would use the senator's threat to retaliate against you, I wouldn't even consider rejecting him."

"And if I thought the man was that devious I would personally fling him from the top of Sleeping Lion to keep you from marrying him."

When she still balked, he confided, "I've already spoken with the rock mason Klaus Jamus in Chihuahua about putting me up a building." He patted her on the shoulder. "Go head, my dear. Do it now. It's time you got this behind you."

"I'd thought . . . maybe tomorrow night."

"Come up afterward," he offered, "if you need someone to talk to. I'll be here late."

Now tomorrow night had arrived. She had dressed carefully in a subdued gray percale and pinned her braid into a neat coil. Then she waited on the porch for over an hour, stewing inside, wishing there were any other way, knowing there wasn't. She hadn't expected it to be so hard. She had never wanted to marry Lon. She'd never wanted to hurt him, either.

Get it over with, she prodded. *Don't dally.*

"I'm ready to answer your question." They stood shoulder to shoulder at the porch rail. She spoke to the parade ground. A quarter moon cast a hazy glow over the autumn-dead grass.

"A Christmas wedding? That'll lift your mother's spirits. She's still reworking that green gown. Red bows, I think—"

"Flowers," Sabrina corrected. "Red flowers. But I can't marry you, Lon."

She felt him turn to face her, but she dared not look. "Can't?" He sounded confused.

"No, Lon, I . . ." Her voice was strong. She thought oddly that it might have come from someone else's body, someone who wasn't trembling so hard she had a death grip on the porch rail. Drawing on that false strength, she chanced a glance in time to see his brows pop a time or two, dislodging a shock of blond hair. It fell over his fore-head. She thought how uncharacteristic of him, to look mussed.

"I understand," he was saying. "It's the gossip. Once we're married it'll die down. You'll see. I shocked a lot of people by putting up with it, but I never believed it for a minute, Sabrina. Not for a—"

"I can't marry you, Lon. I mean . . . I won't." She changed verbs, hoping to clarify the matter. How strange that he hadn't been prepared for her rejection. She had never given him the slightest encouragement. He should have known.

"Won't?"

"Won't." Her voice came weaker now. She felt like an engine that had suddenly run out of steam. Despondent, she watched him shake his head, saw when truth began to dawn.

"You're rejecting my offer of marriage?"

She nodded. To speak the words again would only add insult to injury.

"Rejecting . . ." He frowned, pursed his lips, and when he spoke, his voice held an unfamiliar edge.

"Do you have any idea what you're turning down, Sabrina? What I've offered you? Don't you understand how far I'm going with this career? With Carmichael in the lead, I'm headed for the top. And you would make the perfect partner." He popped his brows again. The edge came off his voice. "Age will help, you'll see. In a few years

age will curtail that tendency you have to throw convention
to the wind. Yes," he repeated, as if to formalize the statement, "age will help you adjust to your rightful place."

"My rightful place?" He hadn't understood. "What
about love, Lon?"

"Love? What about it?"

"You don't *love* me?"

"If you're talking about lust, I have lusted for you for a
long time. Even though you certainly haven't returned the
feeling. That's why the gossip is so ludicrous."

"Ludicrous? That I could feel passion?"

"Your mother is right. You've read too many romances.
The kind of love you're talking about grows out of respect,
Sabrina. Respect takes years to build. It isn't some instanta-
neous, sock-you-in-the-gut thing like those stories make
out."

*Sock-you-in-the-gut? Yes, that was the feeling. Love socked you
in the gut.* "There must be a seed to start it growing," she
argued. "Even in the beginning, there must be an inkling
of passion, of . . ." *Butterfly wings or . . .*

"Too many romances."

"Not fiction, Lon. Real feelings." She closed her eyes
and was swept away by a yearning so intense it burned into
her chilled soul. That foolish smidgen of hope tried to
sneak from beneath the dead butterflies. "Heat," she whispered, clutching her arms about her chest. "Longing,
yearning, need, sizzling heat, and—"

"What?" Startled, he sounded like a man who had just
seen a ghost. But Lon Jasper was not the type to believe
in spirits. "Who's been talking gibberish to you?"

"Gibberish? These are real feelings, Lon." She pressed
a hand to her heart. "They exist, and if we're to be married,
we should feel them."

He stared at her as if a boulder had crashed down from
Sleeping Lion Mountain and bowled him over. "Damna-

tion, Sabrina, you did it, didn't you? By God, you did it! You crawled into bed with that savage?"

"I didn't say I crawled into bed with anyone. I said—"

"Deny it, then. Deny that you slept with that squaw man."

"Lon!"

"Don't pretend outrage, deny the gossip. Go ahead, I'm waiting."

Fear sizzled through her. What had she done now?

Not a lick of sense.

She agreed. After fourteen years, she agreed. She didn't have a lick of sense. Not where Tremayne was concerned. And she didn't care. All she cared about was being with him. In his arms. In his life—

"Damnation! I've been made the everlasting fool. Do you know that? You've made me look like a damned fool. I should have listened to Neil."

"Neil? Carrie's husband?" Sabrina had never confided in Carrie. Nor in anyone. "What could Neil Young possibly know about my life?"

"It was plain as day. That's what he said. Said Carrie said you just had to take one look at you and Tremayne at that soiree to know there was something between you. I should have seen it! Damn! I should have seen it that day you came running over to Headquarters. . . ." He struck the porch post with a doubled fist. "Treating his daughter! Sure you were. Damnation."

She didn't know what to say, so she said nothing. For Carrie had seen the truth. She couldn't keep her eyes off Tremayne, not at the soiree, not any time since. But Tremayne hadn't been able to resist her, either. Memories of those heated exchanges brought a flush to her cheeks and anticipation fluttering in her stomach. Butterflies?

Oh, yes. She felt butterflies. Sadly, she knew now they would never truly die. But they would always be for him.

If he were here right now, she would throw herself in his arms and never let him go. She needed him. Never more than at this moment.

Never more than for the rest of her life.

"You threw your reputation out the window like so much dishwater for a damned squaw man."

"I've asked you not to disparage—"

"Hah! *I've asked you, Lon* . . . Go to them, then. Go live with the savages. And die with them. I don't want you. Your mother must have known the truth, too, as hard as she tried to pawn damaged goods off on me. I've been had by the lot of you."

"My mother had nothing to do with this. She knows nothing—"

"And Edward. Oh, the signs I missed. What a fool! The way you took up with that whore in Chihuahua should have warned me."

"Rosa Ramériz? Are you calling Rosa a . . . Rosa is a fine woman, upstanding—"

"Sure, and she's about to give birth to someone's babe. I wonder whose?"

"Her husband's."

"That's not the way I heard it."

"Then you heard wrong. You know how gossip—"

"I certainly do. I've been hit over the head with that brickbat once too often. I'm still reeling from your going to bed with a savage. It probably all started with your association with Rosa."

"You're wrong."

"Wrong? Why don't you ask Tremayne who fathered that whore's child?"

Cold chills raced down Sabrina's arms. "That's a lie."

"Ask him. I dare you. Next time you're in bed with that squaw man, ask him who fathered Rosa's child."

"You're disgusting."

"And you, my dear Sabrina, are a slut. Maybe that's the way you prefer it. A threesome?"

It took a moment for his meaning to register. When it did, she became truly angry for the first time tonight. "Lon Jasper, how can you be so crude? And my mother thinks you're my chance of a lifetime."

"You need one," he returned. "You're just not smart enough or moral enough to know it."

"Sabrina, child, what is it?" Martha came onto the porch.

Seeing her, Lon found another target for his frustration. "Find someone else to pawn your daughter off on. I'm leaving."

"Sabrina . . . ? Captain Jasper, wait . . . Sabrina, what . . . ? You refused Captain Jasper?" The realization poured out, ending on a high gasp that once it left her body seemed to have been her last breath. "Child, child. How could you . . . ?" Martha crumpled to the floor without finishing her sentence.

"Mama!" Sabrina rushed to her mother, calling through the screen, "Papa! Papa, come quick."

By the time they got Martha to bed she had come around, but she refused to look at Sabrina.

"What the hell happened?" Edward wanted to know.

"I rejected Lon's marriage proposal."

"She had her heart set on that, sugar."

Sabrina felt his censure to the soles of her feet. "I know, Papa."

"But then I guess your heart is set on something different."

"I guess."

She went for Doc Henry, and by the time they returned Edward had gotten Martha into a flannel nightgown and had the covers pulled up to her chin. The doctor prescribed laudanum, told her to get some rest, and took his leave. Sabrina followed him into the parlor. They stood by the fireplace, beneath the portrait.

"She'll come around, my dear."

Sabrina gazed up at the likeness of her sister. "It's ironic. The first time I really and truly stand on my own two feet, no possible good can come of it."

"Give it time," he suggested. "Perhaps . . ."

After Doc Henry left, Papa remained with Mama and Sabrina returned to her room. Gloom covered the house like a shroud. She thought it heavy enough to suffocate on, except that death would be too good an ending for someone like her.

She had failed her mother.

She had failed Lon.

She even failed Papa.

But most of all, she failed herself. Lon was right to call her a fallen woman. Plagued by lust and uncontrollable erotic cravings, she had fallen into the depths of despair. Was there no hope for her?

No redemption? Ket's screams echoed in her mind. *Evil! Evil! Evil!*

She felt the child lunge for her, jerk her braid in the air for the whole village to disparage its color, a color Tremayne said Apaches would see as spiritual. Mama had always cautioned her to cover her head, else she would be thought coarse.

Serena's soft curls tamed the color; Sabrina's plank-straight hair accentuated its scandalous hue. . . .

Yes, she was coarse. Mama was right, Lon was right, Serena had always been right. Tears poured from her eyes. She wiped them with the back of her fist and became suddenly aware of something in her hand.

One lamp burned in her small room. Tentatively, filled with trepidation, she glanced around. She sat on the floor, legs crossed. And all around her . . .

Absently, she lifted a handful of hair. Focusing on her lap, she stared dumbly at the mess—lanks of red hair covered her skirt and the floor around her. In the midst of it all lay her braid. It was no longer attached to her head. When she focused on the object in her right hand she saw it to be her father's straight-edge.

But there were no gold bows . . . Only the one in the wickiup.

Her hair. As in a trance, she ran her fingers across her head. It felt strange. Soft and short. And there in her hand, she held the braid. Panicked she fetched Papa's shaving mirror from the porch. When she had taken the straight-edge, she couldn't say.

One look in the mirror made her cringe in horror. Her long red hair had been chopped off; it was shorter than Lon's. It looked like Ket's. Could she have cut her hair and been totally oblivious to the act?

And why?

Apache women chop off their hair . . . an expression of pain and loss.

Pain and loss. Oh, yes, she was in pain—she had lost. Reverently she reached under the bed for her rag sack and withdrew Tremayne's red headband. Holding it to her face, she inhaled deep drafts of the scent of him, the strength of him. Finally, she lay the braid lengthwise upon it and rolled the red fabric around the red hair. Then she cleaned up the mess and covered her head with a kerchief.

The grief didn't let up as the days dragged by with no change. Martha remained in bed most of the time, more despondent than Sabrina had ever seen her. And Papa was distant. He went through his days as though Sabrina wasn't there. His occasional glance at her kerchief-covered head brought a frown that hurt more than a tongue-lashing would have done.

On the bright side, Lon Jasper stopped calling. But that

small gain had been won at a heavy price. Without him around no one played the piano. No one laughed. They had returned to the bad old days, Sabrina thought guiltily. And it was all her fault.

Finally the treaty was negotiated, a solemn occasion for Sabrina, even though she knew how important it was to Tremayne, for it signaled the end of his trips to the post. Not that she had seen him or even the black lately. She wasn't even certain he was still part of the team.

The days were getting cold now, as fall turned into winter. The treaty signing had been set for the day before Thanksgiving.

"Wouldn't surprise me to wake up to snow one of these days," Doc Henry commented one morning when Sabrina arrived at the hospital, blowing on her hands to warm them.

"We haven't aired our winter clothes," she commented. "This gown smells of moth balls."

Just before noon, Felipe, Rosa's younger son, raced into the dispensary.

"Señorita, venga, por favor. Vengase."

"Rosa?"

"Mama needs you," Felipe cried. *"El bebé—"*

"I'm coming. Run. Tell her I'm coming." She found Doc Henry. "It's too early for the baby to come."

"Go on ahead, my dear. I'll send Hedgewick with a wagon. We must get her to the hospital."

By the time Sabrina arrived at Rosa's shack on the far side of Chihuahua, the baby's head was already pushing its way into the world, leaving Sabrina with little to do. Tying the cord, she washed the tiny body and wrapped it in a clean piece of flannel.

"It's a girl, Rosa. A beautiful baby girl." When she placed the swaddled child in Rosa's arms, the woman wept.

"Pobrecita. Pobrecita."

"Hush now," Sabrina crooned. "She'll be fine. She's small, but listen to that cry. It means her lungs are strong. What will you name her?" Sabrina strove to bring joy to the moment, but her attention was on the baby. Even in the dim light the child's hair was brown, not black, with a hint of waves.

"Neeta," Rosa whispered. "Manuel always wanted a daughter to name after his mother." Rosa kissed the top of the tiny child's head, while tears continued to fall from her eyes.

"Doc Henry is sending the wagon. We'll take you and little Neeta to the hospital."

When Rosa objected, Sabrina declared that Manuel would expect her to do everything necessary to care for his mother's namesake. She called the boys to see their sister.

They knelt to either side of Rosa. "She is small," Felipe said. "Will she live?"

"We'll do our best to see that she does," Sabrina assured him.

By then, Doc Henry and Hedgewick had arrived. Sabrina held the baby while the men loaded Rosa onto a pallet in the wagon bed. Rosa's sons turned grim.

"She should not go to the post. Everyone will see the truth."

Sabrina froze, dreading to hear the gossip repeated. It couldn't be true, but the post gossip mill had spread the same tale Lon had told her. "The only truth that matters is that your mother and baby sister need a doctor's care."

"Look at that hair," Diego said. "It is true, Mama. You cannot deny it any longer. This child was gotten by Tremayne."

"No!"

Afterward, Sabrina wasn't sure whether she cried the word, or whether it was Rosa's denial that echoed in her own heart. As weak as she was, Rosa reached out for Sabrina.

"It is not true, *chica.*"

"I know."

Two days later, the boys burst into Rosa's hospital room.

"Shh, your little sister is sleeping." Sabrina had spent the night to be on hand to help Rosa with the baby, whom Doc Henry said needed to nurse more often, being premature. The boys arrived just after Rosa and little Neeta had fallen asleep. "Don't wake her yet. Your mother needs the rest."

"We have come to see her eyes," Felipe demanded.

"Two bits'll get you four they're green."

"Please," Sabrina pled.

But Felipe had already scooped the tiny bundle in his arms. When the baby opened her eyes, it was with a shriek that sounded far too loud to come from a body so minute.

"You've frightened her." Sabrina reached for the baby, but Diego grabbed her away.

"Damn! They're blue."

"Of course they're blue." She omitted the fact that newborns almost always had blue eyes. The boys, however, were not convinced.

"Doesn't mean Tremayne ain't the one who got her."

Sabrina fought to control her anger. "Give me the baby," she demanded. Diego handed Neeta over without further argument. "Don't do anything foolish," she added. "Think of your mother. You'll make things worse—"

"We don't have to do anything," Felipe boasted. "Captain Jasper is going to take care of Tremayne."

Sabrina almost dropped the baby. "What do you mean?"

The boys exchanged smug glances, then shrugged indifferently. "Won't hurt to tell it now," Felipe said. "They've already left."

"What do you mean?" Sabrina demanded again.

"After the treaty is signed, Captain Jasper is going to kill Tremayne for us."

"For you?"

"Not for us, stupid," Diego rebuked his brother. "For himself. You heard him say he has a private matter to settle with that savage."

Chapter Eighteen

Had she caused Tremayne's death? That fear chased Sabrina on her mad race from the hospital and across the clearing. Halfway to the stables, she realized she had rushed off without medicines or even consulting Doc Henry.

Should she go back? How much time did she have? At breakfast Papa said the negotiating party left just after daybreak. It was now almost high noon.

Pray God, she wouldn't be too late.

Pray God, she wouldn't need medicine.

"What's the hurry, sugar? And where's your cloak? You shouldn't be running around in this cold—"

Already out of breath, the sight of Edward coming from the warehouses beyond the stables momentarily stopped her. "Lon is going to kill Tremayne."

"What?"

"Lon has gone—"

Edward reached her. "They've gone to sign the peace treaty."

"After the signing. Lon intends to kill Tremayne afterwards. Rosa's boys said—"

"Sabrina, sugar—"

"Turn me loose, Papa, please. I have to get there in time to prevent it. It's all my fault."

"Nonsense. Even if that were true, you can't traipse out there—"

"I'm going, Papa. I have to."

Edward stared into space a moment, thoughtful, before snapping, "Rosa's boys?"

She nodded.

"Why would you believe them? They hate Tremayne."

"Lon told them." She watched him take note of that. "I have to go."

"Not alone." Papa had been distant for so long, when he pursed his lips and frowned she fully expected him to continue the argument. But he surprised her. "I'll come with you."

Gratitude welled in her eyes. "Thank you."

"Run home and get your cloak," he was saying. "Tell your mama we're riding out, but no need to mention where we're headed. I'll saddle us some horses."

The stage station at Van Horn Wells, a site west of the post and south of the Apachería, had been chosen for the treaty signing. The long road there crossed desolate, winter-barren mountains and drab desertland, but at least it was a road. Setting and holding the pace, Sabrina berated herself the whole way. Could Lon be irrational enough to retaliate against Tremayne for her rejection? Would he murder Tremayne because of her?

"For the first time in my life I stood on my own two feet and look what happened—I sent Mama back into her depression and Lon's going to kill Tremayne."

"You don't know that." She knew he meant the latter.

"Or Tremayne will kill Lon." Shot at, Tremayne would

shoot back. He would have to defend himself. That idea was almost as offensive as the other. Either way she would have caused a death and the certain destruction of the man she loved.

"Even if we get there in time, Lord only knows how we can foil an attempted murder. You can't charge headlong into the middle of a gun battle."

"I'm already in the middle, Papa. If it weren't for me, none of this would have happened."

He shot her a wry assessment that stopped short of I told you so. "Be that as it may, I don't know what you think you can do to stop it."

"Agree to marry Lon."

"The hell you will. If this shenanigan proves true, if that's the kind of man he is, I won't allow you to marry the bastard."

They topped a hill, and her breath caught. A company of returning officers galloped toward them. Panicked, she searched the twenty or so faces, but didn't see him.

"Where's Lon?"

Colonel Merritt glanced from side to side, as though unaware the captain wasn't among them. Senator Carmichael spoke up.

"He'll be along."

"We've been told . . ." While Edward explained, Sabrina spurred her horse. This was no time to dally. Driven by fear she only half-heard her father's call and the horses turning in the road behind her.

Dust rose in a whirlwind when she drew rein in front of the adobe stage station and swung out of the side saddle. The small building looked deserted, but two horses stomped and snorted in the corral—a bay with a US Army brand stamped on its flank and Tremayne's black. The rheumatoid old station master shuffled around inside.

"Better steer clear of them rocks and brush, missy. Got us a full-fledged gun battle goin' on."

Even as he spoke a shot ran through the still cold air. Sabrina's panic clawed its way to the surface. She felt it tear through her throat, but her scream was muffled by the sheer terror of what she had caused. Her only thought to save Tremayne, she rushed outside.

Not a lick of sense!

She agreed. She shouldn't have spurned Lon. "Lon!" she called. "I've changed my mind. I'll marry you."

Her announcement was greeted by a whoop of harsh laughter coming from a jumble of trees and rocks to the right of the station. "Too late, Sabrina. You think I want that savage's damaged goods? But that isn't why you've come, is it? You learned my plan. Well, welcome to the party. You're in time to be our witness."

While Lon gloated, she moved cautiously toward the sound of his voice. She had taken no more than a dozen steps, however, when Tremayne darted from behind a cluster of huge boulders that rose across the road from the station. He grabbed her arm and jerked her back toward the station.

He was unharmed! Her relief was brief, for no sooner had he shown himself than a series of shots rang out.

"Hurry," he encouraged. Bullets spat into the ground around them, kicking up dust and fragments of rock.

Several feet from the station, she felt something tug hard on her left leg. Tremayne must have felt it, too, for he shoved her behind the building and crouched above her, his gun drawn.

"You hit her, damn you, Jasper." With his free hand, he tore back her cloak.

"Serves her right," came the call.

Ignoring Lon, Tremayne pushed up Sabrina's skirts and located the wound. "How bad is it?"

"It's nothing."

"The hell it is. You've been shot." Before she realized what he was doing, he had set aside his gun and torn a strip from one of her petticoats.

A growing circle of blood spread on the leg of her pantaloon, in the vicinity of her calf. Gritting her teeth, she took the cloth from him. "I'll do this. You watch for Lon. He's come to kill you. Where's Nick?"

"Gone to tell Lena good-bye. He's leaving for Europe."

"Oh, no." Lena, pregnant and alone.

Tremayne refocused on the distant outcropping. Horses approached. "What're you doing out here?"

"I came to warn you. I refused Lon's suit, and he's going to kill you. I'll marry him if—"

"Like hell you will. This has nothing to do with you."

"It has everything to do with me. If he kills you I can't marry you."

He glanced around, his green eyes dark. "Sabrina, I told you—" The hood of her cloak had fallen back, exposing her chopped-off hair. His fingers slipped through it. His face grew grim. "Son of a bitch!"

The oath was uttered in that rock solid voice, but in the gentlest of tones. "Look what I've done to you. I never meant to hurt you, Sab—"

"Lon's still out there."

"Then let's get going." He scooped her in his arms and carried her around the far side of the station, headed for the corral. When he whistled softly, the black raised its head. Two steps into the corral, Lon Jasper's voice stopped them.

"For a savage you aren't very savvy," the captain jeered. He had climbed into the corral from the opposite side and strode toward them with a swagger of defiance. Sabrina wondered where his military sharp bearing had gone. Where his sanity had gone.

"Get out of my way, Jasper." Gingerly, Tremayne set Sabrina on her feet. The minute he left her, Jasper dove for him. By now the officers had arrived.

"What's going on, Sabrina?" By the time Edward rounded the building, Lon and Tremayne grappled on the ground. They broke and struggled to their feet.

"I want this to be a fair fight," Lon advised. "Fair and square for all to see." Dusting himself off, he suddenly hauled off and slugged Tremayne on the jaw.

"Fair? You claiming to know the meaning of that word?" Tremayne returned the punch, then staggered with a powerful blow from the captain.

"Lon was boxing champion at West Point," Sabrina called.

"Boxing champ?" Tremayne challenged as the two men wrestled again. "Out here he's champ of the massacre."

"And you're champ of the bastards, right, squaw man? They say Rosa's bastard kid looks just like its father, right down to that sissy wavy hair."

"That's a damned lie and you know it," Tremayne growled. "We both know who raped Rosa and who started the rumor about me, so don't try to divert attention from your own crimes."

"I never murdered anyone." Lon struck a deadly left blow to Tremayne's gullet. "Till now."

"You son of a bitch." Tremayne stepped back, caught his breath, then lunged. "You gave the order that killed my wife." Tremayne slugged him.

Lon dodged to the side. "Prove it." He ducked a right to the jaw, struck with a wicked right of his own.

Tremayne staggered. "And twenty-three other women and children."

"Prove it," Lon challenged again.

"The only reason you didn't kill my daughter was that

she was playing in the hills with a couple of friends. But do you know what, Jasper? Those kids saw you."

The horror of Tremayne's words held Sabrina enthralled. It couldn't be. Not Lon. Her mind echoed Lon's demand, *Prove it. Prove it.*

"Nick's looked into it." Tremayne doubled from a blow to his midsection, backed a couple of steps away, wiping blood from his lip with the back of his hand.

"Holier-than-thou Nick?" Lon jeered. "Way I hear it, Nick has a few morals missing, too."

"That's beside the point."

"He's a foreigner, savage. He couldn't find out anything important about one of our military officers. No more than you could four years ago. You couldn't prove it then, and you won't now."

"We have."

Lon may have stumbled, Sabrina wasn't sure, but suddenly Tremayne had him pinned to the ground. He struck the captain, over and over, again and time and again.

"They were drying roots," Tremayne shouted into the captain's face; his fists hammered the pale, sharp features. "Peacefully drying food for the winter. You gave the damned order, Jasper. Nick found out the truth. I should kill you myself—"

"No!" Dragging her injured leg, Sabrina threw herself on Tremayne. "He isn't worth it. Let him go."

Tremayne kept pounding Lon's face. Then he struck him in the chest.

"Tremayne! Stop." She sought purchase on his arms. "Please stop. Let him go. Please. I love you."

The claim did nothing to stop Tremayne.

"How can I marry you if you're dead or in prison?" she cried. "He isn't worth it. Stop. For me. For Ket. For us."

Whether it was her words, or the combination of fear and truth in her voice, Tremayne's arms suddenly fell slack.

After a long tense moment, he rose, still clutching Jasper by the collar. Then he flung the captain aside and dropped to his knees beside Sabrina. His fingers slipped through her short hair. She saw in his eyes that he knew what had happened.

"I never meant to hurt you," he whispered gently, kissing her lightly in spite of the presence of several officers and her own father. "I've never even told you how much I love you."

She thought she might expire in his arms, not from pain or loss of blood, but from relief. "I've known that for a long time."

"You never give up, do you?"

"How could I? We looked at each other."

"Didn't we, though." He shook his head against the fact that was all too clear. It was a rough and rocky road they would travel. "It's a long shot, sweetheart. A real long shot."

Around them orders were given and Jasper led away, but neither heard. Tremayne knelt on the ground, cradling her in his arms, while she cried. Not over the wound in her leg, not over the battle but over the victory. Why hadn't she done this sooner? She stood up to Lon. She stood up to her mother. Why hadn't she realized she would have to stand up to Tremayne, too?

"No, Tremayne. It's our chance of a lifetime."

His kiss told her he felt the same way.

"Sabrina, child, hurry. We can't be late."

Sabrina stood in her mother's bedroom, mesmerized by the image in the cheval glass. Here she was, staring her fate in the eye, and it had never felt so right.

She smiled, and the image smiled back at her. The green gown fit to perfection; every line of the original was accentuated by the tasteful addition of thousands of tiny white beads.

The gown was pure Worth; the pattern, perfect Apache.

"It's glorious, Mama." In the two months since she'd cut it, her hair had grown back enough to pin at her nape and attach the braid. Her headdress was fashioned from yards of white tulle attached to a headband beaded in the same pattern as the gown.

"Where did you get the pattern?"

"Colonel Merritt's wife found an Apache cloak in the archives at Fort Concho. I copied the design."

"Let's get going, sugar." Papa stuck his head in the door. "You're pretty as a picture." His eyes welled with tears.

"I know."

"How's the leg?"

"Great. Mama's a good nurse." And more.

"Mama's a trooper," Sabrina had told her father one night not long after they returned to the post. She was still in the hospital at the time. Tremayne had brought her there. Then, after being assured she would be all right, he had taken off on a two week trip to Austin.

"Don't be long. You might change your mind."

"No chance. Use this time to mend things with your mother."

"You're the only person in the world who matters to me," she'd claimed.

"No, I'm not." But in his eyes she read a far different response.

What kind of world had they created for themselves and those they loved? For Ket? For Mama? From the way he acted at the time, Sabrina had worried that Papa wouldn't accept her choice, either.

To the surprise of everyone except Edward and Sabrina, Mama adjusted. Past that first day, when she hurried to

Sabrina's hospital bedside, Martha never mentioned Lon Jasper again.

"I just can't believe it. Can't believe it," she had moaned. "Captain Jasper shot you. By mistake, of course."

"Not by mistake, Martha," Papa retorted. "I was there. That murdering bastard didn't care whether he shot our daughter or not. He'll go to prison, with any luck at all, and good riddance."

Bending over the bed, Martha cradled Sabrina's head and cried, "Oh, my baby. Oh, my baby." Her greatest fear had almost been realized. The shock of Lon Jasper committing the dastardly deed was too much to discuss, as was Sabrina's insistence that she intended to marry Tremayne as soon as he returned from Austin.

Martha gave no indication that she even heard the claim, but she must have begun work on the green dress right after that. She kept the door to her bedroom closed most of the time, so Sabrina had no idea what she was doing. She feared the worst, of course—that she had sent Mama into some kind of shock, one she might never shake.

Two weeks later Tremayne returned. He rode right up to the hitching post, stepped down, and walked up the path to their front door as if he did it every day of the week.

She raced to meet him, her heart pounding. He wore his black broadcloth suit, the one he had worn to the soiree, and his hair was pulled back so tightly she thought for a minute he might have cut it.

"Nick taught me to dress for the occasion," he answered her question. His intense green gaze burned away the chill of the winter day. It took a concerted effort to pull enough composure from the depths of all those fluttering butterflies not to throw herself into his arms. She couldn't resist touching him, though, and savored the rocking sensation.

"Occasion?"

"I've come for that talk with your folks."

"My folks?"

"I didn't bring a string of fine horses," he added, when she glanced to the lone black stallion tied to the hitching post. She wished he had at least brought the pinto, but resisted saying so. She could hire a horse from the stable to ride out to Apache Wells. They could bring it back later. Someday.

She felt downright giddy.

"I understand it isn't the custom with you people."

His quip was voiced in a gentle, teasing tone.

"What custom?"

"To bring fine horses in exchange for a maiden's hand in marriage. Guess I'll have to beg."

"You intend to ask them?"

"Of course."

She was nonplused. "What if they refuse?"

"We owe them the courtesy, Sabrina."

She doubted her parents felt the same way about courtesy, but she held her tongue. "It's your funeral."

"Sabrina," Papa called from the parlor. "Who is it?" Turning she saw him step to the door. "Tremayne," he greeted. No *how you doing* or *long time no see* this time.

"Good evening, Edward." He nudged Sabrina with a hot hand to her back. "Come introduce me to your mother."

Sabrina thought she might expire. Tremayne offered his hand, Papa took it, they shook. Solemn.

Inside he called, "Martha, we've got company."

When Mama appeared from the direction of the back porch, Sabrina felt Tremayne's hand tighten at her waist. She looked, hoping to reassure him, but he hadn't even seen her mother.

His attention was on the portrait above the mantel. Time stood still while he took it in.

"That's—" she began.

"I know who that is." His hand moved to her head. He slipped off the kerchief she wore at all times now and let it fall to the floor. With rough fingers, he tenderly sifted her hair. "A beautiful little girl, grown into the most beautiful woman in the world."

Every time she was with this man she found another reason to love him. Edward cleared his throat.

"Tremayne, this is Mrs. Bolton, Sabrina's mother."

A split second later, Tremayne returned his attention to Edward. And to Martha, who stood transfixed in the doorway.

"Mrs. Bolton. I've come to talk with you and Edward."

When Martha didn't budge, Edward took charge. "Sit down, Tremayne, sit down." Papa indicated a chair. "Martha, come, dear. Tremayne's come . . ." His eyes found Sabrina. ". . . calling, I presume."

They sat on the settee, side by side. Across from them Edward assisted Martha into a chair, then took the one beside her. Assigned the task of host by default, he clapped his hands.

"Drink? Could I fetch someone a drink? Coffee? Tea?"

"No." Tremayne reached for Sabrina's hand. "This won't take long." When he glanced at her, she saw his desperation. "One way or another."

"Well, don't keep us in suspense," Edward said with pseudojoviality.

"I've just returned from Austin."

No one responded. Sabrina's hand was wet in his. His was wet, too. She couldn't imagine how hard this was for him. Then she recalled her reception at the Apachería. Even knowing how people could react to those they didn't understand, he had come into her mother's parlor to ask for her hand in marriage.

"I don't have much to offer," he began. "No, that's wrong. I don't have anything to offer."

"Tremayne—"

"Let me finish, Sabrina." He turned back to her waiting parents. "I went down to Austin to check on the land my father owned, back some thirty years ago. All that's left to me is that little valley folks call Apache Wells. The other, several thousand acres, twenty thousand to be accurate, was sold years ago on warranty deeds."

"Sold?" Edward questioned. "How could that happen?"

"It was common practice. Still is, I suppose." He glanced down at Sabrina. "You were right. Carmichael owns it all. That land on top of the hill and the rest of my father's holdings."

"Carmichael? That dad-blasted senator?" Edward's tone left no doubt about how he felt about the man. "The scoundrel's already headed back to Washington."

"Just as well. I wouldn't fight him for it. He isn't worth it. We've had enough misfortune."

"So what do you intend to do?"

"Papa?"

"Shh, Sabrina. He has a right to ask. I've put a bid in for some of that railroad land on the other side of the Rattlesnake Mountains. Nick Bourbon and I have been planning on buying up some of that land for a long time, only I never had the money." To Sabrina, he explained, "I used what the government paid me for helping with the treaty. It won't be much of a living for a while, but—"

"Shh," she whispered, her eyes only for him. When Edward cleared his throat again, Tremayne started.

"I . . . uh, Edward, Mrs. Bolton, I've come to ask permission to marry your daughter."

Martha's hand flew to her bosom as though she were shocked, when in fact Sabrina had reminded her daily of her plan to wed Tremayne.

"Is this what you want, Sabrina?"

"Yes, Papa. More than anything in the world."

"Then I don't see how your mama and I can stand in your way."

It wasn't a blessing, Sabrina realized, but she couldn't have been more happy. Never in her wildest dreams had she expected Tremayne to make the extreme sacrifice of sitting down in her mother's parlor to ask for her hand.

Tremayne broke the heavy silence. "I know this isn't the life you would have chosen for her," he told Martha. "But I'll be good to her. I'll do my best to make her happy. I've never loved anyone the way I love Sabrina."

"I love him, too, Mama."

"It won't be an easy life for a while," he reiterated.

"And I've already said yes," she told him. "We'll have the ceremony at Apache Wells."

"Sabrina—"

"Sh," she said. "I'm the bride, I decide."

"Don't expect a crowd."

"All I need is you." She turned to her parents. "Tomorrow at two o'clock."

"Tomorrow?" It was the first word Martha had spoken. She lifted a stunned face to her husband.

"No," Tremayne told Sabrina. "I need to see Ket first. Try to make things right with her."

"Your daughter?" Edward quizzed.

"She . . ." He favored Martha with a wistful smile. "Keturah is her name. She's ten, and she isn't going to take kindly to this idea, either."

It wasn't the time for small talk. When the conversation faltered again, Tremayne rose. "I'll be going."

"Not before we set the date," Sabrina told him.

"How about the day after Christmas?" he suggested.

"That's two more weeks."

"Don't protest, Sabrina." Martha had come partially to life. "Mister Tremayne knows what he has to do."

"The day after Christmas," she agreed, following him out the door. Before he could reach the black, however, she drew him to a stop. "Don't you dare try to get on that horse without kissing me."

He looked around. Then his gaze softened. He kissed her tenderly on the lips, on the forehead. "You're a strong woman, Sabrina. Think I bit off more than I can chew?"

"We'll see."

After he climbed into the saddle, he peered down at her. "What happened to Jasper?"

"He won't be court-martialed."

Tremayne's eyebrows raised.

"Neither will Doc Henry."

"A trade?"

"We don't know. They put Lon in the guardhouse, but Carmichael got him out. Lon returned to Washington with him."

"Something's rotten there."

"You didn't press charges."

"True, but Colonel Merritt was determined to look into the matter."

"It doesn't concern us," she told him. But of course it did. "I can't believe he was responsible for Nakia's—"

"Like you said, it doesn't concern us. Not anymore."

When he turned to leave, she stopped him. "Wait. Wait right there."

When she returned, it was to hand him the red headband. "Wear it to the wedding," she instructed. "With the rest of it."

He frowned. "To frighten off your parents?"

"To please your bride."

"God, Sabrina." His eyes caressed her face. "I hope you never regret this."

Now the waiting was almost over. The time to pay the piper, as Papa liked to say, only a few short hours away.

"Come on, sugar," Papa urged from the bedroom door. "Your mama's holding your red cape in the living room. The ambulances are packed with guests. Time for the bride to make her entrance. That is, unless you've changed your mind."

Changed her mind?

In the parlor Mama waited in her spot, beneath the portrait. She draped the red velvet cape around Sabrina's shoulders, the cape she had intended Sabrina to wear for Lon Jasper. Yes, Mama was a trooper.

"The gown is exquisite, Mama. I've never seen anything so lovely."

Martha took Sabrina's cheeks in her hands. She kissed one, then the other. "That man was right, child. You are a beautiful woman."

Sabrina squeezed back tears.

"And you were a beautiful little girl, Sabrina."

Make her happy, Sabrina.

The admonition followed them from the house. It trilled through Sabrina's heart like a song, not a sad song, but one filled with love and joy. And hope.

I will, Serena, I will.

"How many people do you think we shocked today?"

Sabrina snuggled deeper into the furry pelt on which she and Tremayne would spend their wedding night. It was all that remained of the cabin's meager furnishings. Lena had offered furniture from the lodge, so instead of stumps for tables and chairs, they now had carved walnut— one table, four chairs, a wardrobe and dresser. Tremayne refused the bed, claiming it would fill up the small cabin.

"I'm never really comfortable in a bed," he had confessed. Sliding under the pelt he nestled against her, wrapping long muscular legs around her, drawing her near with them. "To answer your question, you shocked me."

"Me?"

"Your mother, then. That gown, the beading. It's a perfect Apache pattern. How did she manage?"

Across the room, her green silk wedding gown lay draped across a chair beside Tremayne's buckskin breeches and calico shirt. Dancing flames from the fireplace warmed the small cabin and reflected off the thousands of white beads.

"Mama always rises to the occasion. This time she outdid herself."

"She got it right, down to the bells," Tremayne mused.

"Those were a surprise." Hundreds of tiny bells adorned her petticoats and pantaloons.

"When you walked toward me, it sounded like the wind."

"Or the laughter?" He didn't rise to the topic, so she changed it. She had a lifetime to teach him to believe in the laughter. "You surprised me, too. When you stepped out of the cabin my butterflies set up such a clamor I couldn't have heard the laughter if it'd been screaming at me. You looked exactly like the first time I saw you. Except for . . ." Her words choked with the memory she knew she would hold in her heart for all time—her gold bow pinned to Tremayne's calico shirt.

"Figured I'd surprise you with that one."

"From the day I saw it here beside your bed, I knew I couldn't give up."

He nibbled his way from her lips to her breast.

"When did you know?" she asked.

"Much earlier. That first day, with your red hair flying in the wind. It spooked the black, and you spooked me. Hell, Sabrina, you stunned me so I could hardly move."

"Or stand on your own two feet?"

"I'm glad you learned how to do that." His lips moved lower, following his exploring hands. "How 'bout this?"

"Ahh, it's . . ." When he entered her without preamble, she gasped, then joyously rose to meet him. His rhythm became hers, his throbbing heart echoed hers, and his climax burst inside her, shooting fiery sparks through her head.

"Who else do you think we shocked?" she asked when their hearts slowed and they lay together damply.

"Well, let's see." His breath on her temple felt like butterfly wings. "Colonel Merritt wasn't too eager to get splattered with red water."

She laughed. "But he was honored we asked him to hold the ceremony." It had been a traditional ceremony, albeit one held beside the ancient well instead of in a house of worship.

"A white man's house of worship," Tremayne had objected when Sabrina said that. "I told you once, nature is sacred to the Apache."

Colonel Merritt provided three army ambulances to carry the guests to Apache Wells—including, in addition to the wedding party, himself and his wife, Carrie and Neil Young, Doc Henry and Jedediah.

Jedediah admitted to being squeamish about the legend, but he came. "If the haints ain't got Miz Breena, don't reckon they'll bother a one-legged black feller like me."

To which Doc Henry had groused, "Glad to hear you admit to having a leg."

Also attending were Harry and Reba Applebee, but they didn't bring little Emily. "It will be my project to reunite Emily and Ket," Sabrina related earlier in the week.

Reba had looked wistful, before agreeing. "Every person has the God-given right to know his or her heritage."

Sabrina thought of Keturah. Her refusal to attend the ceremony had put a damper on the occasion for Tremayne, even though he pretended otherwise. If it took forever, Sabrina vowed to never stop trying to gain Ket's trust.

Doc Henry was especially pleased upon entering the valley. "Didn't I tell you to follow your heart, my dear?" He'd looked around the valley with wide eyes. "A lovely place that heart of yours found."

One of Sabrina's hardest tasks had been to persuade Rosa to attend.

"I'd ruin it for you, *chica.*"

"The day won't be complete without you."

"Those rumors—"

"Are rubbish." The rumor about Neeta's parentage had taken a turn since Lon Jasper's fall from grace, convincing Sabrina that he had started them.

Now the gossip mill claimed Carmichael for Neeta's father. It made more sense, but Rosa steadfastly maintained that Neeta was Manuel's daughter.

Sabrina, for one, didn't intend to question the fact.

"Lena is coming to the post a few days early. You and she can ride out together. She'll help you with the baby."

Martha, of course, surprised everyone except her immediate family. In the two weeks since she formally met her future son-in-law, she finished beading the green wedding gown and organized a reception complete with punch and a stack cake, for which each guest provided a layer.

Sabrina never actually saw her smile, but neither did she give any indication of being shocked. Except once.

After Colonel Merritt pronounced them man and wife, Tremayne took Sabrina's hands and in that deep and wonderful, down-from-the-hills voice, recited the ancient legend he had first told her only a few short months earlier.

"After the Great Spirit created the earth and the heavens," he began.

Sabrina gazed into his intense green eyes, and the crowd disappeared. While Tremayne recited the legend, her heart found its home. Around them the red rock mountain rose, protecting, shielding. She felt cradled here, secure, filled with love ... and hope. Her mind spun with the images ...

Before she realized it was time, he dropped her hands and drew from the well. The pulley squawked. A breeze rattled cottonwood branches across the roof of the cabin. All else was still.

"Should this chief become lonely," Tremayne recited.

Mesmerized, she watched him lift the bucket. Before he tipped it, she stepped to his side.

"He has only to bathe in these sacred waters to find love everlasting."

It was hot. So were his eyes. Rivulets of red water coursed down his ruddy cheeks and over his shirt. She felt the same hot liquid trickle down her face. The instant he tossed the bucket aside, she was in his arms.

Applause broke out around them, then scattered cheers.

"The first time I told you this part of the legend," he said, "you thought I was talking about Nakia."

She listened, waiting.

"I wasn't, Sabrina. Even then I was thinking about you. It's always been you. I feel like forever."

Remembering it now, he said, "Your mama may never forgive me for staining that green gown red. In fact, she has yet to speak to me."

"She will." It was one of Martha's specialties, performing up to peak while ignoring the source of her displeasure.

"She probably blames me for taking away your chance of a lifetime."

"You're my chance of a lifetime." When he slipped from under the pelt, she objected.

"Let me throw another log on the fire. Don't want to freeze my bride on her wedding night."

"There's no chance of that."

"When is Lena's baby due?" he asked, returning to bed,

gathering her near. At the mention of a baby she felt his body react against her. Her heart cried for more.

"I'm not sure. A few months. It was lovely, naming Nick your best man in absentia."

"He asked me."

"What?"

"To stand up for him when he and Lena . . ." Tremayne's words trailed off. "Now don't go letting the cat out of the bag."

"Oh! I'm so happy."

"Don't tell her."

"I won't, Tremayne. But when will he return? When will they get married? When—"

He stopped her by pressing her face into his shoulder with a chuckle. "I don't know."

They both knew anything could happen to prevent Nick's return. "Did he know about the baby?"

"He never said."

"Surely he wouldn't have left if he'd known."

"Nick never talked about his life over there. Except once, when he said he intended to ask me to stand up for him. He said he had some things to settle overseas before he could marry her."

"I hope it's soon. Imagine how hard it is for her. Having a baby without being wed is bad enough, but everyone knows this baby's father has left, and no one knows if or when—"

"Sabrina, could we solve the problems of the world some other time?"

"What?"

"I'd like to get on with our wedding night."

She inhaled a long, deep draft of love. It smelled like the hills and the red earth and Tremayne. It occurred to her then that wrapped together here in this cabin, nestled in this sacred valley, they had the one thing neither of them had had before—hope for the future. Thanks to her God and his, and to the guardian of the well, she no longer feared looking her fate in the eye.

"Oh, yes, Tremayne. Let's get on with our wedding night."

Epilogue

Three months later

"It's a boy, Lena." Sabrina and Tremayne had arrived at the post hospital in the nick of time. Papa came for them at the onset of Lena's labor.

"Wash up," Doc Henry greeted her. "She's ready."

From one of the two civilian rooms, Sabrina heard a muffled scream.

"Pity for a woman to have to go through this alone."

"Nick will be back," Tremayne returned. Sabrina wasn't sure whether he took offense at Doc Henry's observation, or whether he was just plain nervous.

"Why don't you go find something to do?" she suggested. "You don't need to hang around here."

It hadn't taken long. "Thank you for coming," Lena mouthed between pains. "I never dreamed it would hurt so bad."

Sabrina mopped her face with a damp cloth. "The hurt won't last. That's the blessing."

"No," Lena said between gasps. "The blessing is our baby."

"He's perfect." Sabrina wiped him clean and placed him on his mother's stomach. "Look at all that black hair. He has your coloring, Lena. He'll be a heartbreaker."

Tears leaked from Lena's eyes. Sabrina watched help-lessly. For the second time in a few short months she had assisted the delivery of a fatherless baby. The babies didn't know it.

But their mothers certainly did.

"He'll be home, Lena." She longed to share the secret Tremayne had told her but dared not. "Have you decided what to name this big boy?"

"Tres Robles," Lena said. "I know it doesn't sound much like a name, but it was my father's."

"It's beautiful. Strong, yet musical and mysterious. Here let me swaddle Tres Robles before he catches cold."

At a knock, Tremayne called, "I brought your mail, Lena."

Holding the baby in one hand, Sabrina opened the door. "Look what we have."

Tremayne stepped inside, tentative, as though he had come face to face with a rattlesnake instead of with this minuscule baby boy.

"Tremayne, meet Tres Robles Bourbon."

"A son. What'd you know?"

The letter was from Nick. Lena read it, then reread it, while Sabrina held the baby.

"He's coming home," she said at length, tears flowing now. "He . . . he asked me to marry him as soon as he arrives."

Sabrina hadn't cried at her own wedding, but now she began to sob. Tremayne caught her from behind, cradling her against him, while she held the baby and Lena contin-ued to tell them about Nick.

"He says he's picked out some land across the mountain from yours, Tremayne." She looked up, questioning.

"We'd sort of hoped things could work out," he admitted shyly.

"I never dreamed . . ." Lena's words trailed off. She squinched her lids, but that did nothing to keep back the flood of tears, until Tres Robles let out a wail that brought them all to attention.

"I think he's hungry," Sabrina said. She handed the baby to Lena. "Call if you need me. We'll be just outside."

In the same hall where once they had been afraid to show their feelings, Tremayne cradled Sabrina in his arms and swayed back and forth. "Things might work out after all."

"Might? How long is it going to take me to rid you that cynicism?"

He tightened his hold on her.

"Think a baby would do it?"

He came to a standstill. "What are you saying?"

"How would you like a son?"

"A baby? I don't care what it is . . . a son, a daughter . . ." He laughed. The sound, and the suddenness of it, stunned Sabrina, for this was no simple laugh. Deep and throaty, it began low in his gut and burst from his mouth like a song.

Oh, yes, she thought. *A joyous heart song, full of love and hope.* She had never heard him laugh before. She doubted he had laughed in a long, long time.

"A son," he said finally. "Wouldn't that be something? A friend for Tres Robles." He shook his head, lost in the wonder of it. "What a friendship that would be."

"We'll ask the guardian for a son." She planted a soft kiss on his lips and felt the butterflies flutter to life inside her. She knew now they had never really died. They'd been dormant from time to time, while she and Tremayne found the strength to admit what they could never really deny, once she'd heard the laughter, once they had looked at each other.

ROMANCE FROM JANELLE TAYLOR

ANYTHING FOR LOVE   (0-8217-4992-7, $5.99)

DESTINY MINE   (0-8217-5185-9, $5.99)

CHASE THE WIND   (0-8217-4740-1, $5.99)

MIDNIGHT SECRETS   (0-8217-5280-4, $5.99)

MOONBEAMS AND MAGIC   (0-8217-0184-4, $5.99)

SWEET SAVAGE HEART   (0-8217-5276-6, $5.99)